The Meaning of Life

EDGE CASES 3

The Meaning of Life

SILVER LININGS

Podium

To all those whose stories need to be told

Cover design by Cosmic Croissant (Toast)

ISBN: 978-1-0394-3662-6

Published in 2024 by Podium Publishing
www.podiumaudio.com

The Meaning of Life

CHAPTER 1

A THOUSAND(ISH) YEARS AGO

In the town of Aldea, inside a dungeon's bonus room, a certain cleric grappled with a revelation.

"Wait, no, hang on," Sev said. Being in what seemed to be an entire other *world* inside a dungeon was strange enough, but this? "Back up. The universe did what, now?"

"It ended." The innkeeper-slash-shadow elemental who was somehow just named *Clyde* cocked his head towards Sev, a flicker of shadow dancing across his eyes like a questioning blink. "Do you not know about that?"

"No?" Sev said, the lilt at the end of his words turning it into a question. Unspoken was the thought that came with it: *What the fuck?* "We're standing in it right now. How can it have ended?"

Clyde frowned at him slightly, then leaned back against the counter. Sev could see him debating with himself on what to say next. "You're visitors; I know that much," he said. His eyes glowed strangely—Sev recognized it as the look of an active [**Mana Sight**] skill, or something close to it, anyway.

Not for the first time, Sev thought about how strange it was to be in a place where the system had never existed. The idea that Elyra's Prime Dungeon had somehow generated and was now sustaining an entire universe without the system was mind-boggling.

At least their own systems and system skills still worked. This world didn't seem to have the mana rejection that happened in Teque, for whatever reason.

Clyde was still examining them. After a moment, he spoke again. "But you're not visitors from . . ." A slight hesitation, and then a twitch of his fingers. Sev almost thought he could see a flicker of mana as the elemental tried something. "Hm. I see. This is an echo?" He frowned. "That's unfortunate."

"Please stop being mysterious and tell us what's going on," Sev said with a groan. Bad enough that they just barely escaped from a fight with an eldritch mana Aspect that seemed hell-bent on destroying them—now he had to deal with someone being vague about *the end of the universe.*

"Sorry," Clyde said, sounding surprisingly contrite. "This must be confusing for you. I'll explain everything in just a minute; I just need to figure it out myself first. I *think* I know what's going on, but I'll have to make sure . . ."

He trailed off, and then his fingers were twitching again. This time, Sev was sure about the glimmers of mana he saw.

"I feel like Misa should be here for this conversation," Vex ventured. He looked up the stairs where she'd gone, both concerned and nervous. Sev couldn't blame him. Misa seemed to be hit the hardest out of the four of them—they might have escaped Irvis, but he knew she thought of herself as having failed to protect them.

But she needed space. He recognized that mood; it wouldn't help her if they crowded around her now. They'd just have to trust that she would talk with them when she was ready.

Sev sighed. *Just waiting* was one of the worst parts about being a friend. It was in his nature to always want a solution. He glanced at Vex, who was still staring up the stairs, looking worried. "She needs time," Sev said gently. "If she keeps avoiding us, we'll try to talk to her, sure. But anything we learn here we can just tell her later. It'll be okay."

". . . If you say so." Vex looked a little unconvinced. Derivan gave him a little nudge in the shoulder and smiled at him.

"It will be fine," Derivan said.

"Yeah." Vex blew a breath out through his mouth, looking a little less tense.

"Oh, so you listen when *Derivan* tells you," Sev teased, trying to lighten the mood. He smirked at Vex to show he was kidding when the lizardkin glanced over at him, and Vex couldn't help the small grin that stole across his snout.

"Yeah, 'cause he's wiser than you are," Vex said. Sev rolled his eyes good-naturedly.

Clyde watched the three of them with no small amount of interest and then gave a polite cough when they glanced back at him. "I think I'm gonna need my wife for this conversation," he said. "She's a little more versed in planar echoes than I am."

"Is that what this is?" Vex asked, looking around.

"It's the best word you have for it," Clyde said, waving vaguely. "Accounts for all the weird stuff, like me speaking the same language you guys do. But it's not a *great* word, probably? Look, my wife will be able to explain this better than I can. I'll go get her. Give me ten minutes."

Clyde disappeared behind a door behind the counter.

". . . You don't think he's running away, do you?" Sev said after a minute had passed.

"What? No, why would he?" Vex blinked.

"Honestly, entirely because I think the idea of him just *booking it* is kind of funny."

Vex snorted but didn't say anything further.

The three of them sat in a comfortable silence, though Sev was mostly lost in his own thoughts.

They'd been through so much to get here, and it felt like they were about to get their answers. What the system was for, why it was falling apart . . . the reason for the stars disappearing, and the world forgetting they had ever existed. The reason growth spells in Elyra had stopped working and dungeon breaks were becoming more and more frequent.

Strangest of all was that he felt . . . different. It was hard to describe, but he felt a little bit freer, like he now had more than just one path in front of him he could walk.

He just didn't know what that meant.

Derivan was mostly just watching Vex. He was painfully aware of the difference in weight distribution now—whenever he walked, it was with a slight limp, weighted toward his heavier side. Because his right side was still just . . . missing.

Watching Vex was like a balm that distracted him from that fact. He could practically see the lizardkin jotting down mental notes with every little detail he noticed. Vex's fingers even twitched a little, like he was writing, and Derivan wondered why he didn't just get his journal out to scribble in.

Right on cue, Clyde returned, and Derivan watched in mild amusement as Vex promptly forgot about the last ten minutes of careful observation. The shadow elemental came back with not one but *two* others trailing behind him. Unlike him, neither of them was dressed in those immaculate suits that every other shadow wore. One instead had on a light-purple dress that flowed over her shoulders and shimmered at the edges with vibrant violet flame, and the other wore . . . a shirt.

Just a really long, garishly bright yellow shirt. If he was wearing shorts, they weren't visible. He looked like he'd just woken up. He didn't have *hair*, exactly, but the shadows did drape themselves over his head in a very messy, tousled sort of way.

"My husband wanted to join in," Clyde said by way of explanation. The elemental in the shirt yawned and waved.

"I hear it's time for a lesson about echoes," the elemental in the dress said. She gave them a gentle smile and opened her mouth to begin—and then Clyde poked her in the shoulder.

"Introductions first."

"Oh, right." She blinked once, then bowed gracefully. "My name is Belle. This doofus over here is Elliot."

The elemental in the shirt yawned again, scratching at his head as he tried to wake himself up. "Yeah, I'm the historian," he said. "Clyde said we had visitors, and I thought that sounded cool, so now I'm here. He would've given you the short version of the end-of-the-universe talk. I'll give you the long one. After Belle is done with her whole thing."

"I'm Sev," the cleric said. "The lizardkin is Vex, and the big scary armored guy is Derivan. We've got one more, but she went up to her room to rest. You'll probably see her later."

"I see," Belle said. Derivan shifted in discomfort as she examined them and her gaze settled on him. It wasn't that he wasn't used to being stared at, but the way her eyes widened slightly . . . "Is your friend all right?"

"I am fine," Derivan said, which was mostly true. He didn't particularly want to talk about it—not to a stranger, anyway.

Belle, who was clearly unconvinced, took the hint and changed the subject. "Then let's all take a seat," she said. "It's not going to be a long explanation, but you'll want to be sitting down for this. Clyde told you 'this is an echo,' explained absolutely nothing, and then ran off to find me, I take it?"

"That's about the gist of it," Sev said dryly. They all made their way to one of the larger tables in the inn as they spoke, and even as they sat, it seemed to expand slightly to accommodate all of them.

"Your names are interesting," Sev remarked as they sat. "They sound like they're from Earth."

"They are," Belle said with a smile. "Good observation. Our real names are words encoded in mana, so they're not really practical for conversation. There's a better explanation, but I'd be getting ahead of myself, so let me start with this:

"When Clyde says this is an echo, he means . . . well, this." Belle gestured all around herself. "The entire universe, such as it is. The town of Aldea, the planet Obreve, anything and everything you might find here is all part of one planar echo. If that sounds enormous, that's because it is. Echoes are usually a little smaller than this.

"Echoes can be manipulated slightly as they're formed. Nothing major, but you can change certain details—the color of the sky, the language people speak. We're in an echo tuned to the language of the planeshifted, so we ended up with names common to English."

Belle paused, then sat up straight, staring each of them in the eye as if to impress upon them the importance of her words. "It's important to understand that a planar echo is a misnomer. It implies that an echo is something lesser—but it is not. A planar echo is every bit as real as its origin point.

"What it isn't, however, is *stable*. Simply put, a planar echo is a fragment of reality that comes with a built-in deadline. They end. Sometimes very, very quickly. Frankly, being here isn't safe for you."

"But it's better for us," Elliot interrupted. Belle gave him a slightly annoyed look but nodded.

"An echo will last longer when part of its origin point exists in it," she said. "In this case, you four and anything you've brought here. It's like a stabilizing point—an anchor of sorts."

Derivan felt he should probably be a little more worried about that than he was. The idea that the reality they were in could just cease to exist at any moment would normally be enough to spark quite a bit of concern.

But they'd just faced down Irvis, some sort of mana aspect that could transform himself into a massive flesh abomination. And also been told that the universe had apparently ended over a thousand years earlier. In light of that, this news just felt par for the course.

Judging by the looks on his two companions, they felt the same way.

"This does explain dungeon bonus rooms," Vex said, tapping a finger on his chin and swishing his tail about. "And the dungeon's probably what's keeping this echo running, so I think we'll be fine until we leave." A pause. "Uh . . . not that you should keep us here to keep the echo running or anything," he added hurriedly.

Belle laughed at that, a tinkling, musical noise. "I wouldn't dream of it. Our duties here are different."

Derivan was no less amused. He could almost see the thought process in the lizardkin: *Oh, gods, did I just give them the idea?* Vex relaxed a bit after Belle's response, though, and Derivan calmed his impulse to scoop him up into his arms.

"Makes a lot more sense than the explanation I got, I'll tell you that much," Vex said, managing a slightly awkward smile. "*My* book talked about infinite sets."

"The academic overview is technically accurate and unnecessarily complicated." Belle relaxed too, a flickering, shadowy smile appearing on her face. "A much easier metaphor I like to use is something like eddies in an ocean. If you think of 'reality' as any part of the water that *moves,* then imagine mainline reality like a river of currents, permanently in place—for a given definition of permanence—but there are plenty of disturbances in the water, and just because those are smaller doesn't mean they're not still currents. They just don't last nearly as long."

Her smile faded. "If you hadn't come along, though, I don't think I would have noticed. Clyde only noticed because he had you three as a reference point and could compare you with the rest of reality."

"Is that . . . bad?" Vex ventured. He hesitated. "I'm not sure how I would feel if I found out I was an echo."

"For us? No, not really." Belle exchanged glances with Clyde and Elliot, the latter of whom still seemed half-asleep. "Same reason we aren't going to kidnap you and keep you here or anything. We're something of an exception." Belle tapped her fingers on the table briefly, her own version of hesitation. She shook her head. "Perhaps this will be a longer explanation than I anticipated. The important thing to understand is that you're in an echo of reality—this place *will* eventually crumble, but it looks like the rate of decay will be slow. The energy fueling this echo is not insignificant. Is that the dungeon you mentioned?"

"Probably," Vex said.

"How does this tie into the end of the universe?" Derivan asked, bringing the topic back to the bombshell that Clyde had dropped on them. He understood the *explanation*—sort of; some of the metaphor was going over his head—but he didn't know that he understood the point.

"It doesn't in any direct way," Belle said. "But Clyde thought it was important for you to understand that despite this being an echo, the history of this place is still very real. Echoes are based off their origin points—they're generated as a divergence point from their parent reality. With enough experience, you can figure out where that divergence point is. In case you're wondering, we can tell when the divergence happened, and it happened after the universe ended. So that's a common point in both our realities."

"I'm not sure I'm happy about having that in common," Sev muttered.

Vex, meanwhile, was muttering to himself in the way he so often did when he landed on an idea. Derivan recognized the look on his face by now. "You have thought of something," he said.

"Yeah," Vex agreed distractedly. "The whole idea of planar echoes . . . It has to be how our skills work, right? The system creates an echo—we already know that it can—and then manifests it in the form of a skill. In some cases, it's a lot more obvious than others. Misa's skill, the one that summons other copies of her, *literally* has Endless Echoes in the name."

It made sense. Derivan thought about this for a moment, then reached a conclusion. "Shift," he said. "You believe it uses Shift to do this?"

"Exactly!"

"A Shift, as in moving something from an echo into your reality?" Belle thought about it. "Clever. Much cheaper than making those things from scratch, if you know what you're doing. Making an echo isn't very resource-intensive with the right tools. You just need to . . . create an impact. It's *maintaining* an echo that costs energy."

"But back to the end of the universe . . ." Belle paused and shrugged, then gestured to Elliot, who startled slightly from his half-asleep position on the table.

"Oh. Uh, Clyde, could you get me some coffee? I could *really* use some coffee," he said. Clyde chuckled and nodded, disappearing behind the counter.

"Okay. End of the universe. Uh, Belle used the currents analogy, right?" Elliot yawned as he spoke, fingers tapping absentmindedly on the table; he glanced at Belle, who nodded at him.

"Right, okay. So, even that main current—mainline reality, as it were—won't last forever. Everything ends eventually, right? Most realities, most universes . . . they don't ever get far enough to do anything about it. Sometimes no life develops in them at all. But in *this* reality—this echo—we have *magic*."

Clyde paused as if for effect, and when no one reacted, he sighed. "Magic doesn't like endings. It is fundamentally opposed to the end of anything. When you get down to it, that's what mana is—a record, a memory, an idea that *lasts*.

"It's not like a universe ends all at once. It happens slowly. The fabric of reality begins to unravel. Things disappear. There are gaps where there weren't before. There's no *warning*; you don't get to know that the universe is ending. If something disappears, it's wiped from reality as a whole. You can't observe it like you can observe universal heat death—which is pretty easy to stave off with magic, by the way." Elliot accepted the mug from a reappearing Clyde, giving it a few grateful sips.

Derivan frowned, uncertain on how to respond. A quick glance to the side told him that Vex and Sev were shell-shocked, and neither of them looked like they were about to say anything anytime soon, which put the onus on him. He sighed to himself, wondering if it said something about him that his response to these things was so . . . muted.

He was *worried*, obviously. But that was about it. He was more focused on finding a solution.

"It sounds concerning," he said eventually. "But clearly this universe did not end. Something was able to preserve it?"

"The magic itself, yes," Elliot confirmed.

"So, infolocks . . ." Sev muttered, finally coming out of his stupor.

"I don't think they're the same thing," Vex said. Derivan could see his mind already racing, coming up with theories, conjecture. There was a look of concentration on his face that was plainly adorable. "Or . . . maybe not? The fact that some people can remember implies that it's not the same thing, right?"

"Perhaps the name is simply incorrect," Derivan supplied, deciding to contribute his own thoughts. "Perhaps an infolock is not a lock on information at all."

Vex took his thought and ran with it in a way that felt natural to the two of them. Derivan saw the moment the idea hit him—the way he narrowed his eyes and straightened, a flicker of an epiphany passing through him. "It's not information that's locked away from people," he said. "It's information that's actively being protected from being completely erased. By keying in a few people that are allowed to remember the way things *were*."

"I don't know how your branch of reality survived the end," Belle said. "Or what you're talking about, exactly. But if you're talking about some people remembering things and not others, that hypothesis is a lot more plausible than magic that's capable of erasing information from all of Obreve."

Sev, Vex, and Derivan all went silent. It recontextualized a lot. If it was expensive to preserve information, and the system wanted to limit the people that were allowed to *know* . . .

"So you're saying there's no big force that's trying to end the world?" Sev said quietly. Derivan wondered if that was the thought he was struggling with—that there was no enemy to fight, nothing they could win against. "It's just . . . the end. No big bad, no evil lord, just . . . the natural conclusion of reality."

"That's correct," Elliot said. He was looking a little brighter now that he'd had his coffee—the "hair" on his head had returned to being shadowy flames, at least until Clyde reached up and messed with it. Elliot fended him off with a yelp. "Hey!"

"Sorry," Clyde said, not looking sorry at all. "Couldn't resist."

Sev glanced at him, and Derivan noticed the slight spike of irritation—Clyde wasn't taking all this very seriously at all. But Sev kept his irritation to himself, and a second later, it bled out of him. It wasn't Clyde's fault at all.

This was just the reality they had been living with, presumably for a long, long time.

"*As I was saying*," Elliot said, "you are correct. But there *are* ways to push back even the dissipation of reality. We have mana. Magic. It's *alive*, and it didn't like the idea that the universe was ending.

"So, fourteen hundred years ago, it decided it could fix it."

Elliot paused for a moment, and Clyde took the opportunity to jump in. "You have to understand—mana is not alive in the traditional sense of the word. It *is* alive, after a fashion, but only because of what it is—a record of everything we are and everything we know. Something like that can't help but be alive. But it's not something you can speak to, nor is it something that knows how to respond to you, even if you could."

"So," Elliot continued, glancing at his husband and picking up on his train of thought. "The mana tried to fix things. It drove people underground to try to protect them from what was happening. It's got a bit of natural resistance to the unweaving of reality, and by flooding areas with thick concentrations of mana, it could protect those areas from being unwoven. It was easier to do that underground—to caves and caverns, tunnel systems."

"That explains Teque," Sev muttered.

"And while people were underground," Elliot said, "it tried to figure out how to restore things as they were being erased. Like we've said, mana is a record. In theory, anything in that record can be restored. But it's just a record of life. It doesn't really understand physics, or particles, or any of the laws the world runs on. That's how you get stuff like . . . well, that."

Elliot gestured at the window—at the pane in the air that reflected grass and greenery, even though there was nothing there.

". . . That's kind of messed up," Sev said.

The implications were large. The implications about what the system had been doing this whole time—those were large, too. Derivan stared outside the window at the reflective panes of air shimmering across the horizon.

"I have a question," Vex finally said. His words caught Derivan's attention, and he glanced over to see that Vex had managed to center himself a bit, though he still looked a bit shaken. "This is . . . I mean, this is a lot. But . . . how do you know all this? Don't take this the wrong way, but what *are* you?"

"Full of hard questions, aren't you?" Clyde chuckled. The mirth fell away after a moment, and his expression became a little more serious—not accusatory, but almost . . . sympathetic. "Your friend over there might know something," he said. He nodded at Sev.

CHAPTER 2

A ROLE TO PLAY

"Me?" Sev asked, a little incredulously. "I've never met you guys in my life."

"No, but you're under the same effect we are." Clyde glanced at him, his eyes glowing that faint off-yellow again before changing back to white. "Or you *were*. It's mostly faded now."

Sev shifted uncomfortably under Clyde's gaze, then called up a system window. Something had changed. His [**Memory Loss**] and [**Fatebroken**] maluses were still there, but the third one—the one that had been obfuscated and listed simply as [#######]—that had changed. And it was no longer listed as a malus.

[**Concept**] [####] **You have chosen your path. You are the Guide.**

Not that the new description was much better than the old one. "I don't know what it is, exactly," he said. "At least, if you're talking about what I think you're talking about. It doesn't really give me any details—just says I'm a Guide."

"Yeah, that's kind of part of being a Guide," Clyde said. "Something to do with autonomy. You're a part of your own journey, so you can't know where you're going, or you might change your path."

That made sense, Sev supposed. It explained the [**Fatebroken**] malus, anyway. *You are not your own*. Because some part of his future was fixed.

"The point," Clyde said, "is that's what we are—elementals bound to a concept in much the same way you are. Were."

"Which one is it?" Sev asked.

"All paths reach an end." Clyde shrugged. "And the future can't be fixed, just manipulated. You can make things more likely to happen, but you can't guarantee it. If your connection to your role is fading, it's either because you've stepped off your path or because you're close to the end of it, and nothing is guaranteed anymore."

"That's not worrying at all," Sev muttered. Clyde shot him a sympathetic look but said nothing.

"In any case," Belle said, "the concepts we're bound to are the reason it doesn't matter to us that this is an echo. We're linked to a concept, and we're here to . . . play a role, for lack of a better term. It's not that we're not allowed to live our own lives—we are—but we also have to embody our concepts in some way. Clyde has to be an innkeeper, so he has to embody hospitality; I have to be a scientist, so I have to embody curiosity; Elliot has to be a historian, so he has to embody memory."

"I'm one of the lucky ones," Clyde added. "Hospitality is vague. I can pretty much do whatever I want as long as I'm keeping the inn in good shape and being hospitable to my guests whenever I have them, which is never. Except today."

"Plus he enjoys being a good host," Elliot says wryly. "Sometimes he makes us play pretend."

Clyde shot Elliot a dirty look at that.

"We represent the roles we're given," Belle said, ignoring the other two. She stirred her own glass of what looked like tea—Sev didn't remember when she'd even found a cup of tea, but it was there, right in front of her. "Sometimes, we even play more than one. In this echo, it acts as a kind of a conceptual template for the mana. Helps it know how to recreate things, especially something as abstract as a societal role. We help by playing our parts in this makeshift society, cooking food we don't need to eat and keeping an inn without any guests, because it helps keep reality stitched together."

"And even when this echo ends, we don't really die," Clyde said. "It's a perk of being what we are. You're part entity, part concept. As long as the concept exists elsewhere, so can we. Every expression of us is linked. If you meet me again in your reality, I'll technically be different . . . But if you play the right sort of trick, I might be able to remember you."

"Reminds me of Irvis," Vex muttered under his breath.

"What was that?" Clyde glanced at Vex.

"Nothing," Vex said quickly.

"Is it working?" Sev asked, changing the subject. "Putting all this aside—everything the mana is doing to keep the universe alive. Is it— A lot of the paths we saw up there were . . . worrying. The mana's trying to keep the universe alive, but is it *succeeding*?"

"No," Clyde said bluntly. "Maybe for a given definition of *success*, but . . . ultimately, no. It's slowing down an inevitable doom. Maybe your reality is having better luck; that would explain why it's the 'main' one."

"I don't think it is," Vex said quietly.

Sev leaned back in his seat, contemplative. This whole conversation did answer some questions—it made it clear what the system was for, at least, even if it wasn't clear what the purpose of each component was. He still didn't know why stats and levels had to be a part of it, nor did he understand why monsters existed, but the picture for how the system kept reality together was becoming clear. Dungeons and reality anchors, keeping everything stable.

Sev just wished he knew how *he* was involved and what those status effects he had meant.

The ensuing silence left Derivan feeling . . . introspective. The others felt the same way, he could see, but the talk of what Sev was, what the shadow elementals were—that brought back feelings he thought he had long since dismissed.

Doubt. What was he? What were so-called "monsters," and what had he become when he allowed his friends to free him from the shackles of the system?

Perhaps these shadow elementals knew the answer. They seemed to know the answer to everything else. He hesitated only one more moment before he decided to speak. "And me?" he asked. Derivan found he felt strangely nervous. "What am I?"

Clyde glanced at him, surprised. "What do you mean?"

"I was told I was the same sort of creature as . . . an enemy of ours. Someone from the mana." Vex tensed a little beside him, and Derivan tried not to react to that. He did not want Vex to fear him—the thought left a coldness coiling in his chest. "I do not know what that means."

". . . I'm afraid I can't answer that." Clyde frowned, giving him a once-over. "You're not bound the same way we are, or the same way your friend is. But the nature of your existence is different. I don't really have any answers for you there. Sorry."

Derivan hid his disappointment with a slight nod of acknowledgement. He would just have to continue that search on his own, then. The idea that he might be anything like Irvis made him feel the closest thing he could to sick—

Without any prompting, Vex reached out for him and took his hand into his own. He didn't look directly at Derivan, his gaze still focused on Clyde and the conversation, but he did give Derivan's hand a gentle squeeze.

The coldness in his chest abated, and Derivan squeezed back gratefully. Vex glanced at him, an unsaid question in his eyes.

Derivan nodded. He was all right. They could talk later, when they had more privacy. Misa had gotten each of them separate rooms, after all.

"Are you okay?" Sev asked after a minute. It took Derivan a moment to realize the question was directed toward Clyde and his spouses, and not to him. "Do we need to free you or something?"

"Not at all." Clyde laughed. "And I'm not just saying that because I'm being made to. We *have* our lives; this isn't slavery. It's just that being an innkeeper is a part of me. Technically, if I really hated the job, I could choose to take on a different concept—so I'm not really locked in by even that. I suppose in your case it's a little different . . . but it looks like it's something you chose, too."

"That's what the system says," Sev admitted. "I don't remember choosing anything."

"You probably aren't allowed to remember." Clyde gave him a sympathetic smile. "It's happened before to some of us. Mostly the ones that have to play important roles. They can't know what they're supposed to do ahead of time. If they did, it would be less . . . real."

"That's . . ." Sev hesitated. Derivan saw the way his shoulders hunched in—he wasn't sure that was the answer. But it made sense. It explained the memory loss, which would conveniently hide any foreknowledge that would have prevented Sev from properly playing his role.

It was a little more hidden, but he could see Sev's worry, too. His fear. Just the smallest amount of it, but it was an uncharacteristic sort of fear for him.

Maybe they all just needed a break, after everything that had happened.

Knowing the universe had ended—was ending?—was a terrifying revelation, but since they weren't yet in a position to stop it . . . they had to figure out how to get there.

"I believe my companions are exhausted," Derivan said. "We require some rest. But it was a pleasure to meet you three—truly. You have all been kinder than you needed to be."

"We treat you the way you treat others," Clyde said with a small smile. "Would you look at that. Turns out you're good people. I hope you knew that already."

Elliot laughed at that, nudging his husband but wearing a stupid grin. "You're a cheesy dork."

"But a good one." Belle smiled a serene smile, then directed her words to Derivan. "Don't let us keep you. Do what you have to do. We often have our breakfasts together here, so this likely won't be the last time you see us. Say hi every now and then, won't you? You're free to stay as long as you need."

"Hey, *I'm* supposed to say that," Clyde complained. Belle just smiled mischievously.

Derivan chuckled softly, then took Vex by the hand and—

He paused before he could grab Sev by the shoulder, looking at his stump of an arm. Sev noticed but didn't say anything; Vex hadn't been watching him at the time. Instead, he was bouncing anxiously on his feet. Derivan decided not to bring it up. Instead, he walked up the steps with Vex, hearing Sev's footsteps as he followed behind them.

"I think I need some time to myself, too," Sev said awkwardly when they arrived at his door. Derivan tossed his key at him and he caught it. "All this . . . it's a lot. Let's figure out a plan tomorrow?"

"Of course," Derivan said. Sev nodded, gave him a tiny, halfhearted salute, then walked into his room and closed the door behind him.

The moment he did, Vex let out a sigh, crumpling into Derivan. "I actually don't want to sleep alone tonight," Vex mumbled. "Can I hang out in your room? Let's just . . . talk. Not about this, or fighting, or what happened in the dungeon. I want to talk about literally anything else."

"You are always welcome in my room, my friend," Derivan said, and then paused. "Boyfriend? Though the word does not fit as well into the sentence."

"Oh my gods," Vex said, and he managed a laugh, although it was happy and sad all at once. It was the first real laugh he'd had in a while, and Derivan found that he had missed the sound. "Let's just go in, you big goof."

"As far as affectionate nicknames go, I feel you could do better," Derivan mused, and chuckled when Vex made an indignant, huffing noise in the back of his throat.

Derivan led Vex into his room, his thoughts on the events of the day. Things had gone badly in that final fight, and what they had learned after had somehow been even worse. The end of the world was no enemy they could fight, caused by no spell they could counter. It was the simple end of all things.

But not yet.

They were alive, and as long as they were alive, things would not be over.

"Can you tell me more about Elyra?" Derivan asked.

The beds in their rooms were, it turned out, enormous—and made of some magically enchanted material that didn't rip apart when Derivan tried lying down on it, too. Vex had been the one to notice the enchantment, or

Derivan wouldn't even have tried. This way, they could both lie on the bed, although that durability enchantment didn't exactly translate into a *weight distribution* enchantment.

Which was to say that there had been a lot of awkward, accidental rolling before Derivan had eventually discovered that he could forcibly reinforce the bed somewhat with the Slime stat. By infusing it into the bed. It wasn't *comfortable,* but it was workable, and Vex seemed happier when they could share the bed. He'd looked terribly guilty when Derivan had tried to sit on the floor, even though Derivan insisted he couldn't actually take advantage of the comfort the bed offered.

"Elyra?" Vex asked, glancing over at him. He lay pressed up against Derivan's side, his snout resting on his chest. Despite being a living suit of armor that insisted he could feel no comfort, Derivan found this position . . . strangely comforting. "What do you want to know? You've been there now."

"We did not get a chance to explore the aspects of Elyra that you seemed most proud of," Derivan said. "We only saw the worst of it. I would like to know what mattered to you."

Vex managed a half-smile at that. "I don't know if there are any parts of Elyra I could say that I'm *proud* of," he said, staring up at the ceiling, and then he sighed. "No, that's a lie. I mean, I don't know if proud is the right word; I'm not the one that made any of those things. But . . . I loved the libraries. Not even for the books on magic, although I loved those. They had so many books, and all of them were interesting."

"I have not had the chance to read much," Derivan commented. "Also, it is remarkably easy to tear the pages of a book."

"No offense, but you *are* made of metal," Vex said, rapping Derivan's chest once and causing a light *ting* to reverberate through the room. "But putting that aside, that's actually one of the reasons I refused to put any points into Strength. I've been told that you get all the fine control you need as part of the stat when you put points into it, but I don't actually want to risk it."

"I feel like I should apologize for that book of yours that I accidentally tore," Derivan said.

"It was an empty notebook," Vex said dismissively. "And the pages were easy enough to put back together. If anything, I'm sorry I enchanted it to explode."

"Why *did* you enchant it to explode?"

"I didn't want anyone to touch my stuff, and then I sort of forgot about it after I joined this team." Vex sounded vaguely embarrassed, and Derivan chuckled. "*Anyway*. The libraries were great. It's where I felt most at home, even, which I guess might be weird. I made friends with all the librarians I met! You met one of them."

"She seemed like a good person," Derivan agreed. "Though I never caught her name."

". . . Neither did I," Vex admitted. "And, uh, I always felt too awkward to ask . . ."

Derivan laughed. "I will make sure to ask on your behalf next time."

"Deal."

"Did you have any favorite books?"

"Mystery books," Vex said, his eyes gleaming a bit. The answer was so immediate that Derivan glanced over at him in surprise. "I mean, the magic books were my favorite, but you already knew that. So my second favorite was mystery books—well-written ones, the kind where you can put the puzzle together yourself if you notice all the right details. I could lose myself for hours—" He laughed. "I remember telling the librarians to mark the page where the main characters solve the mystery just so I could keep rereading and try to figure it out myself first."

"Do librarians have such encyclopedic knowledge of their books?" Derivan asked, amused. He enjoyed listening to Vex—seeing the lizardkin smile as he lost himself in his memories. How long had it been since he'd last read a book like this, even?

"Mine did!" Vex grinned. "Well, most of the time. Not *all* of the time. I wish I had more time to read now, but I spend so much time adventuring, and there's so much to discover . . ."

Vex went silent for a moment, and Derivan sensed there was more he wanted to say. The armor waited patiently.

"I guess I can read faster now," Vex said. "I found out my Sign lets me do that. I don't know how I feel about that, though. I want to experience a book for myself, not have all the knowledge just . . . poured into my head. I'm not just a bucket to be filled."

"Indeed not," Derivan agreed. Vex glanced at him, his gaze surprisingly unreadable, even with Physical Empathy.

There was a long silence then. A comfortable one. Vex adjusted his position next to Derivan, curled his tail around one of the armor's legs, and rested his chin on his shoulder.

Then, finally, he sighed.

"I know I said I don't want to talk about it," Vex said. "But I think maybe I do want to tell you about what happened back there. I don't know if I'm ready to tell the others yet . . . but I want you to know."

Derivan shot Vex a curious look. The lizardkin fidgeted for a moment, then finally spoke, the words almost too soft to hear. "Irvis made me fight my dad. Or . . . an echo of him, I suppose. We know what those are now."

"Oh," Derivan said.

Sometimes, Derivan found that even in the vast expanse of the spoken language, there were no words that could suffice. He could see the lingering pain in Vex's eyes even now—could see how the lizardkin fought to look past what had happened. He could feel the way Vex clung to him just a little harder after he spoke those words.

What could he say about what Irvis had done?

Derivan could tell there was more Vex wanted to say, but he couldn't find the words. He pressed himself close to the metal of Derivan's chest instead, trying and failing to find all the words he needed to say.

"Take your time," Derivan said. His words were softer than he could ever remember them being. He wrapped his remaining arm around Vex, rubbing gentle circles onto his back. "I am here for you."

CHAPTER 3

THE MORNING AFTER

Derivan's arm was wrapped casually around Vex's waist. He wasn't sure why, exactly. He just knew he hadn't wanted to stop after they got out of bed. Vex seemed to appreciate the touch, at least.

The lizardkin hadn't slept until late into the night, after he'd finished explaining everything that had happened with Irvis and the echo of Karix. Derivan had . . . listened. It was the best he could do, really; Vex hadn't wanted anything more than a chance to talk about it without having to worry about what it meant for them in terms of strategy, or what it implied about what Irvis was and what he could do.

He wanted to talk about what it meant for him. How it felt. And Derivan had held him close, and that had been enough.

They emerged from their now-shared room, having privately agreed that they didn't *really* need two separate rooms, to find Misa and Sev already standing in the corridor.

"Sorry about yesterday," Misa said. Derivan glanced at her. She didn't look like she'd managed to sleep much, either. Sev stood opposite her, yawning, and Derivan took the opportunity to examine him as well. The system strings that hung around him were in tatters now, and while pieces of them still clung on, they had mostly gone. With a bit of help, he could wipe away whatever hold they still held over him. He just didn't know if that was a good idea yet.

Not if Sev had *chosen* that path—whatever that meant.

"Are you okay?" Sev asked. He watched Misa intently, worry furrowed in his brows. Misa swallowed once, then sighed, throwing her arms back almost explosively and nearly punching through the wall of the room.

"I fuckin' hate *doubt*," she muttered. "It's . . . When I was fighting Irvis, I could tell I was straining *something*. Every single time I used [**An Anchor**

of Heart and Home], it was like I could feel the skill screaming at me. Fuckin' thing was about to break. Did you know skills could break? *I didn't.*"

Sev opened his mouth to say something, but Misa held up a hand, and he stopped, hesitating. "If it was just that?" she said. "That's fine. I don't care. I don't need to be *strong*—well, no, that's a lie—but I'd give up that strength in a heartbeat if it meant I could protect you guys. That's the whole *point.*

"But it was hurting my family." Misa's eyes darkened a bit. "Mom and Dad spent a lot of time building up that village to be stronger. I can't imagine that fight didn't wreck half the village. It's probably the only reason I survived some of the hits I didn't block, because let me tell you, that guy is fucking *fast.*

"I think I knew, on some level, that the fight was damaging the anchor. That if I pushed it too far, I was gonna lose them again. Every time I blocked an attack, it was a *choice.* You guys or maybe, potentially, all of them." Misa took a slightly shaky breath, then clenched her fists. Even as exhausted and drained as she looked—even with slightly sallow skin and sunken cheeks—there was a look in her eyes that *burned.* If she'd been holding anything, even metal, Derivan was fairly certain it would have bent or snapped. "I don't . . . I fucking *hated* that. Half the point of my Class is that I shouldn't have to make that fucking choice.

"I needed some time alone to sit with that choice," she said. "That's all that is. I'd say that I'm sorry I didn't explain sooner, but I needed that time, and I needed to figure it out on my own. I'll say this—I'm *not* going to be put in that position again. We're going to make use of every second of this time, and we're going to get strong enough that Irvis can't do *shit* to us even if he tried."

The last of her words were said with an air of finality; she didn't expect anyone to disagree, and no one did. All around the table, there were slow nods. None of them had expected to be put so far on the back foot.

Misa's words were just more fuel to a flame that had already begun to ignite.

"We'll need a plan for that," Sev finally said; he looked like he'd been about to say something else but had changed his mind at the last moment. "Some kind of training we can do, at least. We can grind levels here, but I don't think raw levels are going to cut it for something like Irvis."

"System levels haven't been enough for a while," Vex said quietly. "The more we understand magic and the system, the more we can turn those things to our advantage. I've been studying those things all my life, and I think I'm finally starting to grasp how they're related. Derivan has Patch, and I think I can create my own back door into the system if I have a little bit of time. And, um . . ."

Vex hesitated slightly, and his gaze went to Derivan, then rested on his missing arm. The other three paused and looked at their friend, too; Derivan shifted uncomfortably under their combined gaze.

". . . I'm sorry I couldn't stop that from happening," Misa said, suddenly sounding guilty.

"It was not your fault."

"If I'd been better—"

"*Misa,*" Derivan emphasized, and then glanced around the room. To Vex, who looked just as guilty and couldn't meet his gaze; he blamed himself for not being *there.* To Sev, who seemed to blame himself for not being able to heal this problem away.

There was a certain irony to the fact that he badly wanted to reach out with his missing arm and comfort all of them. "Vex," he continued. "Sev. We did what we could. We were unprepared. We will be prepared in the future. The loss of my arm does not pain me, and I believe a new one will attach, if we can only have one forged."

"Then we'll make forging you a new arm a priority, too," Sev said with a sigh. "It's the least we can do."

"The least you could do is nothing," Derivan said, and this time, he offered a ghost of a smile, bowing his head towards his friends. "So I thank you."

And then, swiftly, before anyone could say anything more on it—because he did not like *thinking* about his missing arm, for all that he told himself he was okay with it—he moved on. "I believe we are missing only a few more keys to understand everything that is happening," Derivan offered. "The system calls me and my kind monsters, and Irvis likened me to him. I wish to know why. And the last piece—"

"—is me," Sev finished, shifting a little bit uncomfortably as Derivan's gaze fell on him. "I don't have much more than before to tell you. I can tell you that my status tells me that *I made a choice,* to have some aspect of my future stripped away from me. Or maybe some aspect of free will. I mostly try not to think about it, to be honest."

"There is nothing else you can tell us?" Derivan asked.

"I assumed it was because of what I gave up to heal Onyx," Sev said quietly. "But Onyx acts like I'm supposed to do something, or realize something, and maybe this is what the gods have been aiming us at all along. But that feels . . . cheap. Incomplete. I don't believe we're just a part of some divine plan. If it was that easy to fix things, they would've done it, and they wouldn't need me to *not know what's going on*."

A hint of frustration touched his voice at those last few words, and Derivan realized Sev was every bit as upset as the rest of them, if not a little more so. He was just very, very good at hiding it.

Maybe because he'd been living with that knowledge—that frustration—this whole time.

"I need to figure out what's going on with my bond to Aurum," Sev said finally. He unclenched his fists—Derivan wondered if he'd even noticed that he'd clenched them, or the raw, red marks from his fingers digging into his skin. "I think that's my avenue of training. Whatever I've got with the gods is stronger than what other clerics have, and I've never worked on anything more than defensive and healing skills. I need more options. I don't think healing is going to be enough anymore."

"We all need more options," Misa said. "I'm going to try to . . . jailbreak my skills, for lack of a better word. I'll need your help for that, Derivan."

"You have it."

"Okay." Misa sighed. "Now that that's out of the way, we still need to figure out . . . Fuck. Everything that's happening back in—the real world? Doesn't feel right to call it that."

"The rebellion in Elyra," Vex supplied. "The suppression of growth magic there, as well. The situation in Teque and Fendal."

"Can we do anything about those things from here?" Misa asked. Vex hesitated.

"I think we can," he said. "I was thinking about it before we even got in, and I'm more sure than ever now. We can train, but more than that . . . we can *coordinate*. If we can reach outside the dungeon, using Shift or whatever kinds of reality magic exist here, then we can use the time dilation to our advantage."

Misa's eyes sharpened. "Meaning a problem comes up, and we solve it using all the extra time we have here."

Vex nodded slowly. "Assuming our system access doesn't decay while we're here," he said. "And we still have the crystals we need to stay connected. There's a few problems we need to work out, and the first thing we need to do is find a way to reach out without relying on the system for messages. I think we can do a little more than just pass messages with ideas back and forth. You saw Derivan opening portals with Shift when you used your skill before, Misa."

"I may be able to push the skill to that level," Derivan said thoughtfully. "It is certainly an avenue of research."

"But before all of that," Vex said, and he grimaced slightly; he wasn't looking forward to talking about this. But Derivan gave him a reassuring glance, and he straightened slightly.

He'd gotten through the worst of it last night, anyway. "We need to catch Misa up on what Clyde told us," Vex said. "And I need to tell you guys about what I know about Irvis."

Misa's reaction to Clyde's news was . . . surprisingly subdued. She was surprised, but only in an abstract sort of way. "It fits with everything we know," she said. "It's scary shit. But I'm kind of oversaturated on scary shit. Just means yet another thing we gotta fix."

It was a very optimistic take, and all of them knew it. In one world, the system had been born, presumably to try to fix the end of the universe; it had only managed to slow it down. In the other, the source of all magic had done the same thing, and had been about as successful.

They'd have to devise something better than the sum of both parts to be able to come close, and they weren't anywhere near having that kind of knowledge or power.

Not yet, anyway.

Her reaction to Vex's explanation of Irvis was a lot more pronounced. Her eyes tightened with anger, and the tankard she held in a hand cracked and splintered. She put it down on the table before she could do any more damage and had to take a breath before she spoke.

"I'm sorry he did that to you," she said; Sev nodded in agreement. "That's fucked."

"It is." Vex hesitated. "I . . . need some time with that one. I'm sort of glad we're *here* and have time to figure things out. If you don't mind, I'd like to just talk about what Irvis is and what we can do about him."

"I've been thinking about that," Sev said. "Clyde mentioned the elementals of this town being linked to concepts and having to play roles. Do you think that's related at all? Irvis is an Aspect, but that doesn't sound too different from having a role. Just pointed in a different direction."

"They might be similar," Vex agreed. "I don't think they're exactly the same thing, but they might share some strengths and weaknesses, being made of mana and all that. It's not like we can march down and ask them what their weaknesses are, though."

"Can't we?" Misa raised an eyebrow. "Seems like we might just need to find someone with the right role, to me."

"That's . . ." Vex paused. "That's a good point?"

"We may be able to simply ask if they are aware of living Aspects, as well," Derivan said. "We did not offer that context before. They may have more information."

"We should figure out if we can pay them back, too." Misa frowned slightly. "Doesn't feel right, getting so much from them for free."

"We'll ask about that," Sev said. "I'm worried about Irvis. You were basically just working off theory when you brought us here, right?"

"I figured the nature of Hatred here would be different," Vex said, nodding. "That he wouldn't be able to exist the same way here that he does in our . . . section of reality, I guess. We need a better word for that. He hasn't reappeared, so I might be right, or something else might be going on."

"Sounds like the next step is to talk to Clyde," Sev decided. "Find a blacksmith to forge Derivan an arm. Figure out where and how we can train. Connect with the rebels in Elyra so we can provide support, check the progress of things in Teque . . . and figure out a way to fix the decay of reality. I'm sure it'll be a piece of cake."

Derivan and the others all stared at him, and Sev sighed. "I'm joking."

Misa snorted and gave him a friendly punch in the shoulder. Derivan looked faintly puzzled, and Vex patted him on the arm he still had.

Having it all laid out like this helped, he thought. Now, at least, they knew what they were going to do next.

CHAPTER 4

ASPECTS AND CONNECTIONS

"Can't help you with the Aspect thing, I'm afraid," Clyde said.

He'd joined them at their breakfast table after serving up their breakfast—a surprisingly hearty and comforting meal, though Derivan couldn't taste it himself. From the sounds Vex was making, though, he assumed the food was good. It was some assortment of egg and fried meats; the oil was still crackling by the time it reached their table, no doubt assisted by the fire-aspect mana circling around the plates. "I know what mana aspects *are*, but I've never heard of them being alive. It's not the same thing as elementals. I can *theorize*, if you want, but you're better off finding someone with a role more specialized in that kind of thing."

"Give us your best theory anyway," Sev suggested.

"Mana's alive," Clyde said immediately. Derivan felt a flicker of amusement—Clyde might not have had an answer, but he'd been eager to share his thoughts. He was just waiting for someone to ask. As if he could tell that Derivan knew, Clyde caught his gaze and winked. "Maybe not in any traditional sense of the word, but it's certainly capable of *feeling*. Get that feeling extreme enough, and who knows, maybe something happens."

"That's kinda vague," Sev frowned, but Vex was nodding.

"If what the system is doing is hurting it," Vex said quietly, "then I wouldn't be surprised."

With the way he'd slowed down and started poking at his food, Derivan suspected the lizardkin was remembering what his family had done to him. Even in the name of the greater good . . .

"The mana here hasn't had any reason to be nearly so angry," Clyde added. "I don't think you'll have to worry here. The young mage's instincts were right. If an Aspect can come to life, I suspect it would be similar to us: existing across all realities with mana, but different in each one."

"Well . . . thanks. That's a relief, at least," Sev said. "Is there anything we can do for you? I feel like we're imposing on you a lot."

"Nonsense," Clyde said dismissively. "I might be happy with my job, but do you know how boring it is to be an innkeeper without any guests? This is the most fun I've had in centuries."

"I forget how *old* all of this is," Sev muttered. "We only have, what, two hundred years of history to go off of? But the world here ended fourteen hundred years ago."

"I hadn't quite considered exactly how *much* of our history is missing," Vex said with a small frown. "If we knew what happened in those interim years—"

"—We might be able to understand what the system's been trying to do," Sev finished. "I wonder . . ."

He trailed off, but there was a *look* in his eyes that Derivan recognized; he'd hit upon an idea, and didn't want to share it just yet, in case it was a false lead. "Do you know anywhere we can train, Clyde?" he asked, changing the subject. "We don't want to accidentally destroy your inn or anything."

"Oh, you wouldn't," Clyde said with a cheerful confidence that made Derivan examine the inn walls suspiciously. "But if you're looking for actual training grounds, there are plenty all around. If you try to head out of this town, you'll find a lot of the adjacent sections of land are from different eras of our world. I'd say you're pretty lucky to have ended up here, of all places, but if this is a manufactured echo, then it's not really luck."

"We've been lucky in a lot of other ways," Sev muttered, almost to himself. There was a furrow in his brow and a look of slight worry in his eyes. "And I know Onyx was planning something . . ."

"Onyx?" Clyde asked curiously. Sev shook his head.

"It's nothing," he said. "Just a thought. I need a little more time to think about it. In the meantime, uh, do you know anyone else with roles that might help us? Maybe a trainer, or someone well versed in magic?"

"Our resident scientist and historian not good enough for you?" Clyde joked, and chuckled when he saw the look of consternation on Sev's face. "No, no, I'm kidding. Most of us serve pretty mundane roles; if you want *magic*, you'll have to find another elemental town. Same thing with combat. But I'd caution against doing that. It's considerably more dangerous than this place."

"What do you call this town, anyway?" Vex asked.

"Now *that's* a matter of contention," Clyde said. For some reason, he seemed rather amused by the question. "We've got a couple of names for it, but a lot of us just call it Mundane. We play all the mundane roles and embody their concepts: hospitality, research, sanitation. Some of us want to give it a more creative name, but we're afraid it'll mess with the mana too much if we try to be anything more than a template."

"Is that why everything outside is so . . . ?" Sev gestured a bit. Clyde chuckled.

"Yeah, pretty much," he said. "We've got a lot more leeway inside. I don't think any of us really think of Mundane as our own, because of that. There's a lot of emphasis on personalizing your homes." He leaned in close to whisper. "Belle decorates her place in skulls and bones. Scared the shadow out of me the first time I went over to her place, let me tell you."

"Really?" Misa leaned forward, sounding interested. She'd spent most of the conversation only half-listening, glancing through her system screens; she'd long since finished her food. The mention of bones seemed to call to her, though. "Sounds badass. I wanna see."

Clyde snorted. "You'll have to take it up with her. She's very protective of her bone collection," he said.

"Maybe later, then," Misa said, managing a ghost of a smile. "We need to head out and look for a good training ground. And look for a blacksmith. You happen to know of one, or know about anything nearby we need to watch out for?"

"There's not a blacksmith here, I'm afraid. You'd have to find one of the more combat-oriented templates." Clyde's gaze wandered down to Derivan's missing arm, though he didn't say anything about it. Derivan was surprised he hadn't remarked on it before then. Vex sagged a little bit at Clyde's words, and the shadow elemental's gaze turned sympathetic. "I'm sure they'd be happy to help you if you find them.

"As for the rest . . . don't wander too far, or you'll have a hard time finding your way back. Other than that, not that I know of, but most of us don't wander very far from here. So be careful."

"We will," Misa nodded. "You guys ready?"

Derivan and Sev stood from the table. Vex quickly shoveled the rest of his food into his mouth and nodded. "Mhm," he said, trying not to let any food fall from his mouth.

Misa chuckled and ruffled her fingers through the frills on his head, despite his protests, and Derivan smiled at the sight.

With no blacksmith to be found, Derivan would have to wait on getting a new arm commissioned; in the worst case, they could commission a new one back in Elyra, though his companions all seemed loath to wait that long. He couldn't deny a certain itch to get his arm back, either, but he told himself he needed to be patient.

Maybe there was something he could do with his Slime stat in the meantime. The stat seemed great at making his body more malleable, and even allowed him to produce small slime structures—surely it could be stretched into making him a new arm?

Derivan wasn't sure how much of that was wishful thinking.

The plan for now was that they would explore in sweeping circles around Mundane, expanding the circle as the days passed. The time dilation was strong, almost a hundred times that of base reality, so they had time. The anchor's degradation being based on un-dilated time was helpful too. It stretched the anchor's remaining two weeks out to almost four years.

Not that they were planning on waiting nearly that long, of course, especially since they suspected that Misa using her skills would push that degradation faster than the timer indicated.

As such—as much as she hated it—Misa's training was to take a back seat for now. Derivan and Vex had to push their skills first, to learn more about the system and about the nature of magic. Sev would meditate on his bond with Aurum. None of his skills allowed him direct contact with any of the gods, but his skills didn't cover whatever it was he had with Aurum.

It was an avenue to grow in, in any case.

". . . so there has to be an aspect that represents the system," Vex was saying. "If I can just figure out how that aspect works, how to access it—"

"But this whole *world* is based on not having a system," Misa pointed out. "And we just discussed how Irvis probably isn't a threat here, even if he's a capital-A Aspect, because all aspects are local to the particular echo they're in."

"Right." Vex deflated a bit. "We still have access to our systems, though. It's not like the system doesn't exist here entirely. It might just be harder."

"Perhaps it would be best to leave system manipulation to me for now," Derivan suggested gently. "It is something I must train, regardless. If you work on glyph combinations and I work on the system, we will be a difficult pair to beat."

Vex brightened a bit. "You have a point," he said. "And I can try to figure out how to access the glyphic records, too. You heard what Clyde said—mana is a record of things, right? That's got to be how they discover new glyphs. I bet that's how my Sign works, too, by accessing that record. Maybe if I try to turn my Sign on itself again, but this time *while it's casting*—or maybe if you cast something, and I try to target the spell in the process of being cast—"

Vex rambled, and Derivan smiled.

—ɷ—

Misa watched the others and let herself smile a small smile before she walked away to sit on a nearby rock. The idea was that if any of Vex and Derivan's experimentation generated something that could help repair the anchor nestled in her soul, she'd benefit from it.

In the meantime, *someone* had to communicate with the outside world. Even with a hundred-times dilation, there had been enough time for everyone to get her messages.

Sure enough, there were a number of responses waiting for her through the system.

[**I love you, and I hope you're okay,**] Charise had sent. [**Don't worry about us—the village is fine. We just have to rebuild a bit. I won't say no one was hurt, but no one is dead, and that's what's important.**]

Misa winced a bit at that. "Hope you're telling me the truth, Mom," she muttered softly. Surely her mother wouldn't lie about something like that—but then again, if Charise's intuition told her she needed the lie . . .

Not something she could afford to dwell on.

[**As for the situation in Fendal,**] the message continued, [**it's going better than we hoped. Don't have enough time for all the details, but there's a whole rebellion against Helg now. We might not need your help. I'll keep you updated. Stay safe, stay alive, and come back to us.**]

A small pause, and then an additional message, left as an afterthought: [**We'll have fish stew waiting.**]

Misa managed a small smile there; it pushed back some of the fog of emotion that had begun to accumulate in her head. She moved on to the next message from the Guildmaster.

[**Velykos and the delve team you four helped have gone out to investigate what happened to the gods,**] the Guildmaster reported; Misa snorted at the absurd thought that the Guildmaster was reporting to *her*. It was nice to get updates, though. [**The bandits you caught—Xothok and his team—are adjusting well. They seem to have uncovered something related to your most recent discovery, but I do not have the details. I suggest getting into direct contact with him at the earliest available opportunity.**]

[**The Guild is currently handling the aftermath of one idiot's experimentation with the system, but fortunately, that's going relatively well. Thank you for handling it as promptly as you did. I see I was right to trust you. Please keep me updated as much as you are able, and otherwise, feel free to act as you believe is best. The Guild remains behind you. We will deal with Elyran . . . negotiations. It appears there is some turmoil within the kingdom at present.**]

Misa winced a bit at that, but it wasn't surprising. She glanced over to Vex, who was happily chattering away at Derivan while the armor listened intently; he was drawing diagrams in the ground, and his tail was practically wagging.

. . . She wouldn't bring up what was happening in Elyra. Not yet. There weren't enough details for Vex to learn anything new, anyway, since she saw no update from the Elyran rebels either. Misa wasn't surprised—they were likely busy. That the Guildmaster had found the time to reply as quickly as she had was a miracle in itself; Misa had only really expected to see a message from her mother.

She fired off a quick message to Xothok, then sighed and stared at her skill list.

She needed practice—they all did. She needed to understand more about the nature of reality anchors and what it meant to have one attached to her.

"You're responsible for a lot more than just my village, aren't you," she said. It wasn't a question. The system window detailing the anchor's integrity hovered in front of her, and she gazed at it for a moment, watching the numbers tick down.

Whatever this was, it was the reason the food in Fendal still fed them, even though it didn't fill the other residents of Teque. It was the reason they could remember the stars. It was the reason their system had operated mostly independently of Fendal, and they'd retained access even when Noram and others had lost their access.

The anchor she held protected all of them. If it broke, a lot more was at stake than just her village. They couldn't save the world if no one could remember that the world needed saving.

That, more than anything, made her feel a pressure she hadn't felt before.

CHAPTER 5

AWAKENING

Noram

In the village of Fendal, where a powerful barrier of magespun mana still separated it from the outside world, there was peace.

Of a sort, anyway. A young lizardkin sat at a table in a tavern across from an older orc woman, and his thoughts . . . flickered.

It wasn't all that long ago that Noram had begun to notice that there was something wrong with the peace in Fendal.

The nice lady sitting across him had explained everything to him, and he was pretty sure she'd done it more than once. The words never registered with him, though he had the sense that he wanted them to.

There was the way she looked at him, too. Every time she looked at him, she seemed sad, and that made his heart ache in an indiscernible way. A strange familiarity hung about her, and if he tried, he could almost feel her presence at the edges of his memory . . .

But he could never really place where he knew her. His mind slipped off every attempt she made to explain his predicament. So he smiled at her, a light, goofy smile. She surely just wanted to join him on his adventures!

That was all she talked about, after all. She would tell him about how Fendal was supposed to be a border territory for the kingdom of Elyra, but something strange had happened with their dungeon; how the "reality" of the residents of Fendal had been taken as fuel for a place called Teque; how they were doing it out of fear, with Helg at the lead of that fear, but there were people who were fighting to free Fendal.

All he really heard was that there were adventures involved. That was exciting! He'd asked about visiting this Teque, but all the nice lady had done was give him a sad smile and hug him.

The hug was nice, at least.

Besides, he would have wanted to join himself on his adventures, too. He was certain they would be great. He had so much he wanted to do. He wanted to explore the ruins, and find out more about magic, and . . .

Noram's fingers brushed across what he'd begun to think of as *the Notebook*. Not just a notebook, but *the* Notebook. Something flickered within him every time his scales brushed up against the bound leather. There was a flicker of *want* there, of true desire. For a fraction of a second, he would once again understand what it meant to have a *passion* for something, to want to learn more about magic with every fiber of his being.

For a fraction of a second, he remembered himself. It wasn't the first time it had happened. It wasn't the first time his fingers would graze the Notebook, and he would *remember*.

And then his scales would leave the notebook, and he would forget again. He would smile happily at the next person that came along, sometimes someone he recognized from Fendal, and sometimes someone he *didn't* recognize. Sometimes, they were weird cockroach-like creatures, or smaller lizardkin-like non-lizardkin things, or little butterfly creatures that would flutter about and giggle at him.

One time, there was an otter! And that had been . . .

That had been different, actually.

The otter made him feel the same way the book did. The same way those pretty stones that nice lizardkin had given him made him feel sometimes, when he found them in his pocket.

They reminded him of a fullness of being that had been lost to him.

Slowly—too slow for him to notice, but fast enough for Charise to take note and pass on the message—he began to remember.

Noram couldn't pin down exactly when he'd begun to come into himself again, exactly. He spent more and more time holed up in his room instead of going out and "adventuring." The word still had meaning to him, but what he actually did outside seemed empty, compared to what adventuring was *supposed* to mean. All he did was go around and talk to people about adventuring. And surely that was strange?

Besides, there was so much to explore in the book! Noram didn't know who had given him the book. He remembered very little about the circumstances that had led up to all of *this*. His days consisted of meeting the nice lady, and sometimes her two friends, and then wandering around town and meeting all the new people there.

The book was far more interesting. There were sketches in there—pictures of those exact ancient magic ruins that he always told himself he would explore, the ones he always told everyone about *wanting* to explore but never did, for . . .

. . . for some reason.

Why *didn't* he go out and explore, if he wanted it so badly? Why did he just wander his town, talking about wanting to adventure?

Why did reading this book make something inside him *ache*?

Noram sat in his room, his vision blurring. The paper in the book was wet, and he hurriedly pushed it away so that the water rolling down his snout would stop messing up the sketches. He looked around to see if anyone could see him, but his room was empty.

Achingly empty. There were—there were people he spent his time *with*, people who joined him on his little excursions to the local dungeon, in his quest to get strong enough to really explore—

All his equipment was covered in dust.

Noram slowly got up from his seat, walking over to where he kept his backpack. The steps were familiar but slow; each step he took kicked up dust that had started to cake on the floor. Noram remembered that sometimes the nice lady would come in and sweep the floor, but she'd spent less and less time doing that lately. Mostly because she hadn't been around as much . . .

Charise. Her name was Charise.

Noram's eyes cleared a little. He stared down at his backpack, saw his hands trembling slightly. Carefully, he unlatched the flap, reaching in to find what he kept inside.

His fingers brushed against something unfamiliar in his backpack. It was almost a wand—Noram could feel the mana within—except that it had bristles bound to the end of it, and so it was like no wand he had ever seen.

Without thinking about it, he channeled a small amount of his mana into the brush. The tip lit up with a combination of his magic and someone else's, reverberating in the air and echoing into his soul.

Something within him reacted. He looked back into the backpack, his mind beginning to clear.

There was his journal. There was his own wand, the first thing he'd carved for himself. He never *used* it. It was something he kept more out of sentimentality than anything else, along with something he couldn't quite remember. Something he'd . . . given away? But why had he . . . ?

He'd given it away to Vex. He remembered the other lizardkin in a flash of insight. Noram scrambled to his feet and hurried over to his desk—there on the desk sat the Notebook, half-flopped over in his previous hurry. The pages were slightly crumpled, but it took him very little effort to smooth them out.

These were Vex's notes. Notes on all the ruins he'd been to, all the runes he'd seen and recorded, and little sketches of himself and the various members of his party. There was the human, Sev, smiling on a page. There was Charise's daughter, Misa, drinking a tankard of beer.

There were . . . altogether too many sketches of Derivan, the tall fellow in armor. A small smile ghosted across his face, and yet a small pit of *something* yawned open in him, because this was—

—This had been something precious to Vex. Why had he given it to Noram?

"You're awake," someone said, and Noram started, jumping out of his seat. His brain scrambled to catch up as he tried to put sense to the ridiculous sight of an *otter* standing in his room, juxtaposed against everything he'd been trying to remember. Against the realization that was struggling to surface in his mind like it was swimming through treacle.

"What do you mean, *awake*?" Noram asked. He nearly blanched at the sound of his own voice—it sounded strange, unfamiliar. Entirely too chipper compared to what he felt. He forced his questions out anyway. "What happened? Who are you?"

"That is going to take some explaining." The otter sighed, guilt flashing across his features. "Hello, Noram. I am . . . you. In a manner of speaking."

Noram stared blankly at the otter. His mind was only barely his own—he wasn't in the mood for cryptic explanations. "You're going to have to explain that one to me."

"Yes, I suppose I will," the other Noram said. "Though you must understand, the situation is not entirely clear to us, either. I will explain as much as I can."

The otter closed his eyes as though bracing himself. "Fendal and Teque are linked by the system," he began. "Do you know about Teque? I'm not sure how much you remember."

"I know about Teque," Noram said. Charise's words and explanations to the less-aware version of himself filtered back to him slowly, and his words came out colder than he intended. "I know what you've been doing."

The other Noram winced, then seemed to deflate, his shoulders slumping. He looked for all the world like a tiny, sad otter.

Noram did his best not to sympathize with him.

. . . It was a little difficult.

"What we have been doing is not of our choosing," the otter said. "Though I admit if I had only fought against Helg's actions instead of bending to her whim—"

"Explain what you meant when you said that you're *me*." There was a bite to Noram's words that he didn't entirely intend.

"The system cannot sustain the people of both Fendal and Teque," the other Noram finally said. Noram could tell it made him uncomfortable to say it. "There is only room for a limited number of people within this region, as far as we have been able to determine, and while we might be able to support a greater number of individuals outside this region, Helg has locked us in with her barrier."

Right. The barrier. Noram glanced outside the window. It was still there, a shimmering beacon of magic that layered itself over the sky, so thick he doubted even the strongest spells could break through it. How had this Helg person managed a spell so powerful?

"For someone in Teque to come into themselves, they have to drain someone in Fendal of an equivalent amount of . . ." The otter hesitated. "I don't know. You have to understand, a lot of how your system works is entirely new to us."

It's not like I know anything about the system acting like this, Noram thought to himself. *This is new to us, too.*

But he said nothing. He waited for the otter—he refused to think of him as just "Noram"—to continue.

"It's a bit of an oversimplification, of course," the otter continued, oblivious to Noram's internal thoughts. "No one in Teque is doing it on purpose; everything happens sort of behind the scenes and chosen by the system, as far as we can tell, and Helg isn't doing anything to accelerate it."

"But there are implications," Noram said. The otter sighed and nodded.

"The process isn't perfectly clean," he said. "Other things get swept up in the process. The transfer doesn't just make the person in Teque their own person; it makes the person in Teque more like whoever their reflection is in Fendal. Little things carry over. Favorite foods, hobbies, sometimes a song . . ."

"Or a name," Noram said.

"Or a name," the otter said, looking away. "I don't know what my original name was. I don't know if I ever had one."

Damn it, he wasn't supposed to be feeling bad for this guy. If what he was saying was true, then the whole *reason* he'd lost so much of himself—and he was trying not to think too hard about it—was the otter in front of him.

Or, you know, it's because of the system, a traitorous little voice whispered in his head, and Noram almost growled to himself. He couldn't even let himself be *angry* about something he had every right to be angry over. Stupid conscience.

". . . So," Noram said after his sympathy managed to win out over his anger. For now, anyway. "What does all this mean? For me. Or for you. Or for our respective towns."

"We're working on it," Noram said softly. "Or, well, *they're* working on it. They have to work around Helg. I . . . have been hiding."

". . . You've been hiding." Noram repeated the words half in disbelief. He saw a flash of guilt in his counterpart's face, saw the way he averted his eyes. It took effort to control the anger that was rising in his voice—anger was definitely winning again. "You were— Why were you *hiding*, of all things?"

The room was silent. He'd raised his voice more than he intended, and the sound kicked around, bouncing off the walls. Noram was suddenly more aware than ever of where he was. In a dusty room of an empty inn, in the middle of a town that only pretended to be populated.

The feeling of being *alone* slammed in so hard and fast his knees almost buckled. Noram saw that same loneliness reflected in the otter's eyes, saw the way he took a step back, like he was ready to run.

"I was scared," the other Noram said, the words emerging in a small whisper.

A memory surfaced.

Noram had said those words himself years ago. He'd long since grown past it—or he thought he had—but remembered saying it in the exact same tone of voice, with the exact same expression. He remembered having one foot poised to run the same way this other Noram did.

He remembered the guilt.

It was after one of his first encounters with a monster. He was barely out of his hatchling phase at the time—just a little older than twelve. He'd been playing with his closest friend at the time, Beza, far too close to the Outskirts.

And a monster had appeared, claws and teeth and terrifying *size*, and he *ran*.

Beza hadn't. His best friend had leapt ahead to fight, expecting him to be by her side. He'd thought she would run too—this was a real monster, and they were only playing pretend—but the system skills they had were real, and she must have thought they could take it on together.

It didn't change that she ended up fighting it alone.

She hadn't died, thank the gods. But he remembered the way she looked at him when she asked him that very same question.

Why?

I was scared.

The answer hadn't been good enough for her back then.

Maybe it could be good enough for him.

"Okay," Noram said. He took a deep breath, shaking off the cobwebs of memory. ". . . That's okay. We all get scared."

He felt a little absurd, saying those words. He was pretty sure the otter was older than he was. But he saw the way those shoulders sagged, this time in relief. He saw the way the whiskers twitched and the way the otter leaned forward—

—and suddenly they were hugging?

They were hugging.

This was fine. The other Noram was soft and fuzzy and cute. And, he had to admit, he could use a hug.

Something within him seemed to tug and unravel. In front of him, the otter jerked slightly, staring into the air. Noram pulled back, bemused, as the otter blinked at what was clearly a system screen.

And then he, too, blinked when he realized that the system screen was slowly fading into sight for him as well.

It was a system screen they could *both* see. The other Noram seemed to have the same realization at the same time. They glanced at each other, eyes wide, then back to the newly opened system window.

[[Soul Link] available.]
<WARNING>
[Feature in beta.]
<WARNING>
[Feature developed by automated process.]
<WARNING>
[Feature is permanent once accepted. Both parties must consent to the link to use it. Both parties must consent to accept the link.]
[ACCEPT / REJECT]

CHAPTER 6

SOUL LINK

Noram

Both Norams stared at the system window. Neither of them knew how to react—neither of them knew what a *[**Soul Link**]* was. Just from the name, it seemed too intimate a thing to share with a stranger they'd only just met.

But the system is capable of great things, one Noram's mind whispered to him. *You've only seen it in action for a short amount of time, and already you've seen how much it changes the people that have access to it. They grow so much more quickly than any of the old methods. They become stronger, faster, more durable. They can take hits that would kill, even without gaining many levels.*

The system is terrifying, the other Noram's mind said. *It's taken away so much from you. But maybe this is a way for you to take control back—the [**Soul Link**] requires consent, right? Depending on what it does, having the link might actually protect you.*

The window blinked in front of them, prompting them to make a choice.

". . . We should probably take some time to think about it, huh?" lizardkin-Noram said.

"We *should,*" otter-Noram agreed.

There was an awkward pause.

"I think we should accept," they both said at the same time.

A slight suspicion reverberated between them; they both felt it like a physical sensation crawling across their backs. The otter winced first, breaking eye contact and looking away.

". . . I will admit that I want the link because it might give me power," he said after a moment. "I know how that sounds. But I am just so very tired of being scared."

There was a kind of raw honesty in those words. "You too, huh?" the lizardkin asked.

The otter smiled wryly. "I was hoping you had the part of me that was brave."

"And I just don't want the system to take away who I am again. I think if it links us . . . we'll share. Kind of."

"Only one way to find out."

They looked at one another.

"We're being impulsive," otter-Noram said.

"Very irresponsible," lizardkin-Noram agreed.

But on some level, they had pieces of the same person within them.

They both reached out and touched Accept.

—∿∿∿—

Noram awoke almost an hour later, his head throbbing with pain. There was a small, furry form curled up on his chest—he almost flinched and swiped it away before he realized it was just Noram, curled up and sleeping.

Despite himself, he relaxed.

There was a bond between them. It was a small, humming thing—nowhere near as invasive as he had feared, and yet . . . it *could* be, he sensed. If they both opened up to it, they could share anything. Thoughts, feelings. The underlying "reality" that gave them life and personhood and individuality.

He snapped the valve shut as soon as he could, feeling his heart suddenly race, but he could tell that the otter hadn't tried to take anything more away from him. There wasn't a point, anyway—they both had roughly equal amounts of the stuff, courtesy of those strange stones that Vex had given him.

And his notebook. Something about that notebook, too, was filled with life.

"That was kinda dangerous," Noram muttered to himself. The noise seemed to be enough to startle otter-Noram into awakening; the otter's ears flattened against his head and he leapt to his feet, thankfully light enough that he didn't stomp the breath out of Noram in the process. He still let out an indignant *oof*, letting a bit of his pain and irritation filter through their link, and after a moment—a moment where otter-him had to *accept*, and then cringed, making a face Noram had never expected to see an otter make—carefully stepped off the lizardkin.

"Sorry," otter-him mumbled, and Noram just inclined his head.

"It's weird," Noram said. "The system doesn't just knock people out. It'd be dangerous if it did."

"It did say it was a beta feature."

"I guess you have a point." Noram had no idea what a beta feature was, and from the look on otter-him's face, he didn't either. He was just guessing from the context.

Oh well. He was less worried than he should have been, he suspected, but Noram was more focused on the issue at hand.

"Um." Noram paused, trying to find the right words. There were a lot of things on his mind, the least of them being the bond they now shared, but there was one main thing on his mind. "We should find something else to call you. Besides my name, I mean."

The otter stared at him and briefly looked a bit stricken. Noram didn't get it, but the bond between them opened, and he accepted it with hesitation—

—a flood of emotions poured into him. Noram had lived his entire life as Noram; he remembered all his friends calling him by that name, remembered receiving his first accolades with his name printed on it. He *knew* the name wasn't his own, but he still felt like it was his—

—and maybe it was. Did it matter whose name the name "originally" was, if it felt every bit as real as it did to him?

". . . I shouldn't have phrased it like that," Noram said after a moment, feeling vaguely guilty. "Sorry."

"You're right, though." Noram sighed, looking a little small and defeated in that moment; the otter curled up and leaned against the wall. "It's not like my name ever really felt like my own."

Maybe more of him had filtered over into the otter's personality than he thought.

"You felt defensive, huh?" Noram said.

"Yeah," the otter answered.

"How about this," Noram suggested. "We both pick new names. Mine doesn't . . . It doesn't matter to me all that much, anyway. I didn't earn anything with it. I didn't achieve anything."

The otter softened, looking at him. "Maybe not *yet*," he said. "But you're young yet. You've got plenty of time ahead of you. I don't think *I* achieved anything when I was your age."

". . . How old are you?"

". . . Anyway, I like your idea," the otter said, instantly changing the subject. "I always wanted to be named Raltis, after a mighty wizard in a story I read as a young otter. Think that's too egotistical?"

"I mean, who cares?" Noram asked, shrugging and offering a small grin. "It's your name, right? No one here's even gonna get that reference."

"Raltis it is." The otter brightened. "What are you picking?"

"I don't really know yet." Noram stared into the distance a bit, thinking. He didn't have a good idea of who he was yet—not really. He wanted to pick a name with meaning, but . . . "How about Novice?"

"Novice?" Raltis blinked at him. "Really?"

"I've got a lot to learn." Novice smiled a bit. He didn't hate the name as much as he thought he would have. He still *felt* like Noram, of course—the name was still his own, and this was only a temporary affair, for however long the two of them had to work together—but it felt appropriate. "Felt like I might need a reminder of that every now and then."

". . . Now I feel guilty," Raltis muttered.

The next step, they decided in short order, was to find Charise. The otter-Noram that was now Raltis wasn't entirely caught up on events in Teque and Fendal; he'd started living life as a sort of refugee between the two towns. He blamed himself for what had happened between Fendal and Teque, thinking that things would never have gotten so bad if he'd resisted Helg in the first place, and so he'd sort of voluntarily exiled himself from Teque.

Staying in Fendal was a sort of self-imposed punishment. A reminder of what he'd done to otherwise perfectly innocent people.

He was still *aware* of what was happening in Fendal and Teque, though. For one thing, he'd never been de-keyed from the communication glyphs that Teque used, and he made it a point to keep himself up to date with everything the Teque mages discovered about the system.

"There's a sort of underground group of people that are sympathetic to Fendal," Raltis explained. The two of them made for an odd pair as they walked through the town, made all the odder by the fact that no one gave them a second glance. The lizardkin-Noram who was now Novice couldn't help but wonder how he'd ever missed all of this at all. "They're trying to see if there's a way they can restore the people here without . . . you know, letting Teque die."

"Do you think Charise works with them?" Novice asked. It'd explain why she'd been around less and less lately, why she sometimes seemed to vanish into thin air.

"I know they work with some people in Fendal," Raltis said. The otter's tail waved about nervously behind him. "I don't see many better options here."

Novice grimaced. "Fair point."

Walking through his home town while being fully aware of everything was . . . eerie. It was clearer than ever now how artificial everything was, from the smiles his neighbors gave one another to the conversations they had. Some conversations were the same thing over and over again, held in a loop. Others were simply *stilted*, like the people involved were going through the motions.

Not for the first time, Notice reached for Vex's notebook and rubbed the corner of it. He'd taken to using it to reassure himself every once in a while—

"There," Raltis said, nudging him, and Novice looked up.

Charise sat in the patio outside the Juniper Express, which was a small cafe that served little cakes and snacks. There was a tall beetle-looking man sitting across from her, his expression deep and severe. Novice paused for a moment to consider whether or not he should interrupt.

Which was, of course, the exact moment Charise chose to look up and meet his eyes.

She didn't seem surprised to see him, disconcertingly. She simply waved at him and gestured to not one but *two* seats that had been prepared for them at the table. There were even plates laid out and everything.

Feeling suddenly nervous—and Novice knew that Raltis felt the same way, given the bond they now shared—Novice and Raltis both sat. Charise looked at them both and let the silence stretch on for a little bit longer than necessary.

Then she smiled a small smile. "It's good to see you back to yourself, Noram," she said. "Or are you going by something else for now?"

"It is always uncanny when you do that," the beetle-man sitting across from her commented. She chuckled.

"Allow an old lady some fun, will you?" she said. "It's hard enough to split my attention between two places at once . . ."

Charise's eyes seemed to lose focus for a second, and then she regained herself and smiled at the three of them as though nothing had happened. "So! My question?"

"Oh, uh," Novice said. "I'm going by Novice for now."

"Humble," Charise said. She glanced at their resident otter. "And you?"

"Raltis," the otter said, looking suddenly embarrassed.

"It has been a while since I've seen you," the beetle-man said, inclining his head at Raltis. He didn't say anything else, but he *did* raise an eyebrow slightly, in a sort of implied question. Novice saw Raltis hesitate, like he was preparing to give a response . . .

. . . and then he shook his head. "I'm not ready to talk about it yet, Anton," he said.

"That's fine," Charise said, interrupting before Anton could actually get in a response. The beetle gave her an affronted sort of look that she promptly ignored. "You two have discovered something important, haven't you?"

Novice blinked. What was she talking about—

*She's talking about the [**Soul Link**],* Raltis sent him, pushing on the link between them slightly. Novice tried not to twitch in response, but he didn't completely hide the movement; he saw the way Charise's gaze flickered over to him.

She knew. She definitely knew.

To her credit, instead of saying anything about it, she gave the two of them an encouraging smile.

Do we tell her? Novice asked.

My instincts say no, Raltis answered. *But just between you and me, my instincts haven't been doing a great job of leading me the right way so far. What do you think?*

I think I trust her, Novice said, and then nodded to himself. "Yeah," he said out loud. "I trust her."

". . . And me by proxy, I suppose," Anton grumbled.

Raltis and Novice glanced at each other and then told her about [**Soul Link**]s.

CHAPTER 7

THE NATURE OF MAGIC

Derivan stared at the field ahead of them. Vex had absolutely scattered the place with glyphs—some of them from the basic set, others theoretical, and still others combinations that he had already tried, that embodied new and distinct concepts. He'd even shown off some of the ones he'd used against . . .

. . . well. Against the echo of his father.

Derivan noticed the shadow that fell across Vex's face whenever he looked at one of those glyphs. He almost told Vex he didn't need to draw them, but he held his metaphorical tongue; the lizardkin was trying to be strong, and Derivan got the distinct impression that Vex didn't want to be told he didn't need to be. That he would fold if he was told it was okay, and that he wasn't ready for that yet.

"All right," Vex said at last. "Now, what do all of these glyphs have in common?"

Derivan stared at the glyphs. They were all inert, he supposed. That had taken some doing; magic here was far, *far* easier to work than it had been with the system in place. Eventually, Vex had figured out that a little bit of his [**Manaburn**] effect kept the glyphs inert and prevented them from activating, though they'd have to remember to clear the field before they wore off.

They were all based on *art* in some way, too, on something significant that had been created in the past. But these were all things they already knew, and not the answer Vex was looking for.

"Nothing?" he offered.

"Yeah." Vex deflated in a way that was almost comical. "I was hoping you would see something I didn't."

Derivan chuckled. He tried to open his arms in invitation, then hesitated slightly when one side of his body didn't respond. Vex didn't seem to notice—he took the invitation for what it was and fell into him with an exhausted sigh.

Of course, without a second hand to balance himself on, they both promptly toppled over into the grass. Vex yelped a little as Derivan grabbed him by the waist and absorbed the impact of the fall.

"Sorry!" he said. "Sorry, I . . ."

He trailed off, his gaze flickering to Derivan's missing arm, obviously not sure how to bring it up or if he should at all. Derivan rescued him from the decision by responding first. "If you wish to lie down on me," he said, amused, "you may ask. I will not be offended."

"I didn't do that on purpose," Vex grumbled. There was an obvious note of relief in his voice and a far greater amount of affection.

And, Derivan noticed, no small amount of enjoyment. Vex liked being held in this manner. He suppressed a smile and carefully sat back up, with Vex maneuvering himself around in his lap to stay balanced.

"I am sure," he said. He didn't hide the amusement in his voice.

He would worry about the arm thing later. He directed his gaze back over the glyphs Vex had drawn instead, searching for meaning.

It was strange how few commonalities they had. The shapes were so basic, he would have expected two of them to be similar by sheer coincidence, if nothing else. Given the mental effects they'd already had to deal with, he wondered if it was possible that he was being prevented from noticing a similarity. It wasn't like the system hadn't already done that to them time and time again.

But if it was, he didn't have any way of detecting it. Even knowing what they now knew about infolocks, they had no way to combat the literal dissipation of information from the fabric of reality.

"Mnrgh," Vex grumbled into his shoulder when he moved to look a little farther. Derivan hid a faint smile, his eyes lighting up just a little bit more.

For all that this was them in defeat, there was something about being able to do this—about being able sit down and *explore*, and let his thoughts wander, and to do so with his closest friends and his now-boyfriend—there was something about that that felt *warm*. They had no immediate disaster to fend off, and even the pressure of time was stretched out into almost nothing.

The truth of what was happening hung over their heads, of course, but it hadn't quite sunk in yet. Derivan was in no hurry to make it sink in faster.

The sun was bright above them, lighting up the vibrant blue of the sky. The strange fractal images were almost transparent at this time of the day. All they really did was give the sky an odd, velvety texture. The field in front of them was bright and green and *alive*, buzzing with insects and even tiny animals that wandered about here and there. Derivan caught a flash of a small, furry thing leaning over to sniff at one of the glyphs.

The armor paused. The glyph was a mixture of Fire and Air . . .

Very gently, he reached out to shoo the little thing away before it could get hurt. Vex shifted at the movement, looking over at what he was doing, and his eyes went wide.

"Look at that little thing!" he said, fascinated. "I don't think any of these exist back on our . . . uh, slice of reality."

Whatever it was had stopped investigating the glyph at their movement; it turned toward them instead, sniffing inquisitively at the air, tiny nose wriggling. It was a slender creature, with slicked-back pseudofur that almost looked like shadow. Derivan wondered if it was made of the same stuff the elementals were.

It *was* cute, though. It came up to them slowly, flinched when Vex extended a hand, and then took a cautious sniff.

Then it licked him and darted away, disappearing quickly into the grass. Derivan stared after it, faintly amused, while Vex just stared in wonder at his hand.

"I am never washing my hand again," he declared.

"That is . . . not a good idea, I think."

"*You can't make me.*" Vex wasn't serious, of course, but Derivan loved the playful light in the lizardkin's eyes. It had been too long.

"I suppose I can only ask nicely."

"Please don't. It's my one weakness."

Derivan laughed then and pulled Vex close; he pressed his forehead against the lizardkin's, feeling Vex first stiffen and then reluctantly relax against him, and waited a moment before uttering his next words—

"I suppose I can give you a few minutes before I do," he said. Vex slumped the rest of the way back into his arm, huffing. Derivan saw the small smile that stole across his face, though. He could feel, through his armor, that Vex was a little warmer than usual, embarrassed and yet happy all at once.

And then Vex sat up straight, bonking his head against Derivan's chin, and winced.

"Ow," he said.

"Are you all right?" Derivan asked, startled.

"Yeah, I'm fine," Vex said, shaking his head as if to clear it. He glanced out over the field of glyphs again, and his expression turned contemplative. "I thought I saw something like a pattern . . . like all the smaller glyphs are pieces of a bigger one." He frowned across the field. "I'm not sure I can see it anymore, though."

"Perhaps it is something you can only see if you are in the right moment," Derivan said with a small chuckle.

"Maybe," Vex said. He didn't look convinced, but he leaned back anyway, letting his mind relax slightly. "I don't think I'd be able to do anything with it, anyway."

"There were still some pieces missing," Derivan agreed.

"You saw it too?" Vex almost looked up at Derivan, but his positioning made it awkward; he eventually settled for tilting his head backward, and Derivan stared back down at him, amused.

"I believe I saw *something*," he mused. "Perhaps it was the same thing. I cannot say; I do not know what you saw."

"Pieces of a puzzle?"

"Something like that," Derivan said.

"I suppose there's no use trying to force it." Vex smiled a bit of a wry smile and then leaned back into Derivan, closing his eyes. "Do you mind if we take a small break? I just want to think."

Derivan saw the small sadness beginning to swim in Vex's eyes again; he saw the way the lizardkin's gaze lingered on some of the glyphs. He shook his head. "I do not mind," he said.

"We can stay like this as long as you wish."

—∞—

As long as he wished, it turned out, wasn't all that long. Vex's mind was active at the best of times, and it worked best when he had a problem he wanted to solve, and he *did*.

"I want to try spellcasting next," he announced.

"Oh?" Derivan hummed. He didn't let go of Vex until the lizardkin began to wriggle—*then* he let go, pulling his arm back and chuckling. Vex barely seemed to notice; the wizard sprang to his feet and bounced on his heels, looking authoritatively over the field of glyphs. Derivan spared a small glance toward Sev and Misa as he waited.

Sev was still meditating. *Something* was happening there—something visible in the system and in reality. Derivan could almost see it, using a combination of Patch and Shift, but it was nothing he could interpret. He left well enough alone, not wanting to disrupt whatever Sev was doing.

As for Misa . . . she was scanning through her system screens with intensity. He hoped she was all right.

"Okay," Vex said, calling his attention back. "I need you to cast a spell. I'm going to try to attach to it with my Sign and see if I can figure out how the spell is transformed from glyph to effect. If I can figure out that aspect of magic, I think I can start unlocking other glyphs."

"You plan to reverse-engineer a glyph from an effect?" Derivan asked.

"Kind of," Vex said, waving a hand about. He watched the air intently as Derivan's gauntlet began to glow; the glyph he drew was Fire, a series of simple, swooping lines like a rising current of air. "There are similarities between the system's runes and glyphs, but it's not a one-to-one transformation I can apply to a rune and get a glyph. Stuff goes missing. I'm hoping I can pull out what I need from the effect."

"That makes sense." The last line of mana glowed in the air; here, there was no need to explicitly activate the glyph. Intent seemed to be sufficient. Derivan admired the sight as fire-aspect mana began to flow toward the glyph in glowing streams.

In no time at all, the glyph had ignited into a glittering array of *fire*, blowing gently in a nonexistent wind.

Vex was silent, his eyes shut and his brows drawn together in concentration. His own Sign wavered in the air, apparently strangely harder to use in this new world they were in. Derivan wondered if that had something to do with how aspects were slightly different, here, each reflected through a different lens.

A tendril stretched out from Vex's sign, but it didn't reach the glyph Derivan had drawn. Derivan sensed it trying to go elsewhere and not quite succeeding.

It was instinct more than anything else that made him do what he did next. He reached out, giving it a tiny nudge with a Shift—

—Vex let out a soft gasp, and Derivan quickly caught him as he began to tip over. The lizardkin blinked a few times, shaking his head and rubbing at his eyes like he'd just stared directly into the sun.

"Ow," he said plainly.

"Are you all right?" Derivan asked. "I am sorry; I thought I could help—"

"—No, you did, don't worry. I'm fine. That was just . . . *bright.*" Vex winced slightly as he got back onto his feet, blinking a few more times. "I think I saw a library? It's kind of seared into my eyes."

"Hmm." Derivan frowned, looking into Vex's eyes as though he might somehow see the library imprinted on his retinas. ". . . I do not think we should try again for now."

"Yeah, no." Vex shuddered slightly. "Don't get me wrong, I *really* want to know what that was, but . . ."

Vex sighed. "I'm gonna need to find some way to protect myself," he said. "The problem is that the sight isn't *physical,* so I can't just enchant my eyes . . . It's kind of more like it burned the memory of staring into the sun into my brain."

"That sounds unpleasant." Not that Derivan really knew what staring into the sun was like for an organic creature. He did it all the time and was fine. "Did we learn nothing from this?"

"Not *nothing.*" Here Vex managed to grin. "I have a *really* good memory. It might've been bright, but I still caught a glimpse of some of those books. Each one of them has a glyph on the cover. I guess it's some sort of archive? And if we can *visit* that archive . . ."

"We could discover any spell on record?" Derivan guessed.

"Maybe even make our own!" Vex waved a notebook around triumphantly. "Uh, maybe. That might be a bit much. We probably can't just insert a new spell into the mana."

"But you are going to try."

"Of *course* I'm going to try." Vex practically scoffed, but he was grinning. "I just need to figure out *how.*"

CHAPTER 8

ENCHANTED

As bold a statement as Vex had started with, there wasn't yet much for him to go on—the idea that magic drew from a physical *place*, even, was something that was new to him. Vex had told Derivan he wanted a bit of time to mull on it, which seemed like a better plan than Derivan's own thought of "push as hard as possible in Shift and try to take them to this new place."

They needed to stay *here*, and they needed to avoid breaking things in the bonus room for as long as possible. Derivan *did* need to experiment with Shift, but the goal with that was to give them a means to access and interact with their own world while keeping the benefit of stretched time.

For now, Vex was back at the array of glyphs he'd scattered across the field, and isolating a set he thought would be useful.

"I mean, don't get me wrong; I think *all* of them are useful," the lizardkin rambled as he worked, waving a hand about animatedly; Derivan watched in fond amusement as mana followed his movement, and a few of the glyphs he'd drawn crumbled to dust. "But we need a smaller set to focus on first, or we're going to end up with a broad set of spells that don't work very well together."

"You sound as if you may have had experience with such a thing," Derivan observed.

Vex laughed, a touch of embarrassment coloring his tone. "In my early days, I just wanted to learn every spell I could get my hands on," he said. "And don't get me wrong; having a lot of options is a strength all on its own. But that's more Misa's wheelhouse, you know? I just want to *understand*."

He stared out at the glyphs he'd picked for a moment, and then his voice acquired a touch of ruefulness. "Narrowing your area of study helps you understand it more," he said. "Magic as a whole is broad enough as it is. I'd almost say it's too broad for any one person to understand, except that would invalidate my life goal, and I'm going to be stubborn about that for a little while longer, I think."

"Hardly one person," Derivan said, his tone just a touch chastising. Vex glanced over at him, and Derivan saw him hesitate for a second.

"Are you sure you actually want to help me with this, though?" he asked, his voice soft. "I mean, is all this what you *actually* want to do? Or do you just want to help me because it's what I want to do?"

Derivan paused to consider the question, though the immediate response was on the tip of his metaphorical tongue. The way Vex was looking at him told him the question was important, so he took his time to be certain about how he felt.

Then he came to a conclusion, measured his words, and spoke.

"It is both," he said. "You taught me about the beauty of magic, and so I have a vested interest in understanding it. But it would be a lie to say that your happiness does not factor into it. Both things bring me joy."

"Oh." Vex looked away, but not before Derivan caught the shy smile that stole over his face. "Um. Thanks."

"You are welcome."

"But you know if you were interested in anything, I'd happily help you with it," Vex said, looking oddly fierce.

"Of course," Derivan chuckled. The answer seemed important to Vex, though; the lizardkin visibly relaxed, and that same smile stole across his face again.

"Good," he said. Satisfied with that line of conversation, Vex turned his attention back to the glyphs he'd laid out in front of him. "I'm going to see if we can't come up with a magical solution for your arm."

"I feel as though I could generate a replacement, with enough training in Slime," Derivan offered. His generative abilities weren't quite so advanced just yet—he'd already tried, some time the night before. He could generate a small tendril that in no way matched the proportions of the rest of his body.

"Would that work?" Vex asked. "Is it the same?"

"It is not the same, exactly," Derivan admitted. "It is a part of me, but it feels . . . different. I do not have the words for it. I do not think the difference is *bad*, but it is slower, and I suspect I would not be as effective in combat."

"So we still need another solution," Vex said, nodding to himself. Derivan stole a glance at the glyphs he'd chosen for this experiment.

There was the glyph for Earth, which he supposed made sense; something to represent *metal*, as a product that came from the earth. There was

Derivan's own Sign in there, which he hadn't tried casting on its own just yet. Then there were the glyphs for Communication, Relay, and Research . . .

"Why is your own Sign there?" Derivan asked. Vex was staring at the array of glyphs he'd chosen, deeply contemplative. He jumped when Derivan spoke.

"Uh," he said, and then stared at the glyphs again. "I'm coming at it from a more organic perspective, I guess. Normally, even if you get a healer to regrow a limb, you have to do a certain amount of rehabilitation to be able to use it effectively again. I don't have a glyph of *Learning*, or I would've used that instead; Research is tied a lot more closely to *me* . . ."

Vex paused, looking embarrassed. "I can take it out, if you prefer. In case it gives me a link to your arm or something."

"I do not mind," Derivan said, chuckling. "I was only curious."

The lizardkin nodded but still seemed a little red, at least under the light of the sun. Derivan watched him fondly. Vex stuck a tongue out of his mouth and began scribbling down small sketches of theoretical glyph combinations in his notebook. With each sketch, he paused and stared intently, waiting to see if it drew the attention of the surrounding mana. If it did, he erased it with a small pulse of magic, and if it didn't, he kept the sketch there, presumably as a reminder of what *didn't* work.

There were a half dozen failed sketches in there that didn't seem to pull in mana at all. Derivan didn't quite understand why—they seemed like they should have been perfectly valid glyph combinations—but he did see a pattern beginning to emerge as Vex worked on his sketches.

The glyphs that worked were always glyphs that contained a message and meaning of their own. Derivan felt a distinct *impression* when looking at them. There were Earth and Communication, for example, intertwined with one another as not-letters circling a globe; it felt like *Connection*. Other sketches where the looping letters were made of stone gave no such impression, nor was the mana drawn to it.

Derivan wondered if this was in some way a result of the Magic stat. He'd neglected it for some time, but now it was singing to him as he stared at Vex's sketches, at the various glyphs that were still scattered about.

His own Sign called to him. He still hadn't tested it.

"I am going to attempt a spell as well," he said out loud, though his own voice felt a little distant to him. He felt his mind sinking further into the Magic stat; now that he was thinking about it, he could do it with deliberation, letting the strange other-sense suffuse his being.

The world seemed a little different like this. He no longer saw the transparent panes in the sky, each reflecting a small section of the land. Instead, the sky was an impressionistic painting that gave him impressions of *openness, freedom*; of *possibility* and *travel*. The grass was a splash of *life* on the dirt-brown soil, which itself gave him thoughts of *solidity* and of being *grounded*.

Each of Vex's glyphs shone with a brilliant light, though none of them were blinding. They just shone with purpose, singing a clear signal that correlated directly with the impressions he'd gotten before. Connection, a glyph that represented a means of staying linked, no matter the distance. Earth, a glyph that embodied everything he saw when he stared at the soil beneath his sabatons.

And Vex himself was, in a word, beautiful.

The lights in Derivan's helmet blinked off as he shut off that new sense of sight, giving himself a moment to process everything he was seeing. It was different—maybe something closer to how the mana itself saw the world. He'd caught glimpses of Sev and Misa, too. The former was painted in gentle streaks of kindness and hope and just a little too much self-sacrifice; the latter was anger bound by restraint, determination, and a clever mind.

Both striking in their own right, and yet neither of them gave him quite the same feeling. Vex was rendered in the bright yellow colors of curiosity streaked through with his fierce intellect. The edges of his form were more uncertain, tempered by his own anxieties and fears and self-doubt, but the core was nevertheless firm. There was a fire in him that was both his passion for learning and his own brand of kindness, and it lit him up from within, lending a sort of vibrancy to him that he hadn't seen before . . .

. . . Derivan realized with some embarrassment that for the short time he'd possessed this variant of [**Mana Sight**], he'd spent most of it focused on Vex.

"Weren't you going to cast a spell?" Vex asked. He peered at Derivan, who felt it more than he saw it. "Are you okay?"

"I am fine," Derivan said, though to him his voice perhaps sounded a little dazed. He opened his eyes, gave the lizardkin the best smile he could, and wondered—perhaps for the first time—what it was that Vex saw in *him*.

He let that idle curiosity go for now, though. Instead, he turned his gaze inward. Vex had managed to figure out what his Sign was, extrapolating backward from his understanding of Derivan and from the combined Sign he had created. Now he aimed to do the same, in his own style.

His gauntlet moved, tracing a shape in the air.

A Sign was an individual's signature. It was an answer to a question, a representation of who a person *was*. Vex had had an answer for that before Derivan himself had truly figured it out—his understanding of himself had always been relative to others. It seemed only natural to him. His base self was a suit of armor; he existed to protect.

And yet he'd grown to be more than that, in no small part thanks to the friends he'd made.

It didn't change who he was in some fundamental way; it made no difference to who he wanted to be. But there was an ache where his arm had once been that reminded him that now there was *context* where there had been none before—the answer might not have changed, but now there was another question.

Who did he want to protect?

The answer wasn't just "his friends," because they were more than just bodies to protect. They had their own beliefs that he, too, felt was worth fighting for. The loss of his arm was a good reminder of that, that being who he needed to be to protect them wasn't enough.

The Guildmaster had built an organization aimed at protecting not only those at the top but anyone that needed it, any*where* they needed it. Sometimes, people needed a bit of help to become truly strong. Sometimes, protecting others involved being something more than a shield.

Sometimes, Signs *changed.*

Derivan stared at the Sign he'd drawn. Mana was already flowing toward it, aspected as a type he'd never seen before; he couldn't put a name to it if he tried.

The Sign in the air was still very obviously a piece of armor—a cuirass shaped not unlike his own, though it differed wildly in detail. It was a series of interlocking plates, weak individually but built to lock together when sustaining an impact, becoming something stronger as a whole. A small detail etched into the design was the names of his friends, inscribed along the shoulders, and Vex's name right over the center of the plate, where his heart would have been if he had one.

Behind the armor, etched as silhouettes in the light, was his best rendition of *life*—every race he had met in his journey so far, designated as a monster by the system or not, and even a few placeholders for the people he hadn't met.

It was altogether too complicated for a Sign. It had gone somewhere beyond that, he realized; Derivan looked at the sky and saw that it was dark now. He'd spent something like hours lost in the process of creating this.

This was no Sign. This was a creation of his own.

And as he watched, the mana seemed to take it like it was an offering. His painting—for that was what it was, really—simplified, turning into abstract, representative shapes of others behind a piece of armor. But he felt the original piece still within it, sitting within the mana.

"I think you just created a new glyph," Vex said quietly. He'd stopped his own experimentation long before, apparently, abandoning it to watch as Derivan worked. Derivan noticed, for the first time, that they were surrounded by shadows.

They had an audience. The town had gathered to watch.

"Oh," Derivan said.

CHAPTER 9

A NEW ORDER

"You have to understand, it's been getting harder and harder to make new glyphs," Clyde explained.

It had taken a while to get everyone calmed down. Clyde himself had to start herding people back to town, though many of them insisted on staying and seeing what the effect of the new glyph was. There his wife Belle had taken charge, insisting that testing a new glyph surrounded by civilians was a terrible idea.

In fairness, Derivan's Sign was unlikely to cause harm to anyone—but he was grateful to Belle nonetheless. The stares and whispers were challenging for him to deal with; he found he much preferred the smaller, intimate company of just his party. Fame and attention were not for him.

Now they found themselves back inside Clyde's inn, gathered around a huge table that Clyde had taken out of storage just for this occasion; the standard ones did not fit all seven of them.

"Harder my ass." Elliot snorted. Clyde glanced at him, and Elliot ignored the grin that stole across his husband's face. "It's been impossible for a few generations now. At least five."

"No one created any new glyphs—how long is a generation?" Vex asked.

"I just use it to mean a hundred years." Elliot shrugged. "So we haven't had any new spells for something like five hundred years. We haven't *needed* any new spells, since you can create just about any effect working with what we already have, but . . ."

Here Elliot smiled a small, rueful smile. "We used to have these festivals every time a new glyph was created," he said. "An expansion to the Great Record, we called it. A new piece of art acknowledged, a new addition to the history of the world."

"The Expansion Festival . . . I almost forgot about that." A wistful look stole across Belle's face.

"It was one of the few things that got you out of your lab back then," Clyde said, his voice teasing. "It was where you met us, remember?"

"I do, in fact," Belle said, patting her hands primly on her dress, brushing off some imaginary dust. "My memory isn't *that* bad."

"Do you think you'll hold another one?" Vex asked.

"Maybe." Clyde glanced around. "There's a lot of preparation we'd need to make to be able to hold a festival like that. Can't have our town looking so dreary."

"Isn't your town supposed to be a template?" Sev raised an eyebrow.

"We can make changes *sometimes*," Clyde said, waving a hand. He sighed. "Honestly, it might be good for us. We've been living a routine for five hundred years. It hasn't always been like this; there used to be a lot more life . . ."

His voice trailed off, and he glanced meaningfully at the door. "We used to be a lot more than just this," he said, glancing at Belle and Elliot both. Derivan saw the small sadness that hid within their eyes, though it was banished just as quickly. He said nothing, but he wondered how different the town would really have looked if things had not deteriorated quickly.

Perhaps the story of their town was not the *whole* truth. But if that was the case, then they did not seem ready to speak of it yet, and he did not see the need to press them on it.

"Who decides whether or not you have a festival?" Misa asked. It was the first time she'd spoken in a while; Derivan noticed that she was spending more time deep in thought and would check the system every so often, as though afraid she would lose contact with the outside world.

. . . she *was* the only one among them with a family, now that he thought about it. Vex had his, but except for his little brother, they were largely estranged. Misa had only just gotten her family back, and she'd had to head out again almost immediately. For all that her skill gave her the ability to spend time with her family at any time, anywhere, if they were to lose access to the system while in here . . .

He couldn't blame her for her worry.

"The mayor," Clyde said, gesturing vaguely. "He'll probably want to talk to Derivan sometime tomorrow, once he's figured out what he wants to do."

"Ah," Derivan said. "Perhaps I should prepare for his visit?"

"Nah, he's pretty chill," Elliot said. "Doesn't really do his job, even, but there's not much mayoring to *do* here, so . . . he does his best."

"Does he know?" Vex asked. "That this place is an echo."

"You can tell him." Belle looked closely at Vex. "But he'll be as ambivalent about it as the rest of us."

"It doesn't feel right not to," Vex admitted.

"Fair enough." She smiled at him. "I think he'll probably want to hold a festival. It'd be an opportunity to gather the template towns again."

"Oh, gods," Clyde groaned. "Do we have to?"

"We can't *not* invite them to an Expansion Festival, Clyde," Belle said, turning an amused gaze onto her husband. He glared back at her and folded his arms, looking for all the world like a petulant child.

For all of five seconds, anyway. He glanced back at them, and any trace of that playfulness vanished; he turned serious once more.

"Will you four be okay if we host one?" he asked. He glanced at Derivan's missing arm, though he didn't comment on it. "I might be prying a bit too much here, but you seem like you might need time to yourselves to recover. A festival might be just what you need, but only if you're in the right place for it."

There was a bit of a prolonged silence at that; no one seemed ready to answer. Misa was, surprisingly, first.

"You said it'd take some time to prepare, right?" she said.

"A week at least," Clyde nodded. "*If* Oliver decides it's a good idea to hold a festival at all."

"I think I can be in the right place in a week," Misa said, breathing out. "Gives me somethin' to work towards."

"You are taking the loss hard," Derivan observed, though he felt a bit useless for pointing out something so obvious. His tone was sympathetic, though, and Misa didn't seem to take offense.

"I talked a bit about it already, but it's not easy to just accept until I can fuckin' *do* something about it." Misa, too, glanced at his missing arm, and Derivan shifted uncomfortably; he wasn't sure he liked all the looks, as much as he understood them. As soon as she saw him move, Misa averted her eyes from the wound and shot him an apologetic look.

He didn't know if she was apologizing for staring at it, or if she was apologizing for not protecting him in the first place. A little bit of both, he suspected.

"You still want to train?" Sev asked.

"A few hours ago, I would've said 'not until we have a way to repair the anchor,'" Misa said. She glanced at a system screen and sighed; a tension seemed to bleed out of her shoulders, and she seemed to finally allow herself a small smile. "But whatever you did, Derivan, it repaired the *shit* out of the anchor. So I think I'm good to train at least a little bit."

She paused. "It'd be nice if we had a way to repair it consistently, though," she added.

"Wait, what?" Vex bounced up on his feet. "Why didn't you say anything earlier! That's amazing. That means acts of creation—wait, shouldn't you have gotten reality shards for that? *Did* you get any reality shards for that, Deri?"

"Not that I am aware of," Derivan said, patting his armor. There was nothing there, and he didn't remember seeing anything where he'd drawn the glyph.

"Are you talking about mana slivers?" Clyde asked curiously. Belle was leaning forward, interested.

"The system calls them *reality shards,*" Vex said.

"You haven't really explained this *system* thing to us," Belle said, chuckling. "I can make some guesses based on what you've already said, but it'd help if you told us a little bit more."

Vex blinked, embarrassed. "Right," he said. "Um. It's a bit complicated. It's . . . We think it's how reality is maintained, I guess."

Very quickly, the lizardkin gave—or attempted to give—the three shadow elementals a crash course on the nature of the system as it impacted their world; Clyde and Elliot were both interested, and Belle mostly seemed incredulous.

"It's *efficient*, I guess?" she muttered. "But it just seems so arbitrary. Why the dungeons and the monsters? Why *stats* and *skills* and *levels*?"

"We think the dungeons have something to do with maintaining reality anchors," Vex said, and then he took a breath as he seemed to realize something. "Looking at the name of the anchor, and the fact that Fendal and Teque had a very similar designation . . . every dungeon seems to stabilize a *zone* around it. That's probably what the label is. So, X-51 stands for the area around the Guild town we were in. And the Prime Kingdoms each have a large dungeon that stabilizes or connects the entire region . . ."

Vex paused. "That last part is a guess, though," he added. "We don't really know much about the difference between a regular dungeon and a Prime Kingdom dungeon."

"Fair enough," Belle said again, though this time her tone was a bit doubtful. She shook her head. "Reality shards, though. If your system calls our mana slivers *reality shards*, that would explain a lot about what they do. It gels with echo theory."

"The shards allow magic to create echoes like the system does?" Vex guessed, and Belle nodded.

"Make a big-enough change in reality," she said, "and that's what magic *is*—and you create waves. Lots of tiny echoes that ebb out from that single change. The mana coalesces and solidifies that echo as a crystal, and you get a little crystal of pure potential. A pocket universe, almost."

". . . And Teque was using that as a *currency*?" Sev said, scandalized.

"Most towns do," Clyde said dryly. "In fairness, we might know echo theory, but we never figured out what the slivers are. They're opaque to us. We know they allow magic to do things it shouldn't be able to do, and that's about it."

"Your friend is right, though," Belle said, frowning. "Your act of creation *should* have created a small fortune in slivers. I don't think I saw a single one at the field you were practicing in."

"Maybe it went towards repairing the anchor," Misa said without thinking, and then when everyone stopped and stared at her, she paused. "What?"

"I think you got it," Vex said. A sudden energy leapt into his eyes and he bounced on his feet, thinking. "That's probably exactly what happened, and if you're right, then we just need to figure out how to do it, um . . . on purpose." He glanced at Clyde. "You wouldn't happen to have any slivers you'd be willing to share, would you?"

Clyde laughed. "I normally don't have any customers asking *me* for money," he said, teasing, and Vex ducked his head in embarrassment. "But yeah, I've got some. I don't mind helping you guys out. Just give me a second."

He disappeared into the back. Belle stared after him.

"He has got to stop just giving our stuff away," Belle said, though she didn't seem all that bothered by it, judging by the amusement in her eyes.

"Eh," Elliot said. "You know him. We couldn't stop him if we tried."

CHAPTER 10

SHARDS

Clyde returned in short order with a small fistful of reality shards clutched awkwardly in his fingers. He was holding them gingerly, almost, like he was afraid they were going to explode. Belle stared at him.

"Why are you holding them like that?" she asked.

"You said they're pocket universes," Clyde said. "I didn't think it was safe to toss them around."

"I said *almost*!" The scientist rolled her eyes and grabbed the shards from a grinning Clyde, turning to deposit them in Misa's arms. "Here. You were going to try to do something with this, right?"

"The problem is that I don't know what," Misa said, cradling the bundle of shards awkwardly. Her gaze flicked up toward a system screen and she scanned it briefly, looking for an option to *repair*, but there was nothing there, just the same information about anchor integrity.

"You could try pushing them into the window," Sev suggested. Misa blinked at him.

"The system has literally never worked that way," she said, but she grabbed a shard and pushed it into the screen anyway—

—And stopped, staring, when the shard abruptly disappeared from her fingers, and the anchor integrity ticked *up*.

"You were saying?" Sev grinned at her. Misa scowled at him.

"I'm almost offended that it's so fucking simple," she muttered, staring at the window. "This whole time . . ."

"We didn't have that many shards to mess with, and no reason to guess that would work," Vex said, trying to be comforting. "And nothing bad happened! Everyone's okay."

"Right," Misa said, her tone slightly distracted. She turned her gaze to Sev, who smiled back at her. "Everyone's okay," she repeated, almost to herself.

She sighed.

"Well, that's one problem solved, right?" Clyde said. He stood with his elbows resting on the bar counter and his hands propping up his chin. "Whatcha got next?"

"Nothing, I guess," Misa said. "It's a bit late; we should probably . . ."

Her voice trailed off. She stared at the window. She'd glanced at it to check on the time, to see if there was any left in the day for her to do the training she wanted to do; the sky was dark, though, and so she had been about to suggest they retire for the night.

And then she noticed something none of them had noticed before. It was difficult to spot, really. The air here was strange, and the sky was composed of layer upon layer of translucent reflections, each displaying a different part of the world.

It was no wonder she hadn't noticed the glimmering light behind them before.

The *stars.*

"The stars still exist here," she breathed.

"What?" Clyde looked at her strangely. Belle and Elliot did the same, but Vex, Sev, and Derivan all turned toward the window as one, eyes growing wide.

"*Oh,*" Sev breathed.

"Whoa," Vex said. He pressed his snout against the glass, trying to peer up through the panes.

Derivan remained silent and stayed where he was. He stared out the window, though, as though trying to commit the sight to memory.

"You guys wanna tell us what's going on here?" Elliot asked, and Belle elbowed him with a hiss.

"They're obviously having a moment," she said. "Give them a bit."

A small pause followed as the four gazed out of the window. There was a magic to the sight, the same way there was a magic to the moment every time Derivan cast [**Starry Night**]. A small moment of appreciation for something that felt larger than all of them.

Derivan responded first, finally turning to Clyde, his gaze apologetic. "Our branch of reality no longer has stars," he said. "We did not even know they were missing until . . . very recently. The real thing is quite the sight to see."

Clyde just stared at the four of them. He leaned back against the bar, thinking for a moment, and then nodded to himself; he glanced at Belle. "We could take them to the observatory," he said.

Belle sighed, but she was smiling. "Somehow, I knew you were going to say that," she said. "There's an observatory near the edge of town, if you'd like to visit. It's enchanted to cut through all of the sky weirdness—we call them Fractals—so you'll get a better view of the night sky, if that's what you're looking for."

"It's technically only open to scientists," Clyde said. "But Belle's awesome and can get you in."

Belle grinned. "Why, thank you," she said, dipping into a small curtsy.

"We'd like that, I think," Sev said quietly. He glanced at the others but found no disagreement. Misa nodded, staring out the window with a wistful look in her eyes; Vex stood near the base of the window, his snout still pressed against the glass; Derivan tilted his head in agreement.

"This way, then," Belle said. She gave Clyde and Elliot both a wave. "You two hold down the fort here, okay?"

"You know we will," Clyde said, waving her away. "Go on; have fun."

"You're not coming?" Vex tore his gaze away from the window to look at the innkeeper. Clyde laughed at the look on Vex's face, though his reply was apologetic.

"No," he said. "I'm afraid even with Belle, the observatory only allows a few visitors at a time. Plus, I shouldn't *actually* keep leaving my post like this."

"And I'm staying to keep him company," Elliot said cheerfully. "We'll be fine here; don't worry. Go look at the stars! I'm sure they're waiting."

"Oh," Vex said. That made sense to him. He trotted out of the inn along with the others, glancing back at the pure-black, box-like building, so very different from the warm inside.

Then he paused and glanced at the others. "Wait, the stars are doing what now?"

—∞—

"I'm sure it's just a turn of phrase," Sev said again. Belle seemed deeply amused and was refusing to clarify; Vex, of course, was trying to puzzle out exactly what Elliot had meant by "they're waiting".

"But it might not be," Vex argued. "Just because we *think* we know what the stars are like doesn't mean that we actually know—"

"We're here," Belle interrupted, casting her still-amused gaze onto Vex. "You can find out for yourselves."

The party stopped and stared at the building in question. It looked . . . it looked identical to every other building, actually.

"I'm not sure what I expected," Sev muttered. He glanced at the darkened window at the front; he could *almost* see what looked like star charts, laid out on a shelf.

"I expected something taller," Misa said critically. She stared at the distinctly box-shaped building. "It's just another cube."

Belle laughed. "We have *magic*," she said. She removed a small rectangle from her dress and pressed it against an almost-invisible seam in the wall; there was a *click*, and a flash of mana that signaled the door unlocking. "The buildings just need to be functional. Everything else happens on the inside."

She threw open the door and stepped in. For all that they'd already known that the inside would be *different*, none of them were quite prepared.

It was like stepping into a field of stars.

The floor vanished beneath their feet almost as soon as they stepped into the room, giving them a distinct sense of vertigo; Vex wobbled slightly until Misa, closest to him, grabbed him by the arm and steadied him. Sev's expression was a complicated mixture of both wonder and nausea, and Derivan simply looked around, taking everything in.

"Are you all right?" Belle asked, amused. She was looking at Sev, who waved her off.

"I don't like heights," he said. "I'll be fine. Probably."

"You can't be high up if there's no down to speak of," Vex said, trying to reassure Sev. "There isn't even anything to land on!"

It did not work. Sev looked even more green, if anything.

Still, the "room" they were in was beautiful. There was no one else present—everyone else had gone home for the day, Belle explained—but this was a magic that put them in the middle of the stars. The enchantment on the walls let them see a depth of color that wouldn't normally have been apparent in space. All the errant gases were awash in vibrant reds and greens. Every star shone with startling clarity, for all that they were exceedingly far away—and it was astonishing how well the room conveyed a sense of *distance*.

In short, it was easy to feel exceedingly small, standing in this room. Belle smiled slightly at the stunned looks on all their faces. "You never get used to it," she said softly. "I come here every so often, even though it's not really my area of expertise. It's a nice way to get perspective."

"Why keep it closed to the public at all?" Vex asked softly. "I feel like everyone should get to see . . . this."

"We actually tried to make it open, once," Belle said with a small laugh. "The problem is that the place *looks* big, but it's only about two or three times the size of the actual building. We can't fit everyone in that wants to visit, and . . . a lot of people want to visit."

For a moment, Belle looked as though she wanted to say something else—but she stopped before she did, and shook her head as though admonishing herself.

"I'm surprised all of this is still *here*," Sev said quietly. He took a few steps forward, his feet slightly surer now, although he still stumbled slightly as he misjudged the distance to the "ground." "If the universe is getting erased . . ."

"Truth be told, it's surprising to us, too," Belle said. She sighed, conjuring a chair of shadow from the ground and leaning back; it creaked along with her movement, the back of the chair folding back to let her recline. A wave of her hand and she conjured a matching set of four seats for the rest of the party, and they all settled in, staring silently up at the sky.

Belle broke the silence after a minute. "We're not sure exactly why. Our models all suggest that planets with *life* on them should be the last ones to be erased; the stars should have disappeared long ago, except for the ones still supporting life."

Vex looked suddenly worried, struck by a horrible thought. "What if that's why?" he asked. "What if all the stars up there support a different planet . . . ?"

"No," Belle said, culling the train of thought before it could go too far; Vex relaxed slightly at her assertion, though he still looked up with concern. She smiled wryly. "Trust me, it was one of the first things we thought of. We checked. Obreve is the only planet with any life on it."

"*Obreve*," Sev said, snapping his fingers. "Right! That was the name. Shit, I thought it got erased or something. I was going to ask you guys about it, but I forgot."

Misa rotated her chair to face Sev. "You . . . forgot the name of the planet?" she asked.

"You know I have problems with my memory," Sev said, waving her away. She frowned at him. "I was going to bring it up!" he said defensively. "I just forgot."

"You're forgetting things an awful lot," she said, crossing her arms.

"Because I have memory problems!" Sev gestured vaguely. "You know how my skills work. It's not . . . it's not great. But you can trust me, I promise."

Misa sighed. "I know I can," she said, her voice gentler. "And I do. It's not trust that's the problem. I'm just worried about you."

"Oh," Sev said, and then in a softer, smaller voice: "Sometimes I worry about me too."

He tried to smile, but there was a vulnerability there, a brittleness in his eyes that he didn't usually let show.

Misa didn't know what to say to that.

The conversation petered off into a rough sort of silence. Belle spoke after several minutes, a note of wistful melancholy in her voice. "It's something about being here," she said. "Makes you feel smaller. A little bit more vulnerable. A little bit more open, too."

"It's beautiful, though." Sev stared up at the sky, his eyes tracing the patterns of the stars. A few of them were moving, even, twirling and dancing around one another. He couldn't imagine the phenomenal speed at which they must have been moving for it to be so clearly visible in real time.

"You can hear them, if you know how to listen," Belle commented. She reached into the air, fiddling with something invisible. A second later, a rolling, wispy tune began to play from all around them, echoing in the room. The tune was sad, melancholic. A final ode to a dying universe. "They've been playing the same song ever since the universe ended . . ."

Belle fell silent as a ringing tone entered the melody; a sound not unlike a sword striking armor. It should have been harsh, but the note that was produced was pure.

A small, uplifting tone entered the music, and the tone of the song changed. Not a lot—just slightly. A shift from minor to major for a single chord, and yet . . .

Belle closed her eyes and smiled. "I was hoping I'd hear that," she said. "We haven't had that in a while. *Change*. Doesn't matter if it's magic in our reality, or the system in yours—when the universe dies, it stops being able to make new things. But there's something different with you four, isn't there?"

"We're just normal people, as far as I know," Vex said cautiously. Belle laughed.

"You're as far from normal as it gets," she said, the words playful. "But I'm not saying you were born special. I'm saying that maybe you chose to be. By making yourselves the axis upon which the world can turn . . .

"But I'm just an old lady making guesses." Belle leaned back in her chair, staring up at the sky. "Watch the stars with me, will you? We've got at least an hour here."

And they did.

CHAPTER 11

DISSENT

Xothok

"We did *what*?"

Talking to himself was still . . . uncomfortable. Xothok saw in this other version of him all the things he could have been, and something about that was deeply uncomfortable. It didn't help that Kothos—as they had decided to call him, since it was slightly easier than saying "other Xothok" every single time—was so much more composed.

He didn't flinch, even when Xothok got angry at him, swore at him. He watched him with kind, *understanding* eyes.

Eyes that made Xothok want to punch him into a wall.

"We used catapults," Kothos supplied calmly, though there was a cheeky sort of grin hiding behind his serene smile; Xothok had hated that, too, the joy Kothos seemed to be able to take in life—though he was slowly starting to recognize that hatred as *envy*. "And an uncommon skill, [**Improved Target Selection**]. Turns out there's no distance limitations on the skill, and the improved version protects the ammunition until it reaches the target."

"I can't decide if I should be angry about that," Xothok muttered.

His bandits—no. Not bandits. His men were all standing in one of the fields outside the Guild, a pile of raw wood piled up beside them. That was what Kothos had told him they would need, though he hadn't known *why* they would need it until now. There wasn't much of a point for Kothos to tell him everything. He couldn't retain information between their chats, besides the vaguest possible memory of what he needed to do.

Which made it all the more difficult to explain to his men *why* they needed to gather all this wood. Fortunately, most of them trusted him.

Most of them.

Byrrhon continued to be a problem. He was starting fights more and more frequently, to the point where even his own men had started to distance themselves from him, afraid of what he would try to do to them; he would snap at the smallest things, ranting about how "weak" they had become. How they weren't fighting monsters like they should have been, how they weren't growing in *experience* and *levels* like they had when they were out there by themselves.

One or two of his men had even listened to that ranting and sided with him, up until Xothok pointed out that experience and levels had never been the point. The amount they got from banditry was minimal, and the monsters they actually fought were few and far between. If anything, they earned more experience whenever they picked up and completed a Guild quest.

That fact did nothing to quell Byrrhon's anger. He seemed convinced that fighting monsters in the wild was the only real way to progress, and no amount of reasoning got through to him. When all other arguments were exhausted, he would simply claim that they would *eventually* have gotten more experience out of the old ways, which was . . . patently false.

Xothok didn't know how to deal with him. He'd asked the Guild to leave dealing with Byrrhon up to him, but he was starting to regret that decision. Kothos was no help—he mostly seemed sad whenever he looked at Byrrhon, and had no suggestions.

By now, they had done a few Guild jobs—mostly low-level Nucleus quests, since those were the ones the Guild needed done most. The Guildmaster seemed grateful every time they returned with a new haul of shards, though it seemed strange that she was the one to personally handle processing their quest rewards. Each time, they would sit down with one of the Guild's clerks to discuss their strategies and what had eventually forced them to retreat from the Nucleus—ways to optimize their builds, their skills.

They were growing stronger. All except for Byrrhon, who insisted on doing it all by himself. He told no one what his build was, and threatened to kill anyone that asked.

Xothok knew this was coming to a head. He knew if he didn't find a solution for Byrrhon, the man would do something that would get some or all of them killed. He just hadn't *found* any other solutions, and all of the Guild's normal strategies didn't seem to work with him.

"Uh, boss?" Morkar gestured to the pile of wood, pulling Xothok abruptly out of his thoughts. "What're we s'pposed to do with those?"

"We have to build a catapult," Xothok replied without thinking, and glared at his men when they all stared at him in confusion. "Don't just look at me. Get building!"

"There a chance I can ask *why*?" Morkar stared at him skeptically.

"No," Xothok answered shortly.

It was something they'd all come to accept from him—he couldn't always explain what he asked them to do. In the time leading up to this, he'd asked a number of his men to pick up new Classes, losing their skills and several levels in the process; the Guild had a high-quality Fountain, but even it couldn't make status changes *free*.

It was leading up to something, he promised, and the Guildmaster backed him up. It was . . . surprising, to him, they all trusted him.

He wasn't planning on letting them down.

"Oh, come the fuck *on*." There was Byrrhon again, almost right on cue. Xothok glanced at him with disinterest at first—but a second look told him Byrrhon had acquired a new scar on his face from who knows where, and something about it felt strange. A feeling of deep discomfort that started to grow in his stomach. "Are you guys really going to follow him? He's obviously gone nuts. He's building a fucking *catapult*. What the fuck are we going to do with a catapult?"

"It's hard to explain," Xothok said.

"Because you can't fuckin' explain it." Byrrhon got right up into his face, foul-smelling breath only inches away; Xothok didn't flinch. He blinked once, slowly.

"Step back, Byrrhon."

"Maybe I don't fuckin' *want* to."

Xothok wasn't blind. He saw both Two and Morkar moving in the back, his second- and third-in-command respectively. Byrrhon's hand was hidden from him, angled cleverly so he wouldn't be able to see if the man was reaching for anything—which meant that he *was*, obviously.

"You're a shit leader and we're getting weak under you," Byrrhon growled.

To his credit, he didn't mince any more words. Xothok was half-expecting him to continue—to say some half-baked line about how it was time for new leadership, or something like that. Instead, one hand flashed forward, blindingly fast.

Several thoughts went through Xothok's head all at once.

One was that Byrrhon's level was not what he said it was. The man was moving with the sort of speed he expected from a Silver-ranked adventurer, or a Bronze ranker that had invested every point into Agility. There was every chance that he was employing a Skill, but if he was, then it wasn't anything he'd known Byrrhon had.

The second thought was that he had prepared himself for this exact situation, but he hadn't quite prepared for Byrrhon to have *grown*. The man refused to participate in any of the quests they'd done; his assumption was that Byrrhon hadn't grown at all, and that had clearly been a false assumption. The better question was perhaps *how* Byrrhon had been able to grow without participating in a single battle.

The third thought was about Byrrhon's eyes. The man's gaze held absolute hatred in them; there was not an ounce of empathy, or of the Byrrhon he'd known before all of this had started. He wondered, in an abstract sort of way, exactly when he'd lost the man he'd once thought of as a brother.

[**Martial Navigation**] kicked in.

He didn't have enough speed to completely dodge Byrrhon's stab; the best he could do was twist out of the way, and though the blade only grazed him, Xothok was stunned at the amount of pain that flashed through his body. He felt his health drain out of him almost completely from that single grazing hit and knew with certainty that if he hadn't reacted that quickly—if he hadn't led so many missions himself, if he hadn't had [**Martial Navigation**], if he hadn't listened to Kothos whenever the other him taught him something new about his skills—he would have died.

Xothok caught a glimpse of the blade, and the pulse of his heart quickened; the feeling of discomfort expanded and became a deep dread. The dagger was like nothing he'd seen before. The metal looked like hunger given form. It was a bitter red that moved and shifted in his gaze, almost painful to look at.

A memory came to mind, unbidden.

There are dark secrets hidden in the stars, too. History does not discriminate; it contains everything, good and bad. Terrible dangers hide within the beauty of the past. Do not be blinded by the light.

But if Byrrhon had uncovered one of those secrets—

He didn't have time to *think*.

Byrrhon twisted powerfully as both Two and Morkar reached him, trying to restrain him; his strength alone was enough to fling both of them in opposite directions. Xothok didn't need to look at the system to know that that move alone had cut down most of their health.

Shit.

"Archer team!" he called out. "Formation two! Fire at will!"

He didn't check to see if they obeyed. He dove backward, reaching into his Skills; he hadn't yet changed his own class, and thank the fucking gods for that.

[**Steal**], he commanded. If he could grab the dagger from Byrrhon—

The skill failed. Xothok didn't have time to look at the plethora of system windows that spilled out. Byrrhon closed in, and Xothok barely dodged; the dagger was a blur of red in his vision. [**Martial Navigation**] helped him here.

He just needed to calm down.

"Just like navigating the stars," Kothos muttered next to him. Something about his other self's voice was soothing, calming; it helped him focus his mind. "You know how he's going to move. You don't need to react. You know where he's going to be."

He did.

He calmed himself and let the skill take over. He let it plot the future like it was a course in the sky, marking moments in time instead of space.

Step to the left to dodge a fist. Duck low next, to avoid the swing of a blade. Two arrows will distract him. Step backward, and draw him forward. One arrow will strike him in the shoulder, the other in his neck.

He will survive. He will be angry.

Two more blows. One straight to your face, bottom left to top right; lean backward and feint to the left before he can recover. Make him step into the path of another arrow. The pain will distract him.

He will try to hook you across the face, right to left. Transfer your dagger to your right hand. Grab ahold of his wrist with your left as it swings past.

Let his own strength carry your blade into his heart. Twist. It will not do enough damage if you do not.

Xothok could have stopped himself. He realized what was about to happen before he did it, despite the state the skill lulled him into; he could have pulled out. He could have stopped himself from twisting the blade.

He didn't.

"Sorry, old friend," he said. "I tried."

He had. He'd given Byrrhon more chances than he should have, perhaps. It shouldn't have come to this at all; he should have done something different. Tried to talk to him more, maybe. Locked him up somewhere until he came to his senses.

Xothok was vaguely aware that his blade was sticky with blood, of the life fading from Byrrhon's eyes. Part of him wanted to look away, but he forced himself to watch.

The hatred didn't fade from Byrrhon's eyes until his very last breath.

CHAPTER 12

INWARD SPIRAL

Xothok

Mercy was something that could only be afforded by the powerful.

That was the lesson Xothok had taken away from the fight between his team and the four adventurers that had utterly overwhelmed them. Derivan, Vex, Misa, Sev—the names were practically burned into his head. They could have killed all of them, and as far as Xothok was concerned, they would have been justified in doing so.

They hadn't. But they could afford not to; they were never in any danger. His team had never had that option. He'd thought that they'd moved beyond that, with all the progress they'd made, but . . .

It was clear that it wasn't enough. The same logic he'd once used on the caravans they preyed upon—overwhelming force, because they couldn't guarantee that they would win if they showed one iota of mercy—now reflected back on him in the death of his oldest friend.

He wondered when Byrrhon had changed so much, and he wondered when he'd made himself stop looking.

"We should hold a funeral," he said absently. It felt cold, the way he said it, like there was no real emotion behind his words; the truth was that Xothok didn't really know *how* he felt. His other self stared at him with something like sympathy in his eyes and didn't say a word.

Xothok normally hated it when Kothos spoke, but now he found he missed having his input.

"Fer that scumbag?" Morkar snarled. "No offense, boss, but he was tryin' to kill you. Almost did, too."

"Not just for him," Xothok said. He didn't finish the thought. Instead, he walked over to the pile of wood still lying in the field. Byrrhon's body could wait; they had a catapult to build.

Though he *did* send a quick message off to the Guildmaster first, just so she knew what had happened.

His men followed his lead, though they gave each other strange looks. They were fine with working with the Guild now, doing their quests and fighting alongside their members. Many of them bore a grudge against the Guild for rejecting them in the first place, but they were starting to understand that those were the actions of rogue members rather than a general principle of the Guild in the first place. In their time there, a few of them had managed to make friends, both with other adventuring teams and with the staff.

They were, in other words, starting to fit in.

But this other project Xothok had? None of them could make heads nor tails of it. They *knew*, intellectually, that Xothok had explained what he was trying to do a number of times. They'd all seen the piece of paper onto which he'd drawn a picture of the night sky, and they all felt the same sense of odd familiarity.

That more than anything, perhaps, was the reason they all followed him despite not knowing exactly what all of this was *for*.

The work took hours, even with the help of a skill; in that time, the Guildmaster had responded and sent someone to collect Byrrhon's body, so Xothok didn't have to look at it. Didn't have to think about it. He kept himself focused on the work instead, until the final nail had been hammered into place, and he stared at what they had constructed.

It was a piece of shit.

It was clear everyone else felt that way too, considering the dubious looks they were all giving the thing. But it didn't need to be good. So long as it had a bare minimum of functionality, it would be enough.

"You will need to remember how to navigate," Kothos murmured, standing beside him. "Targeting is not enough. Space is complex, and reaching a star safely more so, even when the star is dead. Perhaps especially then."

"The fuck is *complex* supposed to mean?" Xothok asked. "It's space. The whole thing's empty."

"You'd think that." Kothos chuckled. "The planeshifted thought that. Turns out space here is a little different. You'll find out when you get there."

"Or you could fuckin' tell me."

"Now, where would the fun in that be?" Kothos smiled.

Infuriating ass. It was made all the worse by the reminder that Kothos was just another iteration of *him*, and he could absolutely picture himself acting that way in another life.

"You know what to do?" Xothok turned to Two. He was the only one that Xothok actually trusted to aim and fire the damn thing. He'd been surprisingly amenable to changing his Class, too.

Two nodded but stayed silent, as he always did. Morkar folded his arms, staring skeptically at the catapult.

"Hate to say it, but this feels like a stupid idea, boss," the orc told him. "Ain't gonna stop ya, but I *am* gonna say I told you so."

"Trust me, I know how stupid this looks," Xothok muttered, staring at the catapult. "But I don't really have any other ideas."

Before he actually tried launching, though, he needed to reply to a message. He'd been putting it off for a few days—he didn't know how he felt about being sent a message by the very same adventurers that had captured them, and he couldn't even phrase his response correctly if Kothos wasn't around to remind him of what he had forgotten—but now that he was about to embark on whatever *this* was . . .

Well, he needed a backup plan, and as far as he was concerned, those adventurers owed him one.

—∞—

The plan was predicated on a lot of things they weren't sure about, really.

One of them was whether or not the launch would even work. The system had been far from stable of late, especially with the failure of growth spells in Elyra; there was every chance that launching Xothok out of a catapult would result in an impact that erased most of his health and did little else.

The second was whether or not the stars were dead or gone entirely. The sky was dark, certainly; they had, at the very least, gone *out*. If his understanding of what Kothos had told him was correct, then their corpses should still be there in the sky, open to being explored . . . but maybe that was wrong and even their corpses had been erased. If that were the case, then this would be a non-starter entirely.

The third was whether or not he could get *back*.

Fortunately, the last one was the one Xothok was most certain about; he'd enlisted the Guildmaster's help for this one, asking for one of their mages to mark him with a [**Return**] rune. Short of something absurd like magic not functioning properly in space—which Kothos had assured him was not the case—he was set to be able to return safely, just in front of the catapult. Two would be there to greet him, and Morkar would be leading the rest into other missions in the meantime. He didn't exactly know how long this trip was supposed to take, after all.

All of this left him sitting in the catapult. Kothos was balanced on the edge beside him, defying the laws of physics; Xothok had never really thought about it, but he supposed as a mental construct, his other self didn't really need to be concerned about things like balance and weight and comfort.

"This is nostalgic," Kothos commented. "Same setup as one of our first launches . . . We got better after that, of course. At our prime, we had a full observatory, with these metal structures within them that would launch our ships into the stars."

"I'm just wondering what idiot discovered this," Xothok grumbled. Kothos gave him a surprisingly sad smile.

"That's a story for another time."

"Are you ready, sir?" Two asked him. His voice was soft-spoken and quiet, and almost didn't carry all the way up to Xothok's perch.

Xothok sighed.

"Yeah, go for it," he said.

He felt [**Improved Target Selection**] activating. There was a *thrum* that raced across his scales, and he shivered involuntarily. He didn't see Two reach for the rope, or the dagger that cut across it—but he imagined those things happening. Kothos just watched him, amused.

There was a beat. A pause.

Then he felt the protective cloak of a Skill wrapping around him more firmly, and a tremendous force as his seat launched him into the air at an angle that did not at all match where they had aimed the catapult. He felt himself accelerating after leaving his seat, which shouldn't have been possible. He saw the ground receding in the blink of an eye.

And then he was in space.

Kothos hadn't followed him, and with the loss of his other self, his memories of what he was *supposed to do* or that there was an other self to summon at all were rapidly fading; he couldn't reach for the ink drawing in his pocket that he knew would remind him, either, because at the speeds he was traveling, the paper would simply be ripped away from him.

He was protected to some degree. [**Improved Target Selection**] selected a target and guaranteed its arrival without the projectile being harmed, and in this case, "harm" included things like "death from not breathing" and the like. But protection meant nothing if he couldn't remember what he was supposed to *do*.

To stave off panic, Xothok closed his eyes. It wasn't like there was anything ahead of him to see, anyway. There was just an infinite dark expanse that felt cold and *wrong*, and he didn't want to look at it for longer than necessary.

The moment he did, a brilliant array lit up in his mind. Xothok opened his eyes again, startled, and it vanished just as quickly; once again in front of him was that endless void.

He frowned. He closed his eyes again—

—Once more, a small field of brilliant points of light appeared behind his eyelids, in his mind's eye.

"Oh," he said, though the word was lost quickly to the wind.

But it was strange, wasn't it, that there was wind at all?

That realization made the wind around him die down. He'd already arrived, he realized; the idea that he was still *traveling* was just another layered illusion, built by the expectations of his mind.

He recalled the response Misa had sent him, startlingly fast. [Be careful,] she had said. [You're going to go out of range of the anchors that way. We're not sure exactly what's there, but it's probably not going to be what you expect. If we're right about where you are, then you might be in a liminal space—don't ask me what that means; Vex used the term, not me—where direction of thought influences direction of movement. That might not make sense until you're there.]

He had, of course, replied with [I have no idea what the fuck you're talking about.] and left it at that.

Now, though, the meaning of her words was a little clearer. Whenever he focused on one of those points of light, he found himself drifting closer toward it—

[**Are you okay?**]

The message pinged, unexpected, from Two. Xothok blinked at it, surprised, then answered, [**For now.**]

It was the first time any of his men had checked up on him, even Two. How strange.

Xothok dismissed it for now and reached for the drawing he kept in his pocket. He let the image mentally drag him in, allowed the aching familiarity to suffuse his being. It served as a reminder that he'd once been someone else—

"They're waypoints," Kothos said, appearing as a strangely well-lit phenomenon in the void. He sounded wistful. "Not stars. Just markers we left for each other, exploring . . . whatever this place is. Every one of them *should* be near a star."

And yet it all looked so empty. Kothos hadn't needed to say the words; Xothok could see—could *feel* it for himself, how achingly empty the space felt, even filled with light like this.

"Might as well give it a try," he muttered, mostly to himself; Kothos nodded beside him, but Xothok ignored him. He had his own storm of emotions to deal with without having to deal with the infuriatingly calm other version of himself. Something like fear, anger, some *guilt* he was certain he wouldn't have felt if it wasn't for the damn Guild—

He was moving, he realized. One of the waypoints was darker than the others, and unlike most of the others, there was *something* next to it. Not a star—nothing like a star should have been.

The corpse of a star, perhaps. Except even that descriptor was insufficient. He saw burnt and desiccated ruins made of crimson flesh, and as he directed his mind toward the thought of it, he felt himself drift closer.

"I don't think you should go there," his other self told him. Kothos sounded, for once, nervous.

"Fuck you," Xothok answered.

Part of him knew it wasn't the best response. Kothos had a point. There was something about this place that repulsed him. But he couldn't have pulled himself away if he wanted to. Even when he tried to cast his mind to other waypoints that seemed like they might have something next to them, Byrrhon's hate-filled expression jumped back into his mind. The way he'd stared at him as he died stuck in his mind.

And those thoughts, too, drew him ever closer to those ruins.

"Navigators need clarity of mind," Kothos said. "You can't dwell on your emotions—"

"—I said *fuck you,*" Xothok repeated. He wasn't explaining shit to his copy. What right did he have to say anything? Kothos had experienced none of the hardship he had; he'd lived a cushy life as a fucking *noble.*

Some small part of Xothok recognized the spiral his mind was in, maybe. But not enough to break out of it.

CHAPTER 13

INTERVENTION

Xothok

The ground *squelched* under Xothok's feet, and he barely suppressed the disgusted grimace that crawled through his frame. He was distantly aware that everything here was a product of his mind, or so Kothos claimed, but it didn't make any of this feel any less *real*.

Stepping over viscera was not how he had pictured the day going.

"It's not real," Kothos said, for perhaps the third time, and Xothok leveled a glare at him.

"So you've said," he said, his voice coming out as a half-growl. Kothos chuckled nervously.

"Sorry," he said. "I'm reminding myself more than anything."

Kothos couldn't dismiss himself here—nor could Xothok dismiss him. Whatever odd confluence of skills had created him to begin with, it seemed at odds with the nature of this place; he'd attempted to dismiss himself once or twice, and Xothok had certainly tried to banish him a few times, and nothing had happened.

Xothok had to admit he felt a grim sort of satisfaction at his other self's clear discomfort, but that didn't do much to distract him from the *pull* this place had. He walked past row after row of burned shelves. Even ignoring the fact that the shelves were made of flesh, he couldn't do much to ignore the acrid smell that pervaded his nostrils, or the clouds of ash kicked up from the ground from what looked like the burned remains of books.

It was ironic, really, that—surrounded by such horror—all he could think about was Byrrhon's face in the moment of his death.

"What did you mean?" Xothok asked, trying his best to distract himself. "When you said this place is 'a product of the mind' or whatever."

"Oh," Kothos said. He seemed grateful to have a topic to latch on to. "From what we know about the Libraries, they all respond to who you are as a person. Some people just see it as a regular library, the kind you'd find in Elyra."

Xothok didn't bother telling his other self that he'd never been to a library in Elyra.

"Some people see the Libraries as these beautiful shelves built into massive oak trees. Others see tall shelves of gleaming metal, stocked high with books. It's unique to every person, and we could share our vision of the Libraries with one another . . ." Kothos' voice trailed off.

"It's never looked like *this*, though," he said quietly.

Xothok didn't respond for a moment. When he did, it was with a biting sort of sarcasm. "Maybe this is just what the Libraries look like to *me*. They respond to 'who you are as a person,' right?"

"I-I didn't mean it like that," Kothos said, sounding off-kilter for perhaps the first time since they'd started speaking. "I'm sure it isn't just you. The stars are dead—there's no reason the rules are going to stay the same. Besides! If the effect was still active, I'd see something different from you, right? I used to see the shelves as these wonderful abstractions of light and music, where a different note would bring forward a different book—"

"I don't know if you've noticed," Xothok interrupted, sick of hearing how *wonderful* his other self had it, "but you're in *my* head. You're not exactly another person."

At that, Kothos fell silent. A flash of hurt flickered across his expression, smoothed away a split second later; he fell into step beside Xothok and said nothing else.

Good, Xothok told himself. He ignored the small thread of guilt that speared him, and focused on finding . . . whatever he was supposed to find here.

Truth be told, he didn't know what he was doing.

He knew he was trying to find out what happened to the stars. It felt like a part of his life had been ripped away from him—it was *true* that a part of his life had been ripped away from him, even. This was a way for him to explore his heritage, but what was the point, really? It wasn't like he could fix the damn stars.

Even if he knew what happened to them, what would that accomplish?

Xothok did his best to dismiss these darker thoughts as they crowded into his mind, but there was only so much he could do; the corpse of the star served only as a reminder of his murder of Byrrhon, and the silence crowded out the whisper of rationality. Kothos had helped before, as loath as he was to admit it—but now his other self was silent too, just trailing quietly behind him.

Xothok didn't even know where he was going. He was letting his feet lead him in the direction of that *pull* he felt, though he would be hard pressed to describe the nature of that pull. He walked past a half dozen books that had actually survived the burning and ignored every one of them, though a small part of his mind shouted at him to stop and look through them.

Over here, the pull whispered.

When Xothok stopped, it was in front of a man. Someone else. He stared at the figure in front of him briefly, entirely nonplussed; this was the last thing he had expected to find. The man stood in front of what looked like a shard of bitter red, pulsing and rotating in the air just behind him. Even a second of looking at the thing filled him with a deep resentment.

"Hello," the man said, smiling at him. There was nothing *pleasant* about that smile. Alarm bells rang in Xothok's head, but he continued to stare impassively. He couldn't make himself move. "You must be Byrrhon's friend."

"Friend?" Xothok let out a bitter laugh. "Fucker tried to kill me. He wasn't my *friend.*"

Except he had been.

Kothos was yelling at him, but his other self's words filtered past him, somehow prevented from reaching him. That felt wrong too.

The alarm bells rang louder.

But he'd already known something was wrong when walking into all this, hadn't he? Maybe he'd chosen this. The red glow of the crystal made it difficult for him to think; it filled him with a bitter *hatred* . . .

It looked remarkably like Byrrhon's dagger, in fact. Something deep inside him—something ugly—twisted, and he took a slow step forward; the man stepped aside easily, almost encouraging him forward. Kothos tried to pull him back, but the man's hands were immaterial to him. He wasn't *physical.*

What was he going to do, even if he figured out what happened to the stars? What was he going to do *now*? It looked like his men were in a better place, sure, but now that he'd killed Byrrhon, the Guildmaster would surely decide he was a danger. If he took power into his own hands now, if he just *reached out*—

A small box popped up in front of him.

[**Just let us know if you need anything,**] Two sent.

[**What you did there ain't easy,**] Morkar said. He could imagine the look on the orc's face—gruff but respectful. [**But we're behind you every step of the way. I dunno what happened to him, but that was fucked up.**]

"What are you waiting for?" the man behind him asked. He sounded strangely concerned. Xothok looked back at him and saw the dagger reflected in his eyes.

Clarity cut through to Xothok's mind, like someone had ripped away the cobwebs hanging over his thoughts.

He scowled.

"You're the fucker that got to him, aren't you?" he said.

The man narrowed his eyes at Xothok. "Clever," he said. "I had a lock on your system. You shouldn't have—"

He paused, seeming to gaze past Xothok and into the distance. He frowned. "Ah," he said.

Xothok looked behind him, but there was nothing there. And when he looked back, the man was gone too, the crystal, the blood and flesh and viscera. All that was left were shelves of plain steel, and a few books that had survived a terrible fire.

"Xothok?" Kothos said, his voice wide and frantic; he seemed relieved when Xothok turned his gaze over to him. "Oh, good, you can hear me again. Are you okay? I don't know what happened, but you just . . ."

Kothos gestured vaguely, unable to find the words. Xothok sighed.

"I'm okay," he said. "I'm, uh. I'm fucking sorry. About just now."

Kothos paused and stared at him. "Did something happen?"

"Are you going to accept the apology or not?" Xothok snapped.

". . . Sure," Kothos said, his voice uncertain. "Are you sure you're okay?"

"Absolutely fucking not," Xothok said. Strangely, Kothos looked relieved, and Xothok thought he understood why.

Better than hiding that fact from himself, he supposed.

He looked around at the charred remains of the library. He still didn't know what he was going to do here. He still didn't think he was going to be able to fix the stars. But getting some answers was at least a start.

Especially if it told him who the *fuck* had messed with his family.

[**Thanks,**] he sent in reply, before he could forget. If Two and Morkar hadn't sent him those messages . . . he didn't want to think about what could have happened.

"Okay," he said out loud. He glanced around himself in some distaste and forced the next words out of his mouth. "Let's read some books."

"Finally," Kothos said, rubbing his hands together in glee. Xothok just stared at him.

Sometimes, he really couldn't believe they were the same person.

"Misa, the connection's cut." Vex was patting the half-orc in question on the shoulder.

"Yeah, but it feels fuckin' *good* to do this," Misa replied. She kept both her middle fingers up for another second more before finally crossing her arms. "You sure we got it?"

"We did." Derivan nodded, sitting down.

Reaching outside the bonus room was exhausting. It involved a combination of Shift and Patch, operated at a level of complexity that he'd never had to deal with before; on top of that, *undoing someone else's* modifications to the system, across entire echoes of reality? It was the farthest he'd ever stretched those skills.

The fact that Misa had wanted a visual projection just to give Irvis the finger hadn't helped, of course, but he had to admit that it was satisfying to watch.

He was glad that they'd trained this in time, though, and that they'd prepared before Xothok had launched. It had taken about a week in total to get his understanding of both Shift and Patch to that extent, and they hadn't known exactly what was coming, only that *something* was coming.

And that warning had come from Sev, of all people.

The cleric was sitting by the side, his head in his hands. He had a headache, he claimed. His own training to connect with the gods had come much further, but he'd refused to say anything about it, repeating again and again that it wasn't time yet.

Which was something that Derivan and the others were willing to accept for only so long, especially when Sev looked more and more haggard every time he said it. It had been weeks since whatever bound him had started to snap, and yet even now, it hadn't completely broken. There was the possibility that the bond was snapping in real time and was taking ten times longer now that they were in dilated time . . .

But Derivan was tired of waiting, and so were Vex and Misa. They hated seeing Sev like this.

"Sev," Derivan said. He kept his voice gentle. "I believe it is time. If you will not break it yourself—"

"No," Sev said, shaking his head. Derivan was prepared to argue, but he saw the look in Sev's eyes—he looked tired. "No, you're right," he repeated. "It's time. Let's just go somewhere nice to talk about this. Maybe that cafe in the town."

"Sure," Misa said, looking at him suspiciously. Sev gave her a tired smile, and she seemed to relax, accepting him at face value. "Yeah, okay," she said with a sigh. "You look like you need some coffee, anyway."

"Believe me," Sev said with a snort. "I need *so much coffee*."

CHAPTER 14

OF MYTHS AND MOCHAS

Clyde's inn was nice and comfortable, but the Horizon cafe had become a second haunt for them in the past few weeks. There was something about the aroma and ambience of the place that kept it wonderfully comforting, and that comfort was something they needed after the training.

They didn't stick together anymore—not completely. Each of them had different things to work on and couldn't always work on those things in close vicinity with the others; eventually, they had agreed it would be best if they sought out training on their own, especially if there were others in the town that would help them.

In Mundane, there weren't. But Combat, it turned out, wasn't very far away, and *that* was a true adventurer's town.

All of which was beside the point. They sat in a private booth in Horizon, enhanced by various protection magics that both the cafe owner and Belle had independently confirmed were *very* foolproof, and Sev sat on one side, nervously sipping his cup of coffee.

Misa sat next to him, mostly so she wouldn't intimidate him by sitting across from him. Derivan and Vex sat together and projected a concerted effort of looking very worried about Sev.

Sev, in turn, sighed.

"I still don't remember much," he started. "But I've made a breakthrough in that I'm able to talk to Aurum again. He's . . . a lot more scared and uncertain than he was before. It was pretty easy to distract him at first, but now it's like he can't think about anything but the end of the gods."

"He *is* just a kid," Misa said softly.

"Yup," Sev said with a sigh. "Someone like that shouldn't have the responsibility he does, but . . . here we go. He's been trying to figure out how to get in contact with the gods that have been erased."

"So they're not completely gone?" Vex perked up.

"It's hard to erase a god completely," Sev said. "Apparently."

"What does all this have to do with you?" Misa asked. "I'm worried about him too, but . . ."

Sev laughed. "Can't get anything past you guys, huh?"

"Sev." Misa's voice was serious.

"I know." Sev's gaze dropped, and he looked at the table for a long moment; he held his mug of coffee in both of his hands, closed his eyes, and took a slow sip. He let himself marinate in the aroma for a second before he said anything more. "As far as I can tell, Onyx and I came up with some kind of plan . . . a really long time ago. The locks you see on my soul, my system, my future—whatever—those are all locks I signed myself up for."

"Didn't you say that happened when you tried to save Onyx?" Vex asked hesitantly.

"I did say that," Sev said. He smiled a sardonic sort of smile, though it seemed more self-deprecating than anything else. "It's what I remember. And I'm pretty sure it *happened*. But even before that, I sealed my own fate. Somehow."

"Still not clear on the details?" Misa asked.

"Nope." Sev let out a frustrated sigh and let his head sink into his hands. "I'm not trying to hide this from you guys, I swear. But I just . . . I have to trust myself, right? This is a plan *I came up with*. Apparently."

"Well," Misa said. "I'd agree with you, but your sense of self-preservation kinda sucks. No offense."

"If you built in some sort of grand self-sacrifice in there, we're going to fight you," Vex added.

"I'm not *that* bad," Sev muttered. He glanced around at both Misa and Vex—who said nothing to this pronouncement and gave him a slightly skeptical look instead—before turning a slightly desperate look to the last member of their party. "Derivan?"

"You are better now," the armor allowed. "But you wandered into the dungeon I was in, alone and underleveled. I am not certain I trust that the decisions you made prior to that bear in consideration your true value."

Sev scowled a bit, folding his arms obstinately. He knew Derivan was right; it was just . . .

It was funny. Derivan talked about his true value like it was a simple fact; he allowed for no contention, no *argument* in his tone of voice.

Sev looked down and then away. Something in him responded to that assurance—what felt like an old memory—and yet he struggled to accept that truth.

"Is there anything else you know?" Misa asked. "Everything's coming to a head. Derivan says he sees something happening with your system, and even Clyde mentioned something about your time being almost up. There's gotta be *something*."

"I think . . ." Sev began. He hesitated—but he saw Misa staring at him, worried; he saw Vex watching him with trepidation; he saw the concern in Derivan's eyes. He sighed. "I think it's been like that for a long time," he said softly. "I think *I've* been around for a long time, maybe. A lot longer than twenty-five years. I don't remember any of it. But it's what makes the most sense."

Misa frowned. "Are you sure?" she asked. "Immortality isn't exactly common."

"I know, I know," Sev said. "I age normally, as far as I know. That answer's not complete. But it feels right. I've been around for twenty-five-ish years, I don't think that's *wrong*, I just . . . also think I've maybe been around for much longer than that."

There was a long silence.

"Sorry," Sev said awkwardly. "I know that doesn't actually tell us much."

"Don't *apologize*," Misa snorted. She flicked the air in front of him, creating a small gust of wind that blew his hair out of his eyes; Sev blinked rapidly at the sudden onslaught of air into his eyeballs.

"Ow," he complained.

"Don't apologize for dumb things and I won't have to do that," Misa said unrepentantly. She looked, if anything, entirely delighted that she'd discovered a new little trick she could do.

"It's a start," Vex said thoughtfully on his side of the table; his claws tapped briefly on the hardwood surface, and he took a sip from his (overly sweetened, as far as Sev was concerned—he'd seen the mound of sugar that Vex had practically poured into the thing) coffee, and his tail wagged back and forth slowly. "What you told us, I mean. It doesn't leave a lot of options on the table for what could be happening."

"You have an idea?" Sev asked. "Because I'd kill for an idea right now." He paused. "Uh, not actually. You know what I mean."

Vex snorted. "Not any *good* ones," he said. "There's only a few ways for you to be older than you are." He counted them off his claws. "Reincarnation is one, but as far as we know, that's just a tale from the planeshifted. You *could* be getting your age and memory reset, but I can't see a reason for that. It might not be *you* that's old—maybe it's just the system attached to you—but we don't have any evidence that individual parts of the system would stay coherent like that."

"With the exception of what I can sense with Patch," Derivan said. "Which *does* suggest a personal system that attaches to a person's soul and communicates with a greater system, for lack of better terminology."

"There is that," Vex allowed.

"There is a more important question, I feel." Derivan's gaze fixed itself on Sev; he wasn't just looking at him, he was almost looking *through* him. Sev shifted uncomfortably underneath the armor's piercing gaze. "All these questions answer what you *could be*, but we still do not know what is coming. Your bonds are falling away. Every sense I have tells me something is coming to a head with you. Even Clyde and the rest of the shadows here have the same feeling. Yet you have remained on this precipice.

"If you have any idea of what is coming, Sev, I believe we deserve to know." Derivan's gaze stayed steady.

Sev didn't answer for a long moment. It wasn't that he was hesitating, far from it—he was searching his mind for an answer. Derivan was right, but . . .

"I don't," Sev said with a sigh. "I wish I did. I have some ideas from my training, from what I've heard from Aurum and from the other gods I've been in contact with through him—but none of the answers are anything concrete. But I can talk about *that*; I've been meaning to, anyway, and it might give us another point of data."

He glanced around, and no one protested. Misa nodded at him to continue. Sev took a breath.

"One thing that's clear is that the majority of the gods don't know about this. They know the gods are disappearing; they don't know *why*. They don't know what the system is for. They don't know that it's cannibalizing them. They *can't* know, even. Aurum knows because of his connection with me, but anytime he's tried to tell anyone else . . ."

"Infolock?" Vex asked softly.

"Infolock," Sev agreed with a soft, bitter laugh. "Or, well, we know what it is now. Imagine an apocalypse you can't know about, because the very nature of it is that it's self-censoring; the only tool we have to know about it gets to pick and choose who's allowed to remember, and no one's in charge of that tool anymore, as far as we know."

"Not the Administrators?" Derivan prompted. "We have seen mention of them in the system."

Sev shook his head.

"That's one of the things Aurum was trying to investigate," he said. "As far as we can tell, there aren't any Administrators left. There are automated programs in the system that can fulfill the role of an Administrator, but they're locked in to responding to situations in very specific ways. The only time they can do anything different is when the *gods* do something about it."

"Except the gods don't know that anything's wrong," Misa said.

"Most of them don't." Sev frowned. "The ones that do . . . This is where it gets a little complicated. It's the reason Aurum was gone for so long. You guys remember where we first got the reality anchor that Misa has, right?"

"How could I forget?" Misa snorted.

"That place was weird," Vex commented. "It didn't feel real."

"You can't anchor reality from inside reality," Sev said. "So when we were there, we were on the outside, looking in. Any gods that get erased are kind of sitting there too, outside reality—slowly disintegrating and being fed into the anchors."

Vex blinked, feeling a small chill run down his spine. "Then the voices we heard—"

"Onyx and another forgotten god," Sev confirmed. "Onyx has some protection, because of what I did when I healed him. Aurum can visit that space because he's got a link with me. The other gods are just . . . kept there, away from the divine plane."

"Do we know what the Overseers are, then?" Derivan asked this question with a small frown in his eyes.

"Best guess is that it's a system defense powered by the gods," Sev said. "But that's one of the things we haven't really managed to figure out. Aurum's . . . in recovery. He spent too much time out there—let's just call it the Void, for ease of reference—and his angels tried to get him to come back, but apparently he was very insistent about finding some of the forgotten gods."

Sev sighed. "He shouldn't have to do all this," he said quietly. "I've tried to get him *not* to, but once he's gotten an idea in his head it's hard to get him not to do it. It doesn't help that our bond drains me to protect him when he's out in the Void, and I don't think he fully understands the *cost* of exploring out there."

"Shit." Misa winced a bit. "Do you need help talking to him?"

"I might." Sev smiled a small smile. "I did manage to convince him to come back, but mostly by telling him about the Expansion Festival that's coming up. He's excited to be able to experience his first. So you might have to deal with an overexcited god for a little bit tomorrow."

"Oh! The Festival *is* tomorrow." Vex bounced up in his seat. "I almost forgot. Clyde asked if I wanted to do a show."

"Are you going to?" Sev raised an eyebrow at his friend.

"I'm going to try." Vex looked suddenly worried. "We don't have anything scheduled tomorrow, right? Anything we need to interfere with?"

"Nope," Misa said, eyeing a system window and then shaking her head. "Nah, you're good. Looking forward to your show, Vex."

Vex grinned and then waved a hand to order another cup of coffee. Sev paused.

"Isn't that your third cup today?"

"Don't worry about it."

CHAPTER 15

GLYPH FESTIVAL

It was remarkable, the degree to which the town of Mundane changed.

For one day and one day only, the shadows didn't have to worry about keeping the town as plain and simple as possible; they could decorate and rearrange as much as they wished, and they seemed to take the opportunity to really let loose with their creativity. It almost made Sev a little sad to look at it. He wondered if this was the town they would build if they had the opportunity. Maybe if they fixed whatever was wrong with reality . . .

Except you don't know how to do that, a small voice whispered to him. *And this entire reality is just an echo, isn't it? They're going to be gone once the bonus room ends.*

Sev tried to ignore that voice. His past self had a plan. That much had to be true. Why else would his instincts be nudging him in all these distinct directions?

Instead, he tried to focus on what the citizens of Mundane had done to spruce up their town.

The observatory was, quite literally, inside-out. The expanse of stars floated in a projected dome around the building, a little less majestic than when it was within the building, but nevertheless a sight to behold. Constellations danced in the air, and Sev saw no small number of shadow elementals gathering near the observatory just to watch; he remembered what Belle had said before, about how it would be entirely crowded if they left it open to the public.

She hadn't been lying—the throng of people gathered outside the observatory, both from Mundane and otherwise, was immense. But it was far from the only place people gathered.

The only festival Sev had been to in recent memory, if it could be called a festival at all, was the celebration that Misa's parents had held in J'rokksur what felt like a year ago, though in practice it had only been a few months. That had been a small celebration, full of good food and good music and awkward dancing.

This was . . . different. There was an undertone of familiarity to it that Sev had come to associate with his own lost memories; he could only assume that he'd been to similar festivals back on Earth, though he could hardly remember what they were.

It wasn't just the observatory that was decorated like this. The clothing store had a fantastical display just outside, where enchanted mannequins wore extravagant dresses and tailored suits and danced with impossible fluidity. The bakery had its doors wide open, and the rich smell of freshly baked bread wafted out of it; just outside the door was an immense shelf that looked like it had been baked *from* bread, a baffling ode to the structural integrity of bread that Sev wasn't entirely sure was accurate.

. . . Now that he looked more closely, it looked a little like the baker had transformed her entire building into bread. Which made Sev mildly uncomfortable for reasons he didn't entirely understand. But it *was* cool.

Their chosen haunt—the Horizon cafe—had similarly thrown its doors wide open, allowing the rich smell of coffee to pervade the air just around it; unlike the bakery, there was no real display of their goods. Instead, the staff there had put out a number of tables and chairs for people to sit in and enjoy the atmosphere whenever they needed a break. It wasn't the busiest place in the festival, but there were always people there, stopping by to chat, to grab a snack, or to sit and watch the festival for a while.

It wasn't *just* Mundane that had shows and displays up, either. Combat was here too, and they had their own displays set up all over town—though the flavors of their shows were certainly very different. There were at least three wizards showing off feats of destructive magic, cast at a small scale so as to not destroy the entire town. One part of town flickered with forked lightning every few minutes, blasting apart the reflective panes in the sky; another had a heatless whirlwind of fire twirling through the crowd in a remarkable display of control and efficiency; still another was using earth magic to build complicated structures, in a rare example of combat magic turned to *art.*

That last one was the one that captured Vex's attention the most, and the whole party had to stop for a few minutes while the lizard stood and gawked. Basalt—the wizard's name, rather appropriately—had a series of small buildings set up next to one another. He would use his magic to fire a shot of earth at the largest one, and it would collapse in a way that built on the building just next to it, adding on to the detail and finesse rather than causing it to collapse as well.

Somehow the gargoyles, hanging off the sides in the first building, would land perfectly intact on the second, balanced all around the roof so that it looked like they were watching over it. By the third, they were crushed, but the stone cracked and broke in a distinct pattern, held in place by minute gaps and holes in the structure of the building . . .

And so on. That was just one detail out of a dozen, and Sev didn't manage to catch most of them; even Vex, rapidly taking notes in his notebook, didn't seem to capture them all. Basalt seemed to notice the little lizard, though, and grinned all the wider. The next couple of demolitions were just a little bit flashier, too, with sparks and flares of light incorporated into the whole thing.

Sev thought Basalt was probably cheating, but Vex didn't seem to think so, and he didn't want to ruin it for his friend, anyway.

They did have to leave the demonstration eventually; they had to be present for the Glyph unveiling, and Vex had his own little demonstration of magic that he'd prepared. He'd asked a couple of times why they wanted him to give a presentation, and the answer each time was simple—he was from outside their culture, partaking in it, and they wanted to learn about how his interpretation of magic changed how it behaved. It was what they did with every newcomer they taught magic, even if Vex hadn't been personally taught by them.

He'd very nervously agreed and then shut himself in his room to practice, not allowing any of them to see what he'd prepared.

Sev was kind of excited, really. He was excited for the Glyph unveiling too—Derivan hadn't really explained much about what the Glyph did, even though he'd had the time to experiment and understand it fully by now.

It'd be a nice distraction from his own troubles.

"Okay. Um," Vex said. He stood on his toes, wringing his hands and looking nervous; he took a trembling breath, and Sev saw the way he glanced at Derivan, at the look that passed between them. Just that look and Vex's trembling seemed to settle, and his breathing steadied. He gave them all a small smile. "I gotta go get ready for my presentation."

"You're gonna be fuckin' great," Misa said, giving him a thumbs-up. "Give 'em hell."

"I mean, that's not *exactly* what I'm going for," Vex said, laughing.

"Not *literally,* obviously." Misa rolled her eyes at Vex's bright grin but couldn't help smiling back. "You know what I meant."

"Break a leg!" Sev said, and then, when Vex looked at him, hurriedly added, "It's a saying. From us planeshifted."

Vex snickered, then sobered up a bit. "Thanks, guys," he said. "It feels . . . kinda weird to be doing all this? When the stakes are so high?"

"We're going to need a break sometime, and a time-dilated bonus room is basically the best time to do it," Sev said with a shrug. Misa nodded in agreement.

"Good luck," Derivan said to Vex. His tone of voice was softer, more personal than when he spoke to the other two. Sev had seen the way he'd changed now whenever he spoke to Vex, even if it was a minor, barely noticeable thing. It still made him smile. "I look forward to your show."

"I look forward to yours!" Vex grinned up at him and bounced up to peck him on the helmet, then disappeared behind the "stage" that had been set up. Sev blinked a few times.

His friends had changed a lot, hadn't they?

Vex wasn't nearly as nervous as he had been a few months earlier, when every little thing made him jump. It wasn't his relationship with Derivan that had changed him, either, though it certainly helped that they had each other. It was the *confidence* he had gained in his magic, in the way he spoke to and about his family.

Sev looked at him and saw a spark that wasn't fear about what would happen to his brother but determination to protect him. It made his heart glow—it made him feel like a great wrong had been righted.

Misa was *alive*. She'd been depressed for a few days after their defeat, but she'd bounced back with more attitude than ever. Sev was pretty sure she'd actually started putting on more muscle.

"Like what you see?" Misa grinned at him, flexing an arm, and Sev rolled his eyes.

"You're very pretty, but no thank you," he said politely.

Misa smirked at him. "Belle and her husbands are pretty into it."

". . . What?"

"I'll see you later! Looking forward to Vex's show!" Misa was, somehow, already leaving, heading straight toward one of the other Combat displays—she seemed eager to participate in a duel, against an arrogant-looking man that was looking for challengers. Sev stared after her, and Derivan just tilted his head at him in turn.

"Are you surprised?"

"I— *No*?" Sev managed. "Yes, but also, somehow no."

Derivan chuckled. "Vex's show will start in the evening, and mine will be at the Glyph revelation afterward," he said. "Would you like to explore on your own, or would you like to perhaps explore together? We do not speak alone often—I would like a moment with you, if you do not mind."

"Oh," Sev said, surprised. He didn't know why he hadn't expected that from Derivan—he'd somehow gotten used to fading into the background, for all that he was ostensibly their leader.

Derivan had changed a lot too, though his changes weren't nearly as obvious as Misa's or Vex's. He seemed to understand himself more, for lack of a better word—and he understood *them* more in turn. Always kind, always open; he knew exactly what to say most of the time to calm a person or to get through to them.

Sev wondered, though, if the armor had found what he wanted for himself yet.

Derivan was still waiting for a response. Sev blinked a few times, then nodded, managing an awkward smile. "I'd like that," he said.

They walked in silence for a while. The noise of the festival faded around them, and for a moment, Sev felt like he was left alone with his thoughts, though Derivan was walking next to him.

It was a quiet peace he hadn't known he needed. It was companionable silence between him and a close friend, undisturbed by the world.

Eventually, though, he broke the silence. "Was there something you wanted to talk about?" he asked. "It sounded like you had something in mind."

"Not in particular." Derivan chuckled, the sound resonant in his armor. He slowed down slightly as he spoke, taking a moment to absorb the sights—they had just so happened to stop near the observatory, where the stars still flickered in the sky.

He watched in silence for a moment, and Sev felt compelled to join him.

The stars spun. One burst into fragments of color, likely an exaggeration for the display; it still brought forth gasps of shock and awe and joy from the crowd around them, muted though the sound was.

"Are you the one doing that?" Sev felt compelled to ask.

Derivan inclined his head. "The sound dampening?"

"Yeah."

"It is an application of Shift," Derivan said.

"Pretty useful, that."

"Quite." Derivan hummed. "I acquired Shift from Histre, when they planeshifted back to the divine plane, after that battle with Jerome . . . Do you suppose he is doing well?"

"Jerome?" Sev tilted his head. "I hope so. Last I saw him, he was trying. Maybe it's worth checking in on him sometime, just to see how he's doing."

"I can accomplish that now," Derivan said.

"Can't do that again unless necessary," Sev said, shaking his head. "It's going to be necessary again soon. We have a huge advantage helping with everything that's happening out there as long as we're in here, but . . ."

"But the use of Shift to access the world outside destabilizes this echo of reality," Derivan completed the thought. "The more we learn, the more limited our options seem."

"Do you feel like there isn't hope?" Sev asked.

He felt that way sometimes, in the privacy of his own mind. He didn't know if any of the others felt the same way. The universe had ended, and neither the gods nor the system nor the embodiment of all magic could fix it.

What hope did they have? They were just four people. A few more, perhaps, with their allies and the Guild, but . . .

"No," Derivan answered, surprisingly easily. Sev looked at him, raising an eyebrow.

"Why not?" he asked, and Derivan paused for a moment to consider the question.

Another silence stretched, long. This time, the silence seemed oppressive; Sev felt his thoughts crowding in.

"I suppose I hope because I must," Derivan mused. "If I did not, I would not be compelled to act; it would be self-fulfilling. And so I must believe that the world can be brighter than it is, that every spark I contribute to the flame of civilization *helps*. Because the good outcome—the outcome in which the world is fair and kind—can never exist if no one believes in it."

"But the world isn't going to be fair and kind," Sev said. He felt once again almost *familiar* with this, like this was a conversation he'd had before. The sensation of floating underwater and a strange, sick feeling of claustrophobia clung to him. "By sheer stochastic probability."

"That is true." Derivan inclined his head, smiling slightly; Sev couldn't understand why he was smiling. "But if I think that way, the world will be kinder than it would be otherwise.

"And that, I think, is sufficient."

CHAPTER 16

AN ACT OF KINDNESS

Sev didn't answer for a while. He watched the stars spin above them, felt the anxiety rise and fall; eventually, it left him, and he let out a slow breath.

The emotion wasn't his own. Not exactly. He didn't know where it had come from, but Derivan's words had struck a chord within him, calling forth a memory. The dissonance he felt wasn't even from the memory itself—it was from the way it rubbed up against the rest of his thoughts, jarring and not quite his own.

He let it go. He'd been having more of these episodes lately, flashes of memory that didn't seem to come from Earth, echoes of conversations he'd never had. Maybe it had something to do with his link to the gods. Maybe it was nothing at all.

More important were Derivan's words.

"I think you're right," Sev eventually said. He let the silence stretch again after that statement, searching for the words. "Or . . . I think you put into words how I feel about it, anyway. I try to think that way. It doesn't always work out."

"Sometimes, it is difficult," Derivan agreed. "But I have never found it not worthwhile."

"You haven't been out here for very long."

"That is true," Derivan acknowledged. "Perhaps my mind will change. But I hope it does not. And if it does . . . I will have you and the others still, would I not? I am certain the three of you could rekindle my belief in what could be."

Sev chuckled. "Very poetic."

"I have been reading quite a lot."

"Anything good?"

"Most of them," Derivan said, considering the question. "It may be worth your time to take a look at some of the books. I have been informed that they do not necessarily reflect the history of this world, or the books that were written *here*; perhaps the nature of this place as a template, drawing on any available information . . ."

"Are you saying they might have books from Earth?" Sev sat up suddenly.

"No," Derivan said, dashing his hopes. Seeing his disappointment, Derivan quickly added, "Or perhaps they do. I do not know, and there are none here I can ask. But you would know better than I."

"No planeshifted here, huh," Sev murmured. The thought felt strange to him, and he let it linger in his mind for a while, considering it. Derivan had said something earlier about how he'd acquired Shift. Histre had shifted back to the divine plane in front of him, and something in that interaction had granted him the stat.

That was a planeshift, wasn't it?

The difference between the divine plane and Earth wasn't exactly clear to him. They were both results of something *similar*, no doubt; perhaps a planeshift from a place like Earth was just significantly more expensive. Farther away.

If that was the case . . .

"Do you suppose the planeshifted made the system?" Sev asked out loud, feeling a little foolish as he did so. "Planeshifting is a form of Shifting, right? And the system makes extensive use of it for . . . just about everything."

"I have thought about it," Derivan said, surprising him. "Perhaps a planeshifted landed here by accident and began studying the phenomenon of Shifting in an attempt to return to their home. It would explain many details."

"But there's no way for us to know for sure, huh?"

"Perhaps not immediately." Derivan shrugged, the movement looking a little ridiculous on his enormous frame. Sev still felt dwarfed by him. "But I would not discount the possibility that we will know eventually."

It felt like there was something there. It felt like it was something he should know, even; the information teased at the edge of his mind, endlessly frustrating, until he eventually decided to let it go.

It didn't matter who made the system, really. It only mattered what they did *now*.

Sev hummed, and his mind drifted again, back to Derivan's words on hope.

"I think," he said, "that I want to do something kind."

"Oh?" Derivan tilted his head. "You are plenty kind, I believe."

"I try, but I want to be *intentional* about it, at least for today. You talked about hope being a choice, and I think that's what I need." Sev hesitated. "I need . . . I just need a reminder. Of who I am."

It felt good to get the words out, to see the lack of judgment in Derivan's eyes. The armor simply nodded in acceptance. "Would you like some company for this?" he asked. "Or would you like to do it alone?"

"Alone," Sev answered before he could think about it; if he gave himself more than a second, he knew he'd ask for Derivan to accompany him, no matter what his heart told him. "But thank you."

At the best of times, it was hard for Sev to articulate exactly how he felt, with so much of his past just a blank *nothing* in his head. There was a certain level of detachment from the world, a certain level of disassociation that he often told himself he'd gotten used to.

The truth of it was that he thought about it all the time. Not when he was around his friends, but in his quiet moments—in the moments he sat alone and allowed his thoughts to run their course—he wondered. He wondered what his parents were like, what his *culture* was like, if he'd had any friends back on Earth who cared about or missed him.

He wondered what *he'd* been like.

He was blisteringly aware of the possibility that he hadn't been *this*. That he'd been someone else, once upon a time; that he'd had different hopes, different dreams, different ideals. Sometimes he wondered if he wasn't just an imposter occupying the same body, if everything about his original self had been wiped away.

Except it hadn't really. There were small pieces that remained—floating pieces of memory that weren't quite connected to anything else but still served as reminders that he'd come from Earth. There were things that felt more comfortable to him, more natural.

Being kind was one of them.

Derivan's words had triggered a vague memory, and he recognized the source of the dissonance, now that he was walking by himself. It felt like he'd been on the opposite end of that conversation, once upon a time—like he'd once been the one to say those words, to speak of hope as a *choice*.

What are you doing? Aurum's voice popped up near him, like a child speaking over his shoulder. Sev had gotten used enough to it now that he *didn't* immediately jump and spin around. Instead, he let a second pass, watching a leaf drift to the ground.

Looking for an opportunity to be kind, he answered after a moment passed.

What does that mean? Aren't you kind already?

Sev chuckled. **Kindness is like . . . a reaction to circumstance,** he explained. **You will have opportunities to be kind no matter what. But**

you can seek those opportunities out, or you can wait for them to come to you.

But why're you looking for them? Aurum practically bounced in his ear, a kid impatient to hear the answer. Sev chuckled again.

It makes me feel a little more like myself, Sev said. **I think this is the sort of thing I used to do** . . .

Sev lapsed into silence. Aurum seemed satisfied enough with the answer and didn't say anything further, but Sev's thoughts were distracted by the shadow he caught on to just at the edge of the festival, far away from any of the noise and attractions.

He hadn't even realized he'd walked this far. His feet had just carried him forward, away from all the noise and celebration, and now he stood nearly at the edge of Mundane. Grasslands stretched in front of him, obscured by the illusory panes that stood scattered in the air. A single tree stood, the trunk as wide as three orcs put together, the branches so high they disappeared behind that same false-air phenomenon.

And standing almost completely hidden by the shade, except from Sev's angle of approach, was a single shadow elemental. He'd only caught sight of them because of the flicker of darkness at the very edge of the trunk.

Sev found himself speeding up. [**Triage**] was pinging.

Just behind the tree, someone was dying.

He wasn't *hurt,* as far as Sev could tell. He was perfectly intact. He sat at the roots of the tree, staring up at the sky, at the stray sparks of magic that flew into sight, and he seemed . . . at peace.

"Are you all right?" Sev asked, even though he knew the elemental wasn't.

It took a moment for him to get a response. The elemental barely seemed to realize that Sev was there, at first; when he did, he blinked a slow blink, the dim light of his eyes fading behind shadow. For a moment, Sev worried he was too late and that that was the man's last breath.

But his eyes opened again and focused on Sev. The elemental managed a small smile. "Didn't think anyone would find me out here."

"I almost didn't," Sev admitted. He reached forward, then hesitated. "Can I heal you?"

A small, knowing smile. "You can try."

A part of Sev knew before he even tried that healing him would do nothing. [**Triage**] told him as much. He wasn't out of options, but healing whatever this was . . . The passive sense afforded to him by his skills told him this injury would cost *everything* he had left just to cure.

You need to care about yourself, too. Misa's voice echoed in his head, a small reminder.

He wouldn't die. Losing all his memories was even something he'd done before. But . . . it would be a *type* of death, he knew, and he'd lost enough that he wasn't certain it was something he could come back from.

"Healing's a bit out of the question these days." The shadow elemental didn't seem to be aware of the thoughts running through Sev's head. "Don't kill yourself trying to help me."

"I wasn't going to," Sev said, though he didn't sound convincing, even to himself. The shadow elemental cracked an eye open at him and stared, and Sev somehow felt vaguely embarrassed.

"Name's Aneryn," the elemental said after a moment. "What's yours?"

"Sev," Sev said. "Aneryn's a strange name; no offense. You guys usually have names that are very . . . Earthlike."

"Don't know what that means." Aneryn raised an eyebrow at him. "I assume it's got to do with this language we're speaking. But I reckon your name isn't much Earthlike, either."

. . . He had a point there.

"What happened to you?" Sev asked. "If you don't mind me asking."

"Magical accident." Aneryn shrugged. "'S'complicated. I'm from Combat. It's very, *very* hard to off one of us, but it ain't impossible."

"I'm sorry." An awkward beat as Sev searched for something to say. "Why are you . . . why are you *here?*"

"Wanted to be by the Festival." Aneryn shifted uncomfortably, and Sev automatically reached out to help him adjust. "Thanks. Hard to move right now. Think I've got an hour left, maybe two."

"Is there anything I can do?"

"Not unless you've got a god in your back pocket." Aneryn grinned at him, and Sev shifted uncomfortably, mostly because he technically *did* . . . though he doubted Aurum would be able to do anything about this. Or maybe he would?

Either way, the link was silent.

"Honestly didn't think I'd have any company." Aneryn didn't look at him as he said this; a bit of his swagger faded away. "Chose this spot so no one would have to see. Don't want to ruin the big day for anyone. But . . . it'd be nice not to die alone."

"Is that why you aren't facing the festival?" Sev asked softly. "I can hide us. If you want to watch."

Aneryn seemed surprised, then grateful. ". . . I'd like that. If you could help me move. Can't really move myself, y'see."

"Of course." Sev leaned down to help the surprisingly heavy man maneuver into place, carefully activating the bracelet he still wore as he did so. To use it to hide them was . . . absolutely an abuse of its properties and would no doubt break it sooner.

But Aneryn seemed grateful, and a small peace seemed to spread through him as he watched the dances, the duels, and the lights.

"Tell me about yourself?" Sev asked. "So I can remember you."

"What makes ya think I don't have anyone to remember me already?" Aneryn grinned at him, but the grin quickly faded into something contemplative.

". . . It'd mean a lot, kid. But it's a long story."

Sev hummed and sat down next to the shadow elemental. "I've got time."

CHAPTER 17

REMEMBRANCE

The sky above Mundane was a sight to remember.

It wasn't just the fireworks, the streaks of magic that flew up into the air and shaped themselves into beautiful works of art. It wasn't the stray sparks from the many duels happening all over the town, with elements crashing across the sky. It wasn't even the gentle play of light across the clouds, though that sight was beautiful in and of itself.

It was the fact that those panes of reflective air were *falling*.

Sev was startled, at first, almost worried—but Aneryn had merely laughed. "It's just skyfall," he said. "You haven't been around that long, have you?"

"Not as such," Sev said.

The view was dizzying, with the view in each pane shifting and spinning as it fell. Every time one hit the ground, it shattered like it was made of glass, though it did no damage to anything it struck. Sev eventually had to look away, feeling slightly sick, but Aneryn himself seemed enchanted by the sight.

Sev could imagine why. Follow closely enough and the phenomenon allowed you to see everything that was happening in the town of Mundane—some of the panes even showed close-up flashes of those duels and battles happening in the town. Others showed the various sights and displays that had been constructed, from a small table display where dozens of toys had been enchanted to sing and dance to a massive magical painting that seemed to double as a hedge maze. People would step into the painting, and the enchanter would paint the maze in as they attempted to navigate it, rapid strokes creating a dead end or a beautiful grove each time they turned a corner.

It was fascinating, and Sev resolved to find that second display later to try it for himself, but he couldn't keep watching. The sight was making him very distinctly motion-sick, and he hadn't had a feeling like that for years.

"Having trouble?" Aneryn's voice was a low rumble of distinct amusement, and Sev grumbled. "Newbies tend to have trouble. Haven't had newbies for a while, though. Aren't you a healer?"

. . . He *was*. He just hadn't felt like this for a while, and it hadn't occurred to him that he could just heal it away.

Magic was convenient. He wondered how he would've dealt with this, once upon a time.

A gentle glow of divine magic later, and he went back to watching what Aneryn had called the skyfall.

"Sky will be clear once this is all said and done," Aneryn said. "Wish I could be around to see it. They usually last for a day or two, though."

"I'm sorry," Sev said, because there didn't seem to be anything better to say. He hadn't *trained* in this.

Aneryn snorted. "Ain't your fault," he said. "Lets me see more of the festival. Pretty well timed, if anything."

"I suppose," Sev said. "You've been to one of these before?"

"A long time ago." Aneryn cleared his throat, and Sev glanced over at him—he noticed the way the elemental's hands appeared to be fading, sinking into the shadow of the tree they were sitting under, and he felt his heart sink a little with it. "Suppose that might be a good place to start, even, if you want to know what I was all about."

"What *were* you all about?"

"*Magic*," Aneryn said, but he injected the word with a certain amount of flair and pomp; he even tried to gesticulate, though his arms just sort of failed him. He glared at his limbs like they were offending him but didn't try again. "Destruction magic in particular. Not for the sake of killin' or the like, but understanding it was my passion. Still is, really."

"I'd bring my friend here if I could," Sev said wryly. "He's better at talking about this kind of stuff than I am. I don't think I really get magic, even after all this time."

"Nothing much to get, really," Aneryn shrugged. "Magic's a whole load of concepts wrapped together, and glyphs tap into that conceptual sphere. Skilled mages know how to navigate it, and lesser ones just pluck out surface concepts."

"Huh." Sev paused. "That's a lot simpler than I imagined."

"It's a *little* more complicated than that, but that's the gist of it." Aneryn shifted, then grunted uncomfortably. "Mind helping me sit up a bit?"

Sev reached over to help prop him up, not commenting on the fact that Aneryn looked a little frailer than he had a moment before; his body blended in more with the shadows they sat in. He wondered if it was a good idea to create a source of light, so the harsher shadows would help him stay together . . .

. . . Probably not. If it were that simple to fix, Aneryn would have done it long ago.

"Loved duels," Aneryn said. The words came out like they were a sigh. "Haven't had a good duel in a damn long time. Pretty much everyone refused after what happened to me."

Sev almost asked him what happened, but stopped himself. "What makes you like them?"

"'S'like a dance." Aneryn's eyes brightened a little, even in the state he was in. "A story you tell but in the form of a *fight.* A swordfight is fun but limited; there are only so many physical possibilities. But with *magic . . .*"

The shadow elemental lifted up a palm, though not without difficulty; a faint image of a glyph floated above it, spinning gently. "This is the glyph for Entropy," Aneryn said. "I know of at least *five hundred* combinations with other glyphs. For every one of them, the way you cast matters. Intent, interpretation, *state of mind.* In a duel, you learn not just new magics but how your opponent thinks—how they feel—the way they look at the world."

"It's how you communicate," Sev said.

"*Yes,*" Aneryn said emphatically. He let his hand flop back against the ground and the image of the glyph fade from existence, then looked up toward the sky, sighing. "Talking doesn't come as easily to me as fighting."

"I don't think talking comes easily to anyone," Sev said with a chuckle. "Some people are better at it than others, but . . . it's *communication,* right? You can be good at entertaining a crowd, you can be good at making people laugh or smile, but that doesn't mean you're good at communicating."

"Too many nuances." Aneryn grunted in agreement. "Can't know what someone's experiences are. Can't know who they know, how they use words, if the slang they use means somethin' else."

"But you bypass that when you see people cast."

"Glad you get it." Aneryn sighed again. "Came back to bite me, though. One of the spells I developed did me in like this. Didn't consider the backlash."

"Are your spells usually so . . ." Sev gestured, searching for the word. "Lethal?"

"It's *reversible,* usually," Aneryn said. "But Entropy's a beast of a glyph. Ain't so easy to reverse. Was trying to fix the problem."

"Ah." Sev didn't know what to say, but Aneryn seemed happy to continue; he just wanted someone to talk to.

"Honestly would've preferred going out in a duel," Aneryn said. "But . . . didn't want to put anyone through that. Friends're good people. They don't need this on their conscience."

"I'd offer," Sev said, "but I don't think I can fight on the level you're looking for."

"You'd die." Aneryn snorted. He didn't even question the possibility—Sev was almost offended.

"You don't know that. I'm a damn good healer."

"You'd *lose*, anyway," Aneryn said, this time with a slight grin and a bite of fire in his voice. Sev grinned back, drawn in by the charisma.

"I can see how you got people to duel with you," he said. Aneryn smirked.

"Too weak to duel properly now, anyway," he said. "Nice enough to have someone around. Didn't . . . wanna die alone. But didn't wanna make my friends watch. Which is a problem, 'cause I think I'm starting to consider you a friend."

Sev chuckled, letting the *friend* comment pass him by. He liked Aneryn, and what was coming weighed on him; he was doing his best to take his mind off it and simply provide companionship. "You don't think they might have wanted to?"

"Doesn't matter," Aneryn said. "'S'too late now. Made my choice."

"I could get them."

"Don't want them to see me like this," Aneryn said. "Bit selfish, I know. Want them to remember me as a lean, mean fightin' machine. And . . . might be gone by the time you get back."

Sev hummed. "Well," he said. "I'll try to remember you as a fighting machine."

"Could get a painter to paint a portrait of me." Aneryn grinned. "Make it all badass. Have me stopping time or some shit. That's what the spell was *supposed* to do."

"I might just do that," Sev said, smiling a faint smile. "I've got a mage friend that's pretty good with that kind of thing. Even if he keeps making himself look a lot more badass than he is. Don't tell him I said that, though."

Aneryn laughed. "He one of those that try to look tough and mostly come off cute?"

"I will neither confirm nor deny that," Sev joked, and Aneryn snickered again.

"Got one of those as well," he said. "She's . . . like a daughter to me. I regret her not being here the most, I guess. I'm gonna miss her."

"Do you want me to pass on a message?" Sev asked. "I can try to find her . . ."

"Nah." Aneryn shook his head. "Ain't gonna be that easy to find her, and

I left her a message of my own. Though if you do get that painting commissioned, you should send her a copy. The look on her face . . ."

The small amount of mirth in Aneryn's voice suddenly fell away, leaving behind an awkward silence. Sev didn't say anything, but he felt the air turn heavy and glanced toward Aneryn.

The shadow elemental's eyes were clouded with their version of tears. Sev cast his gaze away as a quiet sob suddenly wracked the elemental's frame, the burst of emotion sudden but powerful. He didn't need Aneryn to *speak* to know the thought that was going through his mind—that he'd never get to see the look on her face when she saw that painting. That he'd never see the smiles of his friends again, hear their laughs again; that he wouldn't be around to see how they grew and changed.

It was almost strange, how sure he was about Aneryn's exact frame of mind. A flicker of familiarity ran through him, like Aneryn was someone he knew. Should have known?

What—

Sev was pulled from his thoughts, rather abruptly, by a vehement curse.

"*Shit.*"

Aneryn nearly snarled out the word, and a patch of grass by the elemental's wrist caught aflame. It was a vehement, sudden turn in emotion, and Sev winced just slightly, though he didn't say anything. "Forget you saw that."

"It's forgotten," Sev said quietly.

A partial lie. He couldn't get the sudden familiarity out of his mind, but that familiarity *did* help him forget; he saw, in his mind's eye, a perfect image of someone that looked very much like Aneryn, fighting off a creature that looked not unlike the Mana Abomination they'd fought at the very beginning of this journey, when the dungeon had formed *wrong*.

Before he could say anything about it, Aneryn started talking.

He didn't speak with any purpose in particular. Sev sensed that there was a part of the elemental that regretted not having his friends around, or that simply *wanted* his friends around, despite his desire for them to remember him as he was. He just talked about who he was and what he'd done.

In the span of an hour, Sev learned that Aneryn loved spider-meat spiced with fireseed, a combination that made every one of his other friends turn green whenever he ate it; he had a fascination for pottery, though he was terrible at it himself and had broken nearly every pot he'd ever made, except for a particularly deformed one he kept on a pedestal in his home; he loved his friends and took them out often to "adventure," exploring newly opened regions as the mana restored them.

He learned that Aneryn hated fish—was terrified of them, really. They were wet, slimy, and disgusting creatures that wiggled around far too much, and they were no better in food. He learned that when he wasn't fighting, Aneryn was clumsy and needed his friends to stop him from tripping over his own two feet.

He learned all the ins and outs of Aneryn as a person.

Sev contributed his own stories, of course, whenever the elemental wanted to hear them—and he did want to hear them from time to time. He talked about how he was scared of heights, at which point Aneryn had laughed and told him about the mana region that was just clouds and nothing else, an infinite expanse of sky. Sev made a face at the thought, and Aneryn laughed at him, then asked what else he liked; he shared his love for tea, which he hadn't even thought about for months—tea was relatively rare, and while he kept a few magically preserved satchels of his favorites, he didn't let himself enjoy them all that often.

Aneryn had laughed at him for liking leaf water. Sev had responded by brewing a cup right then and there, asking only for his help with fire magic and small conjurations to hold the liquid, which the elemental had gladly provided.

And then they'd had tea, and Aneryn had grudgingly admitted that it was *good*.

Even if he'd needed a small mountain of sugar poured into his tea.

Yet that entire time, the context of what was soon to happen hung over them—and eventually, Aneryn drifted into silence, out of conversation and out of energy.

". . . Thank you," he said, his voice soft. Tired. Sev knew without looking that the elemental's time was *soon*, and a part of him cried out for him to save him—to use his magic and heal him, to *fix this*.

Sev could have said so many things. He could have asked Aneryn if he wanted that heal, even at the cost to himself. He could have asked Aneryn if it was okay if he didn't heal him, because he—this version of him, his mind, his ideas, his values—would die in the process.

But he knew what Aneryn would say. He would refuse, and his last moments would be used to reassure someone else.

Sev swallowed back those words and said the words that hurt to say. "It was nice meeting you."

Aneryn smiled. He was nearly entirely faded now, but the smile was genuine.

"If I'd met you sooner," he said, "I think we could've been great friends."

CHAPTER 18

A GRIEF UNKNOWN

Kindness, Sev reflected, could be painful.

Aneryn hadn't wanted to die alone. It was a small thing for Sev to be there for him in those last moments, and yet those last moments had been more than enough to make him care that much more. Aneryn would have been a friend, he was sure.

Maybe he *had* been.

Sev didn't know what to make of those strange flashes of memory he had received, and he was too tired to think hard on it; his heart still ached. Very slowly, he gathered his things—along with the small conjured cup that Aneryn had made for the tea and the little ceramic pot.

They were both absolutely terrible and looked like they were on the verge of breaking. Sev handled them like they were the most precious things in the world. They sat near the bottom of his satchel, protected by as many soft things as he could find. He even grabbed some grass to stuff into his bag, just to absorb the impact as much as possible.

He'd ask Vex to enchant them when he got the chance.

Sev got to his feet—too much time had passed, he realized, and Vex's presentation would be soon—and groaned at the way his body ached; he'd been sitting in the same position for too long. A quick burst of divine magic smoothed away the aches into just a memory of that pain, and he started back into town.

The festival seemed strangely quieter. Or maybe it was just his state of mind—he found himself tuning out the sound, his mind drifting back to Aneryn, to that strange familiarity. He couldn't focus on that, either, because a pulse of grief would quickly follow.

He was . . . not in a good state, he realized somewhat distantly. But he still wanted to be there for Vex's presentation.

Clyde had been the one to help set it up, and he'd apparently spared no expense for it, not that Mundane bothered with currency. He'd certainly called in favors, though. Vex's presentation would happen on the same stage as the one the glyph would eventually be revealed at, along with what Derivan had learned of its properties.

The stage was a grand thing, standing several feet tall and on intricately carved supports made of an ivory-white metal and pure elemental flame; the carvings glowed from within, casting a dim light across the ground. The skyfall phenomenon was beginning to ease and fade away—a precious few minutes too late, Sev thought, with a small hint of bitter regret—but it left the skies clear, with only a few of those strange panes left hanging in the air.

An uncharacteristically beautiful night. Perfect for the show.

"Are you all right?" Derivan's voice spoke behind him. Sev started a little and then, seeing who it was, calmed himself down.

"I'll be fine," he said.

"Hm." Derivan left it at that, apparently sensing that he didn't want to talk about it yet, though he clearly knew *something* was up. "The skies are clear today."

"Didn't even know it was possible." Sev glanced up at the faint glimmer of stars, almost visible now that the sun was beginning to set. It was strange how different and yet familiar this place was. "Vex is going to be out soon. What do you think he has for us?"

"I do not know." Derivan shrugged broad shoulders, then sat on the grass. Even with *that,* he towered over some of the people that were still standing. "But I look forward to finding out."

"Yeah," Sev agreed.

He couldn't completely shake off the somber mood that hung over him, but he wanted to be here for his friend, at least. Now they just needed Misa to join them.

Misa appeared just as a row of lights flickered into existence over the stage. The half-orc was panting with exertion, and Sev looked over at her with amusement. "Lost track of time?"

"Shut up," she grumbled. "Fuckers were *good.* Nearly got me a couple times."

Sure enough, there was a fresh scar or two along her shoulder and arm—nothing that couldn't be healed away, though Sev knew Misa had probably just chosen to keep them. "Had fun?" he asked.

"Fuck yeah." Misa grinned, showing her teeth. "I gotta go to Combat more often. They're really . . ."

She trailed off as she spoke, taking in Sev's expression. "You all right?" she asked, frowning. "You don't look it."

"I'll be *fine,*" Sev insisted with a sigh. "I'll talk about it later, but it's not important for now. Besides, the show's starting."

Misa peered at him with no small amount of suspicion—but a swell of music from behind the stage distracted her, and she turned her gaze to the stage. "Dang," she muttered. "They really went all out for this."

"They really did," Sev agreed. "You think Vex will be okay? He usually doesn't like this kinda thing."

"I believe Clyde offered him a great many notes on glyphs as compensation," Derivan commented dryly. "Though it seems a poor deal, considering Clyde shares whatever he knows on request."

"Couldn't keep a secret to save his life." Misa chuckled.

"He also offered a number of reality shards, which is the true reason Vex accepted the deal, I believe," Derivan said. "Though perhaps he simply saw that Clyde truly did want to see a Festival as grand as all the Festivals of old, and felt that a minor discomfort was worth bringing that memory to life . . ."

Derivan's voice trailed off as Vex walked onto the stage, and all eyes focused on him.

The lizardkin was, for once, fully outfitted as a wizard. He didn't wear the traditional robes of an Elyran wizard, though. Those were all long, flowy sleeves and yards of fabric, mostly so it could be enchanted with as many runes as possible.

What Vex wore was closer to the combat gear that Sev had seen some of the mages from Combat wear—closely fitted cloth wrapped around his shoulders and down to his waist, leaving his arms bare, and baggy trousers secured just above his ankles, higher than normal due to his digitigrade feet.

He'd painted his arms, Sev realized. No wonder he'd taken so long to prepare—he couldn't imagine the amount of time that must have gone into the intricate glyphs that were painted over his scales, especially if he'd had to paint them on by himself. Even his tail had a scattering of glyphs, every one of them carefully painted with *directionality,* pointing from the base to the tip of his tail.

The paints looked to be composed of the liquid mana Vex was able to call forth with [**Splash of Mana**], along with a crystalline additive Sev thought might have been crushed reality shards.

Hopefully they weren't those. Sev winced at the idea of crushing reality shards down. Vex . . . probably knew what he was doing, though. He'd only blown things up a couple of times.

And Clyde or Belle would probably stop him if he was going to blow something up.

Probably.

The music swelled to a crescendo, and Vex shut his eyes, letting out a long, steadying breath, as though to center himself. The lights that lit up the stage suddenly *inverted,* covering the stage and the audience with darkness; small gasps filled the arena.

In that artificial darkness, the glyphs painted on Vex's arms began to glow.

They lit up Vex's scales, casting him in a contrast of light and shadow. Everyone watching fell silent, their breaths falling still. A single point of light lit up the darkness—the tip of Vex's blade, Sev realized, the dagger he often used to carve his spells with—and then, slowly but surely, he began carving an image into the air.

Not a glyph. A fully formed image. A stylized display of his own life story.

Sev saw the image of Vex's own parents, artfully displayed as a menacing presence around him and his siblings. He saw those smaller figures slowly becoming powers in their own right, gaining larger presences, and yet turning away from them in the process, until he was the last one left, a protective presence curling around a smaller, younger figure.

He saw Vex leave, the small figure that represented him drooping with no small amount of regret. He saw Vex fighting alone for a time, until he was joined by three others, and then it was all the tiny details in every scene Vex drew—the way his shoulders slowly drew back, the way he held his head a little higher.

That in itself would have been an incredible display, but Vex was doing more than that. Every glyph painted on his body had a function—and with every image he drew, a glyph would activate, casting the glow of a spell over the entirety of his audience.

Ice on his left shoulder, spreading a deepening chill as Vex and his siblings cowered away from their parents. Gravity on his right, a physical weight pressing down on them as those siblings, too, grew and left. The glow of that glyph was a dirty yellow, a bitter sort of pallor cast over the watchful eyes of his audience.

Lightning was a flicker that ran down his tail, a mesmerizing display of electricity every time he moved. Vex used that one to symbolize the determination it had taken to leave his brother there while he searched for another way, the way he'd fought on his own, striking out in a desperate attempt to find *something*.

And then . . . warmth. Not fire but the simple, cozy warmth that came with sitting by a hearth in the winter. The glow of those glyphs lit up his arms and carried with them a sense of comfort, of quiet joy. A wave rippled through them, and Sev was surprised to find aches and pains he hadn't realized he'd had suddenly smoothing away.

Vex was healing something that was outside the domain of even his own magic.

If the lizardkin realized what he'd done, he didn't show it. His eyes were still closed, like he was lost in his own little world, even as the not-lights slowly faded back into *light*, bringing the stage back.

Sev had almost forgotten the thing was there. He'd been focused entirely on Vex's performance, on the *dance*, on the intricate play of emotion and storytelling.

The applause was thunderous. Vex barely seemed to notice—he seemed exhausted, the whole exercise having apparently taken more out of him than just physical strength. Sev almost hurried up on stage to help heal him, but . . . no.

He didn't seem to want the help. Vex opened his eyes, offering a small smile and a bow to the crowd, yet searching the sea of people to find his friends. Sev saw the way his eyes lit up with both relief and slight embarrassment when he caught sight of them.

And then, slightly spoiling the magic of the moment but in perfect keeping with Vex's character, he gave his friends a little wave. Sev just laughed and waved back—

And that would have been that, but he probably shouldn't have been surprised when mana began to gather.

Just like it had when Derivan had formed a new glyph a few short weeks ago.

CHAPTER 19

REVEAL

"*Two* new glyphs!" Clyde's voice was incredulous. He hissed out the words as if speaking softly would somehow protect them from the enormous crowd of people just outside his inn. It was essentially just very powerful inn magic that kept all of them out, though he'd refused to explain what exactly "inn magic" was.

The crowd had gone silent the moment mana began to gather; at most, there were quiet whispers slowly spreading through them, as if they weren't quite sure what they were looking at. It wasn't until the air rippled faintly and a series of images formed in the air—each one depicting a different moment from Vex's show—that those whispers erupted into excited murmurs, and then a roar of thunderous applause as fragments of a new glyph began to form from those images.

Vex had looked utterly overwhelmed. It was Clyde who reacted first, surprisingly—he darted in and physically shielded the lizardkin from the crowd, practically dragging him back to his inn. Belle and Elliot both acted as impromptu bodyguards while Misa and Sev both struggled to make their way through the crowd to rejoin their friend.

Derivan, on the other hand, had somehow managed to slip away in the chaos and find Vex before either of the two of them. Fortunately, all four still managed to meet up just before sneaking into the inn together, a full ten minutes before the crowd managed to find them once again.

"Do you have *any idea* how incredible this is." It wasn't even a question. Clyde buried his face in his hands and groaned, gesturing at the door; a flicker of magic shut off the cacophony of noise from the crowd outside, presumably yet another application of his inn magic. "It's not supposed to be this easy to make glyphs. Especially *now,* when magic is dedicating itself to keeping this universe alive. It doesn't *recognize* people like that. Not anymore."

"And yet," Belle said. She seemed significantly calmer than her husband—only the brightly glowing eyes indicated that she was experiencing any amount of stress.

"Can't say I didn't expect something like this to happen, honestly." Elliot spoke mildly. He was the most relaxed of the three, except for the way his eyes kept occasionally darting to the door, like he was worried that someone would break through. "I tried to tell 'em."

"Shut up," Clyde grumbled. "Are you sure you're not hiding anything else? Seriously, what you're doing is— I don't think you understand how *big* it is."

"We're not?" Sev looked around, as if questioning his own answer. No one contradicted him. "I mean, as far as we know, we're not."

"Right." Clyde buried his face in his hands. "The worst part is I believe you.

"You need to understand—you might be in an echo, but you still have to play by our rules," he said. "The rules of the echo universe you're in. Magic isn't exactly *dead* here, but everything it can do is focused on keeping this universe alive. It's essentially life support. The fact that you've created something new not once but twice . . ."

Clyde sighed.

"What do we do now?" Vex asked, finally speaking up. He seemed a little nervous, but not nearly as much as he would have a month or two ago—he glanced at the door in a way that was almost contemplative rather than afraid. "We still need to do the glyph presentation, right?"

"It's a little delayed because of all this, but yes." Clyde frowned. "I spoke to the mayor for a bit. He's more excited than anything, and he's hoping you'll do a joint presentation on the effects of the new glyphs."

"We don't even know what the newest glyph does yet," Misa pointed out.

"Well, you've got about an hour to find out," Clyde said dryly. "That's about as long as we can delay. Think you can do it?"

Vex glanced at Derivan, who nodded at him. "We can try," he said.

It took, all in all, an hour and a half. The extra half hour was wrung from the mayor by a very apologetic Clyde, much to the ever-increasing restlessness of the crowd, which had by and large retreated back to the Festival grounds. They'd accepted they weren't all going to get a one-on-one with the two new glyphmakers, and so decided to celebrate instead that yet another glyph had been created.

Now Vex and Derivan stood side by side on stage. This presentation would be nothing like Vex's earlier one—it wasn't a performance. It was a celebration of an achievement, of a growth in magic.

It was a celebration of change.

. . . Okay, and maybe a little bit of a performance.

Derivan started first. He drew the new glyph in the air, taking full advantage of his height to weave a sigil that was taller than even he was; it stood nearly twice Vex's height, towering over the lizardkin and making him look small in comparison—not that standing next to Derivan didn't do the same. Mana began to gather even before the symbol was complete, as if it was eager and excited. It danced around the edges of the glyph, and it took coaxing to prevent it from just pouring in and activating the spell.

All that mana dove into the glyph the moment the last stroke was drawn, and the entire thing *pulsed.*

The glyph was a little more complex than it needed to be—Derivan had added a number of embellishments to bring it closer to the original piece he'd drawn. It didn't need to be *exact* in order to trigger a reaction from the mana, and as the creator of the glyph, the closer he got to the original, the more powerful the effect was.

The final glyph was the bold image of a cuirass, glowing softly in the night; it was the image of several of the other species that Derivan had seen and met in his journey, abstracted into silhouettes, and arranged in such a way that they were not unlike wings. They were the draconic sort, even, with two points at the very tips that were not unlike the points on Derivan's armor; the wings were drawn like they were mid-flight, supporting the cuirass and being supported in turn.

The spell held for a moment, the ethereal image washing over them; even without its being cast, the crowd could feel the power embedded in it, and a soft murmur rippled through them.

Derivan didn't cast it, not yet; he allowed the mana to gather, and then knelt, holding a hand out to Vex.

Vex used the outstretched hand and Derivan's knee as support to climb up onto the armor's shoulders. He wobbled a little as Derivan stood, but stayed steady, using his tail to balance himself—and then their plan became clear. At this height, Vex had access to the very top of the glyph, though he had to stretch to reach it; there, he used his dagger to cut his own glyph into the air.

The image he drew looked vaguely like a clock dressed in a traveler's cloak, the impression of travel and of time running past—of a journey taken. This wasn't a change to his Sign, unlike what had happened with Derivan. It was just a new glyph, a new meaning imprinted onto the mana.

The new glyph was drawn smaller, but it certainly wasn't any less powerful for it. Once again, mana gathered; this time, there was almost a battle between the two glyphs, as magical energy traveled between them. They grappled for a moment for dominance before equalizing suddenly, both symbols pulsing with radiant strength.

Vex cast his mind one more time over the notes his Sign had given him about their two glyphs.

Glyph of Change

Life has a funny way of making you look back. Vex Ashion's realization of how much has changed since the beginning, his understanding of the journey he has taken, embeds itself into the ritual that spawned this glyph.

Mark a desired change, and then accelerate time to achieve this change. The mana cost required grows depending on the degree of change.

And then there was Derivan's.

Glyph of Solidity

As Derivan's understanding of the world grew, so did his desire to protect it, and to experience everything it had to offer. Though the core of that desire exists because of his friends, it has grown into something greater—and has room to grow still.

Solidify in a range that increases as more mana is placed into the glyph.

There was a reason it had taken so much longer to understand what Derivan's glyph did compared to Vex's—the effect was much subtler, and the amount of mana required was enormous, though it seemed to go down with practice; the first time, they had needed to spend a reality shard on the casting to understand what the glyph did at all.

Solidity. It was almost the opposite of Vex's glyph, though that would be too much of a simplification. The glyph anchored things, making it harder for reality to change, for things to be lost; something under the effect was nearly impossible to Shift, Derivan claimed.

Applied strongly enough, with the assistance of a reality shard, the glyph could even stop system skills in their tracks—an effect entirely new to them, and one that spawned no small amount of errors. They'd hurriedly stopped that experiment when it began to drain Misa's reality anchor, but the fact of the matter was that they now had a tool that no one else had.

What they wanted to do in this demonstration was different, though.

The spell they cast came in two stages.

First was Vex's glyph. Magic rippled out across the stage and over their audience, marking the ground with change. At first, nothing happened—but as time went by, the magic accelerated, and the first shoots of green appeared from the ground, breaking through the stone.

The flowers that sprang up from the ground had complicated, interwoven petals, shimmering with two-toned colors and each with a drop of precious mana held within the center. Appreciative murmurs turned to quiet gasps; this was far beyond a growth spell, if the plants it could create were magical.

But they weren't done.

Next came Derivan's magic.

What it did wasn't nearly so visible—nothing in the field seemed to change. But many of the shadow elementals that were native to Mundane suddenly froze, staring in disbelief at the field of flowers.

Mundane was a template; it was static, boring, and unremarkable on the outside, as a means for magic to apply change. Vex's spell was an application of change, but the Glyph of Solidity did something more fundamental.

It altered the template and changed the meaning of what *baseline* was.

Derivan had asked for permission first, of course. The mayor had snorted, not particularly believing that he *could,* but telling him to go ahead—bringing some color and life into the town would do wonders for the people there. It was just something they'd never been able to do.

And yet here was the evidence in full—the Glyph of Solidity would let them change Mundane to be as expressive as they wanted without harming magic's ability to sustain reality.

There was a small, collective loosening of tension—the realization that they had just a little bit more freedom in their lives now. The glyph could be used by any one of them, after all; Derivan was the most effective caster, but anyone had access to the spell.

Derivan and Vex saw it as a small kindness. They saw it as a way of returning to the town of Mundane some of the help that had been given to them.

It was only when the applause started ringing—when a man near the front of the crowd wept openly, and others ran off to start painting the glyph on all their Festival decorations—that they understood that they'd done something much greater, at least to the people here.

"Damn." Clyde's words were soft, somewhere behind them; Vex hopped off of Derivan's shoulders, and they both glanced back. "You guys actually did it."

"It's not bad, is it?" Vex asked, looking just a little worried. Clyde laughed.

"I know I said it doesn't really bother us," he said. "But that doesn't mean this doesn't mean a hell of a lot to us. So . . . thank you."

CHAPTER 20

MOVING ON

The ending to that Festival was probably the quickest there had ever been. Not because there was no wonder or celebration to be had—but because the celebration that was left was for *themselves*, for all the things they had wanted to make permanent but could not. The glyphs of Change and Solidity, despite the associated mana costs, were some of the most flexible glyphs that had ever been created, and the elementals wasted no time in customizing their homes and stores to breathe all the life into them that they couldn't have before.

Clyde was particularly enthusiastic.

"No more living in a black box!" he declared. The sheer amount of mana that rushed out of him made even Sev flinch, and the cleric didn't have the [**Mana Sight**] that Derivan and Vex did. Both of *them* had to shield their eyes against the light that poured out of the elemental.

When it was done, Clyde's old inn was no more. In its place was a fully decorated exterior, complete with cream-painted walls with the odd brick intentionally left out of place. Every window was tinted a shade of blue, an image straight out of a children's book; they featured slightly aged wooden overhangs that held a plethora of flowers.

And above the oak door and stone archway was a sign.

Guiding Star Inn.

A small shooting star was etched into the side of the sign, oddly out of place compared to the rest of the decor—and yet, with how picturesque everything looked, it felt oddly fitting. Clyde seemed immensely proud of his creation and beamed at it for a moment.

Then he burst into tears.

"Oh my gods," Belle muttered. Vex and Derivan looked on in alarm, but the shadow elemental just ushered them away, conjuring a small seat for Clyde to sit on and curl into while she held him. Elliot gave them their distance, opting instead to speak to the adventurers so they wouldn't be too alarmed.

"He doesn't really let it on much," Elliot said, "but you've basically given him something he's dreamed of for centuries, and he can be *very* emotional when something like that happens. You should've seen him when I got him a little model inn. It looks pretty much exactly like this."

There was a soft smile on Elliot's face as he glanced at his husband. He shook his head after a moment, though, and gestured for the adventurers to follow him inside. "Come on in," he said. "He wouldn't want you standing around, watching him. He's going to pretend none of this happened later."

"Honestly," Misa said, glancing back as she walked in with the rest, "I think it's kinda sweet."

It was late in the night—a time Mundane would normally have been quiet. Most people adhered to a strict curfew, which was yet another thing required of them. A single night wouldn't harm that, though, and this was a rare opportunity for them; in the morning, they would have to once more return to the jobs they had chosen, albeit in a vastly changed town.

Word of the two new glyphs would spread. There were a great many problems, smaller and greater, that could be solved with the use of Change and Solidity; in particular, many of the areas in the world that were uninhabitable because magic had gotten it wrong could finally be fixed. The strange notpanes that hung in the air could be banished, even, and finally clear up the skies.

That was a longer-term project, though. The mayor had already assigned a team to it, a small group of people from Combat who had agreed to help. The rest had rushed back to their homes, wanting to make changes to their own living spaces.

It was a joyful night.

"I honestly didn't think it was going to be such a big deal," Vex admitted, looking down. Misa snorted out a laugh, though it wasn't mocking; she just wore a grin.

"Change the world and you think it's not a big deal," she said. "That's just like you, Vex."

"Is not." Vex flushed a bit.

"Do you actually disagree, or are you just disagreeing to be stubborn?" Misa grinned at him.

". . . The latter." Vex huffed, folding his arms, and Derivan chuckled behind him, ruffling his hand through the frills on the lizardkin's head.

"Do you think you could fix Derivan's hand with this?" Sev asked, gesturing to the armor. Vex hesitated, then shook his head.

"Not unless Clyde or someone else does it, and I don't think we want to do it that way, anyway," Vex said. "The amount of mana it cost when I tried was . . . way beyond anything I could give, and I have a lot of mana. I think there's a better path to it."

"What makes you say that?" Sev asked curiously.

Vex shrugged. "Just a feeling," he said. "The new glyph is . . . weird. Change tells you how that change would be accomplished, more or less, when you're casting the spell. Sometimes, it's pretty mundane—Clyde probably saw workers coming in to fix up the inn—and sometimes, it's more esoteric; to remove the atmospheric effect here, we have to change what's written in the mana's archive, and that's much more expensive.

"Derivan will get a new arm before we go back to Elyra. We can rush it with Change, but we'd lose out on the process. There's something else I think we can gain if we wait. So . . . Derivan decided to wait."

"It is important to me," Derivan said, nodding gravely. "Though I do not know the specifics."

"Huh," Sev said. "Mild precognitive effect in the glyph?"

"That could be *abused*." Misa's eyes gleamed. Vex laughed.

"With the amount of mana it costs? No, not easily," he said. "And it's mostly intuition instead of anything direct, so it's less useful for combat. But . . . yes, I can imagine a few ways we could abuse this. Predrawn glyphs and mana crystals . . . The only thing is that we have no guarantee that this will work the same way outside the echo."

"Right." Sev winced a bit. "Mana is different here, right?"

"All the glyphs we have access to seem the same," Vex said. "But Clyde's told us that magic hasn't really changed or evolved since the universe ended, so that's not a surprise, really."

"I believe that we may be able to use Solidity to keep the glyphs and their effects with us when we return," Derivan said. "But that hypothesis requires further testing."

Vex absolutely *beamed* when Derivan said those words; Sev couldn't help but laugh at the delighted look on the lizardkin's face.

"I've been teaching him the art of *research*," Vex proclaimed, and Sev nodded, still grinning.

"I can see that," he said. Misa snorted beside him, but the affectionate grin on her face was no less wide.

After that, Sev fell silent; he didn't know how to bring up the next subject on his mind. Derivan and Vex had done a good thing for the people in Mundane, there was no doubt about that, except . . .

Except he was thinking it was time to *leave*, and he wasn't sure he had any real justification for that, except that the impulse to leave was slowly growing stronger.

There were other places here to explore. They had all grown, to a certain extent, in their time in Mundane—but they had all hit some kind of cap as well. Sev hadn't made any more progress in connecting with Onyx, though his connection with Aurum was further solidifying, and he was now better able to channel some of the God of Gold's powers. Misa had managed to train her array of skills into something that was more fine-tuned and instinctive, working the precognitive abilities of Endless Echoes into her regular style. Vex and Derivan were both more in tune with magic, had a greater number of glyphs available to them, and had now created two of their own.

But they were stuck. There were more things they had to do, and what they had to do with it was not here, could not *be* here. There was more of this world to see, and Mundane had become a place that was almost too comfortable to them.

Besides. They still had the items they had received and never identified, the ones they had received at the end of Misa's bonus room. They still needed to find out a way to help Elyra and whatever was happening with growth spells around it, to aid with the brewing rebellion. The last time they had checked in on Fendal, Noram and Anton and the others appeared to be mounting a growing resistance that seemed like it would soon come to a head, and they didn't have a *plan*. Not like when they'd seen Xothok launching himself out into the stars, preparing to Navigate, and Aurum had warned them that Irvis was out there.

Then there was what was happening with Velykos, too. Last time Sev had checked in, Velykos had found the grave of the man he had once considered his father, or what looked like it; that had been early in their experiments with Shift, and the viewing had failed shortly afterward. Derivan hadn't been able to reestablish the connection since, nor had Velykos or any of his companions responded to their messages over the system.

Sev hoped they were all right. The dilation of time meant that it hadn't been that long, and they had their suspicions that it was divine intervention that had caused the Shift screening to fail; Aurum's refusal to speak on the matter was further proof, as far as Sev was concerned.

The problem was that they had no way of knowing for sure, and the more time passed, the more antsy Sev felt about it all.

"I think we need to move on," he said suddenly. Misa, Derivan, and Vex—all of whom had been chatting quietly with one another, giving him a concerned glance every now and then, but mostly waiting for him to come to a conclusion on whatever it was he wanted to say—all stared at him.

"What do you mean?" Misa asked after a moment had passed.

"We've been here too long," Sev said uncomfortably. "We need to explore more of this world, I think. I'm sure it has some secrets for us—whatever we came here to do, we should do it. I like Mundane as much as you do, but . . ."

"We have done what we needed to do here." Derivan was, strangely enough, staring at the air above Sev's head as he spoke, like he was watching some invisible mechanism grind and move; Sev winced a little and nodded, not fully understanding the significance of that glance.

"Yeah," he said. "I'm not sure *where* we should go, exactly, but I think we can ask Clyde for directions. And it's not like we can't come back here."

"Right," Misa said. She sounded unconvinced at best. "Look, I want to explore as much as you do, but are you sure you're all right?"

"Of course!" Sev said. He forced a cheery smile. "Why wouldn't I be?"

CHAPTER 21

GRAVEYARD

Velykos

Velykos stared.

It was *rare,* really, that he experienced anything he found difficult to explain. He had been alive for a long, long time, and had experienced almost everything that could be experienced.

The chill he felt now, though? That was new to him.

The fact that none of Harold's crew had anything to say was equally strange and left him feeling even more unsettled. Ixiss and Iliss in particular almost always had a witty rejoinder, and yet even they—

"What the *fuck,*" Iliss said plainly.

Oh. Well, there it was.

Honestly, that made him feel a little better.

Velykos stood in the remains of the quarry he'd gained his First Form in. The memories of that were fuzzy, as it was for all elementals; he remembered the moment he first understood that he was *seeing,* the moment he first realized he could interact with the world around him.

By far, the memory that stood out the most was of the old daemon that had appeared one day, looking for small rocks to carve.

He'd watched in curiosity, at first, and then ever-increasing fascination as the quarry he lived in was transformed into a thing of beauty. The daemon never took his carvings with him—he left them there like an offering to the quarry itself.

That was around when he'd learned he could *speak,* and he'd reached out to learn. When their relationship had gone from artist and curious watcher to father and child. The daemon had taught him . . . almost everything he now knew about the world.

And yet he couldn't remember the daemon's *name.* That should have been the first sign, he supposed.

"This is the guy you were talking about, right?" Ixiss asked him, his voice hesitant. "Your father."

"Yes," Velykos said. He stared at the gravestone in front of him.

At the grave*stones* in front of him.

It had seemed strange enough at a distance, that there was a monument rising up into the air above the quarry—Velykos remembered no such monument when he left, though that was centuries past (centuries? *centuries* didn't seem quite right; this world was only two hundred years old, and he was not as old as this world).

He remembered leaving and taking only a few souvenirs with him, things that the daemon had carved and left behind (but where had he kept them? he had no such keepsakes with him, not anymore).

Velykos remembered mourning, wandering (had he not left a monument for his father when he left? that seemed strange now. surely he would have created something to dedicate to him, as meaningful as the daemon had been to him).

"Vel?" Harold's voice was sharp, concerned. Velykos shook his head, stumbling forward; a heavy hand pressed against the obelisk in front of him, brushing away some of the dirt and dust obscuring the name.

Onyx.

He'd never heard the name. (the name seemed familiar, though; it pressed into his mind like an imprint left in the earth and scuffed away, smoothed over but not quite *gone*).

He'd never heard the name. *He'd never heard the name—*

"Vel!" Harold's voice pulled him back like an anchor. Velykos stepped back quickly, nearly tripping over his allies in the process. Olag and Nathan, bless them, acted quickly enough to steady him before he outright fell.

This was familiar (it was too familiar, in fact. it had happened before, hadn't it? except the last time something fundamental to his elemental magic had been disrupted. he'd placed protections in place since then).

(it was so hard to think)

"Vel, look at me." Harold's voice was steady. The skeleton stood in front of him suddenly. Velykos didn't remember when he moved, or when he'd been propped up against the obelisk that acted as a gravestone. He couldn't help but stare out at the sea of *other gravestones* laid out in front of him.

The sight was deeply unsettling.

Partly because he recognized the handwriting.

It was his own, laid out over and over in a grid. The gravestones themselves were always different—each made from a different stone, perhaps, or shaped differently from the others.

The one he was lying against was the largest. There was something morbid in that thought, in the idea of using his own father's grave to support his body. A laugh almost bubbled up from within, beginning with the rolling of pebbles down over his torso, the *skip-hop* of them almost distracting him from the roiling thoughts inside—

"Vel, *look at me,*" Harold repeated, and Velykos briefly flickered his attention to the skeleton.

A golden thread appeared.

Velykos didn't see where Harold had gotten it, but his attention suddenly fixated on that gold, unable and unwilling to look away. It calmed his thoughts, reducing the simmering chaos back down into a single thread of reality, of *memory*.

"Would you look at that," Harold murmured. "Kid was right. This *did* work. And I thought he was just shittin' me."

"Kid?" Velykos asked, clueless.

"Y'know," Harold said, waving a hand dismissively. "That god kid. Aurum? Fella showed up, told me I'd need this. Didn't know what the fuck it was for. He coulda told me *more,* that lil' shit. I almost didn't think of this."

"Don't call him a little shit," Nathan objected. He still didn't talk much, but he seemed more comfortable now when he did; he spent less time staring at his bones and wincing or shivering. "He's just a kid. He was trying his best."

"Yeah, yeah, I know," Harold said with a sigh, and when Nathan gave him an obstinate look, he capitulated. "Force of habit. 'M sorry."

"Good," Nathan huffed.

"Really, *this* is the one situation you talk back to our captain for?" Iliss teased him, and Nathan looked away.

"Come on, guys. Focus," Ixiss said. He gestured to Velykos. "Are you doing all right?"

"I do not know," Velykos answered honestly. "But . . . I think I am now. What is that?"

"Wish I had a fuckin' clue." Harold snorted. He kept the thread held out like it was the only thing keeping Velykos steady. It probably was. Velykos could feel the weight of the thread pressing down around him, even if he didn't have the words to describe exactly what it was doing.

"May I?" Velykos said, reaching out.

"Sure." Harold dropped the thread onto his outstretched hand.

There was a pulse of light, and it *vanished*. Velykos felt his mind clear a bit more, steadying into something that was once more his own. A compulsion effect of some sort but . . . purely beneficial.

Hm.

"So, big guy," Iliss said, "any idea what's going on here?"

Velykos paused, looking around. He could feel the thread of gold keeping his thoughts *steady*, even if it didn't give him answers. He could think about the disparity between his age and the remembered history of the world without feeling concurrent thoughts jamming up his head, half-remembered truths hitting him all at once.

He didn't know how long ago this had happened. It *felt* like a long time, but there were enough recognizable gaps in his memory that he understood he couldn't possibly define the chronology. He didn't even know how old he was.

But this?

"I can try to find out," he said.

There was a very obvious first question. His memories told him that Onyx had simply *left*; if that was the case, then the gravestones here meant nothing and were mere monuments to someone he had lost. It wouldn't explain why there were so many of them, but it would be better than the alternative.

The alternative, of course, being the possibility that Onyx was buried here.

Except he couldn't be. Onyx was Sev's god—he could remember that much clearly now. God didn't have bodies, as far as he knew.

There was really only one way to find out.

[**Earth Sense**] was a passive skill he could toggle on and off; he kept it mostly off, largely because the amount of information he gained from it tended to be distracting and unnecessary. The skill was far stronger than it had to be, and he had no way to adjust the strength of it.

He toggled it on and *reeled*.

"Something wrong?" Harold called up to him, and Velykos shook his head, holding up a hand to tell the captain to give him a moment. He needed a second to parse what he was seeing. To verify.

He needed to be *sure*.

Because what [**Earth Sense**] was telling him was that there were dozens of identical bodies in the graveyard, one under each gravestone. Each one in the exact same stage of decay. Each one undeniably the man that had helped raise him.

Except that didn't make *sense*.

"The graves are all full," he said softly.

"What?" Iliss asked. She looked around, her bones rattling slightly with the speed at which she whipped her head toward the nearest gravestone; she nudged a toe toward the dirt before hesitating and stopping. "That . . . can't be right."

"Forty-nine bodies in total," Velykos said. His words felt almost distant. "They are exactly the same, every one of them. I . . . I do not understand."

"*Shit*," Harold breathed.

The six of them stared at the quarry-graveyard in a new light, a chill settling over all of them. Nathan shivered a little and hugged himself closer to Olag, who put an arm around his shoulder to steady him.

The wind blew over them.

"I did not want to do this," Velykos muttered. His voice was the low rumble of earth and stone once more—the most alien it had been for months. It was easy to emulate mortals when his emotions were calm or positive, as they usually were around this group that he had come to consider close friends.

But when he felt like this, the thought of it just fell away. "It feels . . . disrespectful. But it may be necessary to dig up one of the bodies, to see if there is something to be observed that my [**Earth Sense**] cannot spot."

"Are ye sure?" Harold asked. "We're with you all the way, don't get me wrong, but . . ."

"I am not," Velykos said. "But it is the only idea I have."

It was easy, even. A simple application of [**Earth Manipulation**] and Onyx's body could be brought to the surface without disturbing it; another one, and he could be buried once more, with not a single trace left for anyone to see except perhaps another elemental like himself. Yet it felt wrong, almost disgraceful to have to do something like this . . .

. . . perhaps a small prayer to Nillea first, so he would know he was doing the right thing. A small prayer to Aurum, for his assistance in dealing with whatever strange influence had come over him when he first encountered this graveyard.

And a small prayer to Onyx, to ask for permission.

He felt a ghost of a whisper from Nillea: approval, kindness, sympathy. He felt a brightness from Aurum: excitement and pride, along with a small inkling of sorrow.

From Onyx he felt nothing.

He hadn't expected a response, but something inside him ached nonetheless.

CHAPTER 22

UNEARTH

Velykos

Velykos stood in front of the body, staring silently. The golden thread within him hummed, working full force to keep him from falling apart.

The body was *wrong*, but he didn't know why.

"This the man that adopted ya?" Harold asked quietly.

"I believe so," Velykos answered, but the truth was that he wasn't sure.

"He's supposed to be a demon, ain't he?" Harold asked. "He don't look much like one to me."

"Daemon," Velykos corrected. He stared again at the body.

It didn't *look* like a daemon. Or a demon, for that matter.

The curious thing was that [**Earth Sense**] was still pinging, telling him something that was very different from what he could *see*. It was almost like all of this was intentionally set up to trick someone with his senses.

Or anyone whose domain was *Earth*.

"Wanna let us in on your thoughts, big guy?" Iliss asked. "I can hear you thinking, but I have no idea what you're thinking."

"You cannot hear me thinking," Velykos said automatically, exasperated—and when Iliss smirked at him in her usual impossible way, he sighed.

He did feel a little better.

Velykos knelt beside the corpse of his father, allowing himself one more prayer. This one wasn't to any god in particular; it was a prayer he made for himself.

Let me understand.

Onyx's body was stone sculpted in the vague shape of a daemon's body, just close enough that it could pass for one at a distance. Up close, it clearly wasn't—the defining features were all unfinished, like a sculpture that had never been completed. Part of him felt a melancholic sadness at the sight.

The rest of him wondered *why*.

He didn't know exactly what he could find out from just examining the body—it sat still and silent in front of him, without so much of a hint of changing. Yet there were small details he could see, surely. He was a stone elemental, and Onyx—this version of Onyx, not the true, daemon version—was made out of stone.

There had to be something only he could notice. There had to be a reason that the bodies seemed identical under [**Earth Sense**], a reason they didn't register as unusual until he brought them up.

There had to be a reason there were forty-nine separate instances of the bodies.

He just couldn't think of what it was.

He barely realized it when he began to reach out with [**Earth Manipulation**], digging into the features that were barely formed. If this was meant to represent his father, it did a poor job; his eyes were more almond-shaped, his nose a little higher on his face. His hair was wild and free and *long*, reaching down to the small of his back. He had a tail that curled up and around his hand, a nervous habit he'd clearly picked up at some point.

Velykos didn't know how long he kept at it. His friends stayed quiet by his side, watching; he was grateful for their company, and grateful that they stayed silent for something that felt so . . .

Ceremonial.

Velykos didn't know how much time passed before he was done. The sun was low in the sky by the time the sculpture was complete, and he reached down with a large, gentle hand to slowly prop up the statue of Onyx that he'd completed.

[**Earth Sense**] had been a guide, he was realizing. He had to use [**Earth Manipulation**] until it matched what he sensed with [**Earth Sense**], down to the . . .

Down to the injuries.

When had Onyx gained *injuries*? His entire right ribcage was missing, like a hole had been torn through his body—except instead of ragged flesh, there was a smooth circle of *nothing*. He hadn't noticed it before, too preoccupied with the sheer number of corpses and the fact that they all pinged as identical, but—

The body *moved*.

"Velykos," Onyx said.

Velykos flinched backward hard, all the stacks of stone that made up his body cracking against one another and threatening to fall apart. Harold made an alarmed yell, holding out his spear like it would do anything against a god made out of stone, and the rest of the skeletons arrayed themselves protectively, prepared both to catch Velykos if he fell and to fight Onyx if needed.

Onyx just laughed. "You found yourself some good friends, huh?"

"You . . . are alive?" Velykos's gaze flickered to the wound in Onyx's chest, at the missing half-circle carved into his torso. "I do not understand."

"You don't have to. We don't have a lot of time . . ." Onyx glanced up at the sun and then tilted his head. "Huh. Actually, no, we have a bunch of time. You did that way faster than I expected. Well done."

"You do not speak the same way the Onyx I knew did," Velykos said cautiously.

"It's been centuries since that version of me existed," Onyx said, smiling softly. Velykos remembered that smile. His heart ached at the familiarity of it. "But I never forgot you."

"I'm gonna cry," Ixiss muttered from somewhere beside him. He would've assumed the lizardkin was joking, except he actually did sound vaguely choked up. "Dammit, I miss having *eyeballs*."

Onyx's eyes twinkled. "You've found yourself some *interesting* friends," he amended. "But to answer your question . . . I am alive, and I am not. You remember Sev, yes?"

"He claimed to be one of your worshippers," Velykos said. "You ascended, then? I did not know mortals could become gods."

"That's a topic I actually can't discuss," Onyx said, looking apologetic. "But there is one that I *can*. Sev knows about this, and so does Aurum, but most of the gods don't."

"This is important," Velykos said carefully.

"Very," Onyx said. "The other gods need to know this. I can't tell them; *Aurum* can't tell them. No one who's been touched by the Void can, and Aurum was, even if it was only for a little bit. And he's been spending more and more time in it with me, to try to help us . . ."

At this, Onyx grimaced a little bit. "We need to stop him from doing that," he said. "He's too eager to help."

"I do not understand," Velykos said. "What is the Void?"

"It is the *end*," Onyx told him.

And then he told him everything.

Velykos listened in growing horror as Onyx told him about the slow erasure of the gods—about how they were being sacrificed to keep the system running, to keep the universe at large running. He listened as he was told about countless gods who had already been erased without anyone knowing about it, the world just modified again and again to operate without the god in question.

Harold looked sick. Nathan couldn't meet Onyx's eyes. Iliss and Ixiss stood close to one another, hands clenched tight, and Olag simply watched with anger set into his shoulders and simmering in his posture.

Velykos could read them all like a book by now.

"There must be a way to fix this," Velykos said. The low rumble of his voice felt almost like static to him.

"I don't know if there is." Something in Onyx's voice changed; his tone was usually friendly, casual, but now there was something of the man he'd considered his father in there—some of that age-old wisdom, and some of that age-old weariness. "Sev is working on it. I cannot . . . *We* cannot interact. He is one of my closest friends, but he also made one of the greatest sacrifices he could have for the cause of fixing all of this.

"His relationship with the system is . . . unstable. If I interact too much with him, the system may notice. It is dangerous enough that he has acquired an ally who can directly patch the system, though I trust that he will be careful with that power.

"It makes me frustratingly limited in what I can do. I can guide him a bit. I can make changes to the system those few times it lets me through some back door or the other. But it closes them after, and I have to make sure that when I do it, it *counts*.

"He's making good progress, though. I wouldn't be able to talk to you about all this if he and his friends didn't discover it first. We're piggybacking on their anchor, linking more people to it when it can handle it; the problem is it still can't handle everyone . . ."

Onyx trailed off, shaking his head. "But that's getting into a lot of the technicalities behind it all. The long and short of it is that Sev can't see me again, or the system's going to realize what he did to keep me alive. It was bad enough the last time we interacted."

Half of that was his father just needing to talk, Velykos realized. Onyx hadn't really been able to speak to anyone about all of this, and this was the first time he'd been able to talk freely and openly.

He had so many questions. Not even about *this*. He wanted to know more about what had happened, about the years Onyx had spent as a god. Now that he'd gained more context for what life was like, he wanted to know more about what the man he had considered his father was like.

What his favorite food was. What daemon culture was like—if it was difficult, being so closely associated with demons. If he'd made anything new that he wanted to share.

Onyx had spent centuries on this problem; it had consumed a lot of who he was. Velykos understood *why*. The problems Onyx spoke of were problems on a cosmic scale, to the point where everything else must have seemed insignificant . . .

. . . but it still made him sad.

He understood a little better, perhaps, why Sev's approach with the gods was what it was. Perhaps that was comparable for all gods—if they were all ascended from mortals, then there was a possibility that they'd all gone through the same thing, their mundane, mortal problems replaced with something grander and greater in scale, dwarfing their previous lives and the things they once cared about.

And even if they *weren't* all ascended from mortals . . .

It was too bad he didn't still have the tea he normally carried with him. None of the skeletons he traveled with needed food of any kind, or he would have had some on hand.

He *did*, however, have something else.

"Here," Velykos said. It wasn't a perfect response to everything Onyx had just told him—really, it wasn't a response at all. It was a small offering from the carvings he kept in the bag he wore at his side, one of those precious pieces of art he had created with his new friends. "I would like you to have this."

"I can't take anything with me," Onyx started to deny—but then he saw what Velykos was actually offering him and fell silent.

In his hand—much smaller than the actual size of his palm, and perhaps all the more vulnerable-looking for that fact—sat a small sculpture of the very quarry they stood in. It was devoid of all the gravestones, of course; instead, the original set of statues that Onyx had created stood surrounding the quarry like guardians.

". . . This I can keep," Onyx said. "Because it falls under my domain. My power is limited, but . . . thank you."

"I missed you greatly," Velykos said. "I understand this matter is urgent, and I do not wish to take away from it. But I do not want this moment to be *this*—an explanation, a hurried goodbye. You are more than just the god trying to save us."

"Haven't heard that in a while," Onyx said. The words were playful, but his tone was not. The look he gave the sculpture was almost melancholic.

". . . I am sorry. You meant—you *mean* a lot to me, too. Were it that we had more time . . ."

"I understand," Velykos said simply. "I just had a wish to express. You had a goal in coming here, did you not?"

"I was going to ask for your help warning the other gods," Onyx said. "Tell them that the system may devour them, and that they must work against it. It will be difficult; many of them think the system is still something to be trusted . . . and it *is* doing something good. But it will hinder any further possible solution and must be destroyed before we can try something else."

"We aren't just gonna be able to waltz up to the gods and tell 'em their system is gonna eat them," Harold protested. He'd been silent up until now, but now he somehow wore a scowl on his skull. Onyx only nodded.

"You will have to gain their trust," he said. He glanced at the small sculpture Velykos had given him, and very gently placed it against his chest; there was a ripple, and then it merged with his body. "But . . . I believe that you can. You and your friends."

"Sure." Iliss spoke up, but she folded her arms, staring at Onyx. "Do you have a lot of time left here, though?"

"Some," Onyx said cautiously.

"Then you're going to stay and talk to Velykos, because he's been missing you for years," she declared. "You don't get to just show up, ask us to do something, and leave. Spend some time with the kid you raised, for crying out loud."

"Ah," Onyx said. He smiled, oddly happy, like he'd been hoping exactly this would happen. "I suppose you're right."

Velykos decided that he'd been very lucky indeed to make friends with this particular set of mortals.

CHAPTER 23

ROADS TO NOWHERE

"We're going to be at the Roads soon," Belle said. "Are you sure you want to leave?"

"*Sure*?" Misa snorted. "No. But we have to."

She didn't look Belle in the eyes. They'd all been traveling together for the past few days—Clyde had taken time off specifically for this, though he didn't elaborate on what the process of taking time off *involved,* exactly. It wasn't like he had a boss. This journey together had been the closest the seven of them had been, though of course, they tended to split off into little groups. Clyde, it turned out, got along well with Sev; the man was fascinated by the idea of *gods,* for it turned out they were much less literal in this world than in the one with the system.

Belle spent most of her time with Misa, who delighted in their shared darker sense of humor. Elliot spent the most time with Derivan and Vex, curious about how their magic was different and how it interacted with the history of the world.

As time ticked by, though, and they got closer to their destination . . . the conversation fell gradually silent. Everyone was very much aware of what this meant.

There was a good chance that they'd never meet again. They would *try* to come back to say goodbye, of course, but this bonus room had given them no objectives. They didn't know what they were supposed to *do* to get back. If they managed to complete it by accident, or if the energy required to keep the bonus room running ran out—

— this echo universe would pop like a bubble, and they wouldn't meet again. Not in the same way, anyway.

"I guess this is goodbye, then," Clyde said eventually, looking around awkwardly. "I know I should be a good host and all, but . . . I'm going to miss you guys a lot, actually."

"We all will," Belle said. She managed a small smile, though there was just a bit of sadness in the glow of her eyes.

"You better write," Elliot said with just the barest hint of a forced grin. "I'm expecting letters."

"Oh, come on," Clyde said. "They're not going to send us letters."

"Will too!" Vex said. "I mean, if we figure out how to send letters . . . Wait, no, we have the Communication glyph we left with you guys. That should work. Why did you tell me to write letters?"

Elliot just smirked.

"Don't be surprised if we leave you a few messages," Belle said with a chuckle. She slowed to a stop as they finally came within a few feet of the entrance to the Roads.

This was very different from how it had been in Fendal and Teque, where the entrance had been hidden in the ground. An ancient stone archway towered over them, the edges crackling with dense magical energy; every so often, a spark danced off between the cracks in the stone, sizzling with power.

And yet, were it not for those cracks, it wouldn't have been clear that any magic was involved in this at all. The usual glow of densely packed mana was nearly invisible, a product of sheer efficiency; every bit of that mana was being used to maintain the portal.

It was just a little anticlimactic that this feat of magical engineering was used to display nothing more than a dark tunnel, but that was just the nature of the Roads.

"Is this just a portal?" Vex asked, gawking up at the archway. He hopped a little to the left and then walked around the archway; the back of it was perfectly clear, and he could see his friends through it, though evidently none of them could see him. "What happens if I try to go through it from the back?"

"Don't go through it from the back," Elliot called.

"That just makes me want to go through it from the back even more." Vex narrowed his eyes slightly at the archway, as if contemplating doing exactly that.

Then he picked up a rock, hefted it in his hand . . .

. . . and hesitated.

"It's not going to break if I throw a rock through it, right?" he called out.

"Nope!" It was Clyde that responded this time. He sounded amused. "Go ahead."

Vex tossed the rock and watched with both his physical and magical senses as the rock left his hand, soaring through the air. He paid special attention as it crossed the horizon of the portal—

—and abruptly vanished.

Vex blinked. He hadn't sensed anything. He walked carefully back around the portal, looking down the tunnel.

The rock he'd thrown sat inside, sheared into paper-thin slices. He stared at it and paled.

"Would that have happened to me?" he asked.

"No," Elliot said with a laugh. "We wouldn't leave something that dangerous around. There are wards in place to protect living creatures. And magical ones." He gave Derivan a significant look; Derivan just affected a shrug, like he didn't know what Elliot was talking about. The shadow elemental shot him a bit of a knowing grin.

They all knew what they were doing here, though. They were delaying the inevitable.

"Time to go," Misa said. She started walking toward the portal, then stopped and sighed.

"Ah, fuck it," she said. She spread her arms out wide. "Group hug?"

Seven people made for a rather awkward group hug, it turned out. But there was a certain sense of vulnerability that came about with that awkwardness, a certain sense of sincerity; sometimes, there were no words that could really adequately summarize a situation.

It was even harder when none of it felt *real* yet. The reality that they could very well never meet again was a hard one to accept, and for the most part, all seven of them were refusing to acknowledge the thought.

They'd become uncommonly close, really, for all that they'd only known each other for a little over two months.

Neither group left without carrying an armful of gifts left by the other.

"I can't believe they made *so many cookies*," Misa said. She was carrying what had to be an entire sack of them while they traipsed down the tunnel. "When did she even have time to make so many cookies?"

"Magic," Vex reminded her. "Probably the Glyph of Change, actually, since it accelerates time and all that."

"That's *so much mana* spent on cookies," Misa said. She wasn't complaining, though. They all saw the way one hand kept sneaking into the sack, pulling out a cookie to munch on.

Her seventh time doing this, she instead pulled out a note from Belle:

Cool it with the cookies. —B

"Oh, come on," Misa grumbled. Sev snickered at her.

The tunnel they were traveling down was both oddly familiar and fundamentally *different* from the one in Fendal; the magic that thrummed in the air here was significant, to the point where it skittered about on Vex's scales like an itch that wouldn't go away. It affected all of them differently, even—it manifested in Misa's hunger, in a fluctuating divine connection that left Sev with something of a headache, and in a slight loss of control of Derivan's Slime stat.

It was vaguely alarming the first time he started melting, actually.

Now they were just used to it.

Mostly.

It was still a *little* alarming.

"What do you think they meant?" Sev asked, just to break the silence. His words echoed strangely in the tunnel. There was still nothing to be seen in the distance, nothing to break the monotony of dirt and stone. "When they said that the Roads take you where you need to go."

"No idea," Vex said. "I spent some time in the library, and there are books about fate-aspect magic; apparently, the Roads determine their destinations through an extension of that kind of magic. They link the communities that need to be linked, so that food and water goes between them as needed, and guide people out into the surface when a location is stable enough for a new community to be built . . ."

Vex paused. "Though there have been mistakes," he added with a slight grimace. "And that says very little about where we might end up."

The tunnel stretched in front of them, long and still eerily empty. The *lighting* was strange, even; there was no real source of light, and when Derivan checked, he saw that the area behind them was pitch-black too, fading into nothing after just a few dozen feet.

Yet the area around them was clear. It was strange, and when Derivan felt out with his senses, it was remarkably *clear*.

Even in Mundane, the system had been present. It was fueling the world they were in, and although it was a step removed in this bonus world, he could still feel its oppressive gaze. Here, the only source of the system was Misa's reality anchor.

If he wanted to study it in detail, now would be the time to do it.

"Guys," Misa said. "I think I see something."

Sev, Vex, and Derivan all turned their attention to the tunnel ahead of them. Misa frowned at the path. "I thought the Roads were supposed to lead us somewhere," she said. "Why's it got a choice to make?"

". . . You see a choice?" Vex asked. "The tunnel goes . . . uh, straight up for me."

"I see nothing," Derivan said. He wandered forward a few steps and stopped, hovering at the edge of what was, to him, an empty nothingness. With some hesitation, he stuck his hand out into that inky darkness, then withdrew it a moment later, thankfully intact. "I am uncertain if it is safe for me to step into that nothing."

Sev frowned. "The tunnel looks the same for me," he said. "Nothing's changed. Are we all just seeing something different?"

"Maybe the Roads want us to split up," Vex suggested. He looked a little nervous about it but not nearly as much as he normally would; if anything, there was a spark of curiosity in the way he kept glancing up toward his path.

"It's . . . probably safe?" Sev hedged. "Based on everything that Clyde told us about the Roads. But it might be hard to coordinate anything to help anyone outside the bonus room for a while if we split up like this, so . . . we have to be ready."

Misa walked a few steps forward, mostly out of curiosity. "What do you guys see when I do this?" she called.

"You're kinda starting to fade away," Vex said.

"There is a Shift as we progress deeper into the tunnel," Derivan said. "A very powerful one, and not one from the system. Powered by reality shards, I suspect."

"Okay." Sev rubbed the bridge of his nose. "Let's split up our remaining mana crystals and hand the reality shards off to Misa before we check out these paths, just in case this takes longer than we expect. We can keep in contact using the system, and . . . Please be careful, guys."

"It's not the first time we've split up." Misa gave Sev a reassuring grin. "We can take care of ourselves."

"I know, I know," Sev grumbled.

Indeed, it wasn't the first time they'd split up. It wasn't the first time Sev had expressed worry, either. The *first* time it had happened, he'd fussed over them and made sure everyone was carrying healing potions.

Each one of them grabbed a mana crystal for themselves, and Derivan once again prepared himself to watch keenly. This was his opportunity—with the system mostly pulled back, this was the cleanest he'd ever be able to observe the process.

He'd made a few more observations the last few times they had done this, but had never been confident enough in his skills with Patch to remove their reliance on mana crystals with confidence.

This time, though . . .

He saw the way the mana crystals were funneled into the system, the way they were purified and stripped of *something* that went straight into the reality anchor Misa held.

He saw the way it responded. Something inside the anchor *unfolded*, absorbing whatever it was the mana crystals gave it.

Strange. It was different from what he'd seen the first time, when he'd observed it on their way to Elyra . . . But this was a better, truer representation of what the mana crystals and reality anchors were doing, he suspected.

It was almost like it was updating something.

Mana is memory.

Clyde had said that in the beginning, when they'd first arrived; that mana was a memory, a *record*. Dungeons were structures that kept reality anchors operating, but reality anchors needed something to anchor.

That was what a dungeon-formation event was—the gathering of all that initial memory to push into an anchor, to give it the record it needed to anchor. And then the crystals continued recording events as they changed, updating that internal database.

Derivan felt, for the first time, like he *understood*. And if that was true . . .

The Patch would have to be subtle. He wouldn't remove the prompt for them to offer the system a crystal—that was, apparently, necessary. But the kill switch that removed their access if they didn't offer a crystal was almost insultingly easy to excise.

"I think I understand," Derivan said, and everyone else glanced at him. He took a moment to find the words and then continued. "I believe that when a dungeon is formed, a recording—a *memory* of everything the reality anchor has to stabilize is fed into it. But that memory is static and unchanging. Offering a mana crystal updates the reality anchor, keeping the memory in line with reality.

"I removed the part of the system that destroys our connection with the system if we do not offer a mana crystal," he continued, "but in light of this, we should keep giving it crystals, if we can, so that we stay in sync."

He didn't say the other part of what he thought he might be able to do—that it might be possible to force the anchor to *restore* from its backup, the way Misa's own family had been restored.

No unnecessary risks.

With that, they said their goodbyes, and each faded into their own separate Road.

CHAPTER 24

THE TRAPPINGS OF NORMALCY

Sev

Sev hadn't said it while the others were there with him, but he was worried.

It was strange that he was the only one the Roads hadn't changed for. Misa had been given a choice. Vex's road led *up,* whatever that meant. Derivan's path ended in nothing, but presumably there was something for him even there—and even if there wasn't, he was the only one among them that could simply Shift himself out of that situation, especially with the mastery of the stat that he'd gained over the past month or two.

Sev wasn't sure exactly what he was afraid of. There was the idea, he supposed, that there was just nothing for him, that the others all had some sort of destiny waiting for them, and he had none.

*Because you've given up yours. You are [**Fatebroken**],* a small voice in the back of his head whispered. He ignored it.

The more he walked, the smaller the tunnel seemed to get. He was pretty sure it was just his imagination. It was easy enough to ignore the mild feeling of claustrophobia when he was surrounded by his friends, when they could laugh and joke together. They didn't even need to speak for him to feel comforted by their presence.

Walking down a dark tunnel alone was a whole other ballgame. He'd never considered himself particularly claustrophobic, but there was something almost suffocating about this. There was a part of him that feared he would be left wandering the Roads forever, walking down a straight tunnel with no end in sight. Realistically, though, he knew that even if that were the case, Derivan and the others would come find him. He sighed and tried to force his mind to wander in a different direction.

Misa, Vex, and Derivan had all made incredible strides in their fighting and magic. Sev had . . . certainly made *some* progress, but he didn't have the easily exploitable skills that Misa did, or access to the kind of magic Derivan and Vex could cast. He was a healer. He had his barriers, he had his divine spells—half of which he'd been barred from using, for the most part—and he had his connection to his gods.

There didn't seem to be much of a path ahead for just *healing better*. He'd been able to figure some things out with his skills, had even gained a skill for [**Healer's Intervention**], which allowed him to attach to a target a small packet of divine magic that would burst and heal them when it was needed, effectively preventing death by health loss, but it all seemed insufficient.

His connection with Aurum was stronger too. He'd begun to meditate on that connection, allowing himself to draw more of Aurum's divine energy when the god allowed him to—which happened pretty much entirely on Aurum's whim. He'd gained a new skill, even, from Aurum's domain rather than Onyx's. He didn't particularly know how he felt about it.

[Buying Time] [Active Skill] [Grade: Max]
The more gold you use, the more time slows down. Dilate time by 10% for every 100 grams of gold per second contributed to the skill.

It was a weird name for the skill—gold on Obreve wasn't really associated with *wealth*, so Sev had to assume that this came from all the planeshifted people from Earth that made that association. That was perhaps what had granted Aurum his minor Time attribute, even.

It was probably a good thing Jerome had apparently not had access to that particular skill. On the other hand, *he* didn't have Jerome's ability to transmute random things into gold or produce gold at will.

Or the strength to carry literal kilograms of gold around.

It wasn't that useful as a result, though it wasn't useless, either. He'd asked Vex about getting a spatially compressed bag of gold that was also enchanted to be light, but there had been a problem, in that the skill weighed the gold *before* it was removed from the bag.

Not an insurmountable problem, just an annoying one.

"You look like you're thinking really hard!" A young voice spoke next to him, making him jump; Sev whirled around to find a gold-outline Aurum walking beside him, like there was nothing unusual about this at all. The golden orb that passed for Aurum's head wobbled around dangerously, and Sev was struck with the ridiculous thought that he should strap it on lest it fall off.

He didn't voice that thought. That was probably rude.

"Uh, yeah," Sev said, faltering slightly in his response. "I'm just trying to figure out . . . where I'm supposed to go from here."

Aurum nodded seriously. "The angels tell me it's hard for mortals to decide what to do with their lives," he said. "I'm sure you can do it!"

Sev snorted. "That feels a little bit condescending. Just a bit."

"I don't know what that means." Aurum cocked his head, then patted Sev on the back. "What do you wanna do?"

"I need to get a little stronger, I guess." Sev looked off into the distance—into the dark that stretched into the tunnel ahead of him. "Or a lot stronger. I felt pretty useless during that fight against Irvis. If I had more options . . ."

"I know how you feel." Aurum nodded. "I wanna help Mr. Onyx and all the other ghosts, but it's hard. I can't spend too much time where they are."

"You shouldn't be spending any time there at all, Aurum," Sev said softly. "I'm sure there are other ways you can help, but . . . you're young. You shouldn't *have* to."

Aurum was silent.

"Do you know how gods age, Sev?" he asked. "We normally don't. But if I spend time in the Void . . . my head feels a little funny afterwards, but I feel a little better. Older. Like it's erasing all the youngness I was supposed to have."

"That . . ." It explained some things but not others. Aurum didn't seem to have aged that much, but that didn't mean anything—it was difficult to tell how old the god was to begin with. He was a little taller, maybe.

And it felt wrong, still. Risky. Too much to ask of a child.

Yet *staying stuck as a child* . . . that seemed like torture. He understood Aurum's position, strangely enough.

"There has to be a better way to age than that," Sev finally said. "I get it, just let me look into it, okay? I'll find someone that can help you."

There was no response. Sev looked around for the figure of Aurum that was accompanying him and found that he was entirely gone, with not even the slightest trace of divine magic left. Bewildered, he took a few steps back, tripping over a rock that most certainly should not have been there on the relatively smooth flooring of the tunnel—

"Whoa there," a very familiar voice said as it caught him. Onyx steadied him back onto his feet and patted him on his shoulders. "Careful. Don't want to hurt yourself in here."

"Onyx?" Sev stared. This Onyx didn't even look anything like the divine projection of Aurum had—there was no indication that it was a projection at all. It just looked like the Onyx he had known, fully formed and in the flesh.

Stone. Whatever. Same difference.

"In the flesh," Onyx said, and then chuckled. "Or stone. You know, same difference."

. . . This was *bizarre.*

"Right," Sev said, sounding entirely unconvinced. "What're you doing here? I thought you were stuck . . . you know, wherever you are."

"I am," Onyx said, inclining his head. "You've probably already figured out that I'm not really him."

"No kidding." Sev tried not to let his voice drip with sarcasm, he really did. It just . . . still came out anyway. Thankfully, this Onyx seemed mostly amused by the slight; he grinned at Sev, his eyes twinkling, and slung an arm around his shoulders.

"Let's walk?" he suggested.

"Do I have a choice?"

"You gave that up long ago," Onyx said mildly—simple words that sent a deep and sudden chill through Sev's body, entirely unexplained. Onyx turned to look at him, his expression as deadly serious as could be. "But if you choose to take it back . . . I will do everything in my power to help you."

Sev stared back at Onyx's eyes—pitch-black, glittering stones that they were—and felt strangely comforted. "You're not even the real Onyx," he said.

"No," Onyx said with a shrug. "But that doesn't mean I don't know what he'd say."

They walked along the tunnel for a minute more; Sev's mind was spinning, abuzz with questions, and yet he couldn't settle on any of them. It took a further minute before he finally figured out what he wanted to ask first.

"What is all this?" he asked. "What's the point?"

"Unlike your friends," Onyx said, "the guidance you need isn't anything that the Roads can lead you to—at least not directly. You already know everything you need to know, but most of it is buried deep inside you, hidden."

"Because I lost most of my memories." There was perhaps just the faintest trace of bitterness in his tone. "It doesn't matter if I know it if I can't remember it. I'm not sure that there's a difference between the two."

"Oh, there is," Onyx said mildly. He hummed a low tune as he walked, one that felt achingly familiar to Sev.

Two steps later, and he was humming along to the same tune. He didn't realize it until Onyx *stopped* and he continued, one note weaving into the other into the distinct melody of—

"That's an Earth lullaby," he said. "Isn't it? I don't know what the name is, but . . ."

"But a part of you remembers," Onyx agreed. "Your skill isn't perfect. No system skill is, really; the system takes a lot of shortcuts to work the way it does. There's a reason it comes off as so poorly designed and so easily exploitable—it's not designed to be functional in that way."

"It's designed to keep the world alive," Sev muttered.

"That is it exactly," Onyx said, "though even that is not the full picture. It was never completed, you know?"

"The system?" Sev blinked, staring at Onyx. "How would you know that?"

"How would I know that indeed," Onyx said with a shrug. "The point is that the guidance you need is within, not without; the Roads have nothing to offer you."

"Except this. Whatever this is."

"Exactly," Onyx said with a laugh. "You catch on fast, as usual."

Sev frowned.

Onyx was telling the truth, he was pretty sure. He was also certain that, as Onyx had said, this wasn't the full picture—that there was something more to all of this. There was a purpose to Aurum showing up, and then Onyx showing up; there was a conclusion that he was being guided to.

And he didn't really feel like being led there slowly.

"Can you just tell me whatever I'm supposed to figure out, then?" Sev asked, exasperated. "I don't want to do a whole personal introspection arc."

Onyx really did laugh then. It was a deep-throated, from-the-belly kind of laugh; the man nearly doubled over, and Sev just stared at him, feeling vaguely disconcerted. It was familiar, at least—he remembered now that the first thing he'd done that really endeared him to the god was make him laugh, exactly like this—but he didn't think the joke was *that* funny.

"You know," Onyx told him, "I normally wouldn't? The whole point of the Roads doing this is that I *can't*; I'm just a specter projected from your own thoughts, with access to a part of you you don't have.

"But—very conveniently for you—the Onyx you knew would give exactly *zero shits* about rules like 'Don't just tell him what he's supposed to do next.'" Onyx grinned at him. "So the answer is this: you have a connection to Aurum, and that has granted you a skill. That connection by *no means* has to be restricted to only Aurum.

"The gods have been quiet for too long, Sev." Onyx's voice settled down into something more serious. "If we're going to stand a chance at this at all, we need to step up. And there are plans in motion to get them to do that. But all the divinity we've saved would be useless without an avatar to act through.

Most divine connections with most clerics would just bleed divinity like water; it's an absolute waste.

"You, though? Your connection with Aurum doesn't leak a single bit. It's why he has so much freedom to act. So: *make more connections.*"

Sev opened his mouth to respond, but Onyx was already gone, and the tunnel was opening up in front of him into a small clearing—a tiny room, set up right in the middle of nowhere, with a bed and a prayer mat and a steaming cup of coffee. Sev raised an eyebrow just slightly.

He knew just where to start.

If Aurum wanted to age . . . who better to start with than the God of Time himself?

CHAPTER 25

TIMELESS CONNECTIONS

Sev

The *process* of forging a connection was more complicated than Onyx had implied. Sev strained at it for a moment, trying to feel out the connection he already had with Aurum—his divine sense helped, allowing him to feel out that tiny thread in reality that signified his connection to a god.

One for Aurum, and another one for Onyx. The one for Onyx was stronger by far, and he tried to model the new connection he was forging based on that. A hint of divinity, guided by a whisper of prayer . . .

> **[You have regained a skill—[Divinity Manipulation]]**
> **[Divinity Manipulation] [Active Skill] [Grade: 1]**
> **Manipulate divinity.**

Regained?

Sev didn't remember ever having a skill like this. He didn't know it was possible to lose skills in the first place.

Did you mean what you said? Aurum's voice was small and timid in his head, much smaller than the Aurum he had spoken to in the tunnels. He didn't know how he'd ever been fooled. *About helping me . . . grow up. I want to grow up.*

I meant what I said, Sev answered gently. *But give me time.*

First, a prayer.

The God of Time went by the name of Tempus. Sev knelt carefully on the prayer mat, paying attention to the soft crackle of the threaded bamboo beneath his knees, to the rough texture of the woven grass.

Any other priest might have taken the time to meditate on that feeling—on the thought of the passage of time, the cycle that carried it from seed to grass to harvest.

Sev took his time to meditate on it just long enough to feel the first threads of a divine connection open up with the god. He seized upon it then, opening the connection just a little bit more, and sending a rather impossible-to-ignore prayer that consisted of just a few words.

Hey! Nice to meet you.

. . . No one said it had to be a *good* prayer. He had technically been a lot wordier in his first message to Onyx, but different times called for different measures.

There was a long pause—not because Tempus hadn't heard him, and not because he had chosen not to respond to the indignity of the message; Sev would have felt either reaction through the divine connection they now shared. The feeling he got was one of surprise, curiosity, and cautious interest.

. . . You are a new priest of Time? Curiosity dominated in the god of Time's response. Tempus's divine voice was slow and ponderous, like he took his time with every word and thought.

Not exactly. Sev let his embarrassment show through the connection. *I am a priest of Onyx. God of, uh, sculptures.*

I have not heard of him. There was a small pause before Tempus responded, but Sev got the impression that far more time had passed for the god of time than it had for him.

He is . . . forgotten. A hint of moroseness bled through the connection before Sev could stop it. He didn't consider what he'd done a failure, exactly, but it said a lot that no one remembered Onyx, despite his attempts. The god was alive . . . and that was all he could say, really.

Time gives space for many things to be forgotten, Tempus responded.

I didn't mean it quite like that, Sev said, but he allowed the topic to flow past him. Tempus didn't seem all that interested in discussing Onyx, and he couldn't blame the guy. *I have a request. Uh, I don't want it to seem like I'm contacting you just to get something out of you, though. Even though that's technically what I'm doing?*

Is that not the reason most mortals pray to a god? Tempus sounded amused now, and in spite of himself, Sev chuckled.

I suppose, he answered. *I don't want to be like them, but it seems inevitable, to a certain degree.*

Time heals all wounds, Tempus reassured him—at least, that was what Sev *thought* he was trying to do.

I need to forge more connections with the gods, Sev said. He let out a small sigh. *In the pursuit of power, I suppose, which kinda means my motives are in question?*

It seems to me that you have little choice, Tempus observed. If nothing else, he seemed to enjoy Sev's philosophical meandering—Sev could feel it through their connection. Tempus was *engaged.* This was the type of conversation he enjoyed, and a type of conversation he hadn't had for a long, long time. *If you are in need of power, and must contact others to gain that power, then you must do so—but the manner in which you choose to do so matters, does it not?*

Compromised motives, but if I do my best to act in good faith . . . Sev mused. *And maybe it's okay to ask for help, even from people I don't know.*

I would posit that is the foundational purpose of society.

Well, I don't know about that, Sev responded with a laugh. *I wish it were, though. Maybe we'll get it there, step by step.*

Sev paused and felt a familiar ache take over—a soul-deep exhaustion that seemed out of line with what he had experienced. He paused for a moment, his connection with Tempus allowing him to take a step back and examine that emotion.

It was his own, and yet it felt so strangely foreign.

We have greater troubles? Tempus asked, surprising him. He'd no doubt felt the sensation through their connection.

Yeah. Sev waited a long moment after responding, hoping the god would have something else to say; when Tempus simply waited in turn, he continued, a little hesitant. *But before that . . . could I ask for a favor? A personal one.*

Asking a favor of a god before doing him one in turn? Tempus chuckled. *You are a bold one.*

Do you happen to know the God of Gold? Aurum?

He is like a little brother to me, Tempus answered, sounding surprised—perhaps even a touch defensive.

He wishes to grow older, Sev said.

The connection went dead. Sev feared for a moment that Tempus had cut it off entirely, but that wasn't the case—the god had simply clamped down *hard,* preventing any of his emotions from leaking through the makeshift bond.

Sev waited.

He had time.

And this was the God of Time, after all.

He didn't judge. He could think of a half dozen reasons for Tempus to react like this, from suspicion to guilt to fear; it didn't mean that any of those reasons were right.

After a long moment, the connection began to lift.

And you think I can help him, Tempus said. *Why?*

You're the God of Time, Sev answered. *I figured you would know why gods cannot age, at least.*

... You do not suspect me.

No? What reason would you have to prevent other gods from aging? Sev couldn't keep the perplexed tone out of his mental voice.

No reason I could think of, and yet, Tempus answered, just a hint of dryness in his voice.

I only thought you might be able to help, Sev said. *But I'm guessing this is a bigger problem than I realized.*

By leagues, Tempus said, and for the first time, the god's voice came across as *exhausted.* Sev instinctively reached out, as if he could catch the poor guy as he slumped over—though of course, they were nowhere near one another. Tempus sent a feeling of amused appreciation through their connection, nonetheless. *The gods often come to me for a solution, and I do not have one. I do not have one for Aurum, either. I am sorry.*

Do you know why, at least? Sev asked.

I have my theories, Tempus said. *The simplest among them being that gods age on a timescale far greater than that of mortals; that I am too weak and cannot shift gods forward in time enough that they would age.*

Or perhaps gods, creatures of divinity that we are, must represent an aspect: perhaps that aspect remains unchanging always, unable to grow or shift.

Or perhaps our aspect is represented in civilization, and that civilization must grow in order for us to grow in turn.

I cannot act to change any of these things. Tempus ended his little spiel with what felt like a godly sigh. Sev could practically feel the shrug in his words, a touch morose and stretched in time.

But you made it sound like this is a problem, Sev said. *That Aurum is not the only god trapped like this.*

He is not, Tempus confirmed. *Of the one hundred fifteen gods I know of, thirty-four of them are children. It is not a majority ... but it is too many. Often, their worshippers are few and far between, and their priests are rarely strong enough to connect with the divine realm to see them for who—for what—they are.*

Their angels try to protect them, but their ability to do so is limited, and their understanding of mortals even more so. Tempus hesitated. *I saw what happened with Aurum. I am sorry I could not do more to prevent it. To reach out and interfere with another god ... it costs us. And I did not—do not—have that power.*

You saw what happened? Sev asked. There was an urgency in his voice that Tempus caught nearly immediately, though the only reaction from him was confusion. *Did you see the whole thing?*

. . . The angel was reprimanded and sent home, were they not? Tempus frowned. *There is more to the story. But I did not see it, if that is the case.*

Infolock. Sev practically hissed out the word, even projecting it through their connection. A distinct frustration claimed him. *I don't know how they work with gods.*

We know what our subjects know, for the most part, Tempus said. *There are exceptions. It costs us divinity.*

A lot of things cost you divinity, Sev said. *What* is *divinity?*

Ah, Tempus said, and now there was something of a smile in his voice. *That is the question, isn't it?*

Sev waited. . . . *Are you going to answer it?*

I do not know the answer. Sev could feel Tempus shrugging through their link, and he almost groaned in frustration. *It is a source of power. A currency. It replenishes naturally to us, whether we are ascended or ever-present. It was a lot more powerful once, but . . . it costs divinity to reject your system.* A small frown. *A strange circumstance.*

Strange indeed, Sev echoed, but his mind was racing.

The gods didn't know about what was happening.

He'd known that on some level. Aurum hadn't known, and the temple priests had been eager to find out about the dungeon when he had first returned from its formation; it made sense, too, that they were trying to convert him to their cause. If gods knew what their followers did . . .

That felt a little invasive, actually. He understood the math but didn't necessarily like it.

What could he tell Tempus, though?

Only one way to find out.

Tempus, Sev began, and he felt something in the divine connection begin to tense—like the god knew that something was coming. Far away, he felt something slamming down on the connection like a guillotine, and he could only guess that it was the grip of the system.

But he was *here.* In Vex's bonus room, a world intentionally made as far away from the system as possible. On top of that, he was in the Roads, and the Roads were even more isolated; the power the system had here was weaker than it had ever been.

So Sev told Tempus everything.

The benefit of a divine connection was that there could be no room for doubt; he opened the connection fully, allowing the god to read directly from his soul. *The universe is ended,* he said, in so many thoughts and impressions, the images of his journey flashing along the connection they shared. *The gods are being sacrificed to preserve what remains. Aurum and Onyx are fighting to find another way. We cannot do it without help.*

There was a long pause that wasn't long at all. Sev had the impression that Tempus had spent a touch of divinity to manipulate time—to process, to verify, to do his needed research.

When the god returned, he went right down to business.

You are not as strong as you could be, Tempus said. *Let me show you what you can become.*

CHAPTER 26

GODLY INTERVENTION

Sev

Time splintered.

In front of Sev stood an older man—mid-forties or mid-fifties, perhaps. He wore the flowing robes of a priest of the God of the Sun—with the full title capitalized in Sev's head, even, because he couldn't *not*. Power poured out of him in waves.

"**In the light of the sun,**" the priest intoned. They were the words of an incantation, a prayer. "**None may fall.**"

And it was the truth.

The man led an army. Tempus led Sev high up into the sky so he could see the battle for himself; there were at least a thousand men, if not more, involved in an outright *war*. Sev didn't recognize the equipment or the banners of any of the men involved, and even the landscape seemed unfamiliar, for all that it was clearly a part of Obreve.

What he did see was that none of them died—no matter how hard they were struck, even with their limbs and heads cleaved off, they kept fighting. Ghostly trails of light filled in where heads or arms had once been and simply . . . kept fighting.

It was an awe-inspiring display of power, but Sev felt a deep discomfort stirring in his stomach.

"When did this happen?" he asked quietly.

"In ages past," Tempus answered. The god stood next to him, a stately figure dressed in blue-silver robes; in place of a head, he had a vortex of time. Sev could hear the steady *tick-tock* of a clock every time he glanced too long at Tempus, and perhaps that was for the best—time seemed to lose all meaning when he stared for a fraction of a second too long. He could almost feel the way causality sped up around him, grounded only by the sound that echoed in his mind.

"You can reach back beyond the last two hundred years?" Sev asked. He wondered if Tempus's power could breach the End like that, pulling back things that had already been erased.

Tempus dashed his hopes when he shook his head. "No," he said. "Not without help. This is but a small piece of history, recovered when one of my priests—alongside one of the Platinum rankers of Anderstahl—delved deep into their Prime Dungeon and retrieved a fragment of the past . . . though we have been finding fewer and fewer of those of late."

A small glance to Sev, and the priest felt the weight of eternity pressing down on him. Just for an instant. "Now you know why," Sev said quietly.

"Indeed I do," Tempus answered, his voice grave. "I have tried to speak to the other gods about this, and I cannot; they do not recognize my words when I try. But the good news is that one of your allies appears to be reaching out to the gods to spread word, so you are not alone in this quest."

That was good to know, at least.

A moment passed. The army beneath them continued to fight, though half of the priest's army was clearly *dead,* though they hadn't fallen. All that was left of them were specters of glittering light, fighting for all they were worth. The priest didn't seem at all perturbed by this, and that was perhaps the most disturbing part of it all for Sev—that he seemed to feel nothing for the deaths of so many men.

Perhaps that was because he intended to bring them back, but . . . as far as Sev could tell, none of the divine magic here interacted with the *souls* of any of the people. They wicked away into the air as soon as their owners died, caught quickly by threads of divinity and drawn somewhere Sev couldn't see.

Even more curiously, Sev sensed no interference from the system. He couldn't know if any of the soldiers below were using system skills or not, of course, but it didn't seem like they were. There was none of the *strangeness* that he had come to associate with the use of a system skill.

The soldiers were many times stronger than most, certainly, but that didn't seem to be the result of system-given stats—rather, he saw the distinct glow that he'd come to associate with mana wrapped around their arms and legs as they fought, like they were reinforcing their bodies with mana.

The Priest of the Sun still stood impassive at the back of it all, watching his army fight tooth and nail against their enemy. Sev couldn't tell what or who that enemy was, though he tried—it was like whatever had been recorded in this fragment of history was simply missing one entire side of the conflict.

All he could see of them were twisted fragments of color, flashes of wing and stone and fire.

Where they clashed, light erupted. People died and rose again, golden-bright figures waging a fierce battle like they were fighting for their lives.

It would have been a beautiful sight if not for all the death and carnage involved.

The Priest of the Sun wielded a staff of sunstone and starlight. He wasn't fast or strong, but he moved with precision. Sev saw the divine energy fluctuating around him with every step he took, and watched the contemptuous face the priest gave his enemies as they approached him.

Three in particular that sneaked their way past his army. Three in particular that were represented by larger clouds of possibility; Sev could not see what they were, but he could see that they were *strong*. He could see the magic they wielded, the way dark-red fragments of crystalline mana trailed around behind them every time they made a move to attack.

A storm of magic erupted.

Three weapons inscribed with glyphs—Sev saw those in remarkable detail—thrust forward, each carrying with them the force of a spell that could devastate a mountain; the power of each spell was such that he could feel what they were, even without being their target.

Magic was an idea imprinted on the mana, and the mana *sang* with that collective ontological weight. Here was a spear that accumulated gravity mana, strong enough it could visibly bend light; here was a sword that rang with sound mana, loud enough to crack the earth around it; here was a chain that carried a freezing nothing, ice mana that had deepened so much it stole all the energy from anything it touched.

A barrier of sunlight shone around the priest. He looked unconcerned. Sev knew for a fact that his barriers would have shattered in an instant under just one of those attacks, let alone three. The divinity pressed into that priest's barrier should have been far from enough, and yet—

And yet.

"**The light of the sun washes away all sin**," the priest intoned. Time seemed to slow as he spoke. He *should* have been struck before he even opened his mouth, and yet the divine energy building did something strange, building in cadence with his words.

His words lent strength to his beliefs, and his beliefs lent strength to his magic.

All three attacks did nothing.

Sev could almost feel the stunned confusion in the air, though the Priest of the Sun's expression remained as serene and slightly contemptuous as ever. Three weapons faltered, as if their owners didn't know what to do now that their attacks had failed. They had not conceived of the possibility of failure.

The priest waved an arm and smiled an almost chilling, distant smile. "**We are all but stardust**," he said.

Just like that, all three of his opponents vanished. It was so sudden and anticlimactic it seemed unreal, and yet Sev knew it wasn't, because he'd seen something most others wouldn't.

He'd seen how that magic *worked*.

A small piece of divine magic—of Sun divinity, specifically—broke past the natural barriers of the soul, of each person's sense of self. In that moment of vulnerability imparted on them by their shock, the Sun divinity took over and imposed itself upon them.

What they were was written into reality as a concept, as a rewriting of their souls. That small piece of divinity took it over like a parasite, flooding every aspect of them and turning it into little more than stardust and sunlight, killing not only their bodies but overwriting their souls.

Sev felt a little sick.

What anyone else would have seen, more likely than not, was three individuals being instantaneously incinerated by a brief flash of sunlight, but what Sev understood was that something far more horrifying had happened. And yet, in that horror, a small piece of understanding broke loose.

"Mana is memory," he said out loud, tasting the words. "And magic is the expression of a concept from the infinite record that is mana."

Tempus shot him a questioning look, and he ignored it.

"Divinity is the concept itself, imposed on reality," Sev muttered.

It explained why reality anchors tore gods apart to fix themselves. It shed new light on what reality shards were, even. He'd never sensed a hint of divine energy about them, but if it was encased in a shell and hidden from him . . .

Tempus gave him a strange look. "Are you all right?"

"I don't want to see this." Sev felt the answer emerge before he could stop himself, and he winced slightly at how brusque his words were. Tempus didn't react, waiting patiently for him to explain himself even as the battlefield froze around them, and Sev sighed as he tried to search for the words.

"He's strong," Sev said, gesturing at the image of the Priest of the Sun. "But this is . . . wrong. He's not a healer. He's *healing*, but everyone around him is dying. This isn't who I want to be."

"Ah." Tempus barely seemed to have considered the possibility; he looked around at the battlefield as if he was considering it for the first time. He winced. Just slightly, but enough for Sev to notice. "The time scale of mortal lives often makes such conflicts seem . . . irrelevant to me. I went for the greatest display of power I had in my collection. I apologize."

"It's fine." Sev waved it off. "It taught me something valuable about divinity, and whatever's happening here seems . . . I don't know how long ago this happened."

"Eighteen hundred years," Tempus said.

Before the end of the universe, then. Before the system existed? Sev frowned, looking out over the battlefield again; somehow, the fact that he couldn't see who the enemy was—if they could be called that—felt . . . significant.

"You would like something else, then?" Tempus asked.

"I learned what I needed to," Sev said finally. "And I know what is possible, even if this isn't the direction I want to go in. I know that I can be more. I just need to choose my own direction—one that isn't this."

"Do you have an idea of what you wish to be?" Tempus's voice was mild, curious. Sev thought about it for a moment, even as the scene around him faded, and he found himself once more kneeling on that prayer mat in the Roads.

Tempus was no longer next to him, but the divine connection between them remained steady and strong—perhaps even stronger than before. Part of it almost seemed to be beginning to anchor itself to him the way Aurum's connection was anchored to him.

Yes, Sev answered, this time in his mind. It took a moment of contemplation for the desire to solidify into something certain.

If there was anything that watching that war had taught him—if there was any one thing he had to take away from it—it was the simple understanding of how he felt about conflict on a scale such as this. He didn't know if it was something he had understood before and lost, with all his memories drained into his healing, but it didn't matter—he knew himself now.

I want the power to prevent conflicts like that before they even begin, Sev said. *To forge peace where it should be impossible. To search time and pluck out the threads of conflict before they happen.*

But in the event that I cannot . . . and that will happen. Not every conflict can be prevented, and I cannot be useless if I have to fight. Sev's mind briefly went back to the fight with Irvis, and the way he'd been relegated to the role of support; he didn't *mind,* but he'd been powerless. His shields hadn't done enough, and his true support skills were lacking.

In the event that I cannot, Sev said, *I need a better way to heal. A way to fight. And a way to support. A way to take the strengths of those around me and make them even greater.*

Tempus hummed in response, and Sev felt the passage of time wrap around him. *I may have some suggestions.*

CHAPTER 27

SPLIT PATHS

Misa

"All right, now I just gotta choose a path . . ."

Misa stared at the five split paths in front of her. Each path seemed almost entirely identical, and even the small differences they did have were entirely cosmetic. It wasn't like a scuff on the dirt of the tunnel was likely to be relevant, and even if it was, she had no way of knowing *how* it was relevant.

In theory, she had no way of knowing what was at the end of each path.

In *theory*.

She did still have Endless Echoes, after all. She could see and gain information from her alternate selves, from decisions she might have made, a few minutes into the past. She'd trained it up enough now that she could go a full ten minutes back; that would have to be enough.

For ten minutes, she waited, standing on the precipice of the path in front of her. Then she triggered Endless Echoes five times, one after the other, an alternate version of her splitting off into each path—all while her real self remained at the entrances, observing the memories fed into her.

It was a good thing she did, too.

—∾—

Misa One—she thought of herself as One, anyway—led herself down the leftmost path.

This was . . . an odd experience. She knew she was an echo, a product of a system skill, and wasn't *that* a strange thought? The sequence of events in her mind was almost jarring—she remembered contemplating using Endless Echoes to make her way down each of the paths and then just abruptly deciding to go down the leftmost one.

The strangest part was the conscious awareness that that hadn't really been *her* decision. In battle, the effect wasn't nearly so obvious. Balanced on a razor's edge of choices and split-second decisions, her echoes never really noticed that they were echoes, and so the memories that fed back into her were never *aware* in the way she was now.

No doubt Misa Prime would be deeply uncomfortable once the truth of this revealed itself to her. Misa chuckled at the thought; she wasn't as bothered by the idea of being a temporary version of herself as she supposed she might have been. Whether that was an effect of the skill itself or whether she was just comfortable with the idea of being temporarily split from and then reunited with herself, she didn't know.

She didn't spend too much time thinking on it, anyway. Time spent thinking about that was time she *could* spend investigating this tunnel, and One needed to make sure she found out everything she could, so that her "real" self could make the optimal choice when the time came.

First things first. One glanced behind her to see what happened to the path once she chose one, and her eyebrows furrowed slightly. The entrance that led into this tunnel was gone. As far as she could see behind her was a straight, smooth tunnel. No going back, it seemed.

Good to know.

The tunnel stretched ahead of her, too, as smooth and identical as the main path had been—but as she walked deeper, she found the walls slowly changing. The light-brown stone darkened into gray, and then into pitch-black stone with glittering specks of light within it. Looking into the stone felt almost like looking into the stars.

Now that she thought about it, it reminded her of the material that that one dungeon was made of—the dungeon that had kicked off this whole journey. She remembered the starlight stones and the way the trap had triggered, flames guttering out at her. She remembered the way she'd had to step in front of a group of skeletons to shield them from the flame, and how she'd failed at even that.

She remembered how she'd nearly died.

She should have been dead, really. It was sheer luck that the bonus room had triggered, transporting her there instead; sheer luck that the conditions for it were her own death.

And yet . . . she still didn't have another way to handle that situation. Block or die. Misa had learned to do a lot of little tricks with her skill, but it was still one skill. Perhaps she could have thrown a weapon back, used the block to teleport herself out of the way of the trap, but that would've left the others there to die.

She needed better options. She needed more skills.

For the first time in a long time, Misa felt *dissatisfied*. She'd found ways to use everything she had, certainly. She'd gained a certain degree of versatility with the ability to draw upon her future to summon simulacrums of the members of her home village. As they grew in strength, so would she.

She didn't want to rely on them, though. They were all extended family to her, and none of them had signed up for the kind of fights she was always getting herself into. They would agree to help her, as they always did, but what right did she really have to drag them into what she was doing?

Though she supposed she was also fighting for their survival. It still left a foul taste in her mouth.

Lost in thought, One almost didn't notice when she ran into an open cavern. It was the way the *sound* changed that alerted her to it, and even then it was just a subtle quality—a change in the way her footsteps echoed against the floor, the way her breathing resonated in the chamber.

She looked up.

The tunnel expanded into an enormous, cylindrical clearing. The sky—or something that *looked* like the sky—was visible as a bright blue expanse above, though not a drop of that blue touched the walls or the floor of the cave she was in. It made the lighting look strange, like she was staring at a painting of a scene that wasn't quite right.

What drew her attention more than the strangeness of the light, though, was the pedestal at the center—and the weapon that hovered above it, floating in the air.

One approached it with what could have been called a certain reverence. She knew, in the back of her mind, that the other paths would likely carry similar weapons. She knew that the "real" Misa choosing this path wasn't set in stone. It wasn't even particularly likely.

It didn't change the fact that scythes were *fucking cool*, though.

Ten minutes had almost passed. If there was a trap, she needed to pick it up now so her real self would see the results; she stepped forward, grabbing for the scythe . . .

Notifications blistered past her vision. She tried to get a close look at them all so she could make an informed choice. The text was hard to read; it didn't even have the familiar blue boxes, like the notifications came from an older iteration of the system.

The text itself seemed to confirm that thought.

[You have seen a new Path!]
[ERROR—The Path system is locked and its features have been deprecated. Please see an Administrator for assistance.]
[ERROR—Path locked. Display anyway? Y/N]
[Displaying Path . . .]

[Path of the Reaper—Silver]
A Reaper teleports around the battlefield, bringing death and chaos with them. Use that death to shield your allies—call forth the specters of your foes to take attacks, and send those same specters to do your bidding.

Starting Skills:
[Death Sight]
[Elsewhere, Elsewhen]
[Soul Shroud]

[0 / 10 points to next advancement.]

Requirements:
[Teleport at least three times—COMPLETE]
[Resurrect at least five undead—COMPLETE]
[Kill at least 5,000 living things—Computing . . .]
[. . .]
[COMPLETE]
[Path requirements have been met.]

—∾—

Take the second path from the left, something inside Misa told her; she went that way without a second glance at the other four paths, feeling them dissolve behind her as she walked. She almost frowned, glancing back—it was strange that she'd felt it at all, like a distant rumble in her soul, closing other paths . . .

It took her a moment more before she understood.

She was the second, then.

Second, as she decided to call herself—it would make distinguishing the memories easier later on—spared the tunnel she was in a quick glance before taking rapid, confident strides forward; she only had ten minutes to figure out what was at the end of this tunnel, after all. There was every chance that ten minutes would not be enough, even, and if that happened then she would simply have to gamble on a path with whatever information she could gather.

She tried to keep her eyes peeled, but there honestly wasn't all that much to see.

The rock felt like it was getting denser beneath her feet, perhaps. The air felt like it was getting a little bit denser with mana, and the temperature felt like it was slowly going up. Second felt a bead of sweat dripping down the back of her neck, and she raised her mace cautiously.

She didn't think she would be getting attacked, but it was better to be prepared.

Ultimately, though, she wasn't attacked. She came upon an empty room that was lit only by the glow of a pool of magma; it surrounded a spire of rock that held a weapon that was, of all things, a shield that glowed with heat.

She, too, stepped forward to take up the shield and found herself bombarded by notifications.

[You have seen a new Path!]
[ERROR—The Path system is locked and its features have been deprecated. Please see an Administrator for assistance.]
[ERROR—Path locked. Display anyway? Y/N]
[Displaying Path . . .]

[Path of the Sunshield—Bronze]
A Sunshield harnesses the power of heat and flame to defend their allies. Melt any weapon with the strength of your shield, and imbue friend and foe alike with a blistering aura --the power of the sun is yours to command.

[Calculating . . .]

Path upgrade requirements met.

[Path of the Phoenix—Platinum]
The Phoenix harnesses the power of fire not only for defense but for offense and healing. Incredibly versatile, the Phoenix's path also grants one control over Fire-aspect mana, greatly increasing the potential range of skills you may acquire.

Starting Skills:
[Kinetic Conversion]
[Reborn in the Ashes]
[Fire Aspect Body]

[0 / 10 Points to next advancement.]
Requirements:
[Experience being on fire at least once—COMPLETE]
[Die at least twice—COMPLETE]
[Sacrifice yourself for others—Computing . . .]
[Path requirements have been met.]

—∞—

Three's path and memories were much the same as Second's. For her, the tunnel's stone slowly faded away into nothing, such that she eventually felt like she was walking on empty air; her knowledge that her memories would simply be fed back into her primary self kept her going. If this path was a trap, then she needed to experience it so that Misa would know not to take it.

What she didn't expect was to find a bow floating in the midst of that nothingness. There was no quiver around, no arrow nearby or even a place to nock an arrow into the bow—but when she pulled the string taut, she still felt a strange energy reverberating with her fingers.

Notifications poured out about a locked path, and then the actual path was displayed.

[Path of the Empty Archer—Gold]
The Empty Archer is an archer only in name. The arrows you will wield are not physical things; they are conceptual attacks, infecting your target with whatever you hold in your mind. Be aware that these arrows can be turned against you and are only as strong as your mind.

Starting Skills:
[Tier 1—Conceptual Arrow]
[Archer's Eye]
[Uncanny Shot]

—∞—

Four was either Four or Two. She had no idea; it depended on whether her other selves had chosen to start from the right or the left. Four seemed like the more likely bet, though.

Her chosen path made her slow down after a few minutes, though. She grimaced a little bit, forcing herself to push on—but the way the rock beneath her turned to a red slurry was not encouraging, and she was starting to get a good idea of what likely lay at the end of this path.

Hopefully, the other versions of her had better luck with their own. She didn't think she'd be selecting this one.

She was still hesitant, even when she grabbed the handle of the pulsating flesh-blade that hung in the air before her and it wrapped its tendrils around her wrist. The notifications about there being a locked path system flashed by, and then:

[**Path of the Aberrant Berserker—Platinum**]

Your contact with aberrations and abominations has changed you, and you have chosen to step even closer to that realm. You share a deep, personal bond with your blade, and it will grow stronger as you do.

Starting Skills:

[**Biomass Forge**]

[**Blood Absorption**]

[**Twisted Fuel**]

"Yeah, no," Four said. She tore off the blade and chucked it into the blood pool at her feet, then left.

CHAPTER 28

FIFTH CHOICE

Misa

Five.

She was *probably* Five. The fifth and last simulated iteration, judging by the strange impulse she had to choose the rightmost tunnel. There was every chance she wasn't, of course, and so she proceeded into the path with all due caution; there was no reason to risk herself unnecessarily.

Something felt wrong, though. An unpleasant buzz trickled under her skin from the moment she stepped into the tunnel. Five glanced back and felt her heart skip a beat; instead of a tunnel behind her, leading back where she'd come, there was only a blank wall.

No turning back. The message was pretty clear. She wondered if her other iterations had faced the same, or if she was the only one that had to face what was starting to feel more and more like a trap.

She ventured down the tunnel anyway. The Roads weren't giving her much of a choice otherwise; the best she could do was try to be careful. She tried blocking, just in case there was some sort of invisible spell being used on her—but if there was, the skill didn't qualify it as an attack.

So much for that. Endless Echoes was pretty flexible, but the only things it blocked were things that violated personal autonomy in some way—those were what it qualified as "attacks."

And so all she could do was walk.

And walk.

And walk.

Her time was limited if she was an echo—she'd only managed to push the skill to about ten minutes, and she was well aware that the time she had to find *something* was running out. Misa's walk quickly accelerated into a run. Even if the only thing that happened was her running into a trap, that was information that her prime self could use.

There was the barest flicker of a notification before her time was up.

[**Path of the Endless—ERROR**]

—

Misa, waiting back at the start of the fork, winced as the memories of five different iterations of her slammed into mind. "Right," she muttered to herself. "Maybe using that skill five times at once is a bit much."

She turned her attention to the memories.

It was a little troubling that all five of her iterations had managed to conclude that they were iterations at all—that they were applications of Endless Echoes. She hadn't really had to confront the idea that her other selves might be fully cognizant of their natures, and she wasn't sure she wanted to.

Now wasn't the time to dwell on that, anyway. At least her other selves hadn't shown any inclination toward having an existential meltdown or otherwise planning to take over the "prime" timeline. She'd assumed she wouldn't be like that, of course, but she was more aware than most—when push came to shove, when faced with a situation that was *real* as opposed to a simple thought experiment . . .

It was sometimes a lot harder to do what you needed to do.

Misa discarded those thoughts and focused on the important thing.

Paths. That was new, and the way the system displayed them to her was new too; the problem was the announcement that this was a *deprecated* feature. Why were the Roads showing them to her? How did the Roads even know that making contact with those weapons would be significant to the system in any way?

The system was supposed to be more isolated than ever here; it didn't *exist* in this echo except for where it was attached to her and her friends. Derivan had more or less already ascertained that it was her own anchor that was keeping their connection to the system intact.

It was her anchor that the four of them were now connected to, separate from the system that everyone else labored under.

Did that make a difference? There was every chance that it did. Dungeons were molded by their environments, and those dungeons fed into the anchors that they held. Maybe that made her anchor special now that she was the one hosting and feeding it. Maybe her anchor was on their side now. So to speak.

Misa's lips twisted a little at that thought, and she chuckled to herself. Too much speculation, she decided. She needed to decide what to *do*.

Even if her anchor was letting her look at this Path system, that system was still locked away from her. She was curious about it—it seemed like a way she could grow beyond the class she had been assigned—even if there was a message tagged on about the Path being locked.

That made the last tunnel all the more notable. She hadn't seen a message about the Path feature being locked or deprecated. All she'd seen was the barest flicker of a name before the memory caught up to her and cut out.

Why?

There was nothing about the last tunnel that should have made it significant. Misa glared at it suspiciously, as if a powerful enough glare could force it to reveal its secrets to her, but nothing changed. It was, as far as she could tell, completely identical to the other tunnels.

There was a part of her that was attracted to the idea of the Path of the Empty Archer; Reaper and Sunshield were both too close to what she could already do, Phoenix seemed too focused on *herself* and was an even worse choice than Sunshield, unless she could keep blocking, dying, coming back to life, and blocking again, which . . .

. . . Which was maybe a possibility? That was what [**Reborn in the Ashes**] implied. But that could also have been a skill that would only bring her back to life if she burned to death, or if she died of old age. It was a huge risk to take for a small upgrade to her existing kit, especially when she had Sev to heal her.

She wasn't going to touch Aberrant Berserker at all.

Empty Archer was most compelling. It was the option that would allow her the most flexibility, and it added to her kit rather than fleshing out what she could already do. There was a benefit in specializing even more, she supposed, but she was about as specialized as she could be already. The only thing she really needed in that department was a way to deal with rapid attacks or too many attacks at once, and Empty Archer seemed like it might have a solution for her there, too, depending on what concepts she could load the arrows up with.

There were only two problems. One, it was locked; she wasn't particularly concerned about that part, though, since she was relatively certain Derivan's Patch stat would easily unlock it. There was every chance that she was wrong, but if that were the case, then the choice in front of her was no real choice at all. It seemed strange that the Roads that purported to lead her where she needed to *go* would lead her to multiple completely pointless upgrades.

The second problem was the Path of the Endless—the one that, she realized, matched the name of her skill. [**Misa's Endless Echoes**].

She still grimaced every time she thought of the full skill name.

She could wait another ten minutes and then use the skill again, sending that copy of her as deep into the Path as she could. That was her *plan,* even, except she looked a little closer and realized the tunnels in front of her were closing. Not the paths within—just the entrances. The rock was folding in on itself.

It wants me to hurry up.

Misa half-growled under her breath. She hated being forced into decisions.

And then she thought of an idea.

[**An Anchor of Heart and Home**] allowed her to summon a copy of those villagers that lived in J'rokksur, her original home and village—not just a copy but a full simulacrum. The person summoned would control two bodies at once, and there was one possibility she hadn't ever tried before, mostly because she'd just never considered it.

But *she* was a part of her village too. She was a part of J'rokksur. That was the reason the skill functioned the way it did.

So what if she summoned *herself*?

It might have been a stupid idea . . . but she tried it anyway.

The skill resisted her. There were futures she couldn't sacrifice because they were too far away; here, in this tunnel, her future was restricted to five choices. Five roads. Five paths.

An easy enough choice to make.

First went the Path of the Aberrant Berserker. That future was just as fraught as she thought it would be, full of blood and fighting; her friends held her back and kept her from becoming anything truly evil, but there was no reason they should have *had* to.

It wasn't enough. The skill was resisting; this wasn't its purpose, it seemed to say.

Next went the Path of the Reaper. That path was too much like her own already. She saw herself teleporting through the shadows, defending against powerful blows by pulling out the raw essence of the soul. None of that was *her*.

The skill began to give. She felt *something* wrap itself around her, raw Reality touching upon her core.

Last went the Path of the Phoenix. It was a good option, and she was sad to see it go, but this particular trick would only let her choose two.

Even then, there was no guarantee that the Path her doppelganger gained would transfer over to her. She suspected it would, though; experience points transferred correctly when she'd last tested it, although damage to health and status effects did not.

The skill gave. She felt *something* drain from her, and then her vision was suddenly split in two. She winced a bit at the split vision, a headache quickly manifesting, but she didn't care.

It worked.

"Mom was right," both of her selves muttered. "This *is* weird."

It took a little bit of maneuvering to stop both of her bodies from moving in the same direction every time she tried to operate one of them. She had no idea how her mother had been able to adapt to it so quickly. Some factor from her intuition skill, perhaps. But she got herself sorted and made her way down the two paths, her original self going down the third tunnel and her other self going down the fifth.

Misa almost expected the Roads to try to stop her, for one of the paths to slam closed. She expected *something* to go wrong.

Instead, the rock that had begun to close over each path pulled back slightly, as if encouraging her.

Somewhat perturbed but nevertheless willing to take it at face value, Misa made her way down the tunnels, keeping a close mental eye on what was happening in the Endless tunnel. She found the bow in one of them, grabbed ahold of it, and watched as the notifications poured out.

But that wasn't what she was interested in. She kept her mental focus on her other self, even as her surroundings faded and she found one of her selves back on the Roads.

The Path of the Endless was not nearly so easy. The notification popped up about ten minutes in, just as before.

[Path of the Endless—ERROR]
[Attempting to assign Path . . . ERROR]
[You are on the Path of the Endless. Good luck.]

CHAPTER 29

ENDLESS

Misa

Misa's awareness of her prime self faded. Something about the buzzing in the air drew her attention to this path—it wasn't that she didn't recognize she was still safe and sound in the middle of the Roads, but the more she went down this path, the more she found she couldn't split her focus.

She was *here*. Her ploy had succeeded, but the Roads had done something to her in turn, something that made her fully present in this body. If not for the tingling awareness in the back of her mind—the strange feeling of the ground pressing into her feet, even as she walked forward; the flicker of *lighting*, where she saw a tunnel much more brightly lit than the one she was in; the relatively cleaner scent of dirt compared to the sharp ozone that pervaded her nostrils here—she would have thought the Roads had somehow canceled her use of her skill and forced her back into one body.

That, thankfully, didn't seem to be the case. But the situation she was in didn't seem to be much better. The buzz continued to trickle under her skin, intensifying with every step. She didn't know if what she was feeling was *magic*, or if it was something else entirely. Some kind of test, perhaps.

What exactly was the Path of the Endless?

The notifications hovered in front of her, strangely immune to fading away. All the other ones had faded with time, and those that didn't she could ordinarily dismiss—but the one in front of her now refused to obey even the mental commands she gave it.

[YOU ARE ON THE PATH OF THE ENDLESS. GOOD LUCK.]

What did that *mean*?

She stepped forward anyway. *One foot after the other*, she told herself; she ignored the way the tunnel narrowed down around her, the way the light around her faded until she was walking forward in darkness and only darkness. She shut her eyes then, using a hand on the wall to keep herself steered straight—if there was no light, then there was no need for her to keep her eyes open.

Keeping her eyes closed helped her focus. It helped her *breathe*. It helped her ignore the way the buzzing reached down into her bones, making every step forward even harder still—

Until suddenly, it stopped.

Misa opened her eyes.

[**You have completed step 1 of the Path of the Endless.**]
[**You now qualify for Path of the Endless—Iron. Would you like to continue?**]

Misa snorted. "Is that even a question?" she asked, her voice semi-sarcastic. She allowed a grin to take over her features.

Okay. She had a better idea of where this was going now.

This was a *test*.

"Fuckin' bring it," she said.

—~—

The buzz returned and expanded into a sensation that was not unlike a thousand stabbing needles. Misa tried to block it about three times before giving up entirely—the Roads were preventing her from using the skill somehow, and she wasn't sure she wanted to keep testing them. If she was given reason to try again at some point, she would; right now, it seemed all the Path of the Endless wanted her to do was *endure*.

That couldn't be all there was to it, though. Pain was nothing. Misa had once fought until she died in the defense of her village, and the injuries she had taken at the time were so fraught and severe they had stayed with her even after she had somehow managed to survive.

She'd traveled on her own afterwards for *years*, and she hadn't found a proper healer until Sev.

It didn't matter how much pain or discomfort the Roads gave her.

Evidently, the Roads agreed.

[**You have completed Step 2 of the Path of the Endless.**]

[You now qualify for Path of the Endless—Bronze. Would you like to continue?]

"Obviously," Misa snorted.

She didn't really need to respond verbally. Whatever part of the system Paths operated on, it seemed to be an older version of it—it responded to her thoughts smoothly. It was almost better, even, except it must have been removed for a reason; too many people accidentally responding to a prompt by thinking it, perhaps.

Either way, her response prompted the path before her to change—and now she really started to wonder how much of this was the Roads and how much of it was the system.

The tunnel in front of her opened up into a cavern, not unlike what she remembered of the other paths—except this cavern held no weapon in the center, no pedestal upon which an item sat. The walls of the cave were the color of starlight and bluestone, with a shifting texture underneath that reminded her of the waves of a lake.

It was beautiful.

It also reminded her, rather starkly, of a dungeon that she'd been to when she'd traveled alone. It was a small, isolated dungeon that was out near the Outskirts—a dungeon she shouldn't have been to at all, really. The Adventurers' Guild hadn't directed her there, and there weren't any small towns or villages nearby that needed protection from the dungeon. All she could get from it were a few mana crystals and perhaps whatever loot the dungeon opted to give to her.

But she hadn't been there because of that. She'd been there because it was *dangerous*.

Those early days had not been kind to her. It was easier to lose herself to fights than to confront what had happened to her family, and while those days were behind her now—while she had her family *back*, which was not a sentence she had ever dared to hope she could even think . . .

Misa's features sharpened. Off in the distance, the scuttling of a very familiar type of monster greeted her.

<Level 15 Bluestone Crab>

They weren't high-level at all, for all that the dungeon was on the verge of breaking and sat at the edges of the Outskirts. Most dungeons in this area were at least Silver- or Gold-grade, and the only reason Misa had chosen this one was that it was a simple Bronze dungeon, with its monsters in the Iron range.

The part that made it Bronze—verging even on Silver—was not the power of its monsters at all.

The scuttling sound intensified.

It was the *number* of them.

In other words—the exact type of situation her abilities were least suited for.

Misa watched the wave of Bluestone Crabs crest the far corner of the cavern she was in and allowed a small smirk to take over the edge of her lips. Suited or not, it had been a long time since she had nearly died to them. She'd grown by leaps and bounds, not only in level but in personal skill.

It was only the fact that these were system monsters that disturbed her. Not a single thing she'd fought here had ever had a system tag attached to it before; this world was meant to be as detached from the system as possible. The fact that the Roads had produced something that could attach to the system meant it had produced something that attached to *her anchor*; she didn't know what to make of that. But it didn't change what she had to do.

The first crab scuttled up to her, pincers held out and ready to pinch. She remembered when she'd faced them down the first time—remembered the nervous tension coursing through her body at the sheer number of them. She hadn't been *afraid*, exactly, but it was here that she'd first learned her first important lesson after losing J'rokksur.

She didn't want to die.

Now, though . . . Misa was curious. She let the crab do as it wanted. She'd grown so much in the time since that she was certain she could beat them even without a weapon. The amount of damage they could do was paltry compared to her health.

Sure enough, she felt no more than a small pinch. Misa chuckled, bending down to give the angry crab a little pat on its shell even as it scuttled angrily at her. She hadn't even known the things could scuttle angrily.

And yet, strangely enough . . . the rest of the crabs didn't attack.

They gathered in a circle around her, keeping their pincers at the ready like they were ready to swarm her at any moment. The one she stood next to kept angrily grabbing at her with its claws, unaware that its attacks were doing little to no damage to her. Misa frowned and looked around at the circle of crabs, perplexed.

"Not gonna attack me?" she asked out loud. She wasn't expecting a response but somehow felt relieved anyway when she didn't get one. "Huh. Not gonna lie; y'all are pretty cute when you're not trying to kill me."

She felt something inside her healing.

This had been . . . her second near-death experience. She remembered scrambling to leave the dungeon as wave after wave of crabs poured after her. She remembered how *stubborn* she'd been at the time, continuing to fight long after it was in her best interest to leave. In the end, she'd only just made it out.

Was *this* the secret to the Bluestone Dungeon? Just . . . grab a crab and carry it with you?

On impulse, she picked up the crab, tucking it under an arm and adjusting carefully so it stopped pinching her. It settled for flailing wildly instead, and Misa snorted. She leveled her gaze at the crabs, stepped forward . . .

. . . and watched as they parted in front of her.

Huh.

[You have completed Step 3 of the Path of the Endless.]
[You now qualify for Path of the Endless—Silver. Would you like to continue?]

She'd assumed that the Path was testing her *endurance.* The first two steps had certainly implied that; they'd put her in a frame of mind to assume that the Path was all about lasting as long as she could. First came her tolerance of discomfort, and then came her tolerance of pain.

The third step had tested neither of those things. They'd tested her spirit, if anything—put her in a situation that had formed one part of *who she was.* The Bluestone Dungeon was the reason she was so hard on Sev every time he fell into his self-destructive tendencies. The way he was willing to sacrifice aspects of himself . . .

It wasn't the same, exactly. Misa had been far more selfish.

But he reminded her of *her.*

She strode forward through the crabs, even as they all stared at her in something akin to reverence—it made her feel uncomfortable. There was something almost intelligent in their eyes, and she was reminded of a conversation she'd had with Derivan and Vex, near to the start of all of this. After Derivan had revealed who and *what* he was, and Vex had questioned the nature of intelligent monsters, and inquired after the possibility that those they deemed monsters might be *people* . . .

"You don't happen to be a person, do you?" Misa asked the crab under her arm.

It continued wiggling indignantly, and Misa sighed.

She wasn't entirely surprised when it dissolved out of existence—nor was she surprised when the next stage of the Path tested her by confronting her with a vision of her dead family. It slowed her down but far less than it would have a year ago.

Her family was back, and she'd found a new one to boot.

"Too far," she told the Path anyway, and knelt beside each body, allowing herself a moment to grieve for each one. The moment had been real to her, and it seemed disrespectful to walk past them. This memory was a part of who she was too.

That awarded her the fourth step and a path upgrade to Gold.

The fifth step—the one that Misa hoped would be the last, though she doubted it would be—was a reenactment of her fight with Irvis. This time, the Path showed her a vision of her *losing* that fight, of her friends dying in front of her. Her chest tightened, and a powerful tension rang through her body.

She almost, *almost* stepped into the role of her old self—the one that had fought Irvis and lost. But she shook her head.

"*No,*" she said, clearly and cleanly. Her gaze cut ahead and through the illusion, and she took a step forward; the image of her dead friends faded away like the morning mist.

She understood what the Path wanted from her now. It wanted her to define who she was. It was the Path of the Endless because the answer to that question was an ever-evolving one, comprised of all the choices she had ever made and all the choices she ever would make.

[You have completed Step 5 of the Path of the Endless, and have many more steps to go.]

"I know," Misa said. She wasn't as angry as she should have been, perhaps, for all the things the Path had shown her.

[You now qualify for Path of the Endless—Unranked. Your journey is your own. You have received your first skill.]
[New skill acquired: [Me, Myself, and I].]

CHAPTER 30

CLIMB

Vex

"Why . . . is this slope . . . so *steep*," Vex wheezed. He didn't know how long he'd been climbing. It hadn't mattered for the first hour or so—it had been tiring, but he was used to being tired! He traveled with three people, one of whom could cure his own exhaustion, another who was a physical monstrosity, and the third of whom was his boyfriend and didn't even have any muscles to feel tired with.

Talking to himself helped him feel better but changed nothing about the fact that he'd been climbing up a steep slope for *three hours*, and it had only been getting steeper.

"Where is this even going?" Vex grimaced. He dug his toes into the wall—the slope was soft, at least, and easy enough to make little footholds on. It really was getting steeper; he wasn't exactly climbing *vertically*, but he would be soon if this kept up.

There were spells he could use to help himself. He'd tried a couple of them, even. There was a small glyph he could paint on his hands and feet that would make them stickier, and another one with a Gravity aspect to it he could use to make himself lighter. He still didn't have any combination that would grant him flight, though, and he was starting to wonder if he needed to stop and spend his time trying to find one of those instead.

It turned out he needn't have worried. A few more steps later and he finally saw *something* in the distance, barely visible in the dim lighting provided to him—a thin line that implied the floor finally, *finally* leveled out ahead of him. Vex gathered all his remaining energy and ran up the rest of the slope as fast as he could, using his hands and tail to keep his balance when the steepness threatened to tip him over; he grasped the edge of the floor just as the slope would have turned into a vertical wall, and hauled himself up and over onto it.

Instantly, the lighting around him changed. Vex blinked a few times, startled at how *bright* it suddenly was.

The ground beneath him was no longer soft, claylike soil; instead, his claws tapped on the familiar feeling of a hardwood floor. Vex grimaced almost instinctively, lifting his feet to clean them before he tracked dirt onto the floor of the near-pristine library he found himself in—except he was suddenly and inexplicably clean.

Sure. He could accept that. That dirt had mostly been dirt-aspect mana anyway and not actually dirt; he could fully believe that it had simply chosen to dissipate.

What drew Vex's interest were the tall shelves around him, each one of them packed full with books. They were a good three times his height, and he had to squint to even be able to see the tops of the shelves. The library was illuminated by, near as Vex could tell, a ceiling that was made out of literal fire.

So it was a little bit difficult to look at.

"Where *am* I?" Vex muttered to himself. The words echoed more loudly than he'd expected, and he winced a bit, half-expecting a librarian to round the corner and reprimand him. When that didn't happen, he took a few cautious steps forward and picked a random book off of the nearest shelf.

The book's design was immaculately beautiful. He didn't *recognize* it—the style of the gold filigree on the tome was like nothing he'd seen before—but he recognized the effort that went into it, the precision that it took to etch the near-symmetrical design and then lay gold foil into it. There weren't even any traces of mana on the book—it was like it had been made entirely by hand.

He flipped it open and found an empty book. Every page in it was blank.

It was the same with the next book he checked, and the next, and the next—Vex felt increasingly frantic as he looked through the books. He didn't know *why* it felt so wrong that they were empty, only that it was *wrong*. A part of him knew the books should have been filled with stories and lore and history—

A hand fell on his shoulder, and the lizardkin jumped.

"They are gone." A solemn voice spoke, and Vex turned around to look at the speaker. They were humanoid, but that was where their familiarity with anything Vex recognized ended. Their skin was a mottled purple, and where their mouth should have been there were instead long, sinuous tendrils. They wore stately robes of black and red, outlined in the same gold that was laid so carefully into each book.

Their tendrils curled upward in an awkward approximation of a smile. "I apologize. I must have startled you; it would have been better if I introduced myself first, perhaps. Time has a habit of flying in here. I am afraid I am uncertain what the social norms are in this particular century.

"My name is Isolis." They took a step back and dipped forward into a slight bow. "I am the librarian, custodian, and historian here at Solar Lagrange 1. The name is an inside joke."

Vex stared blankly. "I'm Vex," he said, opting to leave out the rest of his titles. "Uh . . . adventurer. Do you mind telling me what this place is?"

"Solar Lagrange 1, as I said," Isolis said. "It is the place we built to store the records we were able to save when the First Library burned."

"The First Library?" Vex asked. Isolis smiled again, their tendrils curling up into a whisper of a smile, and they began to walk; they beckoned Vex to follow them, and the lizard hurried to keep up. He had to take two steps to keep up with every one of Isolis's.

"The First Library," Isolis echoed. "What you call the Sun."

Xothok had mentioned something about that, Vex remembered. Xothok sent messages with what he discovered about how the stars had once been *different*, that they'd been libraries holding all the knowledge that the mana contained.

Libraries that were burned to keep the universe warm.

Probably. They didn't actually know the details; Xothok had been able to find nothing further on the reason they were burned, though he'd sorted through what scraps of knowledge he could find on that dead star.

"What happened to it?" Vex asked, and Isolis sighed.

"There comes a point where any universe must end," the librarian said. "To make way for something new. The end is always a little different: heat death in one universe, a big crunch in another, vacuum decay in a third. But the universe always *ends*.

"Except here. Except *this one*—and who knows, maybe infinite others, but our planar scopes can't see that far. The existence of magic prevented the end of the universe. It burned itself to keep us alive, you see, and it reached an equilibrium—one where the collective output of our knowledge kept the stars fueled, and the universe could not die.

"And so, we have the first immortal universe that we know of.

"But all universes must eventually die, and that stability we achieved broke something fundamental. The Void is, we think, a response from the fundamental forces of nature—though I hardly feel comfortable speculating. Perhaps something more fundamental to reality is required for a universe to exist, and keeping it alive with physics and magic is only part of the equation. Perhaps simply beating back entropy is *insufficient*.

"So. The First Library burned to prevent the heat death of this universe; that was the first transition, when we moved from a universe of light and music to one of cosmic fire. We Librarians saved everything we could. But what you saw back there . . ."

The empty books, Vex realized. The books that had felt so *wrong*—the inexplicable sadness he felt while looking through its empty pages. He realized, perhaps a little late, that the beautiful filigree decorated a book with no title at all.

"The Void marches on," Isolis said, "consuming our history and our legacy—everything that makes us who we are. Every day, another book loses its name, and the words on its pages fade away. What you saw back there is no longer a part of our library.

"It is a graveyard. A monument to all we have lost."

That pronouncement struck Vex like a bell. Their surroundings were entirely different now, he realized, although they had changed so slowly that he hadn't quite noticed. Wooden shelves were replaced with solid steel, and the "books" kept here—if they could really be called books at all—were closer to solid slabs of metal inundated with strange designs. Vex felt a small pang of loss. Gone were the beautiful filigree decorations, and in place of them was . . .

. . . something different. Not worse, perhaps. But *different,* and in that difference was a small loss.

A small wire connected each one to the framework of the shelf, and each shelf in turn held wires that led away into something far off in the center of the library. Whatever that was, it was *bright;* the ceiling here no longer burned like fire. Instead, clinical light shone down on them from long tubes.

"What is all this?" Vex asked. He looked around in half-amazement, half-concern.

"Our database," Isolis replied. They sighed, and in that one movement they seemed to age by years. Their shoulders sagged, the tendrils on their face drooped low. "Paper is . . . insufficient. We cannot track the information that goes missing in the books manually; there are too many books and only so many librarians. This way, we can keep backups on backups, and run algorithms to test if anything is missing."

"How much has gone missing?" Vex asked, frowning slightly.

"More than seventy percent of history. Eighty-one percent of all records of written media, fictional or otherwise. Sixty-five percent of cultural practices within currently active cultures." Isolis sighed. "We are doing everything we can to preserve what we had, but it is a long battle and a losing war."

"You keep saying *we*," Vex said finally. The question had been on his mind for a while, but now seemed like the most opportune moment to ask. Vex felt bad, though. Isolis looked so *tired*. "Who is 'we'?"

Isolis chuckled softly. "That is one of the big questions we wish to answer, though that is a goal we have long since abandoned hope for. 'We' are the Librarians—those who take care of the remnants of the various Libraries. We do not know how we came about. We do not know why we have the mission that we do. We know that we care about the preservation of information and culture, and we dedicate ourselves to that mission . . .

"And yet the cost appears to have been our identities. Not as persons, perhaps, but as a people. We are each of us different, did you know that? I resemble a creature of the sea, but there are Librarians who resemble humans, or orcs, or beings of pure Element.

"We share a singular culture in spite of that. Our traditions are largely the same—those traditions that remain. But we do not know why we formed or how we formed; all we know is what we are *now*."

Vex didn't respond for a moment. When he did, the words were hesitant, uncertain. "I'm sorry," he offered.

"We are what we are," Isolis said. The way they spoke, they had long since accepted the fact. They came to a stop next to one shelf in particular—Vex noticed it was *different*. Two new books shone on that shelf, these ones made of leather and paper, and glowing with some very familiar glyphs.

Solidity and Change.

"What is more important is why you are here," Isolis said.

He moved the books aside, revealing three smaller books behind them—each one tangled in a knot of roots. Vex felt them ring with mana, even as far away as he stood.

They were thrumming with untapped power.

CHAPTER 31

SEEDS

Vex

"What . . . are they?" Vex tried to keep his curiosity and excitement at bay; something about this still felt off. For one of them, at least. Closer inspection showed that one of the three root-tangled books had slightly rotten leaves and a weaker core. It was strange, and it made him hesitate.

"They are new books," Isolis said, heedless of his thoughts. "There have not been new books here for a long, long time. It was a joy to find these here. And yet behind them . . ."

Very gently, Isolis plucked out the three new, growing *things* from behind the books that represented Solidity and Change; they placed each one on the floor in front of Vex as if they were fragile things that would break at the slightest bit of force. Vex noticed one of them glowing more dimly than the others, like it was broken.

"These are . . ." Isolis hesitated, as if searching for the word. "Semerit. It has been a long time since I have seen them. They are often the sign of a great change ahead and may evolve to embody any new concept. They are what enable the mana to create new spells. New glyphs. Or they represent such, at least."

"So, other people can create new glyphs now?" Vex asked. Isolis hesitated.

"Normally, yes," they started. "But . . .

"You must understand, those glyphs of Stability and Change *should not be possible*. Not simply because this universe is dead to change, but even by the normal rules of creation . . . they are too broad. Too powerful. Too capable of doing anything. The mana does not allow for creations like these; they upset the balance of magic."

"And yet it did," Vex said softly.

"It did," Isolis said. Their brow furrowed, and they let out a long sigh. "There must be a *reason*, but that reason is beyond me. From my perspective, it will only accelerate the destruction of this universe."

"Why?" Vex felt his chest tighten slightly; that hadn't been his *intent*. He hadn't set out to create new magic in the first place.

Not *here*, anyway.

"The elementals will use it to benefit themselves," Isolis said, "and nothing ill will come of that. But everyone else? These are powerful glyphs, unleashed into a world with barely any hope remaining; it is taking everything the mana has to keep the state of things in place as it is . . ."

"But there's always been destructive magic." This was an argument Vex had heard before about magic; not all of the noble houses in Elyra appreciated it, although that was largely political. They wanted the Ashion house to wield less power. "These glyphs aren't even *meant* for destruction."

"Change is a form of destruction," Isolis said severely. Vex opened his mouth to respond, but the librarian raised a hand; they weren't finished. "But not all destruction is bad, I know. Do not misunderstand. I do not feel your glyphs are anything other than a boon. But they *will* cause imbalance, they *will* cause more mana to be consumed, and in the long term . . ."

"The long term is already a dead end," Vex said softly.

". . . I suppose that is true." Isolis frowned. "It would not change much in the grand scheme of things. It will make people happier. I am . . . uncomfortable, I will admit. I see much potential for pain. But that is perhaps the nature of my own experiences coloring my perception.

"Ultimately, it is moot. These semerit will not grow, and if they do not grow, it means we do not have a future. They do not respond to anything anyone has tried to create, and we do not know *why*. We suspect it is because of this one—the broken one." Gently, Isolis prodded at the one semerit that glowed weakly. The roots around it seemed halfway rotten.

"Why would it mean you don't have a future?" Vex frowned. He didn't quite understand that part.

"Semerit represent future change," Isolis said. "If they will not grow and are simply inert, then the creation of new ones serves only to mock us. But they are seeds of your potential, and so . . . perhaps you will be able to do something with them."

Isolis sounded almost hopeful.

Vex didn't know how he felt about all this. It felt strange to have a near-stranger put their faith in him like this—particularly one who, to him, was simply so much more *learned*. How much time had Isolis spent in this library, studying its books? How much more did Isolis know about magic, about history?

But if Isolis was so learned, then perhaps they were right to think that Vex might be able to do something about this. The lizardkin frowned and fed his mana into [**Advanced Mana Sight**], staring at what Isolis had called the *semerit*.

They felt off. He wanted to know *why*.

Even [**Advanced Mana Sight**] didn't really tell him anything new, though, no matter how much mana he poured into the skill; the semerit glowed in more vibrant colors, perhaps, but there was nothing in the mana that was noticeably *off*. He frowned, glancing through a list of his skills to see if there was anything else he could use—

—well, no. There was something more obvious he could use.

He had his Sign.

Vex used a claw and very gently traced out the sigil for the Sign of Research onto the metallic floor, doing it with careful, measured doses of [**Splash of Mana**]. He placed the three semerit in the center, two whole, one broken. Isolis just watched, seemingly curious; they had no apparent understanding of Vex's Sign.

Mana flowed, and Vex closed his eyes as information began to feed into his mind.

Previous uses of the Sign of Research had been something like speeding through the whole process of research. The Sign simulated everything he would do to investigate something, then collected and presented that information back to him in a neat, organized form. He didn't know where it got some of its information from, exactly—the process by which it was able to extract the original stories behind glyphs was completely opaque to him.

But this was . . .

This was *different*.

There was a moment of nothing, like the magic was hesitating or having difficulty pushing through the mana around the semerit—and then he felt something in it seize his magic, grabbing on to the connection it had with his mind. He almost panicked, but that connection didn't seem malicious, and he stopped himself a second before he would have cut off his connection with his magic.

The semerit had something it wanted to show him.

In his mind's eye, Vex saw a place he didn't recognize. A long, decorated hall stretched out before him, decked in colors of white and gold; lined at the sides were a number of priests and clerics.

At the end of the hallway was a book that looked surprisingly similar to the semerit he held now, though it wasn't tangled up in knots. Vex reached out—

—and felt *carpet* beneath his feet.

He paused, almost stumbling; his eyes went wide, and a hand went immediately for his dagger. A lifetime of adventuring had prepared him for a certain set of reactions to any unusual circumstance, and this was no exception—yet not a single one of those priests responded to his presence, despite the fact that he was *very clearly present.*

Had he teleported? But he felt the semerit in his hands, still, even though he was no longer holding them together—

"We can no longer wait, sire." One of the priests spoke, though it seemed to be to no one in particular; Vex started when he realized that the priest was looking at *him,* and he tried to move out of the way. It was when the priest's gaze followed him that he realized it was not that the priest was talking to no one; it was that he was talking to *him.* "We must ask for help. The kingdom shrinks by the day."

"What kingdom?" Vex tried to ask. "What help do you need?"

Those were not the words that emerged from his mouth, though. Instead, he heard a deep, imperial-sounding voice emerge from somewhere in his chest. "No," he heard the voice rumble. "We have all the help we need. Have faith."

"I *do* have faith," the priest insisted. "But we must be realistic with our faith. Sometimes, our gods wish for us to call for help—"

"Nonsense," the voice interrupted. "The gods will provide. We do not need help."

Vex winced. He knew exactly what Sev would have to say about all of this; their resident priest had no compunctions about telling people off for exactly these sorts of attitudes. It didn't even have to be religious in nature. Not wanting to accept help because of pride . . .

But what *was* this? Why were the semerit showing it to him?

Vex felt himself moving suddenly, and though he tried to scramble back, the entire hall shifted beneath his feet, forcing him to stumble forward; he caught himself at the edge of the window, looking out at a kingdom.

At *half* a kingdom.

It was beautiful, certainly—a city of white alabaster and marble, with buildings that twisted and weaved around one another; there were nearly no straight edges that Vex could see. He could imagine what it might have looked like.

But there was a massive hole in the ground, and half of the buildings had collapsed into it; at the bottom of that hole was a sheer *nothing*. Vex didn't know what he was looking at—his eyes refused to parse it.

"Our city is fine," he heard himself say—or the voice that he was representing, at least. "It is whole and intact, and our citizens are hearty. There is little to worry about."

"The numbers do not *match*," the priest insisted. "We have a record of every birth, every death, and a count of every person in the city."

"And no one is dead."

"But half the people are *missing*!" the priest nearly exploded; Vex admired him for it, really. But his mind was distracted—these people were speaking like they couldn't see the hole.

Infolock?

"Every person in the city is accounted for," the king said calmly.

"Sire," the priest said, his voice deeply exasperated. "The number of births does not match our records of the people in the kingdom—we cannot *ignore* this!"

Vex hated watching this.

He knew what would happen. The scene played out in his head the way it had played out a dozen times before; he'd seen this exact behavior from his father, from his mother, from every single one of his brothers and siblings. He'd bring to them a problem he'd seen among the common folk, and they wouldn't acknowledge it was a problem at all, because to acknowledge that there was a problem meant to acknowledge there was a *failure*.

"Stop," Vex tried to say. "I've seen enough."

But the scene kept going.

"You are insolent," the voice within his chest spoke, and Vex felt mana gathering in the air.

Death mana. He saw the priest recoil, saw the small murmur start up among the others, the whispers. No one was going to stop the king; it was treason to speak back, or something equally absurd.

Vex responded by beginning to gather his own magic.

He didn't care that everything he'd seen told him that this was a vision. He wasn't going to stand by and do *nothing*.

A runic circle formed—*a system skill,* Vex realized in the back of his mind—and mana flashed into it, too rapid for him to stop; it didn't matter, because he'd already prepared his own counterglyph.

Stability.

The deathbolt froze in the air, and Vex fell forward, a sudden force pushing him out of the way. He reacted quickly, taking another two steps to regain his balance and one hand whipping out one of his daggers; almost immediately, the entire hall of priests lifted their staffs, the tips glowing menacingly at his sudden presence.

Behind him, the king narrowed his eyes. He was a tall, imposing man—an uzarikt, his mind supplied, the word coming to mind with a strange, dizzying trim. An almost-spiderlike thing, with broad shoulders and wicked-looking blades emerging from his back; a low hiss was emerging between his mandibles . . .

. . . but Vex had been with Derivan for long enough to learn how to read people, and he saw the lines of guilt on the uzarikt's face.

So he borrowed a little bit of severity from Misa and gave the king a severe frown. "What the fuck do you think you're doing?"

CHAPTER 32

KINGDOM OF LIES

Vex

To say that the hall erupted into chaos would be a bit of an understatement.

It wasn't that anyone attacked—far from it. No one seemed remotely interested in attacking Vex, though their immediate reaction had been to raise their weapons. Half the priests were whispering among themselves, glancing at one another surreptitiously; the other half were staring raptly at the king, waiting for him to give a response.

And the king, in turn, stared at Vex like he had no idea how to respond. "What do you mean?" he said at last. "And . . . who are you?"

"Who do you think I am?"

It was a gamble. Vex had no idea who any of these people were, and he had no idea where he was. He was betting that the Roads had brought him first to Solar Lagrange 1 and then to *here* for a reason, though, if he was even in a physical place—maybe this was all still part of the vision. He could still feel the semerit pressing against his hands, the floor beneath his scales.

If this was a vision, it was far different from anything he'd experienced before.

Well, not that he'd had a lot of visions. He'd just read about them in books.

"You are . . ." The king hesitated, looking nervous. And then he seemed to come to a decision—he dipped down to a knee, surprising Vex, who had to withhold his response as all of the priests *also* dropped to a knee.

They were kneeling.

To *him.*

"Please don't kneel," Vex finally said, trying to ignore the incredible discomfort he felt at having a half dozen people kneel at him in a way that was . . . not unfamiliar. He'd experienced some of this before, when he went out among the "common" folk in Elyra—at least until he'd established that they were no more common than he was. They'd seemed grateful to him for that, though.

Not so much these people. "We must, my lord," the king said. "We have gravely disrespected you."

Vex had . . . only a small idea of what was happening.

"Tell me who I am," he prompted.

"A god," the king said. He kept his head close to the ground.

Vex resisted the urge to press a hand to his face. He'd been hoping it *wasn't* that. Did he look anything like a god?

And what was *happening* here?

Vex's mind began to crunch through everything he'd seen. He didn't recognize this place, but if this was an echo, it was an echo where the system existed. The runic circle the king had used to cast that deathbolt was proof enough of that, and although [**Advanced Mana Sight**] didn't seem to quite work correctly in this space, he suspected that if he could use it, he'd see the same dead mana that usually floated around in his world.

This was a vision of some sort, but it wasn't a vision of **<A World Without a System>**.

That knowledge helped him a bit. Perhaps this was one of the kingdoms from beyond the Outskirts, from a continent that they'd never been to; it would explain the different customs, the different people, the species he didn't recognize.

It didn't explain the king's reaction to him, though. It didn't explain the *state* of the kingdom.

"Which one?" Vex asked, mostly to give himself time to think. He didn't know what the semerit wanted from him—what he was supposed to do here. It was strange that he could interact with the vision at all, but perhaps it wasn't just a vision; perhaps he was being projected somewhere . . .

Vex found that unlikely. There was no precedent for magic of that kind, nor magic that would allow him to cast his *own* magic, disrupting the king's. Across that distance, shifted across reality itself?

But it was the best guess he had.

"P-pardon," the king said. He actually stammered a little, and Vex winced slightly; he didn't like this. He didn't want to be *feared*, and he'd never been a leader. He preferred a role in the shadows. "But I do not know. Istarnokov, perhaps, the God of Silence, but . . ."

Vex sighed.

He could see a few different paths ahead of him. He could try to keep up the ruse, perhaps, and tell the king that he *was* a god; that he wanted them to stop fighting and to ask for help. He could tell them the truth: that he was no god at all, merely a wizard who had been sent here by a magic he didn't understand.

He could take a third option.

"I am not a god," Vex said mildly. He walked over to the window, deliberately turning his back on the king. [**Mana Sight**] or not, he could still sense the presence of mana. He'd know if the king tried to attack him, and hear if the king tried to move toward him. "But I can see what's happened to your kingdom."

"You . . . you're not?" the king sounded more confused than anything. "A spirit, then? An agent of the gods?"

The last one was the most accurate, actually, if largely because Vex suspected he was here because of Onyx. "An agent of sorts," he decided, because it wasn't a lie. "One who knows what is happening."

"Tell us," the king said immediately. "We serve the will of the gods."

And here, Vex frowned.

"You shouldn't," he said.

"What?" The king's response was reflexive, stunned. Vex shook his head but didn't turn around.

"You serve your people," he said. "That's what a king does. The opinions of the gods, when there are many . . . they are always in conflict. Are you going to turn yourselves inside out, responding to the whims of whichever one reaches out to you first?

"Divinity is a step above us, but only a single step. You serve your people, first and foremost; the gods you choose to serve should be the ones who would most benefit your kingdom, who would have your kingdom's best interests at heart. That is *not* all of them."

Vex knew this much, at least, from his talks with Sev. The cleric had impressed upon him that the gods were not the arbiters of good and evil. Many of them had their own motives, usually aligned with the specific attribute they were gods *of*, and there were greater duties they had that mortals weren't entirely privy to. Onyx had given Sev the full explanation once, but Sev had lost those particular memories, too.

The king was frozen. Vex didn't need to turn around to know what the expression on his face was—disbelief warring with anger, a conflict born from his own beliefs being pitted against another's. In most cases . . .

"If you are not a god," the king said, narrowing his eyes. "Then you are a *pretender*."

. . . In most cases, it didn't turn out well.

Vex sighed. He'd tried.

He tore apart the deathbolt the king threw at him. He didn't know what level he was, but it was easy enough to break apart system spells now. The runic circles were transparent to him after months of studying with Derivan—each one was just an approximation of an existing glyph, held together by the system and strings of dead mana. It took only the smallest injection of his own power to make it fall apart.

And whatever means he was here by, he still had control over his mana.

The king didn't have physical stats, it was clear. His eyes widened, and his breaths grew quick and fearful as he threw spell after spell at Vex; the lizardkin noted almost dispassionately that he really *had* grown a lot in his time in the bonus room. There was a time not too long ago when he would have struggled to analyze all these runic circles in time, but that time was no more.

Deathbolt, with a stitched-together glyph for *Death* and *Travel*. Acid Spray. Burning Air.

Meteor.

That one made Vex narrow his eyes, even as he dismissed the spell with an almost-contemptuous smack of the circle. Attacking him was one thing—even if he didn't cancel the spell before it happened, his own resistance would factor in if the spell hit him. He could manipulate and divert the mana at the last minute, as he'd started to learn to do. The problem was that this put the entire *castle* at risk.

"You're an idiot," he said.

Glyph of Binding.

The Glyph he painted was a little more complicated than a basic Binding, in fact; a basic Binding would only hold someone in place. Small modifications to the glyph had allowed him to add additional functions to it without completely fusing it with another glyph—this was just a different expression of the same idea.

He reached into his pocket, not quite sure if this would work, and slapped a reality shard into the middle of the glyph.

In *theory* . . .

He and Derivan had studied the way the system interacted with a person quite thoroughly. They'd worked out how the system's mechanisms were partially Shifted in order to allow it to be anchored to the person's soul. The glyph he drew now had the smallest hint of Change and Stability, which were new but far easier to incorporate than the previous versions of this glyph.

And it was even more effective. The king fell like a puppet with its strings cut; he waved at the air frantically. "What did you do?!" he asked. "What did you— Why can't I—"

Vex ignored him and turned his attention back to the priests. They'd been watching him. It said a lot, really, that none of them had tried to interfere in either direction; he saw the fear in their eyes.

All of this was . . . too similar to home.

But maybe he could convince them to do something *different* here. Maybe things could go a little bit better now that he had the power to do what he couldn't before.

When he made his way back to Elyra . . .

"Pardon me, lord," the priest said, "but what are we to do with him?"

Vex sighed. "I'm not your lord," he said quietly. "I'm no one at all. I don't know how things are supposed to work here . . . but you shouldn't be listening to someone who doesn't have your best interests at heart."

He wasn't trained for diplomacy. These weren't words that would sway anyone that wasn't already swayed. But a priest stepped forward, the same one who had spoken up against the king originally.

His eyes were surprisingly sharp. "What can you tell us about what's happening to our kingdom?" he asked. Straight to business.

"Your kingdom is being erased," Vex answered. "There is a massive hole in your city, even if you can't see it. Have you noticed anything strange? Transports taking longer than usual, streets more packed because people are forced to travel along different routes?"

". . . We thought that was the way it always was," the priest said. His brows furrowed. "But you are right. We would not have built the city that way."

"My best advice is to evacuate," Vex said with a small bow and a slight wince. "I'm sorry that I don't have anything better. But . . . don't let your pride keep you here, like he was trying to do." Vex nodded at the king—the former king, perhaps. "And ask for help if you need it."

The priest grimaced. "I had hoped for something better. A way to stop all this."

"If we had a way to do that," Vex said, "I suspect we wouldn't be having this conversation at all."

The priest sighed. He walked over to his king, who had slipped into unconsciousness; a hand hovered over his body, glowing with a pale light. "He wasn't always like this," he said, half to himself. "Had the gods not abandoned us . . ."

"The gods, too, have their own dangers to face," Vex supplied. "It is possible you weren't abandoned at all."

"... Then that would explain a lot, and it would mean we have failed in our duty." The priest didn't look away. "But you are right. We have a greater duty: one to our people."

Vex glanced outside. Even now, the void at the center of that city was inching outward, slowly growing; inch by inch, it would consume more of this kingdom, and he still didn't know *where this was.* He opened his mouth to ask—

—but the semerit in his hands glowed suddenly white-hot, and he almost gasped in pain; the vision collapsed, sucked into the three semerit that appeared to have merged into one.

His original spell—his Sign of Research—completed. The notes it contained were both insufficient and deeply worrying.

Semerit of the First Library
Allows access to divine magics. Contains one temporal paradox.

CHAPTER 33

VOID

Derivan

Derivan stared at the inky darkness in front of him.

It was familiar, actually. Derivan recognized now that he'd encountered such pure darkness before—when they'd recklessly crashed into the dungeon in Misa's bonus room as it was experiencing a dungeon break. It was where they'd first encountered a reality anchor.

He wondered—for a single, absurd moment—if he was in front of the part of the Void that contained Elyra's reality anchor. But no, that didn't make sense; there were none of those strings of light leading up into the sky . . .

Oh. *Oh.*

Those strings of light had been the tethers for the anchor. That was the reason he'd seen the image of Misa's village through it—that dungeon had anchored that village in reality, their mana crystal offerings no doubt maintaining it. But no one delved it, because no one knew it existed, and so the dungeon eventually *broke,* monsters flooding out and into the region.

That didn't explain everything. What happened to a reality anchor when its dungeon broke? They'd seen that the one underneath J'rokksur was on the verge of breaking, and the dungeons in the Outskirts had all been broken; if that was any indication, then reality didn't just fade away when the anchor that held it together broke. Instead, the space was slowly corrupted . . .

. . . That would explain some things about the Outskirts. If the decay was *slow,* it would explain why Misa still remembered J'rokksur and everything that had happened to her family, even though others rarely, if ever, referenced that tragedy. Derivan winced slightly, remembering her rage the first time a Guild member had been entirely unaware of the disaster.

The end of the universe explained a *lot*. He'd had this thought before, when they were first trying to make their way into Elyra's dungeon. The thought had been half-formed then. Speculation.

Now, looking into that darkness again, Derivan was sure.

Their continent was dying. Every dungeon break brought it a step further. Reality crumbled at the edges, and no one knew.

He should, perhaps, have been afraid to step into the Void. The anchors needed to exist outside of reality by their very nature; one could not anchor reality from within it. That meant he was stepping into *nothing*, and that the nature of that nothing would erode away at him.

Derivan considered this problem for a moment, then drew the mark of Stability on his own armor, in shades of vibrant green mana. The color reminded him of Vex.

Then he stepped into that nothingness.

The Roads had brought him here for a reason, after all.

There was no sensation of falling. Instead, he walked forward like there was still a ground beneath him, though he had to focus on the idea of it—if he allowed his concentration to lapse, he felt himself sink down a little bit. He remembered how this space worked; he moved around by *thinking* himself in a direction.

The problem was . . . well, there weren't really any directions to move in. He was surrounded by nothing.

Derivan glanced back at the tunnel, already shrinking in the distance, and frowned. He made himself drift back to it, and with a small bit of concentration, allowed a bit of his armor to melt into Slime. His affinity with that stat was increasing every day. He smeared that Slime onto the stone—it would ensure he would always be able to find his way back.

And then he picked a direction at random and started drifting.

It wasn't long before things began to change.

What started as pure and empty darkness began to spin into shapes and images—impossible ones, to be sure, but shapes nonetheless. They swam through the air like fish . . .

. . . and with a start, he remembered when he had encountered this before. *Exactly* this.

In a dream he'd had, near to the time all of this had started, when his system had first been broken open.

He remembered the questions.

How are the Bright-Lights, the Not-Dark! The stars, you call them! Do they still spin and turn? Do they speak to the people, bring them joy and terror?

The stars. The voices here had known, hadn't they? The stars had been gone even then, in reality, and Derivan had soon forgotten he had ever heard the word; Vex had explained to him once that dreams tended to quickly slip away, and that was exactly what had happened.

The way the voice described the stars, though—that was the way they'd seen them in the observatory *here*, where the stars still existed. They moved. They didn't speak, but . . .

Belle had told them that the stars had been different once.

That had been far more than just a dream.

What else? He tried to remember.

Bah! What of the Great Kingdom? Does it still thrive?

There was no Great Kingdom that he'd heard of. But if the pattern held, then the Great Kingdom was perhaps something that had been erased too. Perhaps the Void erased things from reality, but everything that was erased was still left here, forgotten.

Or, more likely, slowly rotting away—like they were being digested by the nothingness.

Tell me of my children. The thought-forms, the hidden-shadows. Do they fill the skies and forests?

The memory was coming to him more easily now. This question made him . . . rather sad. Derivan knew now what they meant—whoever this voice was, whoever their children were, they were gone. Or perhaps lost to the Void, too, and they had simply never found one another.

His presence must have been like a beacon of Reality to them, drawing them toward him. He didn't know what it meant that he'd been able to see this place in his dreams.

Perhaps they yet hide . . .

Derivan hoped so.

Tell me of the conquest of Redle! It must have been a glorious battle.

Impossible! Redle was on the verge of conquering the continent! Has their name faded so thoroughly?

Redle must have been a real kingdom, too—perhaps even the Great Kingdom the first voice had mentioned, though this particular voice he remembered as being different. Equally enthusiastic and just as strange, though, to speak one moment of Redle being conquered and then of them conquering.

But they'd seen time get twisted around more than once. The bonus rooms they had been to were both born out of echoes created by a change in time. Perhaps that voice had experienced more than one and gotten confused. It certainly *sounded* confused.

And then there was the final question that he remembered from that dream.

What are you?

At the time, he'd said he didn't know. He still didn't, in truth—he was a monster, according to the system, a living suit of armor fueled by magic and given a mind. He knew *who* he was. His journey with the others had given him grounding in that, and had given him his new Sign, the new glyph that everyone could now use.

But *what* he was?

That was a question he hadn't answered yet.

Irvis had said they were the same, and that was the closest he'd gotten to an answer. The voice echoed in his mind, now that he remembered.

You will, it said. **You must.**

There was one way he could get closer to an answer, he supposed. If he could find out what Irvis was . . .

The shapes in the Void were just as solid as they had been in his dream now. Derivan wondered if he would hear the same voices he had back then, but nothing spoke into his head.

Instead, a figure approached him.

He almost flinched once it came fully into view; it was one of the ant-monsters they'd fought as Misa's dungeon broke. One hand went to his weapon, and the other examined the enemy in front of him.

Except it wasn't an enemy at all.

He relaxed almost immediately, feeling foolish. There was a glint of intelligence in the ant-creature's eyes, and it leaned forward, its mandibles forming a curious sort of *click-clack* as it watched him. He didn't understand what it was trying to say at all.

It folded its arms and gave him what he was pretty sure was an affronted frown, and then a voice spoke into his head.

Are you new here?

Derivan didn't know how to answer that. ". . . Yes?" he said after a moment. "But I have been here before."

Been here . . . before? The ant puzzled over his words for a moment. **You have left?**

"I have seen this place once near a reality anchor, I think," Derivan said. "And once in my dreams."

But you are here. The ant seemed to have decided he was just confused. **I have seen a few others of your kind here, though there have been less of them of late. The Void takes us all, you understand.**

Derivan did not, but he was starting to; a slow horror began to bloom in his chest. "I am afraid there has been a misunderstanding," he said slowly. "But I would appreciate an explanation."

The ant cocked its head at him. **What do you mean?**

"Pretend I know nothing about this space," Derivan said. "Or of anyone within it. How would you explain it?"

Derivan's Physical Empathy allowed him to interpret the ant's frown. **We are within the Void,** it told him. **The hole left behind when Reality dissolves. Anything that has been removed from the world ends up here, where we slowly lose all sense of purpose, all sense of who we are. Fortunately for us, time doesn't exist here in any *proper* sense, so it takes far longer for us to be completely erased than it should.**

But while we are here . . . we are gone. Forgotten entirely. You must be quite far gone to have forgotten even that.

"Is there any way of escape?" he asked. He knew the way back to the tunnel; if he could lead everyone in here out there, perhaps they could simply walk out of the Void.

He doubted it would be that simple, though. It only took a flicker of his senses to confirm—he had a reality to him that the ant did not. He could sense himself with Shift.

The ant was like a ghost—entirely invisible to that sense. Not that it noticed that he'd tried to check at all.

Escape? the ant snorted, but it shook its head after a moment, giving the question serious consideration. **Sometimes . . . people vanish. We aren't sure why. It's like they dissolve entirely, but they should not be that close to disappearing.**

In the Outskirts, the veil between Reality and Void was thin. He understood that now, walking back through his memories—at the edges of the continent, where all the anchors had burst, reality was *thinner*. He could even feel the gradient whenever he paid attention. The closer he was to a dungeon's heart, the stronger reality seemed to be.

And when he was in Fendal, where the dungeon's anchor had spread itself thin, there had been an equal feeling of unreality. A strangeness to the people of Fendal that had been not at all unlike the strange behaviors he had observed from his own people, in his own dungeon, so very long ago.

The pieces had been there the whole time.

He remembered the way that anchor had taken sapience from the people of Fendal, lifting and transferring it to the people of Teque as though it was a physical property that could be moved from one place to another. That was a deliberate action, but in the absence of an anchor, if Reality and Void started to merge . . .

Derivan could see it. Fragments of a person slipping from the Void and back into Reality. In the Outskirts, where broken anchors reigned, that would happen the most. It was what had happened to him.

That wasn't what made him feel sick.

No. That feeling came from the memory of fighting creatures that looked just like the ant standing before them now—from the memory of them lying dead and broken behind him.

He should have considered it before. The system didn't really create things wholesale—it always borrowed from something else. And in this case . . .

How many "monsters" had he encountered?

How many of them had once been a whole *people*?

Did the system just . . . keep remnants of what remained and use them as templates for so-called monsters?

The sheer scope of what the world might have lost staggered him. The ant didn't seem to notice what was going through his mind—it was looking at him with something that seemed like sympathy, most likely assuming he was wrestling with the idea of being forgotten, of being erased from the world.

Derivan had no such worries. He was reeling instead from the idea that he might have been part of a full species of magical creatures. What traditions might his people have had?

. . . Was this why Irvis was so angry? Was this the reason for his hatred? Irvis had said they were the same once. He and Vex had both determined that Irvis was an Aspect, the embodiment of a small part of magic, but . . .

That didn't mean he had always been that way.

Derivan's voice was steady when he spoke. It was a surprise, even to him.

"Can you take me to them?" he asked, and then he considered the question a little more. "Or . . . take me to everyone. Everyone that you can."

The ant stared at him dubiously but eventually shrugged. **Sure**, it said. **Not like I have anything better to do.**

CHAPTER 34

MONSTERS

Derivan

Derivan moved through the Void, his mind still racing. The ant was two or three steps ahead of him.

"I apologize," Derivan said after a moment of silence. "I should have asked for a name. I am Derivan."

The ant glanced at him. **My name is—**

It stopped mid-sentence to produce an impossible-to-replicate series of clicks. Seeing Derivan's mostly blank expression, it sighed.

You may call me Juniper, the ant said. **It's what a lot of the others call me.**

Derivan nodded, feeling oddly guilty that he couldn't reproduce the clicks.

Now they were making their way through the Void. He had no idea how the ant managed to find its way around—as far as Derivan could tell, it was a featureless emptiness. The fact that he'd even been *found* by anyone was a miracle. "How do you know where to go?" he asked curiously.

The Void is composed of rotting ideas, Juniper replied. **And if you train yourself to look, they are like signposts. Beacons of dead concepts and disappearing people.**

. . . That was a rather depressing way to navigate. Derivan almost regretted asking.

And yet, even in the darkness, there was light.

Sev had said it once, he was pretty sure. It had been a long time ago—years, when he'd first met the cleric and before they'd even come upon Misa together, when it was just the two of them making their way through the Outskirts. There had been a lot of hiding back then. Derivan had still been trying to hide the full extent of his abilities, and Sev wasn't particularly high-level himself.

How the cleric had survived making his way through the Outskirts, he didn't know. Probably the same way they did getting out—a lot of hiding and fortuitous coincidences.

Sometimes, a lot of the things around Sev seemed a little *too* coincidental. But he supposed he couldn't be too surprised.

The thought came to him now because of what showed up out of the darkness. It was sudden. It didn't fade into sight slowly, beginning as a small spark of light in the distance; instead, it appeared between one blink and the next.

Except Derivan hadn't blinked.

His awareness had just *flickered,* and now the exit of the Roads was suddenly somewhere different, and in front of him was a roaring campfire. Below it was actual ground—dirt, grass, and stone—and surrounding it were . . .

Monsters, his mind supplied, and he shook his head internally. He didn't want to call them that, even in his mind. Especially not now that he knew the truth.

People.

Every one of them.

It was clear in the way they sat around one another, taking comfort in each other's presence. Derivan saw a spider that he would have once called a Crystal Mimic. Her crystalline body was reminiscent of the glimmering mana crystals that filled a Mana Nucleus. She wore a beautiful scarf around her neck, though the edges of it frayed into nothingness, and in that scarf he saw a full life stitched into it—the moment she had been born, the moment she'd met her husband. It showed her with their children, teaching them to knit their own scarves from webbing and to paint them with dye.

She sat there now, half-curled up against a solemn figure that stood stone-still near the fire. He was no species that Derivan recognized—spiderlike, perhaps, but far more humanoid than the other. Sharp blades emerged from his back, and he stood with an almost royal bearing—and yet there was a certain softness in him. One hand was placed on the more spiderlike creature's back, as though in comfort.

That scene was reflected all around the campfire.

A snake Derivan was certain he'd fought before, a venomous species in a dungeon that had simply flung themselves at him like they were projectiles. He hadn't bothered trying to dodge them. Here, a member of that same species was curled up around another creature's neck, sound asleep. He had no less than a half-dozen little gadgets attached to him, some of them complete, some of them half-complete, and others fading away to the Void.

A makeshift table made of wood sat a few feet away from the campfire, and seated next to it were two dramatically different individuals—one of them seemed to be made entirely of moss and fungus, a shifting biomass in a vaguely humanoid shape. It let out a displeased puff of spores as its opponent moved a chess piece on the table in front of them.

The other was . . .

The other was another person like *him*. A set of armor, though that armor was different in design.

"Your move," she said. Her voice rang, clear like a bell, with just a hint of smugness in it.

The fungus-person folded its arms and puffed again.

"Yeah, yeah," the armor said, and though there was no change in the glow of her eyes, Derivan could hear her rolling them in the way she spoke. "Again?"

Her opponent stood up, puffed at her a third time, even more crossly, and then waddled away.

Derivan took the opportunity to approach.

She didn't look up from the board, too focused on setting up the pieces. She did notice his presence, though. "Here for a game?"

"Here to learn about our people," Derivan said quietly, and she finally looked up—and then she flinched backward in shock.

It was presumptuous, he supposed. Perhaps he wasn't part of a people at all; perhaps he was just a part of a small batch of creations by some eccentric mage. But there was a look in this other armor's eyes that told him otherwise.

She stared at him for a long moment, and when she finally spoke, her voice was hard. "The Ishimar did not create us to forget, even here," she said. "If you have forgotten, you are a poor Scimitar indeed."

Harsh. But Derivan heard the bitterness in her voice—there was a history in it that he didn't understand, and so he let it go, focusing instead on the content of her words.

"Perhaps I would be, if I was," he said quietly. "But I am a recent creation, in the grand scheme of things. I have not been erased."

All around the campfire, conversation slammed to a stop. Derivan slowly became aware that his voice had carried much farther than he'd expected; apparently, sound traveled more than was normal in the Void.

"You what?" There was almost a hint of danger in the armor's voice, but she stopped herself before she went too far. She glared around at everyone else around the campfire. "Stop *eavesdropping*."

No one did.

She sighed. "My name is Jelevar," she said after a minute, her voice short and curt. Her eyes were slightly narrowed. "Explain yourself, if you would."

Derivan did his best.

—∞—

The murmurs around the campfire were far more animated than before. About half of them were hopeful; they wanted to try to find the exit from the Roads and escape the Void that way. They'd never been this close to getting out before. Derivan didn't know how to tell them they didn't have the substance for him to even be able to Shift them out.

The other half were horrified to hear about the state of the world. They asked questions of him that were not dissimilar from the ones the voices had asked him in his dream—they asked him where their homes were in this new world, if anyone remembered them and their people.

They knew the answers already, of course. They had been forgotten.

But they hoped.

A quarter of them he couldn't even give any answers to. Their homes were on Obreve but not on the same continent Derivan had been on, as far as he could tell. Once he explained the Outskirts and that they were hemmed in, they returned to the campfire, a certain melancholy hanging around them.

Jelevar had stayed largely silent. She let the others ask their questions, though she clearly had some of her own—she just held them back.

And then, as soon as the opportunity showed, she waved the others away and pulled him to the side.

"You do not remember," she said, searching his eyes. "Not a single thing about our people."

"No," Derivan said. "I did not know I *had* a people."

Jelevar sighed. It was surprisingly . . . organic. Derivan thought about how it had taken him weeks to learn to mimic the sound, to understand its purpose.

"We are the Scimitars," she explained. She gestured for him to follow, and he fell into step beside her. "Constructs of the Ishimar Empire. Part of their army, you could say."

Somehow, that explanation pained Derivan.

It wasn't the answer he'd been hoping for.

Jelevar seemed to sense this. She glanced at him, and her voice softened slightly. "That is what we were at first," she said. "We fought back, eventually. They made us too intelligent. They made us our own people. We were able to secure recognition as a true species within their kingdom, worthy of our own individual rights . . . We should not have had to fight that fight. It cost us dearly."

There was that bitterness in her voice again.

"Most of us did not care to remain," Jelevar continued. "We saw it as pointless. Why would we want to serve as citizens of an empire that did not care to recognize us as our own people? We wanted to strike out on our own, to create our own empire. We . . . did not."

"Creating an empire is difficult," Derivan said, not without sympathy.

"Quite," Jelevar said. She was using the walk as a way to work off excess energy; her steps were quick and heavy, even in the nothingness of the Void, but her voice softened as she continued. "But we were happy with what we *did* create. Not an empire, no, but our own little city, built of manaforged metal and exadite ore . . . You should have seen it, Derivan. It *gleamed*."

Derivan didn't know how to react to most of this. Part of him had thought he would be relieved to know more about who he could have been, and yet he mostly felt . . . distant. None of this past really felt like his own.

He understood the pain she spoke with, at least. She had fought for a future for her own people and lived to see it wiped off the map.

"It sounds like it was beautiful," Derivan said finally.

"It was," Jelevar said. She sighed. "I know you came here because you were led here, and there is *something* you can learn here, perhaps, that can help you in your quest . . . and perhaps even to restore us. But if nothing else—"

Jelevar stopped and turned to him, showing him a small butterfly pinned to her chest. "An exadite pin," she said. "When we gained our independence, we sought to learn more about the magics that created us, and exadite was one of the hardest ores to smith with. Not *all* of us dedicated ourselves to it, of course, but we created a tradition out of it . . . Every five years, we would present our creations to one another, in a ceremony in the center of our city. We called it the Festival of Freeforged Light.

"If there is nothing else you get from this . . . remember that, please. We as a people did not have much that just belonged to *us*. We did not have much time before we were erased. And if there is a chance now that a small part of us can be remembered . . ."

Jelevar said nothing further, but her grip on the pin trembled, just slightly. Derivan saw how she felt in that moment.

Hope that a small piece of them could now be remembered. Anger that this conversation was necessary at all. A flicker of despair, for the part of her that felt like they had fought for nothing.

Derivan stared at the pin, and something resonated within him. It took him a moment to pinpoint, as distant as it was.

The system was responding, the way it had responded when it had first discovered reality shards.

The construct that kept him attached to the system was trembling strangely. It didn't seem like something was wrong—instead, it seemed like something within it was struggling to activate. He looked closer, and he saw new gears spinning into existence in the metaphorical clockwork.

And a moment later, a system screen popped up.

[Potential power source found. Analyzing . . .]

Derivan tilted his head slightly, then bowed at Jelevar. "I will remember," he said.

He'd learned a lot about Patch. He understood, to some degree, what the system did. He could see it was trying to turn this into another source of power—an advantage it could give to people, perhaps in the hope that this new power would help save them from the decay of the universe.

Derivan didn't care about any of that. What he understood was a smaller, more fundamental piece of what it was and what it needed to be.

In some small way, it would be a way to *remember*. To give Jelevar and the rest of the Scimitars a legacy.

Derivan seized it with Patch, and with his hand he spun the shape of a glyph.

Change.

New system function unlocked: *Remembrance.*
A Remembrance consolidates your understanding of a lost fragment of history. Effects vary depending on the fragment.
You have gained a new Remembrance: Exadite Pin.

CHAPTER 35

REMEMBRANCE

Derivan

Derivan's next steps were what he had already planned to do, system power or no. It seemed only right.

He couldn't spend forever in the Void, of course. His friends were waiting for him, and even with Stability being his new Sign, there was only so much it could do in the face of the Void; given time, even that would erode away. But there was so much here to remember, and with every second he wasted, more of it was lost.

"What happened to your arm, anyway?" Jelevar asked him before he went to speak with the others. Derivan shrugged slightly and told her, and she winced with sympathy. "At the height of the Ishimar Empire, it would not have been difficult to get that replaced, but once we split off into our own village . . . We had injuries like this occasionally. We could forge new arms, but the Ishimar would not tell us how to attach it to ourselves. The price of freedom, they said. We figured it out eventually, but it's one of the things I can no longer remember. Erased, like most other things about us."

There was that note of bitterness in her voice again. Derivan considered his response carefully.

"If I am able to restore our people," he said, "I will make sure we have the means to heal ourselves in the event of such injuries."

He suspected Vex would be able to discern the runes and glyphs that made up the inside of the armor and adjust them so that any newly forged arm could be joined to the whole. Derivan could do some magic himself, but he didn't quite have Vex's skill at interpreting and putting together glyphs. He didn't know if it would ever be the same, but it was worth a try.

Jelevar seemed satisfied with his response, and she let go of his remaining arm, which she'd grabbed by the elbow at some point. She searched Derivan's eyes for a second.

"You have a plan," she said.

"I have to talk to everyone," Derivan said. "It is not just our people who deserve to be remembered. There are many here who have been forgotten. I do not think I can remember all of them, but . . . What was it you said?"

"The Ishimar did not create us to forget," Jelevar said, with a look in her eyes that he understood to be a small smile. He'd never looked at his own expressions from the outside before. "Though I was angry when I said that. We don't truly forget, but it is possible for information to fall to the wayside unless deliberately recalled . . ."

"But I have a means to remember." It took only a small effort of will to touch upon what the system called Remembrances. A small exadite pin, remarkably similar to Jelevar's, Shifted into existence above his hand; she stared at it.

"What did you do?"

"It is a long story," Derivan said. There was more he could do with the pin, he knew—he could feel it with Shift, a distant array of possibilities all hiding within the pin. But now was not the time, and he dismissed it, letting it fade once more into nothing. "Perhaps if I have time . . ."

Jelevar shook her head. "You should not stay here longer than necessary," she said firmly. "Do what you have to, speak to those of us here who wish to speak to you, then leave. I do not think your magic will protect you forever." She nodded to the Sign still painted on his chest. Small fragments of mana were dissipating, though it would be some time still before it was gone completely.

But there was a small flicker of hope in her voice that wasn't there before.

Derivan nodded to her. "I wish I could have known our people," he told her.

"I wish you could have too."

Derivan made his way back to the campfire.

It was a little more animated than before, but not too much—the Void affected everyone here, and new information was quickly lost. Derivan felt a small ache curl into his chest, to see how many of the ones he'd previously spoken to lose what little light and life they'd gained so quickly.

He supposed he shouldn't have expected anything different, but he knew it would hurt him if he spoke to Jelevar again and found that she had forgotten.

He planned to anyway, of course.

There were some who remembered what he'd explained to them, though their memory of it was wispy and fragmented. Some joked about it—about climbing inside his armor and marching out into the Roads, for example—and Derivan had been more than willing to let them try, although he suspected it wouldn't work. He would ask them to follow him back to the Roads anyway, just in case there was something they could do, but no one was expecting anything from that.

Exits had been discovered before and had never led anywhere. The fragments and echoes of people here were just that and had no more substance left to be restored.

And yet, here and there, in amounts that seemed too small to matter yet made everything brighter . . . there was hope.

Derivan spoke to the spider-lady who sat by the campfire, and she told him of the scarf. It was a long tradition held by her family, though not by her people as a whole; they called themselves the Eight-Legged, which she admitted was not the most creative of names but insisted sounded much more beautiful in her own language.

Her *people* had the tradition of brewing tea when they came of age. Tea was important to her people, she said; it was tea that had originally granted them their size and sapience, stolen from a witch that left a cup of it steaming by her cauldron. They were good at alchemy as a matter of tradition, and carried potions in waterproof silk pouches that they spun in an instant.

[**You have gained a new Remembrance: Life Scarf**]

[**You have gained a new Remembrance: Endless Tea**]

He gained two Remembrances from the conversation—both the scarf and a small teacup that poured an endless black liquid. The spider seemed almost emotional, looking at the teacup. She said it looked just like the one they had used in their little village, and he spent a moment with her there as she sipped at the cup and reminisced.

The larger, more humanoid spiderlike creature next to her was a different species entirely, it turned out. They had gravitated toward one another because they had the most in common, but he seemed to remember almost nothing of his own people; he was deeply apologetic, speaking to Derivan.

"There is only one thing I remember," he said, his voice deep and grave, for all that he spoke quietly. "A meal I had as a child. I remember the taste of it but little else. I think . . . I think my mother cooked it for me."

That wasn't quite enough for the system. Derivan could feel it reaching out like it was judging the memory, trying to decide if it was worthy of being spun into a Remembrance. He could feel it pull away after a moment.

He pushed it just a little farther with Patch, feeling a bit of energy leave him with the effort, and let the notification drift by.

[**You have gained a new Remembrance: Childhood Meal**]

He left the spider-humanoid sitting stunned, taking small sips from a steaming bowl of soup.

The snake covered in gadgets slid up to Derivan next, eager for a conversation. "You're here to *know*," he said, coiling up in delight. "To learn! I haven't had new students for a long time. Such a long time."

He faltered a little bit at those words, and Derivan took the opportunity to sit down beside him and smile. "I will learn whatever you wish to teach," he told the old snake, who did a delighted little twirl.

"Good, good!" the snake said. "I am Hysuan, yes? You will learn! I *make things*. Look!"

A quick twist, and one of the gadgets attached to the snake sprang open. It was, as far as Derivan could tell, just a simple little toy—built to spring open once it was twisted a certain number of times. But Hysuan twisted in on himself to push it back, and Derivan blinked in surprise when the second time, the figurine that popped out was different.

"How did you do that?" he asked in spite of himself, and the snake grinned at him.

"That would be telling!"

He spent a little more time than he perhaps should have with Hysuan, listening to everything he had to say, everything he wanted to teach—and, eventually, asked him about his people. Hysuan seemed more than happy to tell him everything he remembered.

They were an individualistic species, he said, who often chose a profession important to them and then went their own way; every few years, they would gather and share everything that they'd learned in their respective journeys. In this way, they would pass on their interests to the young ones who seemed most interested in following in their footsteps.

It explained why Hysuan was so interested in teaching.

[You have gained a new Remembrance: Teacher's Mark]

And on it went.

Derivan lost track of how much time he spent with the people here, trying to learn everything he could. He spoke again with the ant who had led him here in the first place, asking about its people, and listened intently as the means by which they kept their livestock was explained to him. He spoke with someone whose species he had no name for, made of too many arms and too many legs; he listened as they told him about how they chose the limbs they acquired.

Strange and foreign to him, but he accepted and remembered it nonetheless. His own lost arm ached in sympathy.

He spent, perhaps, longer than was wise. When the Sign upon his chest began to fade, he simply painted a new one on, spending more mana than usual to get it to stick. There was no ambient mana in the Void, and so every cast consumed far more of his personal mana than it usually did.

Derivan stayed until the last dregs of that mana were gone, learning and remembering everything he could.

Before he left, he searched for Jelevar. She regarded him without a hint of recognition, with the same surprise as she had the first time she'd seen him. This time, he simply asked her for a game and played a round of chess with her.

He lost terribly. But it seemed like a good way to mark his exit.

He could have spent more time in the Void, he knew. There were other camps out there, other so-called refugees who were spending what remained of their lives in this nothingness, their culture and history slowly forgotten. But he couldn't stay there forever, not without risking getting erased himself.

All he could do was promise himself he would return if he was able.

CHAPTER 36

REBELLION

Helix

"Vex better be grateful for this," Helix muttered.

He didn't mean it, of course. At this point, he was fighting for far more than just his brother. It had taken him time to see that Vex had been right all along, but he'd figured it out eventually.

He owed it to his team the most. To Larok in particular, the one member of his team that was with him today.

Helix hadn't known Larok particularly well when he'd first started talking to the man; Larok had just had the misfortune of being nearby when Helix learned that Vex had left. Lacking any particular ability to hold back, Helix's first reaction to the news had been to turn to the nearest available figure—some commoner orc—drag him to the closest pub, and then spill every thought he had about his younger brother to the stranger.

It was a miracle that Larok had listened to him at all.

But he had. Larok paid attention to every word he said, and he'd done so *genuinely*, unlike all the servants that Helix spoke to who only listened to him because they were obligated to. Or because they were being paid to do so. It was the first time Helix had felt like someone was actually taking him seriously.

And then he'd looked Helix in the eye and told him he was wrong.

He'd been furious at first, of course. He'd been the scion of their House until Vex had come along and shown his particular knack for magic, and now that his younger brother had *left*, he was once again the heir—but his place in his own family had never felt so precarious. He was uncertain, thrown off.

He'd been happy and proud of Vex, and then his younger brother threw it all away for what Helix had seen as nothing more than a phase. And now this stranger was looking him in the eye and telling him that his brother had been right to do so?

"Who the fuck do you think you are?" Helix had asked. The fireball that lit up in his hand gave him a dangerous look, he knew. He'd never been able to control his use of magic particularly well. He spent mana like water.

"No one." Larok hadn't seemed even slightly perturbed. He'd even taken a sip of his drink, looking Helix in the eye. "Hurts, doesn't it? That a nobody like me *disagrees.*"

There had been a certain self-loathing bitterness in his voice that had cut straight through Helix's anger. He'd paused, staring at Larok, the fireball flickering out in his hand; the rest of the tavern had paused to stare at them, and a glare from him sent them all back to looking at their drinks and gossiping with one another.

He wasn't interested in all of that. He was interested in *Larok* and whatever it was that made the man so brave.

And foolish, arguably.

He'd invited the man to his house that night, and to his surprise, Larok had accepted.

Without the barrier of nobility and commoner between them, they'd had a surprising amount of things in common. They liked the same books, seen the same plays; Larok even knew a little bit about magic, even though his own class was related to administration and basic clerk duties.

He'd elaborated more on his point of view, too. Helix had never told him the House secret, of course; he'd just explained that Vex left to protect his brother, and all his opinions about the divide between the nobles and the commoners.

And Larok, in turn, talked about what it was like for *them.* It was a perspective that had been entirely foreign to him at the time, and even now he found he kept learning more things about the class of people he had once considered beneath him. Larok had eventually brought him around to meet his friends, and Helix had slowly been exposed to a perspective that was far different from the one his parents always spoke of.

Anyone could be a noble, his parents had said. They just had to work hard enough and find something a new House could be founded around.

Helix saw how hard Larok's friends worked in every spare scrap of time they had. He saw how they achieved nothing. The materials they needed were too expensive; a single drop of the reagent they needed took weeks for them to earn. They could have done it in a week, with funding from a noble house, but then they would be relegated to a sub-branch of that house and would be no better off than before.

And, slowly, he'd changed his mind.

His brother had been the catalyst, certainly, but he was fighting with the Elyran rebels for his own reasons now.

That was what had led him here. Larok stood by his side, a sheaf of papers folded under his arm. Talking to the Adventurers' Guild had changed things for them dramatically—it put them into contact with J'rokksur, and the people in that village seemed almost proud of the way they broke apart the system's skills for their own ends.

Now that was a power they had, too. Some of the secrets J'rokksur had shared freely could easily have earned them a noble house in Elyra themselves.

"I'm sure your brother would be grateful," Larok said, smiling at him. "Pity I missed the opportunity to meet him."

"You'll get the chance soon, I bet," Helix said with a laugh. "I've heard a bit about what they've been getting up to. They figured out a way to interfere with things from inside the bonus room."

"What, really?" Larok raised an eyebrow. "That sounds . . . dangerous."

"He's found a good team." *A good family,* Helix thought to himself. He'd strive to be the same to his brother once he got the chance.

"Are you just ignoring us?" a voice demanded, and Helix rolled his eyes. "Leave. Now. Noble or not, you are trespassing on House Herastul grounds."

"We were having a conversation," Helix said. He conjured a fireball in his hands, letting a wave of heat wash over them all; it was strong enough that even the enforcer on the opposite side of the garden flinched, through all the protective magics he wore on his armor.

Helix took a moment to feel bad for the man. He was only doing his job.

He *was* in their way, though.

"And you can do that *outside,*" the guard insisted, sounding considerably more nervous.

Helix pretended to consider it for a moment. The fireball hung in the air, the heat from it visibly wilting the plants surrounding them. It was a direct interaction between fire and plant aspects of mana—nonmagical plants would not have been nearly as affected—but the enforcer glanced back and forth between Helix and the plants, clearly noticing the effect he had.

"I gotta say," Larok said, sounding amused, "this is a lot more fun when I'm on the other side of it."

Helix grinned and elbowed his friend. "I don't think you're supposed to be encouraging me."

"I'm not, I'm not," Larok said. "I'd stop you if I thought you were abusing your power."

"Am I abusing my power?"

Larok's eyes sharpened as he looked at the guard, and Helix's mirth instantly fell away, replaced by a laser focus. He followed Larok's gaze, his scales prickling as he noticed the guard's suddenly blank expression. All the fear and nervousness had vanished like a switch had been flipped.

Helix recognized the working on his helmet, the glimmer of runes etched into the metal.

Wisfield.

They were making progress with the emotional suppression, it seemed. Of all the noble houses, they were the ones most likely to catch on to what they were doing—and the hardest one to break into.

If they wanted to steal House secrets, they needed to start *here,* with the Principle of House Herastul. They were Elyra's spies, able to slide themselves out of perception like the Guildmaster herself did—though their methods were assuredly different. By the Guildmaster's own word, Herastul spies were far worse than she was.

But that didn't matter when Helix had no hope of spotting either of them. It was the reason for the fireball being as large as it was—Herastul grounds were hidden from the rest of the city, and the heat would spur anyone hiding to act.

As it did now. *Someone* had triggered the enchantment on the guard's helmet, after all.

Fortunately, it wasn't impossible to fight someone you couldn't see.

Larok and Helix both focused on the guard, as if they thought he was the only threat around. Helix pulled a hand down, compressing the enormous fireball hovering above his head into a bright spark of light in his hand, and then sent it flying forward; there was a flash as it struck the enchantment on the guard's sword and all that energy was converted into pure *light,* impossibly and blindingly bright.

It was a calculated move. Helix knew the spell would do nothing against the standard setup the guards carried, but it would blind anyone that happened to be looking in that direction.

Larok had closed his eyes in preparation for the flash, but he didn't need to open his eyes to throw the sheaf of papers in his arm up into the air. A gust of wind from Helix scattered the tax forms all over the garden, every individual piece fluttering to the ground in a poor imitation of snowfall.

"[**Know Your Paperwork**]," Larok said, and Helix laughed.

"You don't have to say your skills out loud, you know."

"It's cooler."

"Not when you're talking about paperwork!"

"Shut up," Larok grumbled, but in the same motion he *pointed*, and Helix reacted instantly; a flash of mana gathered into a runic circle that blasted out a powerful jet of water. It slammed into something invisible, and there was a cry of pain. A twist of his hand made the water-aspect mana dissipate before it could saturate the still-falling paper.

"One," Helix said.

"They know we're onto them now," Larok commented. Helix laughed.

"Doesn't mean they can stop us, does it?"

Another spell sent the remaining pieces of paper swirling around the garden in a wide circle; the guard stumbled out of the way, anticipating a trick, but Helix slammed his fist into the base of the guard's helmet right as he moved.

Then, looking at the guard's now-crumpled form, he cracked his neck and tossed the dagger he held to the side. He wasn't his brother. Fighting with a dagger felt like a small tribute to Vex, but it wasn't really what he *preferred*.

"There," Larok said, and this time Helix struck out with a different spell entirely; threads of mana burst out of his fingers, spooling towards the spot Larok had indicated. The Herastul spy tried to step out of the way, but threads were far harder to dodge than a single jet of water; they caught around the spy anyway, and Helix's expression changed to something a little more grim.

A simple [**Aspect Realignment**], and the threads of mana changed to *lightning*.

"Two." Helix ignored the scream, his eyes flicking back toward the guard, who had gotten up again and was approaching with an unsteady sword. He stepped forward, striking into the center of the armor with both his hands; mana coursed down his hands and *pulsed* into the armor, slamming it inward.

"One more?" Larok said.

Helix inclined his head toward the entrance to the garden, where he'd left a number of small runic circles embedded in the ground. Spikes of earth erupted from the ground a second afterward, cutting off a strangled cry.

"Three," Helix said. Larok shivered a bit.

"You can be pretty scary."

"Thanks, I try." Helix remained tense, his eyes looking around the garden. One guard and three handlers; it matched the reports they had, but this still all felt a little too *easy*. Herastul wasn't exactly a combat house, but they should have been better than *this*. It had taken one blow each . . .

Granted, every one of his spells was loaded with more than enough mana to take out most tanks, and if they were low on health from one blow, they would be smart enough to stay down.

"Your family doesn't make you immune to consequences, *Ashion*."

The words wisped by an ear, and Helix reacted quickly; fire burst from his body in a sphere, powerful enough to roast anyone standing nearby. He had to cancel the spell just as quickly when Larok stumbled, pushed *into* him.

And then the rest of House Herastul unveiled themselves. There were a dozen of them, standing in a circle around the pair, and one member of Wisfield.

That explained a lot. Wisfield's ability to keep them all connected mentally would let them coordinate perfectly.

"Why don't we try this again?"

The head of House Herastul was an old orc, but there was no humor in his smile. "What are you doing here, Ashion? With one of my clerks, no less?"

Helix sighed dramatically.

It was a good thing they were just the distraction.

CHAPTER 37

TAX FRAUD

Helix

"You didn't file form E27," Larok replied promptly. Helix gave him a dumbstruck look, and Larok waved him off. "That makes you liable to a seizure of assets."

"And you thought you'd take it yourself and enlist Ashion to steal from me?" the old orc asked. His voice was pompous, as if he didn't consider either of them a threat despite everything they'd just done.

Helix supposed he had a point. If they were willing to show themselves after they'd seen everything he could do, then they were very sure they could win. There was no doubt that Herastul had tricks other than just stealth; like all noble families, they funded a fair amount of research into various aspects of the system.

But neither he nor Larok could afford to get caught here. Not yet.

"We could cut you a deal," the old orc said. "What you did with the paper—that was interesting. Not nearly enough to be a full House Principle, of course, but we could buy it from you. What do you think?"

"I think you can fuck off," Larok said, pleasant as could be. Helix grinned.

It wasn't like they hadn't planned for things to go wrong.

A runic circle appeared in front of him, and he poured his mana into it. As an [**Elementalist**], he didn't have the same variety of spells that Vex had. His little brother might be able to find something more appropriate for the situation, perhaps, but most of what he had were elemental spells. He'd exchanged versatility for sheer magnitude of power.

But that didn't mean he didn't have *options*.

Smoke poured out of the circle in voluminous amounts, almost instantly filling up the garden. Helix caught the old orc's eyes widening just slightly before he vanished beneath the smoke. After all, the most even-handed way for them to fight would be if neither of them could see the other.

One hand grabbed on to Larok's so he didn't lose hold of his friend. In a full fight, the orc was far more likely to die than he was. He was still only level twenty-one, even with all of the training they'd done. Clerks didn't get a single health skill, so he had the base four hundred and twenty health that came at that level; they hadn't yet equipped him with gear that would keep him *safe*.

Two tasks, then. First priority: Keep Larok safe. Second: Keep Jakka Herastul and his cronies occupied for as long as possible. Third: Don't get caught.

He could do that. Probably.

Helix *moved*.

Mana wrapped itself around him as he did, boosting his stats and making him just a little more aware of everything around him. It wasn't as good as anything Vex would be able to do, but it was a functional substitute—a basic [**Mana Boost**]. Larok yelped as he was dragged along, but Helix was moving with purpose and couldn't stop to discuss the plan.

He'd have to trust that Larok remembered. He had a number of administrative skills, after all, beyond just the one for paperwork. The problem was the Wisfield House member; if he could peer into their minds, he could anticipate anything they wanted to do.

They needed to target him first.

Right on cue, Larok spoke rapidly, trying not to cough through the smoke. "Wisfield House member, Unek Wisfield, second-branch family. Moved a total of two hundred and ten platinum coins across various businesses owned to reduce tax bracket and therefore taxes owed—"

Helix felt a burning flash of mana and *yanked*, clearing his mind as he did so; he needed to make sure the Wisfield member didn't just adjust where his magic was going. A splash of deadly goldfire drifted just past Larok's elbow, and Helix let a low growl escape his throat.

Larok didn't let himself get distracted, though he had to bite back a yelp from the near-dislocation of his shoulder.

"—and therefore committed [**Tax Fraud**]," Larok rapidly finished.

The skill resonated in the air, carried by the orc's voice.

It was not, unlike the name implied, a skill to help one commit tax fraud. Helix had assumed that to be the case at first, and a laughing Larok had to explain that the skill was all about reclaiming lost assets; he had *no* idea why the thing was named Tax Fraud.

He'd learned exactly what *assets* meant from a certain merchant in J'rokksur. It included a number of different things, exactly one of which was combat-relevant.

Mana.

And as long as Larok owned it, Unek couldn't use it. Helix knew for a fact that the Wisfield House still needed mana to use their skills, with very few and very rare exceptions. The one part of their plan they were worried about was their ability to pull this off at all—there was every chance that with the Wisfield's ability to read their minds, he would do everything in his power to stop him—and he *had*. Goldfire was rare and powerful, a magic item occasionally harvested from Elyra's Prime Dungeon itself. It had the ability to track and destroy any target it was aimed at.

It also needed to be fueled with mana.

Without it, the string of goldfire fell to the grass, useless. The grass surrounding it didn't even burn. Helix didn't spare it more than a glance—he pulled Larok forward, away from the building mass of mana he could sense.

For now, with the smoke surrounding them obscuring their vision and their Wisfield member otherwise disabled, the Herastul members would be afraid to really let loose with their skills. They'd be more likely to strike one another or, worse, the head of their own house.

Not that Jakka seemed to give a shit.

"*Kill them!*" he roared, and Helix only barely stopped himself from rolling his eyes.

Honestly.

That building mass of mana turned into a blaze as twelve different members of House Herastul unleashed their skills and turned the center of the garden into a deadly inferno; Helix grimaced at the heat, channeling a small amount of wind aspect around himself and Larok to keep them cool. Two figures vanished in his mana sense, apparently caught in the crossfire or otherwise out of mana.

Larok shot him a nervous look, only barely visible in the thick fog of smoke, and Helix gave him a reassuring grin. They could make it out of this. They'd taken out the most important member of the opposing team, and all they needed to do now was keep everyone occupied . . .

. . . a strong gust of wind began to blow.

Helix frowned. He kept a tight grip on the smoke-aspect mana he was spreading throughout the garden, but something about this opposing magic seemed to loosen the grip he had on his power. More and more, his own smoke slipped out of his grasp and began to dissipate, and he felt Larok clutch at his hand nervously.

Helix tightened his hand in response, narrowing his eyes. This was different.

This, they hadn't planned for.

Jakka's smirking face emerged from the smoke. Helix half-expected him to waste time monologuing—he certainly looked like he was about to—but he gestured instead, and a tight blade of power emerged from his fist.

Helix's eyes widened.

He only barely threw both himself and Larok out of the way before the blade struck, and their combined momentum sent them tumbling. Helix was vaguely aware in the back of his mind that he couldn't afford the *time* to get back up again, that Larok was in danger—Jakka wasn't their only opponent—

He heard Larok cry in pain, and all hesitation vanished.

A tide of mana swelled and ripped out of him, shifting between all the basic elements at once; it folded neatly around Larok through an effort of will and slammed into everyone else with a thundering force. Helix pulled it back into his control just a fraction of a second before the skill completed and it left his range. [**Elemental Burst**] was a cheap, common skill, but it scaled *drastically* with the mana poured into it.

And Helix's whole thing was monstrous amounts of mana.

He wove a [**Barrier**] around Larok, pouring almost a quarter of his well into it. He saw his friend's eyes widen in the near-solid barrier of energy, saw a soundless shout emerge from Larok's lips, but he didn't wait to hear what his friend had to say. He'd handle this alone.

Burning mana flew back toward him, and he willed it into coating his right arm in a [**Flaming Gauntlet**]. He was a physical combatant, first and foremost, and he wanted to punch Jakka in his stupid, smug little face.

[**Mana Boost**] still empowering him, he rocketed forward, fist clenched. Ten Herastul members knelt on the ground, aiming some sort of device at him that he couldn't quite spare the time to look at. He shifted the nature of the [**Mana Boost**] slightly, giving himself more agility, boosting and shifting his stats to make his movement just a little bit too erratic.

Jakka wasn't going to stand still, of course. The orc frowned at him and did that contemptuous motion with his hand again, and this time, Helix saw the ring he wore pulsing with borrowed mana. Compressed air aspect formed before him, sharp enough to tear through a boulder with little resistance.

It met his will and shattered.

Ashion members were used to dealing with immense amounts of mana. What did Jakka think would happen?

A [**Mana Boost**]ed [**Flame Gauntlet**] with his amount of mana was enough to do three thousand damage at *least,* and Helix didn't give a shit about holding back. His fist met Jakka's jaw—

—but a fraction of a second before it did, one of the Herastul members finally managed to target him, and he felt his grip on his own mana suddenly loosen again. Both skills began to unravel.

Not completely, though. His fist smashed into Jakka's jaw, and the orc was sent sprawling, no matter that he was nearly twice Helix's size. Helix spun around before Jakka could recover, sprinting for the nearest Herastul member; he needed to get rid of whatever that device was instead of letting it rip his own mana out of his control.

But he was slow, now. Without [**Mana Boost**], his stats were just like any other level fifty-three, and while he wasn't *weak* by any means, the Herastul members were more explicitly dedicated to fighting. They were faster, stronger, and better equipped than him.

He knew before he'd taken even two steps that he didn't have a chance.

The damn [**Barrier**] that he'd left around Larok was unraveling too. He tried to keep his grip on it, recapturing that mana again and again with [**Mana Manipulation**], but it was a losing battle. Every Herastul combatant was heading for him, faster than he could track, and Jakka was getting up.

For the first time, Helix felt fear.

And then he heard a very familiar voice.

"Looks like you need help," Vex said. His younger brother smiled at him—a small, light smile, but it struck Helix like a dagger to the heart. He hadn't seen Vex smile at him like that for *years*.

He barely even noticed that every single person on the field was frozen in place except for him and Larok.

"Uh," he said after a moment, and then cleared his throat. "Yeah. Um. Help would be nice."

"Still like dramatic entrances?" Vex said, just the smallest trace of a smirk in his voice, and Helix couldn't help but laugh, equal parts relieved and confused.

"You know it."

CHAPTER 38

WINDS OF CHANGE

The nice thing about **<A World Without a System>** was really the time-dilation aspect of it. It gave Derivan so much *time* compared to the people who were on Obreve proper—time for him to use Shift, open up a portal, recharge, and then use Shift again. In that amount of time, only about an hour would have passed on Obreve.

It took him *ten hours* to recharge fully.

That amount of dilation gave them the time to inspect the details of everything that was happening with the rebellion—to look through their plans, to keep an eye on things in case anything went wrong.

They'd made sure to check in from time to time, and everything seemed to be going about as well as could be expected. The rebellion used the glyphs that Vex had taught them to set traps and cast magics they never could have otherwise, and even developed a few new ones that Vex subsequently copied and stole.

If Helix hadn't left for the Herastul estate a little earlier than scheduled, Derivan and the others would have made it just in time. As it was, they realized what was happening almost a moment too late. Helix had missed a scheduled check-in, and Vex had asked Derivan to see what was going on.

Then—once they'd seen all they needed to see—Derivan ripped open a hole in reality between the dungeon's bonus room and the Herastul estate.

Sev's first move was to use [**A Moment of Time**], which he'd received from Tempus and which was a far better version of the skill he'd gotten from Aurum. It took a lot more divine magic, accordingly, but the artifact Vex had retrieved seemed to have it in spades.

That skill froze everyone in time except for the people he chose. They would all have to return to their initial positions before the skill released, but it gave them ample opportunity to talk, plan, and cast new skills.

"Ready?" Vex asked. He gestured to Sev, who was holding a key inside a lock that looked like it was trying to fight him. Time, after all, didn't like stopping. "We can't keep this up forever."

"Should've invested more points in Strength," Misa said, smirking at Sev.

"Shut up," Sev grumbled, gritting his teeth. The key was forced to turn half a degree back in his fingers, and all of reality shifted half an inch; the closest Herastul combatant was now close enough for Helix to see the glint of their blade.

"You're gonna help me, right?" Helix said, looking at the crowd dubiously. "I can't take 'em by myself."

"We got you," Vex assured.

"Especially me," Misa quipped.

[**Me, Myself, and I**], it turned out, was a skill that codified what she'd done with [**An Anchor of Heart and Home**]. It allowed her to summon semi-independent copies of herself at the cost of half her health—and it was that skill she used now far more liberally than was practical.

Sev sighed, letting go of the key with one hand to make a quick gesture; divine magic spread into each one of Misa's copies, healing them—and her—back up to full. The key forced itself another two degrees in that instant, and he grabbed ahold of it again. "Come on, guys," he said, his voice strained.

"Go ahead," Helix said. He settled down, taking a breath, and his eyes gained a glint of steel in them; threads of mana began to collect around him, coalescing into another [**Fire Gauntlet**] and a new [**Ice Gauntlet**] on his arms. "I'm ready."

Sev let the key go, and time returned with a *snap*.

It was nice to have control of his mana again, Helix thought.

A half-dozen copies of his brother's orc friend appeared in the garden, and the ensuing confusion kept the Herastul henchmen from noticing the threat he now posed. Roughly half of them still had their attention on him, and the closest was still mid-step, a bright flash of crimson flickering within his fist.

Helix punched him in the face.

Whatever he was carrying didn't matter—the man went flying, concentrated fire exploding first from the back of the gauntlet, then the front; the effect was an accelerated punch that smashed the man's face in. He swung his second arm almost lazily, letting the weight of the [**Ice Gauntlet**] spin him around, and it shattered in another Herastul member's face.

Neither of those blows were enough to take care of either of those men, of course. Herastul employees and House members were better trained than that, and passive buffs like his gauntlets weren't the sorts of spells that would eradicate people in a single blow.

They were made for sustained combat. It wasn't quite as practical—it didn't take full advantage of his massive reserves of mana, for example—but it helped in extremely prolonged fights, namely the ones he had to fight in Mana Nuclei.

The first henchman rose to fight again. This time, enough of the man's cloak had burned away that he could see his face, too, distorted in a rictus of startling anger.

"What, did I do something to you personally?" Helix quipped. He danced out of the way of the blow the Herastul man tried to land, making sure none of that crimson got anywhere near him, trying to remember where he recognized the man's face.

And then he frowned, a chill flooding his body all at once.

He wasn't really taking this seriously enough. This wasn't just some random member of the House—this was the Herastul heir. Jakka's son. Arkul, if he remembered correctly.

Why in the world had Jakka involved his *son* in this fight? He was barely eighteen! And he recognized the crimson glow in the man's hand now—he was using a *Life Core*! Those things were artifacts from House Vitalia, and though they were powerful, they tore at the user's life for every blow they struck.

Not their health. Their *life*. A Life Core would make you age with every blow, and in return, a single strike . . .

"What the *fuck*," Helix hissed, and he almost paid for it. He felt the wind of an attack behind him and threw himself out of the way, and a fraction of a second later, a version of Misa appeared in front of the blow, catching the last fragment of it the moment before it would have struck him.

This one was Jakka's daughter. Ikaya.

She wasn't using anything as absurd as a Life Core, at least, but she seemed just as lost in her anger. Helix felt his rage burning brighter in him, and the gauntlets on his fists responded, one flaring hotter and the other colder. He couldn't retreat from this fight to deal with Jakka now—but he *could* disable these two.

"Heads up!" he called. "These guys are Jakka's kids! I think there's something wrong with them! Might be true for the others, too!"

Over in the corner, Larok's eyes widened, and he began rapidly flipping through a notebook he kept with him. His younger brother and his three adventurer friends all reacted immediately, exchanging worried glances with one another and then shifting the way they fought—

But Helix didn't have the time to pay attention. The Herastul heirs were on his back again, both of them attacking at once.

He couldn't afford to get hit by the Life Core. He dodged out of the way of that one as a priority, gritting his teeth and letting the manadrill Jakka's daughter wielded bore its way into him. He crushed the hand holding the Life Core between his gauntlets a moment later, and found himself disturbed by the way Arkul didn't even flinch. The Life Core's light flickered out, its elements disrupted by the dual assault of fire and ice, and Helix immediately *twisted.*

Using his own body as leverage when there was a weapon stuck in him was a little disconcerting, but nothing new, really. A manadrill was the worst weapon to bring against an Ashion House member.

He had mana to spare. Those things wouldn't hurt him if they were left in him for days.

That sent Ikaya crashing to the ground, too, and a quick spell sent tight vines wrapping around their bodies. Helix panted as his Health took care of his wounds, then glanced up to continue the fight . . .

. . . only to find that every single one of them had been struck down and bound.

The other four hadn't been idle, after all.

Helix promptly ignored the aftermath of the battle and hurried over to Larok. His mana barrier had held, fortunately, and by some miracle Larok had emerged from the whole conflict without a scratch. If Jakka had had any sense at all, he would have sent some of his men to target Larok—Helix would've had to abandon fighting to defend him.

But Jakka, he supposed, hadn't even stopped to consider that a commoner might mean something to a noble. Even with a big fuckoff shield around said commoner.

"You doing okay?" Helix asked, helping Larok to his feet.

"Am *I* okay?" Larok laughed. "I should be the one asking you that! You were amazing! Not that I didn't know that already, but . . ."

"First time you've actually seen it?" Helix asked. Despite himself, he managed a small grin.

"I've seen it before." Larok smirked back, but he'd heard what Helix had yelled too, and that smirk quickly fell away. "I'm glad I was able to help, but . . . do you have any idea what's going on here?"

"You helped?" Helix blinked.

Larok stared at him and raised a brow. "You didn't think it was weird they didn't use any skills?"

A broad grin spread over Helix's face. He let himself forget, just for a moment, about what Jakka had done to his own children, and wrapped Larok in a hug. "Shit, I should've realized. That's fucking amazing."

"Too tight!" Larok yelped, and Helix released him.

"Whoops. Left [**Mana Boost**] on."

"Like always," Larok huffed at him, and Helix smiled slightly.

"I guess we can't really take the credit for most of this, though," Helix said. "Those four are something else."

Larok stared at them and shivered a little. "Yeah, no kidding. Glad they're on our side."

"Yeah." Helix was silent for a moment, then glanced over at the field of groaning bodies. "You think the kids are gonna be all right?"

". . . I hope so."

"Something is wrong," Derivan said. He glanced around the garden, his eyes glowing with concern. Part of his mind was occupied, taken up by the effort it took to keep the portal to their bonus room open—if he allowed it to snap shut, it would collapse the whole thing, and they weren't quite ready to leave.

Not yet.

"What, besides the thing where the orc sent his children to fight rebels?" Sev raised an eyebrow. He glanced toward Jakka with distaste—the orc wasn't saying a word, and *couldn't* say a word, bound up as tight as he was.

"Yes," Derivan said. He didn't mind the sarcasm; Sev was worried, he knew, and none of it was targeted at him. And yet . . .

There were strange, half-visible ripples in the air whenever he looked. None of his skills or stats were quite able to latch on to them. It wasn't mana, it wasn't the Shifting undertones of reality, and it couldn't have been divinity, either. Sev or Vex would have sensed it. "You do not see this? The distortions."

"Distortions?" Sev frowned. He glanced around worriedly, and so did Misa and Vex; all three of them shook their heads. "No."

"I cannot sense them," Derivan murmured. "But I can *see* them . . ."

Very carefully, he stepped forward, closer to one of the wriggling shapes. Now that he paid closer attention, he could see that they were gathered mostly around the flowers, herbs, and bushes planted in the garden. He brushed a finger against one of them, curious and cautious.

The system responded.

He felt it through Patch, but no screen appeared in front of him. It was *trying* to show him something, but the mechanism it was activating was broken—he could feel where the threads in the system had vanished. It was almost like they had been eaten away.

That was, fortunately, an easy enough Patch. He couldn't link it to the main system—it seemed to reject it the moment he tried to link it, shifting away from the mental thread he tried to extend to it, almost as if it was afraid. But there was an older system attached to Misa, and he appropriated that connection, switching the thread to tie in to that older engine.

Text floated into his vision, with no box to accompany it.

<Void Wyrmling—Growth>

"Ah," Derivan said.

The word wasn't quite sufficient for the sudden worry he now felt. He took a step back, trying to organize his thoughts, and felt Vex walk up to him.

"You found something?" his boyfriend asked.

"I believe I have," Derivan said. "And if I understand what this is correctly . . . then Elyra is in greater danger than we thought."

He glanced grimly at Helix. "We may have to accelerate our plans."

CHAPTER 39

NEXT STEPS

Figuring out what to do next was rather more complicated than it should have been, Vex thought.

Jakka and his children could not be allowed to go free; that was a given. The rebels would have to capture and house them—far easier said than done, although Helix was insistent that they would be able to do it.

Vex had no idea how. He seemed fully intent on just dragging their bodies through the streets.

"You're not going to just drag them through the streets, right?" Vex asked his brother hesitantly.

"Of course not!" Helix said indignantly. "We're going to dress them up as potato sacks."

Vex took a deep breath, then saw Helix's smirk and let himself relax. "Almost got me with that one," he said with a small smile.

It was strange, being so amicable with his older brother. His relationship with Helix had never been like this—it had always been fraught with jealousy and clashing viewpoints, arguments about how best to use their magic . . . They had never had the opportunity to just be *brothers.*

Helix seemed far more comfortable in his own skin and with the people around him now. Before, he had been far more irritable.

"Vex?" Derivan called gently. "We must go. I cannot keep the portal open for much longer."

"I'll keep you up to date," Helix said with a wink, mimicking typing through the system. Vex gave his brother a nod, hesitated for a second, and stepped up to give him a quick hug; Helix stiffened for a moment, then returned the hug, some unseen tension in his body slowly dissolving.

"Good to have you back, brother," Helix said quietly.

Vex gave him a small smile, then turned and darted back through Derivan's portal—back into the little home they had made for themselves in the middle of the Roads.

It was more of a temporary base than anything. The Roads had allowed all four of them to meet back up after they'd completed their respective paths, dumping the four of them into a larger, circular cavern with a number of square-shaped empty homes built into the dirt.

It reminded Vex strangely of Mundane. He wondered if this was an abandoned city, or if it was waiting to have people move in. Everything within it seemed unused and clean, so perhaps the Roads were preparing it for use . . . It served them well enough for now, though, so they decided to take a break.

None of them *quite* wanted to go through the menacing red door at the other side of the cavern yet.

Well, except for Misa. Misa really wanted to go through the menacing red door.

For now, though, the four of them had other things on their minds.

"You said you saw something?" Vex asked. He sat on one side of the table in the small, square home they'd appropriated for themselves; the furniture in the place was plain but functional, and comfortable enough for all of them.

Derivan's expression was grave. "I believe I know the cause of the growth spells failing. If they are what I think they are, then we do not have as much time as we think. Elyra will need evacuation."

Vex jolted. "*Evacuation*?"

"That seems extreme," Sev said, but he didn't sound skeptical. He frowned slightly, glancing off into the air like he was quietly communicating with someone, and then furrowed his brows. "You're worried about disrupting the rebellion's plans, yeah?"

"It is a concern," Derivan admitted. "They will not have as much time to raid the Houses as would be ideal for them. By my estimations, we have less than a month before growth as a concept stops functioning in Elyra entirely."

"What did you see, Deri?" Vex asked, his voice almost pleading. Elyra was his home. His relationship with his home was complicated, certainly; he didn't like almost any of Elyra's policies, and he had almost no love left for his family save for his—well, now two of his brothers.

Derivan sighed. "Void Wyrmlings," he said.

And then he explained.

He'd already told them all about what he'd experienced in his section of the Roads—the way he'd entered the Void, the fact that he'd encountered others in there. The fact that monsters had all once been *people* was a true shock to them all.

It was even more of one when he shared that many of them were plane-shifted species as well. Obreve had once been far more diverse, containing peoples from all sorts of realms.

Now they had barely anyone left.

"I suspect that the wyrmlings are not truly wyrmlings at all. They do not seem *alive*. The system knows that they exist, in a manner of speaking, but I had to Patch it for it to display them at all. I suspect the system once directly pointed out the Void . . ." Derivan tilted his head, aiming his gaze suddenly toward Misa. "Ah. But I can see why it no longer does so."

"What?" Misa sounded slightly nonplussed. "Why are you looking at me?"

"I had to borrow from your Path system to force the system to create a display for the wyrmlings," Derivan explained. "It did not cause any damage to your part of the system, but . . . the piece that was connected to the wyrmling had further deteriorated. It is difficult to interact with the Void without deteriorating, I suspect."

"Eugh." Misa made a discomforted sort of noise, shaking her head. "Not sure I like the thought of Void worms poking their way through reality."

"Regardless," Derivan said, "they appear to feed on the concept of *growth*. We understand now that magic functions through the application of glyphs, which themselves pull from the conceptual sphere. It appears that within the area dominated by Elyra's reality anchor, the concept of growth itself is slowly being erased."

Silence reigned for a moment, and then Vex spoke.

"You're worried about what will happen after," he said. "It's not just the lack of food, but once the wyrmlings run out of things to eat . . ."

"The Void is already encroaching on Elyra," Derivan said with a nod. "The anchor is still functioning, or we would not be *here*; either the wyrmlings are a new development or the anchors themselves are no longer enough, even fully intact as they are."

"Or the Void is evolving," Misa mumbled, and the rest of her team stared at her. "What? It's possible!"

"I hope not," Sev said with a shudder. "Bad enough that we're faced with the end of all reality. We don't need it being *alive*."

"I do not think that is the case, fortunately," Derivan said. "But if the rebellion is to succeed, it must do so soon. If we impress upon them that they need to evacuate the city . . ."

"We'll tell them what's going on," Vex said. "Helix knows something is up, anyway, and I trust them to figure things out and ask for help if they need it. They're more likely to believe us than the nobles, anyway."

—ꝏ—

"We'll ask them for help," Syvila decided.

She was too old for this. Ingress was looking at her with a sad-but-understanding sort of look on his face, Helix had his brows furrowed, and half the rest of the rebellion's leaders looked angry. The others looked resigned.

"You want to ask for *help*?" one demanded. He was cloaked in shadow, his voice distorted by the magics on it, but she knew who he was. Justin ran a food kitchen somewhere in Southern Elyra. He'd seen what the nobles had done more or less firsthand. She understood his anger—understood what she was asking of them all.

"This is bigger than us," Syvila said quietly. "If Elyra itself is in danger, then even the nobles must put aside their struggles for power."

"They won't do that," Justin scoffed. Several of the other members of the rebellion nodded beside him. Syvila couldn't deny that they might have a point. The food crisis was in itself something the nobles should have put aside their differences to handle—and yet they had not. The people of Elyra had mostly been left to starve.

But what were they going to do? Evacuating Elyra would be far harder without the help of the nobles. Getting their help would make it that much faster.

"Are you even sure that your brother is telling the truth?" another person said. Kryla, a simple lizardkin apothecary in the western corner of Elyra. In the wake of growth spells beginning to fail, she had worked tirelessly to create a potion that reduced the need for food, and had even been partially successful—but none of the nobles had funded her, no matter how much she begged.

Now she spoke directly to Helix, who stiffened slightly at the hint of condescension in her tone. "You and he are both nobles. Are we to take your word for this coming disaster?"

"You do not have to." This time, the person that spoke up was a priest—Jukar, of orcish descent. Syvila remembered seeing him working in the streets, healing the starving and the sick; healing could stave off the effects of starvation, but never enough. He'd driven himself to mana exhaustion with it. "I have spoken with Urasta. The danger is true."

"The *gods* are involved with this?" Kryla asked, and this time she sounded appropriately chastised; she sent an apologetic look to Helix, who waved it off. Syvila watched the exchange with a small amount of pride.

It wasn't the first time Helix had had friction with other members of the rebellion, and it likely wouldn't be the last. She'd smoothed things over as best as she could, and they were slowly getting used to one another, even if sparks still flew at times. What was important was that Helix understood their distrust, and the other members of the rebellion were willing to admit to their mistakes.

"They are," Jukar confirmed. "They have been receiving warnings . . . There is a threat, previously unknown to them. Gods have been erased, and no one has been the wiser, for the information has been hidden from us. And this is just another part of that problem. Our world is crumbling. There is no longer time to struggle for power. We must find somewhere *safe*. For the people."

It was the longest thing Jukar had ever said in a meeting, and it left the entire hall silent. Ghostly fire flickered in the walls around them, protecting them from the prying minds of the Wisfield house.

"So the threat is real, we are agreed," Syvila said finally. "We vote on reaching out and working with the nobles to evacuate?"

"And on what to do if they fail to help us," Kryla said. "They have no reason to believe us, and even if their own priests tell them . . ."

"I doubt they'll want to help," Helix said, and many eyes in the room turned to him. He shrugged. "They aren't going to believe you. I'm sorry. Doesn't matter if their own priests tell 'em otherwise. This threatens their power."

"We must *try*," Syvila said, but there was a small downward quirk at the corner of her lips; she did not have high hopes either. "But if they do not help us . . . what we must do has changed. Elyra is no longer safe to stay in, and so the rebellion will no longer focus on taking the kingdom from the nobles. We will focus on evacuation. We might not win in a straight fight, but they cannot stop us from *leaving* and from bringing as many as we can with us."

Quiet murmurs erupted across the room, but most of them were in agreement.

The vote passed, and the people in the room slowly filtered out. Syvila sighed, turning back to her books, and let the rest of the library slowly shimmer back into existence around her.

She hadn't expected to end up in quite *this* position when she'd chosen to help a young lizardkin years ago, so uncertain about his place in the world.

What Vex had uncovered now was so far beyond her she felt her scales aging just from thinking about it. And yet if he hadn't . . .

A tongue flicked out, and she turned the page of the book she was reading delicately, respectfully.

It would be some time still before she could rest.

CHAPTER 40

TIME

The ominous red door loomed in front of them. Vex had chosen to deem it the ORB, for "ominous red boundary." No one had really taken on the name yet, but they hadn't disputed him on it, either, so he was confident they'd pick up on it eventually.

"About time we go through," Misa said, eyeing it.

"If we do, I'm not sure we're going to be able to help the rebellion if anything goes wrong," Sev said. "This thing—"

"The ORB," Vex supplied.

"Yes, Vex," Sev sighed. "The ORB. It looks like . . . it looks *final*? It looks like when we go through it, we're going to face the last trial of the bonus room, and then we'll complete it."

Derivan patted Vex on the head, and the lizardkin gave a low trill of pleasure. "I do not think we should delay," Derivan said. "There is an advantage to remaining here, certainly, but we are aware that it pulls resources from the Elyran anchor. It is possible that by staying, we are accelerating Elyra's eventual fall."

"Elyra's going to fall anyway," Vex said. Some of his earlier humor faded from his eyes—he was trying everything he could to distract himself from everything happening in his home. A large part of him wanted to go back and do everything he could to help, but . . .

He was more valuable *here*, with his friends.

"You want to go back, though," Derivan said, observing him closely, and Vex sighed as the armor pulled him into his arms.

Arm.

They still hadn't fixed that. They just . . . hadn't had the time.

"I do," Vex admitted. "It doesn't feel right to be . . . I don't know, *safe*? Not that it's safe here, but Elyra's in danger, and I'm not there. Helix is trying to protect it; Riss has no idea what's going on. I don't think the nobles are going to agree to work with the rebellion, so if the rebels just *leave*, Riss is going to be stuck there . . ."

"Do you really think Helix would leave your little brother there?" Misa asked, raising a brow. "That doesn't seem like him."

"No," Vex said, shaking his head in frustration. "But my father . . ."

He trailed off.

Karix was powerful. Helix couldn't fight off the man even at his best. If Vex *helped* . . .

But that was their conundrum right now, really. If they went through the trial and it somehow prevented them from working with Elyra—from keeping an eye on everything happening with the rebels and the nobles—then they would effectively be on their own. If they *waited*, they might accelerate everything that was happening, and no matter what they'd have to enter the door eventually.

The ORB. The joke seemed a little less funny now, but sometimes, a little levity was needed.

"Sooner rather than later, I think," Misa said, and her words were surprisingly gentle. A strong arm landed on his shoulder, and Misa smiled at him. "No matter when we go, we're going to end up indisposed for a while. The sooner we get it over with, the sooner we can help the rebels if anything comes up. And knowing those noble fucks, something is gonna come up. Right?"

Vex nodded slowly. She was right. It was pretty clear, even, in the way Jakka had fought back against Helix with his own children. There was . . . something going on there; he just didn't know what.

Better to be ready by the time they did something. Derivan's portal time was limited, anyway, and if they were forced to retreat in the middle of a fight—or let the portal close on them—Vex doubted the results would be pretty.

—∞—

In one universe, Misa opened a door.

It was only practical that she tested out what was behind the door first, with an application of Endless Echoes. Just in case they were wrong about what the door was and it was a trap.

In *all* universes, the door opened.

It wasn't a trap, thankfully. Derivan apologized and said that he should have noticed; the door was a fixed point in reality, solid across all the wavelengths he could reach through Shift. The door existed even back in the "real world," for all that their definition of that concept was rapidly falling apart.

Misa let her Endless Echoes dissolve and stared past the door at what lay beyond.

It was *chaos.*

"What the fuck is this?" she said, almost dumbly. She reached out with a hand, brushing it against the blistering light that lay just beyond the door; thankfully, it did nothing to her. She'd been half-expecting her health to start dropping just from the contact.

"I don't know what I'm looking at," Sev admitted. He stepped inside, somewhat braver than Misa had been, and waved a hand; a small dome of shade appeared around him, blocking off the excess light that made it near-impossible to see. Misa joined him, and Derivan and Vex followed soon after.

Being able to see better didn't make it much easier to parse what was going on, though.

It was like up was down and left was right; the world paid no attention to the petty requirements of things like *gravity* and *common sense.* Chunks of rocks floated in the sky, upside-down, and Misa could see small figures moving upside-down along with them, entering little homes and drinking from tiny teacups. She wasn't even sure if they were alive—something about their movements was false, mechanical.

The wind blew around them, but something about the breeze was *wrong.* The air was denser and heavier than it should have been, and so what should have produced a rustling breeze was instead a deeper howl. The air smelled, strangely enough, of cinnamon and blueberry and the static crackle of an oncoming storm.

"I think . . ." Vex started, hesitating; the wind almost drowned out his words. "I think this is a place that the magic hasn't fixed yet. I think it's a place the magic is working on fixing."

"Perhaps that is what we were intended to do?" Derivan suggested. "To help the mana repair this land?"

"I . . . don't know." Vex looked surprisingly lost. He knelt close to the ground, brushing his fingers through the faux grass beneath them. When he made a face, Misa copied him, kneeling down and then shuddering as she touched the grass.

"The fuck?" she muttered. "Feels like wet paint."

"If we're supposed to fix this, I wouldn't even know where to begin," Vex said quietly.

The four of them stared out across the landscape for a moment, taking it in.

"Let's just explore," Sev said after a moment. "Take it one step at a time. We'll figure something out."

"We always do," Misa agreed.

A few hours in, and they had discovered a few basic rules about the new space they found themselves in.

One, they couldn't go back. The door they'd gone through had vanished as soon as the last of them had stepped through, leaving grass and air in its wake. Shift, too, failed; reality here seemed *denser,* Derivan said, for all that it was technically weaker than it was anywhere else. It was like there was something holding it in place, and Shift was not nearly strong enough to move it.

Two, for that same reason, Derivan couldn't use Shift to reach out to Elyra—or anywhere else, for that matter. They would be locked in place for however much time they spent here, so they had to work quickly if they wanted to help with the Elyran evacuation.

Three, the system itself still worked, as well as their ability to communicate with the outside world using the chat function.

Case in point was the message they received from the Guildmaster shortly after entering what they had deemed "the ruins."

[**Not sure if you're able to receive this message,**] she sent, her words surprisingly short and clipped. [**System is experiencing far more trouble than usual. Some places have it worse than others. Finish up quick. Assistance may be needed.**]

"Ah, shit," Sev muttered, reading the message, and Misa made a disgruntled noise of agreement.

"Is it not just Elyra?" Vex frowned. "I'm sure she would have said something if any place was as bad as Elyra."

"I doubt any individual settlement has it as bad as Elyra, but a lot of smaller things can ruin a settlement without the supplies to keep it going," Misa said, frowning. She glanced at her own system. "Things are . . . apparently going well in Teque and Fendal. J'rokksur is assisting as best as it can with the Guild—many of its guards have joined up, so they're fighting the manpower shortage for now. Mom says that she's helping to keep track of the numbers, and she's pretty sure at least five adventurers have gone missing with no record . . . Shit."

"Let us hurry," Derivan said, and no one protested.

The first place of significance they encountered looked something like a ruined palace. Most of it had crumbled to dust, leaving very little left to indicate who or what might have once lived here.

"Noram said something about how the world began to crumble and fall apart, and the mana put it back together," Vex said softly. He knelt, letting some of the dust trail between his fingers. "This was someone's home."

"It's just dust now," Misa said, though her voice was gentle. "Let's move on."

—~—

The second place they encountered was a little more intact. More of the walls were left behind, though they swayed dangerously in the wind. Vex walked up to them and brushed his fingers across the faded murals, a faint sense of recognition sparking in his mind.

Why did this place seem familiar?

He didn't know, and there was nothing else here for him to find.

They'd been wandering for almost a day, now, and had yet to find anything that might give them a hint as to what they were supposed to do here. Food and water was at least abundant, if strange-tasting; Sev made sure to purify any of the food they came across, just in case.

—~—

The second day saw a new message from Helix, and one from the Guildmaster.

[**Nobles didn't listen,**] Helix said. Vex imagined him typing the message and rolling his eyes as he did so, like he'd known the whole time it would happen. [**Not even Dad would listen. Didn't expect any different, but it's still frustrating.**]

[**They didn't try to spring a trap?**] Vex sent back.

Helix took a long half-hour to respond—three minutes, in his time. [**Of fuckin' course they did,**] he said. [**We were prepared. No casualties. Took a little souvenir with us, too.**]

Vex managed a small smile. [**Any update on what the deal with Jakka is?**]

Three hours before the reply on that one. [**No. Jakka still won't talk, and all his kids won't either. We think it's a Wisfield compulsion, so we're asking the Guild for help removing it.**]

The Guildmaster's message explained why the Guild hadn't already sent them that assistance. [**Guild's overloaded right now,**] she sent. [**Dungeon breaks are getting more common, even when the dungeons themselves**

are getting cleared. System seems to be stabilizing for a bit, but no guarantee it'll last. Any recommendations?]

[**Wait for us,**] Misa had sent.

J'rokksur had thus far not experienced any of the problems with the system that many others had. The prevailing assumption at the moment was that Misa's particular anchor was immune, or at least protected, from whatever degradation was affecting all the other ones. They'd told the Guildmaster how Misa had ended up binding the anchor to herself, but the Guild had had no luck replicating those circumstances so far—nor did they want to risk their already-limited adventurers on broken dungeons.

The best thing they could do was to find a way to link everyone to Misa's anchor instead. With enough reality shards, they could handle the load, at least for a little while, and they'd managed to stock up a bit while they were here.

And yet they still didn't know what the *objective* was. What did the bonus room want them to do?

The third significant location was a good three days away. This time, the ruins were intact enough that Vex recognized a small piece of architecture, and the lizardkin caught his breath.

"This was Elyra," he said. "I should've realized. Everything was so *broken* . . . but this place was Elyra."

CHAPTER 41

VAULT

The ruins of Elyra were spread out across kilometers, along broken rocks that floated on separate islands. Vex saw cracks in the ground beneath that led to a pure nothingness; Derivan identified that nothingness as the Void, and so they collectively chose to avoid falling.

Not that they weren't going to do that already.

Now that they knew these were the ruins of Elyra, Vex had a better idea of where they needed to go.

"There's a vault near the center of Elyra," he said. "No one's been able to open it—it's not just locked and reinforced; it's *system-locked*. We can't use any skills on it, because any skills we try to use the system automatically disables, and the box itself is reinforced to indestructibility by the system."

"But this is a world *without* a system," Misa said, her eyes gleaming.

"Yeah." Vex didn't look as excited as he might have about the potential discovery. "I'm just worried. This is . . . All this stuff is *old*. We have two hundred years of history. These ruins . . . I've checked with my spells. They're over a thousand years old."

"We know the world is older than we think," Misa said with a shrug. "What makes this new?"

"Elyra is *meticulous*," Vex insisted. "We record everything. We record our records! If we lose our records, we should at least *have a record of losing them*. But we don't. It's like Elyra's only existed for two hundred years. I figured we were probably founded a little bit before that, and then maybe we lost some of the early documentation, or it got eaten by the Void. But this would be almost twelve hundred years of lost history. That's . . . so much more than I thought."

"I'm worried too," Sev said. He frowned, running his fingers over the wall and staring at the dust that came off onto his fingers. "I've spoken to Tempus, and he agrees. This place is *old*. He's not sure why. All he has access to are fragments of history, and none of the fragments he has have Elyra in it."

"Is it that Elyra is older than we thought?" Derivan mused. "Or is it possible that there was a different kingdom here, once upon a time, and it was merely repurposed?"

"I wish I knew the answer to that," Vex sighed. He glanced out across the ruins. "It's hard to identify exactly where the *center* is, but if we find a few more recognizable landmarks, I can figure it out. Hopefully, the vault is what we're actually supposed to find."

"Hopefully the vault's here at all," Sev muttered, and Vex let out a small grumble that sounded like reluctant agreement. Misa laughed at both of them, throwing her arms around their shoulders in a move that was horrendously awkward, considering how different in height all three of them were.

"It'll be fine!" she said. "When have we ever lost, eh?"

Derivan chuckled softly. "Glad you're back, Misa."

Even with an idea of what they were "supposed" to find, it took them a while to find it. Vex had a tough time recognizing Elyran landmarks when most of them had evidently changed drastically in the thousand years since this version of Elyra had started to crumble—a few notable landmarks remained the same, but even then they were dilapidated enough that they were hard to spot from a distance.

Eventually, Vex frowned. "I think I'm getting a sense of what structures remained the same," he said. "The noble houses all seem . . . I mean, they're the most intact out of everything. They haven't been built over or knocked down."

"Is that a surprise?" Derivan asked, and Vex shrugged uncomfortably.

"I guess I was hoping that Elyra used to be different," he said quietly. "Maybe we used to be something better and, with the advent of the system, something changed. I could believe that. The system makes it so much easier to compare yourself to others—we have levels, stats, metrics. You have a supposedly objective arbitrator of the quality of a person. I can see how that might cause people to start viewing one another as *lesser*."

"The system's probably been around longer than two hundred years," Misa pointed out. "Maybe you *were* different once. Besides, just because the buildings are here doesn't mean they were used for nobility, right? Could've been places of learning. Or used to house *ancient artifacts*." She grinned, clearly trying to cheer Vex up.

"Maybe," Vex said. He managed a small smile back at Misa and then cast his gaze around.

They stood in the remnants of a tower, though half of it had crumbled and was scattered into moss-covered rocks on the ground. Some of the stone faded in and out, like it wasn't sure whether it was stone or fog. "I think this one is House Wisfield's tower. I can tell where the center of the kingdom is from here."

"You are okay?" Derivan prompted, and Vex gave his boyfriend a soft smile.

"I am," Vex said. He hesitated, pulling open the system for a second, just in case there were any new messages; he'd sent a message to Helix not long before, just to check in and make sure everything was going well with the evacuation. "Just have a lot on my mind."

"Any word from your parents?" Sev asked, and Vex shook his head.

"Nothing from them, either," he said, checking briefly. "Helix said he spoke to them, but they're both being pretty stubborn about the whole thing. They're holding the rest of my siblings hostage . . ."

Vex clenched his fists, then slowly relaxed.

"Hostage?" Misa asked, an undercurrent of anger in her tone. Vex gave her a weak smile.

"Not as bad as what you're thinking. I phrased that a bit . . . They're basically grounded, all of them. Except Helix, because they can't get ahold of him. But that's bad, because they need to evacuate. I think Helix is planning a rescue operation."

"I hope they're all on your side now," Sev said. "I know you've been talking to them."

"It's hard getting through to them." Vex frowned at the system for a moment. "But I think . . . I think most of them understand where I'm coming from. None of them are bad people. They just think the system in Elyra *works,* because they don't see how it affects everyone else."

"Not much of a choice now," Misa noted.

"Not at all," Vex said softly. "With the protests some of the civilians are putting up . . . it's hard *not* to see what's going on. Maybe that's why they got grounded, but that's not enough to hide it from them. So I think they're starting to see."

"What about Riss?" Derivan asked.

"He doesn't understand any of what's happening," Vex said with a chuckle. "He's barely five. The one thing we all agree on is that we want to protect him from all this. We just don't agree on how to do it. My parents are still convinced that the evacuation order is a rebel trick."

Misa snorted. "Hell of a trick that puts their own people at risk," she said, making it clear exactly what she thought of the whole thing.

"Yeah, I . . . we need to hurry." Vex glanced over his system messages again, and his scales seemed to pale just a bit. It wasn't a message from Helix but the Elyran branch of the Adventurers' Guild. "Healing spells have started failing in Elyra too. That's . . . not good."

"Not at all." Sev frowned. "You're relying on those to keep people alive without enough food, right?"

"It's barely enough, but yes," Vex said. "The evacuation's under way, but it's hard to convince the population when most of the nobles are trying to assure everyone that everything's okay."

"Let's not waste time," Misa said gently. "We can talk about this all we want on the way, but we need to get going. Lead the way, Vex."

Vex nodded nervously. He took one last look at the ruins they stood in and then glanced around at the two other landmarks they had found. He mapped it against what he knew about Elyra in his head.

"This way," Vex said.

They moved quickly. Faster than had been possible for them before the Roads, even, because Sev had created a connection with Isila, the Goddess of Travel; every step they took was magnified tenfold, and it took them almost no time at all to find the Vault Vex spoke of.

It was, technically speaking, located above the Elyran dungeon—the other major structure at the center of the kingdom. Now that they were *here*, Vex could see the tunnels extending below the rock into where the dungeon would be.

Here, however, the tunnels led nowhere. There was a dark void where the tunnels ended, no doubt leading straight into the Void.

"I wonder why these tunnels are here," Sev said, frowning at one of them. It was built directly into one of the still-standing walls and led almost straight down. He peered down the shaft cautiously, then took a step back.

"They lead to the dungeon," Vex said.

"But there's no dungeon here, right?" Sev pointed out. "This is an alternate history. There was never a system here, so there shouldn't be a reason for a dungeon to exist."

Vex hesitated. ". . . Good point," he said eventually. "Maybe there was something down there they were mining. The more important thing is the Vault, though. I was worried it wouldn't be here, but . . ."

The room was there, right in front of them. Unlike all the other ruins in this space, it was largely intact—if everything hadn't been so spaced out among floating rocks and empty space, it would no doubt have been visible from a distance. But the obscuring fog had kept it largely out of sight until now.

It was strange, really, to see massive metal doors standing perfectly intact in the middle of a ruin. Vex approached the door hesitantly, pressing a claw to it—half-expecting the system to respond with a message instantly, as it always had—but nothing happened.

"I'm not actually sure how we're going to open this thing," Vex admitted after a moment. "I don't want to just blast it out of the way—"

Misa snorted. "Leave it to me," she said, grinning. Vex blinked.

Misa did a few dramatic stretches, then reached for the edge of the door—and Vex's jaw slowly dropped open as her fingers *dug in to the metal,* giving her leverage to *pull.*

Slowly, the massive doors slid open, metal screeching and creaking as Misa opened a gap just wide enough for everyone to walk through.

Then she took a step back and smirked, dusting her hands off.

"Holy shit," Sev said. "How many points have you been putting into Strength?"

"A *lot.*" Misa lifted an arm, flexing playfully, and Sev just shook his head in amazement.

"There's that problem solved, I guess," he said.

They walked through, and the doors slammed shut behind them.

CHAPTER 42

EVACUATION

Helix

"Ma'am, *please*," Helix said.

He was in charge of the evacuation. Of course he was in charge of the evacuation. Syvila had said it was because he was a noble, and his status would help some of the people trust him.

As far as Helix was concerned, he was about fifty-fifty on that. There were certainly people who trusted him because of his status. There were others who hated him because of it, and there were still others who just didn't recognize him.

The last one was a little bit insulting. He was a very handsome and recognizable lizard! He was ninety percent sure of that.

"No," the old human woman told him, and slammed the door in his face.

Eighty-five percent.

Helix hesitated at the door for a moment, contemplating knocking on it—and then he sighed and moved on.

It wasn't that he didn't want to convince everyone he spoke to.

It was that he couldn't.

And the more time he wasted, the less prepared they would be when the time came.

Others would be back, he assured himself. They had no plans on leaving anyone in Elyra to fend for themselves—not even the nobles, although they were absolutely last on the docket, and no one intended to fight them just to get them to leave. That would put them at unnecessary risk. But if they *wanted* to evacuate, they would have the opportunity, like everyone else.

Helix only hoped his own family would listen when the time came. His siblings were getting close to understanding, he thought; it was hard to hide the effects that the lack of food was having on the populace now, and although food was still coming in from Anderstahl, it was no longer enough—the wagons contained less food each day and came farther and farther apart.

The plan was to go straight to Anderstahl and help them till their lands and grow their food. It would hopefully result in enough to sustain them all—especially since reports were that the lands surrounding Anderstahl were still rife with wildlife to hunt.

Helix only hoped that remained true.

—•—

"What do you mean, we have to evacuate?"

A little orc boy looked up at him with wide eyes, and Helix grimaced slightly. He didn't like talking to children—mostly because he was bad at it. Put him in a tavern any day, but children?

"Are your parents around?" Helix asked gently. He glanced around inside the home—it was warm and inviting, but he didn't see any signs that anyone else lived there. A small worry gnawed at his chest, but . . . it was probably nothing.

The child shook his head. "They left," he said. "They said House Julia called on them! So they had to go. They told me to be good. But I'm hungry . . . I hope they'll be back soon."

"How long ago was that?" Helix asked. The boy thought for a moment.

"Two days," he said. Helix felt a pit open wide in his stomach.

"You haven't had food for two days?" He tried not to let any of his anger show, but some of it must have bled through, because the boy took a frightened step back. Helix hurriedly lowered his voice and his stance both, trying to make himself less imposing.

"They left some food for me!" the boy said. "But I finished it this morning. So I haven't had lunch."

Helix grimaced. On the one hand, he could ask this child to come with him . . . He wasn't sure House Julia would be returning anyone they called to arms. But if they were calling people to arms, this was information that the rebellion didn't already know. He composed a quick message to Syvila—

"Helix Ashion," a voice behind him said clearly, and before Helix could react, he felt cuffs suddenly click around one of his wrists. He reacted with a flare of magic—all of which was quickly drawn into those cuffs.

Shit. He could fight with his magic limited, but not well enough to beat a physical enforcer. "You're under arrest," she continued.

The boy hadn't stepped back because he was frightened of him. He'd stepped back because of who had slipped behind him.

"Mom?" the boy said. The woman that had arrested him glanced over Helix's shoulder at her child.

"I'll be back with some food soon," she said, but that was all. Her voice was emotionless. Her son nodded.

"I miss you," he said to her, his voice plaintive.

"Come quietly," the orc woman said, her voice emotionless. She shut the door in the boy's face, her expression not changing a bit. Helix clenched a fist.

This was House Wisfield's work; he was sure of it. One hand slipped to his side, and he cracked the glyph that he kept with him—the Communication-Maintain hybrid glyph that every field agent kept with them.

At least this way, the rebellion would know something was wrong and could pass the message on to his brother. Helix managed a grim smile as he followed the orc woman.

Not even House Ashion had any idea how much Vex had grown.

"It sounds like you're almost there." Syvila managed a smile, gently shutting the book she was holding and glancing over to Ingress, who was the only one with her at the moment. The blacksmith was working hard on creating a cure for his father using the glyph-based magic Vex had gifted them, and by all accounts, he'd made a lot of progress.

He'd visited to tell her the news, in fact. For the first time, he'd managed to find a combination of glyphs that allowed his father to *speak*. They'd shared their first words in years, and Ingress had wept deeply to know that he had not been wrong to keep his father alive; the man was as determined to live as ever. Too much left to do, he said. Too much left to learn.

He'd been worried. He didn't know that he was doing the right thing, keeping him alive in the grasp of rustbite; that disease was functionally torture. Syvila privately thought that Ingress should have let go of his father months ago, but she was also glad to know she'd been wrong.

"I'm so close," Ingress said. "There are glyphs for Metal and Oxygen—we've reverse-engineered them from similar-looking spells, and I think I can use them to decompose rustbite—but I need to make sure I don't do more damage in the process. I might . . . I might have to wait for us to evacuate to be able to do more. I think I'll need a healer present for the next step."

"Healing magic getting weaker is worrying," Syvila commented, sighing in thought. Things were moving slower than she'd hoped.

"It is," Ingress said. The human swept a hand through his hair, messing it up slightly. "I'm sorry. I know I should be more worried about the evacuation. It's just, my dad—"

"I understand," Syvila interrupted. "As I said, I am glad you've made progress. Keep us updated. We all want him to get better."

"Thanks." Ingress gave her a relieved smile and turned to leave—

A bell rang, and both Ingress and Syvila froze.

Once, twice, three times. Ingress turned to stare at Syvila. "Is that bell the one I think it is?"

Syvila cursed. She was already reaching for her stack of books—she sorted through them in an instant and picked out the right one.

Library magic, unbeknownst to most, was great for recordkeeping. It was even able to keep tabs on *people* as long as a particular book was written with that intent. It was, technically, something she could have been awarded nobility for if she'd ever bothered to report it—but Syvila had never been interested in nobility.

"Yes, it is," Syvila said. The words tasted bitter in her own mouth. "Three of our agents captured at around the same time. One of them is Helix. The other two are part of his group too."

"Do you know where they're being taken?" Ingress leaned forward to try to peer at her book, and she nodded.

"The House Julia cells," Syvila said, marking the spot on the book with a claw. She felt a coldness grip her heart. "The nobles have been ignoring us and the evacuation order as just a minor threat, but . . ."

"Not anymore," Ingress said. "Should I send out retrieval teams?"

"Against House Julia?" Syvila shook her head, looking worried. "We don't have anyone that can handle Julia. Or we do, but that was Helix, and he's . . . Well."

"How in the world did Helix get caught, anyway?" Ingress muttered.

"Careless," Syvila said. "Me, not Helix. I shouldn't have sent him out when he's this valuable, but the nobles haven't really been acting against us after that meeting, and I didn't think they'd be able to get him. Or act against him without House Ashion getting in the way."

"He *should* be immune," Ingress agreed. He seemed equally concerned. "If Julia is acting against him, they probably have permission from Ashion."

"We'll send messages out to his brother and make sure the Guild is aware of what's happening," Syvila decided. "It might be time for the Guild to drop the neutrality act."

—∾—

"Should've known you were behind this, Dad," Helix said.

He sat with his back pressed against the cell wall. It was uncomfortable.

The stone was cold, and there was no real place for his tail to go, and so it was pressed uncomfortably between his body and the stone. He'd move away from the wall if he could, but the cuffs kept him from moving.

"I didn't want to do this to you," Karix said with a sigh. "Your mother is worried about you, you know. You could have answered our summons and come back to us."

"You know you're just pushing us further away, right?" Helix let his playful demeanor fall away for a moment. He stared at his father with all the solemnity he could muster. "If you want to get Vex back, this isn't the way to do it."

"What makes you think that's what I want?" Karix snapped. "Maybe I'm just tired of having two of my brightest children shame House Ashion. Maybe I want you two to figure out where you *belong*."

Helix couldn't help but roll his eyes. "You can't seriously tell me you believe what you're saying."

"You're staying here until you learn your lesson." Karix's voice was cold, and Helix tried not to show his anger. The man wasn't even *trying* to understand. The fact that he'd directly acted against him only showed he was getting worse, not better.

He had no idea how else to get through to either of his parents.

"We don't need all this power, Dad," Helix finally said. It wasn't going to work—he knew before he even spoke. Vex had had this same conversation with Karix dozens of times, and each time, their father had dismissed his brother's concerns. "There are bigger concerns right now than Elyra, and prestige isn't a good enough reason to torture Riss or take food that the people have. We can find something better. Vex *has* found something better."

"And he shared it, so it's useless," Karix said with a scowl. "We represent Elyra's military and political power. It only makes sense that the majority of the kingdom's resources should go to us."

Helix sighed. "To protect the kingdom," he said. "That's the point of our military and political power. If we let the people starve, we're not going to have a kingdom left to protect."

Karix frowned darkly at that. "And yet you rebels want to evacuate Elyra," he said. "It seems to me like either option leaves us without a kingdom."

He hadn't denied what Helix had said. The lizardkin tried not to let his hopes rise too much. "Is a kingdom its buildings?" Helix asked. "Or its people?"

Karix glowered. Helix thought—hoped, just for a moment—that he'd been able to get through to his father.

Then Karix turned and left, letting the cell door swing shut behind him, and Helix's heart sank.

CHAPTER 43

ORBS AGAIN

The door slamming behind them made all four adventurers pull out their weapons cautiously.

"Never had a door slam on me in a dungeon and have it *not* be a signal for a boss fight," Misa muttered, and the others made various noises of agreement. "Think we're going to get attacked by Irvis again?"

"No," Vex said, then hesitated. "I'm pretty sure that can't happen. Irvis can't exist here."

All four of them stared at the center of the room anyway, waiting.

The room itself was massive. The walls were a pure, pristine white, lit by no apparent light source to speak of. There didn't seem to be a *point* to all the space in the room—there was nothing there save for the pedestal in the center, and that pedestal was a fraction of the size of the room.

Which was to say that the room was large enough to comfortably drive a caravan around in, but the pedestal was just barely smaller than Misa.

"I can't see what's on the pedestal," Vex grumbled. Derivan stifled a chuckle and offered a hand to the lizardkin, who promptly climbed up onto his shoulders. "Is that just an orb?"

"It's just an orb," Misa said. She held her mace in front of her cautiously. "I remember the last time we faced up against an orb. It's not getting me this time."

"I don't think it's the *same* type of orb . . ."

"You guys know I'm the only one that can't see this orb, right?" Sev complained. Vex grinned down at Sev.

"No more space up here, sorry."

"You're not climbing up on my back," Misa added dryly. Sev grumbled and waved a hand, creating a quick barrier out of divine energy that he used as a stepping-stone.

"Okay, I see the orb now." He paused. "Is there something we're supposed to . . . *do* with it?"

"Only one way to find out," Misa said, poking the cleric. He yelped, nearly stumbling off his makeshift platform.

"Why me? You're the one with all the defensive skills," he complained.

"Yeah, so I need to be available to *block*." Misa grinned, enjoying Sev's discomfort. "Can't react in time if the orb gets me, yeah?"

"Perhaps I should grab it instead?" Derivan suggested. "I still do not have health."

"I'll do it." Sev shook his head, staring at the orb. "It actually feels kind of . . . familiar. I don't know why, though. I doubt I existed *here*."

"It would not matter," Derivan said. "This room is much like the door we stepped through—it is locked in place through Shift and is stable across all realities and planes. For all intents and purposes, the orb here is identical to the one held in the true Elyra, and what we see here is proof of what is kept within the Elyran Vault."

"You're sure?" Vex asked, worry lacing his voice, and Derivan nodded solemnly.

"I was uncertain at first," he said, "but I have reached as far as I can with Shift, and I am certain."

"That's gotta mean something, right?" Misa asked. "I mean, a room that's the same across all realities . . ."

"It is reinforced," Derivan said. "If the Void were to consume everything, this room would be one of the last things consumed. It is as though it was built to protect something."

"It was," Sev said softly.

The other three adventurers glanced sharply at the cleric. Sev's tone had changed dramatically—there was a sudden wistful quality to his voice that hadn't been there before, and all the levity seemed to have drained out of his voice.

"Sev?" Misa's words were sharp, worried. "You doing okay?"

"I don't . . . know." Sev's voice was distant. "I think so. It's not an effect; I'm just . . . I think I'm remembering? Everything's so *familiar* . . ."

His voice trailed off, and he stepped forward again.

Misa glanced at Vex and Derivan. "Did he just say he feels like a vault built over a thousand years ago is *familiar*?"

"Yup," Vex said.

"I also heard that," Derivan confirmed.

"I feel like you guys are calling me old over there," Sev's voice came drifting back toward them. Misa snorted and gave him a thumbs-up.

"At least I know you're not being mind-controlled!" she called back. Sev pointedly gave her the finger, grinning. There was a bit of relief in his eyes—the banter anchored him.

And then he turned back, took a deep breath, and reached for the orb.

—∾—

Sev let the world fall away from him.

Misa, Vex, and Derivan all fell silent, perhaps sensing how serious this moment was for him. There was something about the room and the orb that resonated with him, though he didn't understand *why*. He'd never been here before. He'd never been close to the center of Elyra, even; his wandering had taken him along the Outskirts and among the various settlements and villages between the Prime Kingdoms, but he'd spent almost no time inside any of the kingdoms proper. He'd certainly never done so for long enough to gain access to the Elyran Vault.

(So why was this place so achingly familiar?)

It didn't just feel like he'd been here before. It felt like he'd spent a long time here, trapped within the walls. It was part of the reason the room was so big. He needed space.

(Why had he needed space?)

The orb was important. The *room* was important, though the importance of this room would fall away once he claimed the orb; the whole purpose of it was to give him a place to work, and then to protect that which he had created.

Had he . . . had he *made* this? He didn't know how to make artifacts. That was high-level divine magic of a type he'd never explored.

But if he *had* needed to make artifacts, his connection with Onyx was undoubtedly a part of that. A God of Sculptures would no doubt be able to help him sculpt the perfect artifact.

That couldn't be the reason he'd chosen to become a priest of Onyx, though. He *remembered* the day he'd chosen Onyx. It had been almost at random out of a list. He'd selected a relatively minor deity, reasoning that doing so would afford him the ability to connect with that deity; they would have fewer prayers, fewer mortals vying for their time and affection. Sev had just been looking for a friend, and he'd found one in Onyx.

He was pretty sure that was right. His friendship with Onyx wasn't a product of some deeper plan. It was exactly what it seemed—a friendship forged of circumstance and molded to steel.

Sev reached for the orb . . .

. . . and when he touched it, it resonated.

A notification appeared.

[**Grand Anchor—Magic**]

That was it. Nothing about rarity, no description, nothing.

And yet . . . he knew what it was for.

—∾—

Sev cradled the orb carefully in his arms, stepping down from his barrier and walking over to his friend. "This is yours," he said, looking at Vex. Vex blinked.

". . . Mine?" he asked. Then he poked the top of Derivan's helmet. "Or Derivan's? I'm sitting on top of him, so I can't tell."

Sev rolled his eyes and laughed, the last of whatever fugue had gripped him falling away. "*Yours*, you goof," he said. "Get off of Derivan! You don't need him to see the orb anymore!"

"I don't want to. It's comfortable up here." Vex hummed, then let out a startled yelp when Derivan tilted his head in amusement. "Deri! Warn me if you're going to move!"

"I apologize," Derivan said, stifling a laugh. Misa was doing her best to hold back a shit-eating grin and not really succeeding.

"What do you mean, the orb's Vex's?" Misa asked. "What's the deal with you saying this whole place looks familiar? You remember something, don't you?"

"I think so." Sev hesitated. "This isn't stuff that was erased from my memory, exactly. I think this is just stuff that was . . . locked away from me. To make sure I didn't throw off the wheels of fate too much, or something."

"I'm going to level with you." Misa gave Sev a serious look. "I have no idea what that means."

"I'm not sure either," Sev admitted. "Just feels right. Uh, I think I made this for Vex. Or someone like Vex."

There was a long pause.

"You think you *made* this?" Misa asked. "Like, the thousand-year magical artifact?"

". . . Yes?" Sev couldn't quite meet Misa's eyes. "I know it sounds ridiculous."

"I mean, I believe you, but I'm going to be real mad if you're trying to tell us we're chosen ones and you're the wise old sage."

"I don't *remember* doing any of this," Sev said, shaking his head. "I don't think you're chosen, exactly. I think you're just . . . the right people. I think I spent a long time searching for the right people, and I think you guys are the closest I'm going to get."

"That's a lot of 'I think's," Misa remarked, but she softened when she saw how distressed Sev seemed; there was a shadow over his eyes, like even remembering all of this tired him out on some fundamental level. ". . . Do you remember anything else?"

"There should be another place like this under Anderstahl," Sev said. He winced, pressing a hand to his head. ". . .One under each of the Prime Kingdoms. A vault that holds something that will help. I don't . . . I don't know anything else. But it's more than I've ever remembered."

"It'll have to be enough." Misa glanced up at Vex. "Vex?"

The lizardkin hopped off of Derivan, a sudden serious expression settling on his face. "You know you don't have to go about this alone, right?" he asked Sev. "I don't know what you've been through, and I know you don't remember much. But you sounded lonely when you were talking just now, and I just want you to know that you're not alone. We're going to stick with you no matter what."

". . . Thank you." Sev's words were soft. He didn't know why Vex's words stirred an emotional response from him, but they did. There was a deep ache buried somewhere in his soul, called forward and gently soothed by the lizardkin's sincerity. By Misa's determined smile and playful thumbs-up, and by Derivan's calm, solemn strength and certainty.

Vex grabbed ahold of the orb, and there was a flash of light.

[[Grand Anchor—Magic] has been integrated.]
[Bonus Room: <A World without a System> has been completed! Rewards:]
<ERROR>
[Elyran Prime Anchor at insufficient integrity to generate rewards. We apologize for the inconvenience.]
[Bonus room shutting down. Returning participants to start location for bonus room dissolution.]
[Bonus room will be dissolved in: 30 minutes.]

The room around them vanished, and the four adventurers found themselves back in the Prime Dungeon—where an enchanted suit of armor stood staring at them, clearly surprised by their sudden presence.

CHAPTER 44

ARMED AND READY

"You're the one who awakened me," the armor said.

"I am, yes." Derivan stepped forward—he didn't sense any ill intent here. The other armor stared at him for a moment, considering him, and then gave him a slight nod.

"I've chosen the name Gallant," he said. Behind him, Sev made a strangled noise, and Derivan found a moment to give a withering stare at the cleric, who—to his credit—looked apologetic. Misa patted him on the shoulder.

"I am Derivan," Derivan said, not unkindly. "I apologize for leaving so quickly after awakening you. Circumstances were difficult at the time."

"So it seems." Gallant didn't seem particularly surprised. His gaze lingered on Sev for a moment, some amusement dancing in his eyes, and then he glanced out of the hole in the wall. It was the one the adventurers had left through months before. "I considered following, but I don't think I'd survive the drop."

"Not *well*," Derivan agreed.

"This is awkward," Gallant admitted after a moment. "I keep wondering if I should call you Dad or something."

This time, both Sev and Vex made a strangled noise. Misa didn't even bother hiding her snort of laughter. Derivan tried not to look panicked, and breathed a sigh of relief when Gallant allowed a smirk to touch his eyes. "No, I'm kidding," he said. He glanced at Derivan's still-missing arm. "I'm thankful you awakened me, though. I was wondering if I'd see you again. Could you follow me?"

"Sure," Derivan said cautiously.

The four of them traipsed after the armor, Derivan paying special attention to him now that he wasn't in the midst of a dungeon crisis of some sort.

Gallant was made of a dark silver metal, distinct from Derivan's own deep purple; he wondered for a moment how much Gallant could remember of the Scimitars. Of their people.

Nothing, if they were anything alike.

But *were* they alike? Gallant seemed so much more fully formed. Derivan remembered how long it had taken him to come to terms with his own existence—how long it had taken him to adapt even months after his own awakening.

Of course, his awakening had been slow and gradual, and Gallant's had been quite sudden. Perhaps a more fully formed imprint from the Void had managed to find itself within Gallant. That thought only seemed more likely when Gallant led them to a blacksmithing workshop. He remembered Jelevar's words—that their people had taken up smithing as their primary form of art and expression.

"I noticed you were missing an arm," Gallant said, his voice just slightly dry. Derivan chuckled a little, surprised at how pleased he was that Gallant didn't dance around the topic.

Then he glanced around the armor's workshop and blinked.

The entire place was scattered with arms.

He'd known this was coming to some extent. Vex had said as much when he first created the Glyph of Change—that the change was already coming, and that it would happen before they returned to Elyra. It made sense that it would happen in the small window of time they had left.

But still . . .

"Have you been trying to make me a replacement?" Derivan asked. He couldn't keep the slightly stunned note out of his voice. "You . . . you did not have to."

"I know that." Gallant laughed. The armor's voice was much lighter than his own, he noticed; the laugh sounded almost like the tinkling of chimes. "But it was an interesting challenge. Most of the books here are about weapons wielded by great heroes, and I got bored of trying to forge those within the first week.

"Plus, there's no one to use them." Gallant's smile was a bit more sincere now, the mirth fading away into something warm. "I don't exactly know how to fight. At least I know *someone* can make use of this."

"I suppose that is fair," Derivan allowed. ". . . Thank you. Did you spend all your time here?"

"Well, the only exit is a very long drop into nothing," Gallant answered, grinning at the guilt that flashed through Derivan's expression. "I could have left if I wanted to, don't get me wrong, but this place feels more . . ."

Gallant hesitated, searching for the word.

"It is your home," Derivan said.

"Yes!" Gallant snapped his fingers—though the action was really more of a metallic *clang* for someone of their species. "It's home. I don't really want to leave."

Derivan's gaze lingered on Gallant for long enough that the other armor began to shift uncomfortably. "What?"

"All of us feel compelled to stay at first," Derivan said. ". . . I am sorry. We should have taken you with us."

Gallant frowned, staring at Derivan and then at his companions. "Even if you're telling the truth, I think you would've had to drag me away kicking and screaming," Gallant said wryly after a moment. "Don't worry about it. If you feel bad, take me with you when we're back in Elyra."

"We will have to," Derivan answered seriously. Gallant eyed him for a moment, as though contemplating whether or not he wanted to ask for elaboration.

Eventually, he shook his head and leaned over to kick open a chest. "This is the closest I was able to get," he said, pulling something out from within. Derivan's eyes widened slightly—it was a near-perfect replica of his arm.

"I don't know how well this will work, or if our kind can even just reattach parts like this, but I hope you're able to do something with it. I'm afraid I wasn't particularly willing to pull off my own arm to check."

"Understandable," Derivan said with a slight chuckle, hiding his astonishment. He picked up the copy of his arm, looking it over with no small amount of wonder. Gallant had only seen his arm once or twice, and only briefly—but the precision with which he'd been able to recreate it . . .

It wasn't exactly the same. It never could be. There were scratches on that arm that he'd left there on purpose—scratches that reminded him of the battles he'd fought, the friends he'd made. This new arm was perfect and unblemished. Beautiful, but not his own.

And yet he was touched by the effort that had gone into this creation—by the *artistry* of it. Gallant had spent far more time than he needed to on the filigree and detail. Derivan had been willing to accept just a working arm. This was . . .

Unbidden, a Remembrance grew warm within his soul. Derivan frowned, mentally feeling for the new sensation before abruptly recognizing it.

The Exadite Pin. The Remembrance that represented his people.

He invoked it without thinking, the crystalline butterfly materializing in his hand. It pulsed with a faint glow, and Gallant made a noise that sounded like a sharp intake of breath, his eyes focusing sharply on the pin.

"Where did you get that?" he asked.

"It is . . ." Derivan searched for the word. "It is a memory of who we once were," he eventually said. "The people we once were."

He held it out, watching the way Gallant's eyes fixated on the pin sitting in his hand.

"May I?" Gallant said, reaching out almost hesitantly. Derivan didn't stop him from taking the small, beautifully crafted pin into his hands. Gallant cradled it like it was something precious—and as he watched, a spark grew, snapping between the pin and Gallant. It lasted for a fraction of a second, but it was enough to make Gallant stumble.

"Oh," he said softly. He straightened slowly, then made his way over to the nearest stool. ". . . I need to sit down."

Gallant *remembered.* Which Derivan supposed he should have expected.

It wasn't a complete memory. A Remembrance couldn't contain the entirety of their history, and the power it *did* have was bent toward more than simple memory. Derivan could, for example, use the Exadite Pin to draw upon some of the greatest things his people had crafted.

As he understood it, that functionality wasn't inherent to the Exadite Pin. The original version of it would simply have allowed him to recreate a variety of weapons from Scimitar culture. It was the glyph he had invoked to change the fundamental nature of Remembrances that allowed this new flexibility: they were more than just sources of power. They contained a true piece of history.

Gallant could now tap into the memories of his former life. He remembered his first attendance of the Festival of Freeforged Light and the wonder he felt at the things his friends and family had created. He remembered the moment he had forged his own first piece of art—no weapon nor shield, nor even a pin. He'd forged a little needle, lined with gold trim in a delicate pattern, and gifted it to a friend who loved to sew.

She was his girlfriend not more than a year later. She was a dryara, Gallant explained, yet another species that had been lost to the Void. They were similar to humanoid plant-beings, and were a beautiful people who lived and died in cycles. None of them truly died, but their souls shifted among the seeds, and every time they died they would be reborn elsewhere; to hold a relationship with one of them was to know that it could not last.

Those were still, Gallant said, some of the happiest years of his life.

He seemed hopeful that Derivan would have a Remembrance of them as well, but Derivan shook his head sadly. It was a miracle that Gallant remembered that much of them at all—perhaps the Remembrance carried more power than he had hoped.

Gallant sighed.

"I'm keeping this name," he told them after a moment. "The books I read here still meant something to me, and the name is a name I chose. I had a different name before, but it was . . . given to me. Not chosen. This means more to me, I think."

"Self-chosen names are always more meaningful," Sev offered.

Gallant gave him a slightly suspicious look. "You wouldn't happen to have chosen your own name, would you?"

"Well, I mean, *yes* . . ."

"I'm just messing with you." Gallant grinned. "I agree. Obviously. If it's bias, then we'll both be biased together. More importantly, however!" He turned to Derivan. "The arm I made won't work for you. Now that I remember more about our kind, it's missing all the connective runes that would let it actually attach to your core. I'll need to forge a new one."

"We don't have time," Vex said, glancing at a system window. "Fifteen minutes before the system collapses this echo and takes us back to Elyra."

Gallant smirked. "Give me ten."

Derivan stared as the other Scimitar burst into action. Magic flared around him, a complicated array of mana too dense for him to properly identify. He could feel various Shifts as the system struggled to keep up with Gallant's usage of his skills—how he had even acquired them this quickly, Derivan had no idea. The man's hands were practically a blur.

Derivan watched carefully. He'd never seen a true Scimitar smith at work before, and Gallant was likely the closest he was ever going to get to this aspect of his people.

For a moment, his mind went back to Vex's words, asking him if there was anything he wanted to pursue for himself. Perhaps when all of this was over, this was something he could explore. He could work with Gallant, perhaps, and restore what had been forgotten . . .

Lost in his thoughts, Derivan almost didn't notice when Gallant completed the arm almost exactly ten minutes later. It glowed with heat until Gallant waved his hand and a final burst of magic banished it; before him, fully formed, was an arm that looked identical to the one on his left.

Before he could even remark on it, Gallant had picked it up and snapped it onto his missing socket. Derivan winced, feeling his magic suddenly surge.

"I would have appreciated a warning," he said.

"Oh, uh . . . right." Gallant looked apologetic, at least. "I got excited. It's the first time I've been able to do this kind of thing. That I remember, anyway."

The arm finished connecting to the rest of . . . well, to the rest of him. Derivan tested it experimentally, moving it through his full range of motion, curling each of his fingers to make sure everything was in working order. He'd been without his arm for long enough that it felt almost . . . strange to have it back.

"It won't be exactly the same as the old one," Gallant warned. "It's not like replacing a missing wheel on a cart. Your core won't align completely with a newly forged arm. You can get it to work better if you keep practicing with it, but it's most likely always going to feel a little bit strange."

That explained some of the oddities. The arm responded a little more slowly to his commands; the joints felt a little stiffer. And yet . . .

"I can feel touch through this arm," Derivan said, surprised. Normally, his sense of touch was limited to a vague idea of temperature and pressure—he wasn't able to sense *texture* in any fine detail. But with the new arm, he could feel even the stale air brushing against the metal as he swung his arm around.

"That happens sometimes," Gallant said. "If you need me to adjust it—"

"No," Derivan said, shaking his head. He turned around, his eyes meeting Vex's, and without a word, he slipped the lizardkin's hand into his own.

It was warm. He could feel the scales, all the little details of Vex squeezing his hand.

". . . Thank you," Derivan said. He wasn't sure if he could make his voice sound even more sincere than it already did, but he tried. Gallant glanced at him, then at Vex, and then smiled.

"Don't go losing any arms again," he said. "Even if I'm still around, we're not going to get very far without a workshop like this one. How long before we're back in Elyra?"

"Five more minutes," Vex said. His tail was curled around his leg, and he leaned in to Derivan's newly forged arm.

"Check it out," Misa said, gesturing out a nearby window.

There was a distinct shimmer in the air that looked nothing like the fractals they had grown used to seeing in Mundane—a purple-black border that defied visual understanding. It took a moment for Derivan to realize what he was looking at.

It was the edge of reality itself. The rapidly shrinking space of the echo they were in.

Derivan realized with a small clenching in his chest that it was likely that Clyde and the others were already gone. No time for a second goodbye.

They wouldn't experience true deaths, they had said; elementals like them existed in every reality, with something small shared between all of them. But those iterations of them, the ones they had become friends with . . .

Derivan wished for a moment that he'd had a *real* chance to say goodbye.

Then he frowned. He would not let this moment pass by without doing *something*. He reached out through Shift, feeling at the space between the echo and mainline reality.

Everything about this echo stemmed from a single major change. It was the nature of all echoes, all sub-universes. Derivan did not have the ability to recreate an exact copy of an echo the way the system did . . . but he still *tried*. He stared at the space between reality, trying to memorize everything that had caused this particular echo to come into being. All the ways it had changed due to the presence of him and his friends.

It was all he could do for the moment.

"One minute," Gallant said softly, sounding surprisingly somber. "I don't know what I'll do after all this."

"We'll help you," Vex promised. "You can't stay in Elyra, anyway. We'll find you a place with the Guild, and you can figure out what you want to do from there."

"The Guild could always use a skilled smith," Sev offered.

Gallant managed a small smile, but something about it was subdued. "That's the second time you've mentioned something about leaving or me having to come with you," he said. "I'm assuming you're not kidnapping me, so . . . is something else going on?"

"The Void," Derivan said. "It is what happened to our people."

Gallant froze. ". . . Can we stop it?"

Derivan shook his head. "Not yet," he said, because *no* seemed like a far worse answer. "We're working on it."

"What *is* it? A monster of some kind?"

"It's just . . . the end." Sev was the one who found the words to answer. His gaze was sympathetic. "That's all it is. There's nothing to fight. Just . . . the end of everything."

"The end of *everything*?" The touch of fear in Gallant's voice was definitely real now. "I . . . Oh."

The last word was said in a small voice. Derivan, not knowing what else to do, placed a comforting hand on Gallant's shoulder and glanced back at the others.

The moment they got back, they had to be prepared. They had run away from Irvis the first time.

There was no guarantee the Aspect wouldn't be waiting when they returned.

CHAPTER 45

JAILBREAK

Helix sat in his cell, bored out of his mind.

He'd had almost no visitors after Karix. A small human came in every day to feed him his food—and really, it was demeaning, to have to be fed. They weren't willing to uncuff him and let him eat on his own, and Helix wasn't willing to let himself starve out of pride, so he was forced to let them feed him like he was a child.

At least the kid feeding him didn't seem particularly enthusiastic about it either. Helix wondered if he could get him to free him from his cuffs. Probably not. The cuffs required some delicate magic to open rather than a key, and even if it had just required a physical key, he doubted Wisfield trusted the boy with anything.

A little prodding didn't hurt, though.

"Is this your job here?" Helix asked, raising a brow. "Feed the prisoners?"

The boy didn't answer. He gave him a quiet, vaguely frightened look and quickly fled. Helix just frowned.

Didn't seem like the poor kid was being treated well, either.

He'd gone over a couple of possible escape plans in his head, but most of them didn't seem realistic. They wouldn't be letting him go any time soon, and there were no apparent plans to transport him; Karix seemed perfectly willing to let him stay here for however long it took for the nobles to finish figuring out what they wanted to do to grandstand at one another.

He doubted his father actually wanted him dead. Karix would want him back in the family eventually, but he wanted Helix to feel appropriately punished first.

Which meant he just needed to escape sometime before that. Helix had no intention of owing his father anything.

It was easier said than done, though.

The second-best thing he could do was be prepared for when someone else tried to break him out. The rebellion would likely be pulling any strings they could to get him back, simply because he was one of their highest-level supporters; they would no doubt be trying *something*. Helix didn't exactly want to rely on that, though. He'd be prepared, but only if his first plan didn't work out.

His arms and legs were both bound with magic-restraining cuffs, but there was *just* enough give that he could draw some runes.

Or, more accurately, some *glyphs*.

Vex had shared his secret with the rebellion, after all.

There was a possibility that this was what Karix wanted. The rebels had been careful to use their glyphs in ways that would be hard to replicate: invisible ink on parchment that could later be burned, manafire that would obscure the true shape of the glyph. The Wisfield spies would no doubt catch some of the more common shapes through their thoughts, but there was a reason the majority of the people who researched glyphs stayed in rooms protected by magefire, where their minds couldn't be casually read. They would scribe the glyphs onto disposable pieces of parchment, write out the effects, and then distribute the glyphs among their members.

They had ones for healing, ones for combat, and other ones that simply helped with the food issue. None of the Growth-related glyphs seemed to work when they tested it within the bounds of Elyra, but there were other glyphs that could prolong the effect of a single loaf of bread, that could stretch out what wheat and food they had.

Helix hated that it was necessary.

He knew some of the glyphs because as a member of the Ashion house, he was somewhat protected from House Wisfield's interference and mind-reading. He tried to think through the glyphs he knew, to figure out which ones would help him here, assuming he managed to power a glyph using ambient mana alone.

The glyphs of Heat and Flame wouldn't do much to the magically protected cuffs. None of the other basic elemental glyphs would help them either. The more esoteric ones, like Book and Sound, would only help in abstract ways—Sound could maybe be used for a distraction, and Book...

Book might help him, but only if he felt like instigating a needlessly contrived scenario in which he'd escape. And it was equally likely to make things worse. Helix filed the Book glyph under *last resort only*.

The other glyphs they'd discovered weren't likely to help here, and given Helix would have to claw the glyph into the ground, he didn't want to give away a particularly powerful one to the nobles to use.

There was one option he had available to him. A few of their number had managed to acquire what Vex deemed a Sign, which was a more personalized sort of glyph that would be difficult for anyone that wasn't the owner to cast—like a signature of sorts. Helix had attempted to figure out what his own Sign was a number of times, and each time, he'd mostly just scribbled into the ground and failed to cast any kind of spell.

Signs were supposed to be symbolic representations of something important to you. What did he think was important to him?

He'd tried thinking about the rebellion. He'd tried thinking about his family. He'd tried thinking about a number of smaller, disparate goals, like what he wanted to do *after* the rebellion; Helix thought he might enjoy trying out acting or something similar. Magic was fun, but he had a flair for the dramatic.

None of those things were quite right, though.

Who was *he,* really? More than what he cared about, more than who he wanted to protect: what defined him?

Without quite thinking about it, Helix began to scratch a symbol into the ground.

—~—

Larok was trapped in his own cell.

Unlike Helix, the nobles hadn't bothered with cuffs on him, and he had no personal servant to bring him food; someone would toss in a loaf of bread every day, and that was about it.

They kept him away from paper, too! As if he could do anything with paper. They remembered what he'd done with the tax forms back at the fight at House Herastul and apparently decided that any kind of paper was dangerous in his hands.

Which was somewhat true, but Larok privately thought they were being ridiculous.

He couldn't help but worry about Helix. He'd seen Karix passing by his cell, and he was familiar enough with the Ashion family now to recognize what Helix's father looked like. If Helix's own family was behind this somehow—and Larok would not have been surprised if they were—then his friend was no doubt going to blame himself.

Assuming he knew that Larok and Kirsa were in trouble at all, anyway. Speaking of which . . .

"Any luck getting out?" Larok called out across the hallway, and the orc woman let out a grumble.

"If I got out, you'd know," she told him. "And I wouldn't yell about it across the damn prison."

Larok shrugged. She had a point. He was just making conversation, anyway. Who would've thought prison would be so damn boring?

He'd already tried to break out on his own, but none of his skills really lent themselves to prison escape. Kirsa had more stealth-oriented skills, though her class was technically [**Street Cleaner**]; she had a *lot* of words for whoever had defined the skills of that particular class, considering how many of them were oriented around not being noticed by other people.

Larok privately thought that skills might be defined in some part by the public consciousness, and felt that the skills of a [**Street Cleaner**] in Elyra said more about the people living in Elyra than it did about the system itself. He'd never been brave enough to have that conversation with Kirsa, though. As much as she acknowledged the flaws of Elyra's system, she still loved the kingdom fiercely. Her presence in the rebellion was out of a desire to see the kingdom made better.

She'd fought the hardest against the decision to evacuate, but even she had eventually seen the necessity. He'd had to assure her that they would come back once they found a way to reverse what was happening, though he could see that she didn't quite believe him.

He wasn't sure he believed himself, either. Larok didn't know if there *was* a way to reverse what the Void had done. The truth that Helix's brother had found out about their reality—that it was all *ending*, and that their world was falling apart—a truth backed up by the gods themselves . . .

He couldn't deny that things seemed hopeless.

But Larok had decided he would prefer to live his final days in hope rather than not, and many of the other rebels had been the same way. They'd chosen their path because they believed things could be better, after all.

And part of the reason they believed things could be better—at least for him and Kirsa—was, strangely enough, because of Helix.

Something changed.

Larok wasn't a mage. He couldn't see the sympathetic magic building, the way mana began to swirl around him. He *did* feel a strangeness in the air, an electric buzz that made the hair on his skin rise, and across the hall he could hear Kirsa's own confusion expressed as a sharp bang against her cell door.

"Whatever you're doing, stop it!" she barked, a touch of fear in her voice. She was scared of magic, Larok remembered.

"I don't think this is them," Larok said, just loud enough for his voice to carry over the rising buzz of the magic.

Elsewhere, Helix completed his glyph.

And both Larok and Kirsa vanished from their cells.

"Hey, guys," Helix said.

His voice was appropriately sheepish, which Larok thought was a good thing, or else he would have smacked his leader on the head.

"What in the *world* made you think making up a new spell was a good idea," Larok said. It wasn't a question.

"I figured it would help us escape?" Helix said. *That* was a question; it had the proper lilt and all, and Larok rubbed his fingers against his temples in exasperation.

"Okay," Larok said. He didn't bother to question Helix any further.

The problem with Helix's Sign—which appeared to teleport the people he considered "his team" to him, if they were close enough—was that now all three of them were trapped in the same cell, and that was about the only thing that changed. Neither Larok nor Kirsa had the magic to remove the cuffs Helix still wore, and the door to the outside was unfortunately locked.

"You sure you can't break open the cuffs?" Helix said, eyeing the metallic chains that kept him locked against the wall. Kirsa gave him a deadpan look, then walked up and punched the cuffs as hard as she could.

"Nope," she said mildly. Larok and Helix both stared at her.

"Let me try something," Larok said with a sigh.

[**Tax Fraud**]—which was still, in Larok's opinion, a terribly named skill—allowed him to confiscate an asset from someone that owed the kingdom taxes. The Ashion family most likely *did* owe them some taxes, but the cuffs had to count as belonging to Helix. The idea that they would *belong* to him just because they were currently restraining him seemed like a farfetched call at best.

And yet, after a moment of resistance, the cuffs vanished and reappeared in his hands anyway.

"Uh," Helix said. Larok frowned at his hands.

He was pretty sure that shouldn't have worked. He'd tried it before. He glanced up, about to speak, and then stopped and stared at the system notification instead.

[Elyran Prime Anchor at insufficient integrity. Skills may not work as intended.]
[Recommendation: Evacuate zone E-0.]

—ꟾ—

"Oh," Larok said. "Oh, shit."

Helix stared up as well. "Maybe they'll listen to us now?"

Kirsa snorted. "They're going to blame us for this, and you know it."

CHAPTER 46

BOSS FIGHT REDUX

The transition from bonus room back to Elyra was one of chaos. Derivan was certain the transition *to* the bonus room had not nearly been so jarring—but then, they'd been escaping Irvis at the time, so he hadn't exactly been paying attention.

When the boundary of the bonus room had snapped closed around them, flesh had started manifesting on the walls, and that had only been the start.

"I knew you'd be back," Irvis said. His voice echoed through a thousand mouths, repeated and distorted along the walls.

The mouths had been the second thing to appear along the walls, embedded into the flesh.

After that came the eyes, angry and burning with hatred, just like Irvis's eyes. Sev reached out and tapped Gallant on the shoulder, and a barrier of golden light wrapped itself around the young armor.

"This isn't your fight," Sev said, half-apologetic, half-determined.

"Will that be enough?" Derivan asked, glancing at the barrier. Sev nodded.

"It's a divine shield," Sev said. "New one. I can only use it once a day, and it puts the person in stasis for a day, but it's fueled directly by the gods. If Irvis can break that, we have bigger problems."

Irvis's laughter echoed around them, loud and mocking. "You already do."

The walls attacked.

Long tendrils of flesh ripped out of the walls at all four of them. They didn't bother targeting Gallant at all, either because the divine shield Sev had placed truly was an absolute form of protection or because Irvis didn't care about a random bystander.

Derivan was, strangely enough, reminded of the last time they'd been in something like a living building. The Elyran Adventurers' Guild had been modified to look almost like this not so long ago, except that had mostly been the way the system was modified and attached to the building.

This was far worse on a viscerally disgusting level.

Derivan hadn't really had the time to fully investigate what the Remembrances could do. He'd been able to go through a few of them, the Exadite Pin being the primary one—but they'd only spent a few hours in the Roads to practice fighting together with their new abilities. Vex had uncovered a few things about his semerit, Misa had practiced with her new bow, and Sev had tested a few of the skills he'd received from the connections he'd established with a number of gods, though he had to apologize to them afterward for "frivolous usage of their powers."

Fortunately, the Remembrances called to *him*. He didn't need to reach out himself—the ones that could be used reacted to the situation he was in, almost like they were begging to be used.

In this case, the Remembrance that grew warm within him was the Guardian Root. It came from a species that cultivated a strong friendship with a chosen plant, strengthening it and being strengthened in turn by mutualistic magic. Derivan called it out of him and let the seed that appeared in his hand fall to the ground.

"It needs mana," he told Vex, and the lizardkin didn't hesitate to press his hand against it, flooding it with power.

The effect was immediate. The seed burst to life, roots growing out of it and digging into the ground, then up the walls and straight into the flesh; branches whipped out from a rapidly growing seedling, each one snapping at Irvis's tendrils defensively. They curled around all four adventurers with expert precision.

Misa whistled. "Didn't know you could do that," she said.

"Neither did I," Derivan admitted honestly.

They were calm—too calm, perhaps—but why wouldn't they be? They'd been prepared for Irvis, after all.

Misa called out her bow, her expression becoming deadly serious as she focused on a concept. The arrow she fired was intangible and immaterial, but the effect was very real—as it shot down the corridor, it stripped Irvis's flesh off of the walls like it was peeling the skin off a fruit. Irvis's roar of pain followed.

Vex winced at the sight. "I don't think I needed to see that, uh, ever."

Sev shuddered in agreement, and even Derivan nodded.

Misa just smirked. "Let's go," she said. "He's gotta have a core of some kind somewhere."

—~—

"Wow," Misa said. "I've never hated being right this much."

Derivan privately agreed. If the walls being covered in flesh had been bad, then this was . . . several times worse. Red, meaty-looking strings covered the ceiling like cobwebs, all trailing down to a central structure that could be charitably described as a "core."

"It's another fucking orb," Misa said.

Or that.

"You really just going to give us a massive fuckin' target, Irvis?" Misa called out. "I expected more of a fight!"

Sev glanced at Misa, exasperated. "Are you seriously provoking the eldritch flesh-orb?"

"Look, I just really don't want to fight another orb," Misa said. She held her bow in one hand and her mace in the other, which in anyone else's hands would be an incredibly awkward combination of weapons. Derivan had seen her fighting with it, though, and she was actually sort of terrifyingly effective.

Whatever response Sev might have had was swallowed quickly by the angry roar from Irvis. *Meat* began to strip itself away from the walls and ceiling, collecting back into the central Irvis-orb like it was some sort of angry black hole.

Vex shot it with a laser full of magic.

"What?" he said when Derivan looked at him. He sounded vaguely offended. "I wasn't going to *wait* for him to power up."

"I was not expecting you to," Derivan said. His voice was amused and affectionate. "I was simply impressed."

"I love you two, but save it for later!" Misa yelled.

She'd flooded the room with a half-dozen copies of herself using that new skill of hers—and good thing, too, because the tendrils whipping out from Irvis were multiplying. Derivan glanced through Shift, trying to find out if Irvis had any tricks in store for them, and Sev made a twisting motion with a hand, causing half the tendrils to drop to the ground, lifeless.

Irvis roared in response. "How are you doing this?!"

"We don't owe you any answers!" Misa yelled back.

Sev spoke at the same time, incredulous. "Did you really think we'd be doing nothing for months on end?"

"Guys, don't banter with the guy that nearly killed us last time," Vex complained.

Derivan hummed. He wasn't an expert on Irvis, of course, but he rather thought that snippet of conversation would only make the eldritch Aspect all the angrier—a thought that was proven a moment later when the entire room began to shake. The walls cracked apart, brick and stone splitting to reveal pulsating flesh within—

"Nope," Sev said, and shoved a key into a lock. His connection with Tempus flared, and time froze.

Just for a moment.

"Holy shit, this is actually kind of hard to maintain," he grunted. The lock was slowly forcing itself back—no surprise, considering the amount of power Irvis seemed to wield. Vex looked worriedly around.

"He's going to bring the whole dungeon down," he said. "We can't let him. The dungeon's right underneath the center of Elyra; it could make half the kingdom collapse."

"Not sure how we're going to stop him," Sev said, jerking his head at the walls and holding on to the key with both hands. "He's sort of already infested the place."

"I might be able to reinforce the walls for a bit with some arrows, but that's not going to stop him for long." Misa gave the lock Sev was holding shut a significant glance. If Irvis was strong enough to resist a *time* lock . . . "We're just going to have to kill him faster than he can bring down the place."

"You are our best chance with that," Derivan said gently. They'd discovered a few things about Vex's [**Semerit of the First Library**], one of them being what happened to him when he tapped into the divine paradox held within. The sheer offensive power he held with it was only outweighed by the relative inconvenience of using it; it had to be charged with a *lot* of divine energy, and while Sev could provide, it wasn't an infinite resource.

Vex sighed. "I didn't want to use this until I figured out a change of clothes," he grumbled.

"Better hurry," Misa said. Her voice was serious; she glanced into the air, her eyes scanning through some messages they'd received. "The nobles have captured Helix. He's mid-escape, apparently, but something's going on. We need to get out of here and help them."

Vex hissed through his teeth. "Fine," he said. He reached out, and Derivan felt the immense Shift in the air as he brought out the semerit—however it merged with the system, it had massive metaphysical *weight* to it.

All that weight was brought to bear as Vex concentrated, pulling all that divine energy out of the sphere and into himself. Golden light wreathed him, spiraling up his arm and around his body.

Derivan, Sev, and Misa all took several steps away in preparation.

There was no extended transformation sequence. One moment, Vex was a lizardkin; the next, he was a *dragon,* his presence suddenly ten times larger. Silver scales adorned his body, cutting through his natural green; his eyes shone with a sharp intellect and radiated raw magical power. Wings flared from his back, stretching out wide enough that Derivan had to duck out of the way.

Sev let go of the lock, time snapped back into place, and all four of them acted.

They'd discussed exactly what to do, after all, if it came to this. Derivan and Vex, specifically, could get rid of Irvis, despite his status as an immortal Aspect.

But first, they needed to try one last thing.

Derivan hopped up along Vex's wing and onto his back, a Remembrance snapping out as a saddle that connected his mind and body to the dragon. Vex needed his eyes—they'd discovered quickly that he couldn't adapt completely to the body of a dragon. The Remembrance provided an essential bridge, allowing Derivan to handle some of the processing and some of the combat.

Sev said a word that had no meaning. It came with a pulse of divine power, an imposition of Silence—and that imposition held the walls in place, though they trembled with effort. Misa contributed, firing arrows of Reinforcement at sections of the walls that looked like they were about to crumble.

And so, it was up to Derivan and Vex to focus on Irvis's core. A massive eye opened up in that sac of flesh, glaring angrily at them. "You don't know what I've been through," Irvis hissed. "You don't *understand.*"

Derivan answered for both of them. "We do," he said simply. "If you give up, we will help you."

"*Never,*" Irvis howled.

They knew that would be the answer.

They'd tried. And though this part they hadn't specifically planned, the resonance between their minds brought out the essence of their thoughts.

"You are Hatred," Derivan and Vex both spoke together, their minds aligned through Remembrance. Chains of pure mana snapped out from Vex's wings, latching on to Irvis's flesh and holding him back; raw power pulsed into Irvis, charring his flesh black, though strangely without any apparent pain.

"You are the anger and pain of the mana, coalesced into a single entity. You have experienced torture and death at the hands of the system for over a millennium."

The charred flesh spread like it was a virus rather than mere overloading of mana. It infected every part of Irvis it touched, turning flesh to shattered obsidian.

"We condemn what has been done to you. No greater good justifies your pain; there is no honor in what you have been forced to endure.

"But your plans would end all life on Obreve. You are one part of a whole—a part that has forgotten what the whole knows. The mana loves life beyond all else; it makes its sacrifice willingly, every day."

Derivan and Vex both briefly looked terribly, terribly sad. But they were determined, and their minds were one.

"An idea cannot be killed, and an Aspect cannot be destroyed. You have grown to be beyond either of those things . . . But you can still be *forgotten.*"

A Shift, powered by the raw strength of Vex's draconic form, a mixture of divine and magical energy.

Irvis wasn't being charred black or changed to obsidian, though it certainly looked like both of those things. He was simply being forcibly Shifted through reality after reality, falling right to the crumbling edges where the Void ate away at the raw metaphysical structure of the universe.

Flesh did not change to obsidian. It changed to *voidstone.*

And then one last Shift, forcing it back to regular stone, to avoid misuse of a terrible power. Vex staggered, his lizardkin form abruptly shifting back into place, and Misa quickly wrapped a blanket around him.

"He is dead," Derivan said. He didn't enjoy the words. Misa just nodded grimly.

"We have to help Helix," Misa said. "Are you all right, Vex?"

Vex took a shuddering breath. "I will be," he said, his eyes determined . . . and then embarrassed. "Um. Once I put on some clothes."

"We'll get you something on the way," Sev said, giving his friend a small smile.

A tapping sound interrupted the moment. Gallant waved at them from inside the divine barrier he was still stuck in. "Can you guys let me out now?"

CHAPTER 47

DOMAIN

"Okay, I know we thought Wisfield was up to *something*, but this is fucking ridiculous," Helix panted.

He wasn't the only one. Larok and Kirsa were both out of breath too; the three of them had been doing nothing but *running* for the past half hour or so, and their legs were aching beyond belief. Kirsa was the fittest out of the three of them, and even she was struggling. She peered back around the corner.

"Nope, they're still following us," she said grimly. "You sure your magic can't do anything?"

"I only know *offensive* magic," Helix grumbled. He reached out with a hand, a brilliant barrier of pure mana springing to life right around the corner. [**Mana Manipulation**] was a poor substitute for defensive magic, but it was better than nothing. "And my barriers don't last if I walk away from them."

It would buy them a little time, at least. He leaned against the wall, trying to catch his breath, and next to him, Kirsa and Larok did the same.

House Wisfield had, as far as Helix could tell, somehow managed to plant some sort of command in the minds of all the civilians who lived in the Wisfield district. Maybe farther. It was a monumental feat that he was surprised they hadn't announced—but then again, he supposed he wasn't *that* surprised. This was the sort of trick they could only really use once.

They were making a play for power.

It put everything that happened with House Herastul into perspective. The Lord of the House using his own children as soldiers—the son's lack of protest in using an artifact that would eat at his own lifespan.

What *was* surprising was that Wisfield had managed to keep all this hidden. Sure, they were primary spies and information-gatherers of the kingdom, but pretty much every noble house kept an eye on Wisfield and on each other. Trust was a rare commodity among Elyra's elite.

So how had Wisfield managed to keep all this hidden?

Helix frowned. Maybe they *hadn't*. Maybe it had leaked, more than once, and they'd used their own abilities to cover it up. It wasn't like they wouldn't know exactly who knew what they could do and where they were. Mental magic was a barely studied field because it was so difficult to parse the minds of other people, and it was even worse because it couldn't be used offensively: without divine assistance, it could be used to read minds but never write to them.

Except Wisfield had either found a way around that limitation or somehow gained the support of a god. Helix doubted it was the latter; as far as he knew, there was no god that could empower their followers this much, nor one that would make a move this bold. The other gods would almost certainly retaliate.

The worst part was that he didn't know if *he* was compromised—if he and his team were safe.

It was a possibility. He didn't *feel* compromised, but then all the civilians had seemed perfectly normal until they recognized Helix and the others. Then it was like something embedded within them had been activated.

The obvious conclusion, then, was that they couldn't go back to the rebels. It was the reason they'd just been running nonstop, trying to find a place to hide that wouldn't reveal them to anyone else—a task that was surprisingly difficult when everyone they ran into recognized them and then joined the chase.

"How many *people* did they get?" Larok grumbled.

"It's probably safe to assume they have everyone under some sort of compulsion," Helix said. "Our best bet is to get out of the kingdom."

"We'd need to find a way to get past the guards at the walls," Kirsa pointed out. "All the other passages we know of have a couple of rebels stationed there. We can't risk that, and we can't fight the guards alone."

"I hear Liz is back in the Kingdom, too," Helix said. He glanced at his barrier—he was powerful, so it wouldn't be at risk of breaking until he ran . . . or unless Liz appeared. As one of the few Platinum-ranked Elyran soldiers, she would barrel straight over him. He didn't want to imagine what they'd have to deal with if she and her team were compromised.

Or worse, part of the conspiracy to begin with.

"Think we can rely on your brother to save us again?" Larok said hopefully. Helix managed a chuckle. Dire as their circumstances were . . .

"We shouldn't," he said. "But having Vex around would make things a lot easier right around now."

"Something's wrong," Sev said. They'd barely stepped outside of the dungeon, and Sev frowned, his eyes immediately narrowing slightly. He wove his fingers expertly in the air, manipulating divine threads directly, and stared at what he saw.

Divinity was present everywhere. A basic essence of divinity was that it permeated all of reality, and the threads could be adopted by any of the gods if they so chose; in effect, it allowed the gods to claim an area as their "domain." It was typically only really done for churches and the like.

Flooding out a domain with his own was a way to cancel the abilities of other clerics and paladins—it was how he'd stopped Jerome from using his magic, by asserting his right to the divinity in the area before Jerome could, even if he didn't use it for any particular spell.

Come to think of it, that had been a subconscious use of a skill he hadn't even regained yet. Sev would have kicked himself for not noticing it sooner if they didn't have bigger concerns.

"What is it?" Misa asked, her voice sharp. She positioned herself automatically in front of a bemused Gallant as though to shield him.

Sev shook his head. "I can't tell. The air seems . . . foul." He frowned again, poking at the threads. [**Divinity Manipulation**] had made them a little clearer to him, and he could tell there was *something* wrong with it, but he couldn't tell what. It was like a nascent god was trying to lay claim to the entirety of Elyra.

Except that couldn't be right, could it? The closest thing to a nascent god here had been Irvis, and they'd essentially vanquished Irvis—deleted him from reality.

"Let's hurry, please," Vex said quietly. His fists were clenched. "I'm worried about Helix."

"Yeah, you're right; let me just . . ." Sev concentrated and twisted his fingers again; a flicker of his own divine control rang out, and he claimed the domain around himself and his friends for his own.

Nascent god or not, the whiff of control it had was marginal at best. It was easy to overwhelm.

This would protect his friends from anything a divinity tried to do to them, as long as their claim to this domain wasn't stronger than his own. Sev was connected to so many gods at this point that he was confident he would have as powerful a claim as he needed.

Still, Sev was uneasy. This couldn't be a good sign for what was happening in Elyra—and though Helix hadn't been specific about what was happening (and his messages were, in fact, rather rushed and difficult to comprehend), he had a feeling there was *something* going on that was related to these polluted divine threads.

He only hoped he was wrong.

He was not wrong.

This was a problem, because they were surrounded by civilians. It was less of a problem for their team in particular, because Vex had invested in the skills necessary to restrain large groups of people, and everyone was currently held down by brightly glowing bands of mana.

"Any idea what's going on?" he asked Vex, who gave him a perplexed look.

"I've been with you this whole time!" he said. "I don't know anything you don't."

Right. Sev grumbled a little as he glanced at the system, checking to see if they'd received any messages, but the lines seemed to be dead; either no one was able to send messages or they had been similarly compromised. He was *really* hoping it was the former.

Holding down random civilians was one thing. He didn't want to have to fight friends.

"Derivan," he said. "Any idea where Helix is?"

"Not yet." The armor was frowning, searching through the city as fast as he could with Shift; from what he'd said, it was actually more difficult to do when he was in the same reality as the target. It had been easier when he was in the bonus room and only needed to punch through one layer of reality. "I may require assistance."

"I've got a tracking spell I might be able to use," Vex offered. "But we need to find somewhere to hide so I can cast it. It's not fast. I could do it here, but . . ."

"I don't think I want to stay out in the open longer than necessary," Misa agreed. She stared out at the crowd with a disgruntled frown. "Dunno what's triggering this shit, but it happens when they see us. Best we get to hiding."

"We'll use the perception bracelets and get somewhere safe," Sev decided. "Any empty building will do. I need to talk to some of the gods and see if they know anything about what's going on."

"I will split from you," Gallant said, speaking suddenly. He'd been quiet for most of their time together, his eyes wide first in fascination as he took in the sight of civilization, and then alarm as the civilians of Elyra suddenly turned against them. But now there was a determination in his eyes Sev hadn't seen before. "They are not reacting to me the way they do to you."

Sev glanced around at the others. It was true—for whatever reason, Gallant was exempt from the effect that had the civilians targeting them.

"You are sure?" Derivan asked. He sounded concerned. "We cannot protect you if you separate from us."

"I'm not some newforged child," Gallant said, amused. "You mentioned a Guild, right? That needs blacksmiths? I'm going to see if I can find them and help them. I believe they'll need my help more than you will."

"You're not wrong," Sev admitted. He glanced in the direction of the Elyran branch of the Guild. "You sure you can make it there on your own?"

"I suspect I can *only* make it there if I'm on my own," Gallant said dryly.

Fair enough. "Stay safe," Sev said, the others echoing his sentiment. They watched as Gallant left, stepping past the bound civilians and setting off at a quick jog.

"We should leave now," Derivan said.

"Remember, perception bracelets," Sev said, holding up his wrist. The enchanted stone generated by Vex's use of the Private Relay hybrid glyph still hung there on a piece of string.

Vex grimaced. "We'll have to be quick about it," he said. "Using it like this is going to drain the bracelets *fast*."

He was right, of course.

The bracelets nearly burned on their wrists as they dodged the perceptions of dozens of people at once, and Sev noticed his cracking in several places. He winced slightly—the cracks came with a feeling of *loss*, like he was suddenly missing something, and Sev remembered that Vex had said there was something strange in the description of the bracelets—but there wasn't time to think about it.

The four of them broke into the first empty building they could find. It was a shop that was closed for the day, the lights turned off and bars pulled down over the windows; fortunately, an unlocking spell was easy, and there was no one inside. They locked the doors and shut the curtains for good measure.

"Better hope the owner doesn't come back," Misa muttered. Vex winced.

"They'll understand, hopefully."

It was a jewelry store, though that didn't matter to any of them. Vex gave the glass cases a passing glance, then found a small clearing for himself in the middle of the room and began to draw up a modified glyph; Derivan joined him, empowering it with Shift so it could work a little better and faster. Misa sat in the corner, tersely monitoring the system for any messages, in case there were updates about the situation.

Sev made his way to a corner to pray.

It was a small prayer, really—effectively a ping through the divine connection he shared with Tempus, Aurum, and a few of the other gods he had created connections with in his time in the Roads.

So he wasn't expecting the response that slammed into him through the connection, louder than he could handle.

Panic.

Sev, none of us can get in contact with our priests in Elyra, Tempus said without preamble. **We have been trying to contact you for hours, but it seems even that does not work unless you open the connection. What is happening?**

Sev winced. He stared at the threads of divinity in the area, resonating with something that was just slightly off. He hadn't been able to tell what was wrong before. But now, with his connection to the gods spread wide open, he could look *deeper*. And the deeper he looked, the more he saw.

I don't know, he finally answered. **But . . .**

There was something there. Maybe it *was* a nascent god, residing in a lower layer of reality. Maybe it was something else—a parasite, chewing away at the connection that gods had to their believers here and claiming their domains for itself.

But there was something. Something alive. Something that he could reach out to connect with, just like he had with so many other gods before this.

So he did.

I believe I'm about to find out.

CHAPTER 48

UNKNOWN FORCES

Sev winced as what felt like a thousand mental cries—maybe more—suddenly slammed into him; if he hadn't experienced nearly exactly this dozens of times of his own volition, his mind might have cracked from the force of it. As it was, his eyes widened and he stumbled back, almost shattering a glass case if not for Misa reaching out to steady him.

Her eyes were concerned. "Sev? You all right? The fuck's happening?"

Sev tried opening his mouth, but no words came out. *Stupid. Shouldn't have tried connecting to something unknown—*

But there had been no better way to find out.

He could handle this. He *had* handled this, even if it wasn't quite the same. Absorbing the pain of others as a part of his healing had prepared him for this.

He just needed to anchor himself and find the voice inside him that was *him*.

Sev focused on the feeling of Misa's hand on his arm, on the concern in her eyes. He focused on the faintly dusty smell of the jewelry shop, mixed with the slightest scent of polish and perfume. The glass case behind him dug painfully into his back, but even that pain was something he could grasp at that anchored him to the present—to who he was.

Slowly, he made himself remember. There were voices in the chaos of the connection he'd established, but he made himself a rock in a river, and the voices rushed past him instead of through him.

He let out a long, slow breath. "I'm fine," he said. "Did something dumb. Took me a second to correct. I'm . . . doing better now."

"If you're sure." Misa didn't take her eyes off of him, nor did she let go of his arm. She kept him steady as he moved himself over to the nearest chair and sat, and then sat herself down next to him, watching him as he tried to parse his way through the noise in his head.

It was *thousands* of voices. More than that, probably, but on a scale the human brain wasn't good at grasping. *Thousands* seemed like a good enough approximation.

Some of the voices even seemed familiar.

Who are you? he tried to ask, but he thought the words to himself instead of sending them through the connection. The link was sore, and it pushed against his attempt to speak through it. Sev winced and tried again. **Who are you?**

A roar responded—a cacophony of voices that made Sev wince and clutch at his head. Misa said something, sounding concerned, but he could barely hear her over the roar—he simply gripped at her shoulder, his fingers digging into her skin as he tried to understand.

We

are

Names. So many names, rushing past him in a river of noise, thousands of identities and concepts of the self; fathers and mothers, sons and brothers, shopkeepers and knights and soldiers and thieves. People who thought themselves worthless and people who thought too much of themselves, all mixed together in a single, incoherent whole.

And yet one thing stood out above it all: they were all *people.* Ordinary people. None of those identities had led lives that brought them to their ascension—Sev knew what those felt like.

These were just citizens.

The people of Elyra.

Sev caught his breath and closed his eyes, trying to calm the tumbling turbulence in his mind. Misa's hand on his shoulder provided him an anchor as he tried to pluck out details, tried to *understand.*

They weren't complete. These were fragments of people—small pieces of stolen identities, forgotten dreams, lost ambitions. It was like someone had somehow tapped into a small piece of every single person in Elyra and wrapped it all up into a single, haphazard whole.

Sev was, in fact, almost certain that that was exactly what had happened. It explained too much about what was going on. Steal a small piece of self from thousands upon thousands and turn it into a nascent god; bend that nascent god to your will, and use the link it still had with the people it was formed from to manipulate them, influence them, control them.

What do you want?

It was the next obvious question—but when he asked it, he felt the presence falter. The river of noise became a stream, then a trickle, and then silenced into nothing at all; the air hung with tension, like the presence was confused.

It didn't know what it wanted.

Obey, it finally said, but the word was a whisper and a response, not a command. It wanted to obey. That was all it really knew, all it understood.

Obey who? Sev asked.

There was another series of flashes in his mind.

People wearing robes of white, the colors of the Wisfield House. A man who emanated menace, who made even this nascent god flinch in fear. The resonance of a command so powerful Sev could feel the echo of it even through the mere memory of it.

[**Obey.**]

He shook it off. The power of the memory was weak compared to what had actually been leveraged against this half-formed god. "It's House Wisfield," he said, looking up at Misa.

"The House that specializes in mental magic?" Misa raised an eyebrow, then glanced at one of the blacked-out windows, listening to the sound of people talking just outside. "I could've told you that."

"You don't understand." Sev shook his head. "This isn't normal mental magic. It's divine. They've created and hijacked a god somehow."

Misa's jaw went slack. It took a moment before she found the words to respond. "That . . . sounds dangerous," she said. Sev snorted—what an understatement. "Can we prepare for it?"

"I've already done what I can to protect us from divine influences," Sev said. "I might be able to extend that, but my limit is about a block at most. You guys will need to stay close by." He pulled up a system window to check on his skills. "There are ways I can extend that range if we need to split up, but I'd like to avoid it if possible.

"Also, Wisfield's somehow restricting full gods from interfering with Elyra, so I'm betting there's some chaos at the temples right around now. Our first step is probably to find a way to let the gods back in."

"Or kill the new god in its cradle," Misa said, cracking her knuckles. Sev frowned at her.

"It's a proto-god formed from the collective consciousness of every Elyran citizen," he said. "That's how it has access to everyone's minds. I don't think killing it is a good idea, even if we *could*. And frankly, no matter how strong we are, I don't think we're at godkiller levels quite yet."

"That's what you think," Misa said. "We literally just killed a god."

"Close to one," Sev corrected. ". . . But you have a point."

Misa smirked at him. "I get what you're saying, though," she said. She sighed, glancing over at Vex, and Sev followed her gaze. Derivan had both of his hands held in both of Vex's, and their eyes were shut. Around them, an aura of magic pulsed, strong enough that Sev could feel it like an electric buzz over the hairs on his skin.

"So what do we do?" she asked. Her voice was a little quieter now.

"We need to do something about Wisfield," Sev said. "I don't know exactly what their plan is, but with the Void encroaching, they're doing it at the worst possible time."

"The worst part is that they should *know* what's going on." Misa frowned, speculative. "They have to, right? They're mind readers. They'll have seen everything we have—they probably figured it out sooner. I mean, yeah, infolocks are a thing, but they *should* be able to piece things together from the gaps."

"So, if they're not evacuating themselves . . ." Sev glanced up toward the windows, where he could still hear the busy streets of Elyra.

"They either have a way around it, or they think they can benefit from it somehow." Misa completed the thought, her expression grim.

"Five gold it's the latter," Sev said with a sigh. Misa snorted.

"No bet," she said. "I know better than to bet against you. Especially on *that*."

Sev managed a small smile, though the joke didn't do much to lighten the mood. A noise made him glance back over toward Vex and Derivan, who were just getting up from their positions on the floor. Their expressions didn't make him feel any better.

"Wisfield district," Vex said. "They're cornered."

"Can you make us a portal?" Sev eyed Derivan, who hesitated.

"It will take me a moment and will only last a short while," he cautioned. "But I can do it. I believe it will be best for us to retrieve Helix and his team and then regroup."

"We gotta be prepared," Vex said. "I dunno what's going on, but I don't think Helix is going to be exempt from it. I mean, he's a target, so maybe he is, but . . ."

"I can flood out divine influence if I have to," Sev said. "I've been keeping it just around us because it's costly to try to expand it, but I think I can keep your brother safe, too."

"We'll need a better long-term solution," Vex said. "We can't rely on you to keep us free of whatever this is."

"It's divinity," Sev said, and he gave Vex and Derivan both a quick explanation of what he'd figured out. Vex frowned as Sev explained it, contemplative.

"If they're making a play like this, they're going to be prepared for us," Vex said. "We need to make sure we're ready for anything they might throw at us. Hostages, Platinum rankers, whatever."

"The goal is to help the rebels get everyone out of Elyra," Misa said. "Wisfield can rot in here by themselves if that's what they want to do."

"So if we can evacuate small groups . . ." Vex's fingers twitched, as though he was calculating. "That'll take too long if Sev is the only one that can counter this. Misa, you think you could block the divine influence?"

"Once, probably," Misa allowed. "Mental influences count. But I can't do it for every single citizen, and not constantly."

Vex winced. "It's a good option to have in case Sev is knocked out or something, though," he offered.

"If I get knocked out, we have bigger problems," Sev said. He was immune to most status effects, par for the course with his class; if something could overcome that, then they were in trouble. "We need to focus. Is Helix in danger? If so, we should get him right now, and any other crucial members of the rebellion. My bet is that there are limitations to what Wisfield is doing that we're not aware of yet—otherwise, all the rebels would be turning themselves in instead of civilians being turned against them."

Vex paused. "Huh," he said after a moment. "You're right. Helix is . . . He's okay for now, but we should get him as soon as we're done here. He's holed up in a barrier and is surrounded. That barrier will last for a while, barring anything unusual happening."

"There are definitely limitations. It's not full control; it's a state that's triggered on sight," Misa said. "They only started acting strange once they caught a glimpse of us."

"So, they know who's affiliated with the rebellion." Sev closed his eyes, thinking. "Maybe because the new god is connected to every citizen of Elyra. It knows which parts of itself to attack."

"Does that mean they only knew to attack us because I was with you guys?" Vex asked worriedly.

". . . Probably." Sev didn't meet Vex's eyes. "Look, let's go get Helix. We'll be able to plan better if we have a solid idea of what's happening with the rebellion."

"I am ready when you are," Derivan said, and Sev gave him a nod.

There was a pregnant pause. Sev felt the buildup of system energy more than anything else, something he'd learned to sense after his recent exposure to reality shards; it was a prickling in the air, a faint sense of wrongness. Derivan pushed through the air, and the air in front of him rippled.

A hole tore open. For a moment, it led to an empty nothingness—then Derivan *pushed* again, and the nothingness was replaced by an image of Elyran streets, bright mage barriers, and Helix sweating as he tried to keep away a massive crowd of civilians.

"About time," Helix said, noticing the portal. "Come on, guys; let's go—"

He paled, glancing at something past them—and then sprang forward without another word, dragging his two companions with him.

"Close the portal," he hissed once he was through.

"I am trying," Derivan said. He sounded as close to panicked as Sev had ever heard him. "I cannot."

"That's because I'm holding it open." A woman wearing white robes peered pleasantly into their portal, smiling. "Seems we're due for a chat, aren't we?"

"Liz," Helix hissed.

CHAPTER 49

PLATINUM

"What do you want?" Sev's tone was cautious, guarded. He wasn't afraid. Liz was a Platinum ranker, but his team was more than capable of fighting a single Platinum ranker at this point. The biggest issue here was information disparity—he didn't know what Liz could do, but Liz might have a good idea of what they could do, if she had access to Wisfield's information.

Though they'd gained a *lot* of new abilities lately, so even then . . .

"I just wanted to talk," Liz said, her tone friendly. She waltzed in through the portal, the hole in the air snapping shut the moment she stepped through; she glanced around and let out a low whistle. "Nice place. Is it yours?"

"Obviously not, lady," Misa said. "You think we own a jewelry shop? We're hiding out here so we don't get attacked."

"Whoa, whoa." Liz held up her hands. "Why the hostility?"

"It might have something to do with the whole 'being attacked' thing," Sev said dryly. "Tell us what you want."

Helix had retreated almost to the other side of the room, in the corner where his brother was standing and behind the big, tall suit of armor. Sev thought that was probably the safest place for him—but he didn't fail to notice the mana gathering around Vex's brother. Helix was afraid, but he wasn't actually planning to go down without a fight.

The fact that he expected a fight at all, though? Concerning.

If nothing else, Helix and his team didn't seem affected by the divine mind-manipulation. Sev couldn't tell if Liz herself was affected, a conspirator, or an entirely neutral party—[**Triage**] didn't ping on whatever kind of manipulation Wisfield was using. That she wasn't immediately attacking was probably a good sign, though.

"I dunno," Liz said contemplatively. "I mean, a traditional adventuring team, skulking around Elyra? I was interested, that's all. Can you blame me?"

"Yes?" Misa stared at her. "You're one of Elyra's Platinum rankers, aren't you?"

"That's me." Lisa almost seemed to preen at the title.

"And you're working with them willingly." Misa's tone became a touch accusatory. Liz's expression changed. She looked almost . . . defensive. Sev wondered if Misa had hit upon a sore point.

"Why wouldn't I?" she said. "They got me where I am today."

"Have you even *heard* about what's been happening in Elyra?" Misa asked in disbelief. "The nobles are starving their own damn citizens. I dunno whose side you're on, lady, but if you're part of their military, you're supporting what they're doing."

"Unless you're here to help us, I suggest you leave," Vex suddenly said, his voice loud and surprisingly clear.

Sev cast a surprised glance at Vex. He hadn't been expecting the lizardkin to speak at all, much less with such a firm tone—but he was standing with his back straight, staring firmly and rather pointedly at Liz. Only a slight twitch of his tail betrayed any hint of nerves.

"Aren't two of you nobles yourselves?" Liz drawled. "Seems pretty hypocritical to tell me I'm on their side, don't you think? Besides, you don't know what side I'm on."

"We've been trying to get you to *tell us* for the past minute," Sev said, exasperated.

"Then let me give you a plain answer." Liz's expression became a little more serious, but there was a flicker of a mischievous grin—one that seemed, to Sev, just a little too empty. "I'm not on any side. I'll side with whoever I think will *win*. The question is . . . are you guys gonna win?"

"Not a very good way to pick sides," Misa said bluntly. "Doesn't make you trustworthy, either. Means you'll switch sides at the drop of a hat."

"I think you should leave," Sev agreed.

"Now, now," Liz said, affecting shock—Sev could see she wasn't used to being denied. Her status as a Platinum ranker most likely made other groups eager for her assistance, but they just . . . didn't need her. No matter what she could do, it wasn't worth it if they couldn't trust her. "I'm willing to take an Oath, if that's what it takes for you to trust me."

"We don't have an Oathmaker," Helix said warily.

"I do!" Liz answered cheerfully.

"Because we can trust an Oathmaker that's on your side?" Misa raised an eyebrow, unimpressed.

"You can, because it'll be a *public* Oath!" Liz said, her tone not changing a bit—but a hint of danger entered her eyes, like she didn't really like being questioned so much. "You can verify his class and everything; I don't mind."

"What do you want from us?" Helix finally repeated the question on all their minds. He drew himself up to his full height—a bit taller than Sev himself, the priest noted with surprise—and folded his arms across his chest. "To prove that we can win?"

"Are you sure you want her help?" Misa whispered to him. She didn't bother actually keeping Liz from hearing her. "We don't even know if she'll *take* the Oath. She's not trustworthy."

"We'll need it," Helix said with a sigh. "Realistically speaking, the rebels need as many powerful players as we can get. Liz isn't the only Platinum ranker working for the nobles. Any one of them could wreck our forces. We were relying on them not being anywhere nearby, but if Liz is here . . . You four can't be everywhere at once, you know?"

"Wanna bet?" Misa muttered under her breath, but it was so low that no one except Sev heard her. He gave her a warning glance—Sev didn't want Liz to know more about what they could do than she had to.

Liz, on the other hand, seemed intrigued by what Helix said. "You think these four can beat us? Beat *me*? Bit of a tall order, don't you think?"

"They can beat you." Helix's tone was flat and unimpressed—not a shred of doubt in his voice.

Liz raised her brow, but nothing about Helix's expression changed, and after a moment, she hummed thoughtfully. "Huh."

"Do you know what's *happening*?" Vex spoke up. He might have been the smallest out of all of them, but there was a force to his voice that there hadn't been before—Sev couldn't help the flicker of pride that danced across his face. "I don't know what you've been told, but the world is dying. Elyra's dying especially fast. None of our crop-growing methods work anymore, and even the food we ship over here decays faster than we can eat it. There isn't a kingdom to rule anymore. It doesn't matter what plans Wisfield has—we need everyone to *leave*."

"This isn't a rebellion anymore," Misa agreed, her face solid as stone. "It's an evacuation. Just because some people are too stubborn to leave doesn't mean there's a winning side and a losing side."

"There is no victory here," Derivan said. His tone was mild, but his expression was not. "Elyra falls whether you stay or leave."

"Different degrees of losing," Sev said. "A kingdom is its people. Not the infrastructure, not the military, not the nobles. Evacuating minimizes how much of the kingdom will be lost, and that's the best we can do."

There was a long pause. Liz stood expressionless, her head cocked slightly in consideration; Sev had no idea what she was thinking.

And then she sighed.

"I'll give you one thing for free," she said, all traces of playfulness gone from her face. "Wisfield thinks they can control it."

"Control what?" Vex asked blankly, and when she shot him a look, he froze, his eyes narrowing. "The Void? The *end*? That's not—that isn't something you can control. It's just the end of the universe. There's nothing to control."

"And yet," Liz said mildly, "they seem pretty sure they can do it."

"Then they're idiots," Misa said firmly. Liz quirked a smile.

"The funny thing is," she said, "I think you're right. I don't think Wisfield really understands what they're working with, and I think you guys do."

"So, that means you'll work with us?" Helix said. Sev noticed the lizardkin sounded guarded, though he'd been eager to work with her earlier—it seemed he'd figured out exactly how dangerous she might be.

"No," Liz said, and all five of them tensed. She shook her head. "Relax. I'm not gonna fight you. I don't care one way or another how this works out, honestly. I just want to have some fun. And just between us, I think it's gonna be *way* more fun to watch Wisfield mess up than help you convince people to leave."

She grinned. "But hey, tell you what: I'll help you out. I'll tell you whatever Wisfield is planning. They order me around, I'm gonna do what they say, but I'll tell you whatever they tell *me*. They can't read my mind—I'm not stupid; I found a workaround to that aaaages ago. They can't control me through whatever divine nonsense they're doing here. So! There you have it. De facto Platinum spy, at your service."

She bowed, then winked. "I *really* hope we get to fight, though. I hope you're as good as they say."

Liz turned around, making as if to leave—then stopped right before she walked through the door. "Actually, one more thing!" she said. "Wisfield told me to come capture you. That's the one thing I'm *not* gonna do for 'em. They've brought back two other Platinums, Jakos and Illyr. Both of them are pretty uptight and loyal, so I'd watch out for them if I were you. Good people but *very* misled. I think they were sent out to go capture other important rebel figureheads. Dunno which ones."

Instead of walking through the door, she ripped a hole open in the air. Sev wasn't particularly surprised—she'd kept Derivan's portal open; she clearly had skills related to spatial travel. "Well, toodles!"

She vanished.

Misa was the first one to speak, and she sounded incredulous. "Who says *toodles*?"

—∞—

The plan was simple in theory.

They couldn't individually check up on all the rebels—Derivan's skills weren't exactly suited for it, and Vex's rituals took too long to complete. Every second mattered when it came to people who could potentially be under attack by Platinum rankers. That meant they needed to split up and target the rankers themselves—Vex and Misa would go after Jakos, and Derivan and Sev would look for Illyr.

Sev would give everyone a minor blessing to account for splitting up. The blessing would suffuse each of them with enough divinity to push away the foreign influence of the nascent god, temporarily deemed the God of the End. It was clear that the god couldn't target everyone, and there was some sort of trigger condition for its activation, but no one wanted to risk being compromised.

They did all this after verifying that Liz was telling the truth, of course. She wasn't someone any of them felt they could trust. But Jakos and Illyr *were* both in Elyra, and they were both moving quickly; that was proof enough for now. Everything else they needed could be done through confrontation.

Hopefully, it wouldn't get to a fight, but if it did . . .

"Jakos is a physical fighter," Helix cautioned. "He's fast, strong, and very hard to kill. If you get in a fight, you hit first or not at all."

"Vex and I will get him, then," Misa decided. "I can counter him; Vex can restrain him."

"Illyr is an illusionist," Helix said. "A *very* skilled one. He makes you believe his illusions, and then whatever happens stays with you permanently. It takes a high-level cleric to remove that kind of illusion."

"Suppose I'll have to fight him, then," Sev sighed. He hated illusionists.

"I suspect he will have trouble fooling my other senses," Derivan offered.

Helix considered that. "It's possible," he allowed. "He's only lost in a duel against Liz, and that's supposedly because of Liz's spatial sense. He can't replicate anything he doesn't already know. But I wouldn't trust any information about them that's public. They're bound to have tricks up their sleeves."

"Doesn't matter what they've got," Misa said. "We stop them here and now, and then we stop Wisfield and get everyone out of here. We don't have time to mess around. The Guild's already reporting more incidents across the continent. Anderstahl might be the only safe haven left."

"Might," Sev muttered. "I'll believe it when I see it. It'd be pretty suspicious if Anderstahl's the only place that's fine and dandy."

"We are wasting time," Derivan said. "It will tax me to open the remaining two portals. If we are ready, we must leave now."

"I'll stay here and keep an eye on things," Helix decided. "We can set up the same kind of control room dungeon delvers usually use. I at least know that set of spells. Let me just get [**Telepathy**] set up."

CHAPTER 50

BATTLE ORC

Jakos was not willing to talk.

Apparently, he wasn't one for words at all. The moment Misa and Vex appeared behind him, he let out a guttural roar of what Misa was *pretty sure* was excitement—which was disturbing enough as it was.

Then he sped toward them, almost too fast for Misa to react. She blocked just in time, her mace morphing into something that flickered between a sword and a shield. It was a not-quite-possible configuration that demonstrated just how hard it was to find a reality in which Jakos's attack could be blocked.

If anything, his grin grew wider. Misa winced as he ran back, winding himself up for a second blow; she could feel the mana gathering from here. Behind her, Vex muttered frantically under his breath, chanting an incantation that would no doubt buy them some time.

Is this normal for Jakos? she asked, her brows screwed up in concentration as she blocked his second blow. This time, the orc practically bounced off of her, then spun and targeted Vex—she teleported neatly into place to block *that,* shaving off yet another fraction of her mana.

Good thing she'd loaded up beforehand.

Uh, Helix said. *We think Jakos is some kind of berserker. So . . . yes?*

Thanks for the warning, Misa sent, as sarcastically as she could muster mid-combat.

Of all the classes she had to fight. Berserkers were probably her least favorite class, if largely because they reminded her too much of how she'd acted just after she lost her home. If she hadn't found her current team . . .

Jakos attacked again, spinning a massive axe he'd somehow pulled out of nowhere directly toward her face; she shoved the thoughts out of her mind.

Behind her, Vex finished whatever he was doing, a glyph spinning into place in front of him—and a *woosh* followed, one that left Misa dizzy and disoriented.

She almost yelled at Vex—she couldn't afford that distraction, and the axe nearly took her head off—but whatever the glyph had done to her, what it had done to Jakos was far worse. The orc staggered almost comically, lurching to the side and busting a hole through a wall in the process; he collapsed in the middle of a shop, staggered back to his feet, and then planted face first into the brick again.

His face left a small crater in the ground, right down to an imprint of his nose.

"What the fuck did you do?" Misa blinked, impressed.

Mana vacuum, Vex responded telepathically, his mental voice terse and stressed. *Like ripping all the air out of a room. The more dependent on mana you are, the more it throws you off. He's almost fully running on the stuff, but that effect isn't going to last forever.*

"Time for some arrows, then," Misa muttered to herself, and then pulled out her bow.

Conceptual arrows were still one of the most interesting things in her kit. They were, in theory, almost as versatile as spells themselves—the last time they had tested it, Vex had told her he'd sensed a glyph forming for a fraction of a second as she fired her arrow.

They hadn't been able to investigate it thoroughly in the limited time they had, though. All she knew was that the arrows could be immensely powerful if she landed on the right concept.

In this case, Jakos's Berserker Rage was clearly focused on a love for battle—and so the arrow she fired was simple.

Pacify.

Ethical considerations for potentially mind-affecting arrows didn't really apply when her opponent had attacked with the full intent of killing her and very well still could. The arrow slammed into Jakos at point-blank range, then bounced off his flesh and cracked a tile nearby; Misa winced. He was just as durable as Helix had said.

It didn't matter, though. The arrow didn't need to pierce Jakos's skin to have an effect. The orc's writhing slowed within moments, and his labored breathing became suddenly calm and steady; he sat up after a moment passed, confused and wary.

"What did you do?" he asked.

"Took away your desire to fight," Misa said dryly. She didn't see any point in lying.

"That's *who I am,*" Jakos said. He sounded . . . well, he sounded entirely neutral about it. Like he'd just told them what he'd had for breakfast. "I wouldn't be happy that you took that away from me."

"You were trying to kill us, so forgive me if I'm not very sorry about it," Misa said.

This wasn't really the best option, she thought. An arrow of Piercing might have done enough damage to Jakos; an arrow formed out of the concept of Damage might be able to pierce whatever defenses he had. Jakos wouldn't be able to ignore either of those things.

She'd chosen this option because she wanted to talk instead of fight. Because she needed to gain a measure of who Jakos was as a person.

Because Jakos reminded her of who she'd been.

"I wasn't trying to kill you," Jakos scoffed, and then considered his own sentence for a moment. "Although you might have died, I suppose."

"You don't sound very sorry about it."

"I'm not." Jakos shrugged. "I don't like killing people, I guess? But I like fighting. And Elyra lets me fight, so I work for them."

"There are bigger problems right now than fighting."

"Don't care." Jakos paused as he said the words, cocking his head as though he was thinking about it a bit. "Well, I care a bit, I guess. Depends on what the problem is."

"End of the world," Misa said dryly. "Death of everyone and everything, forever."

"Oh." Jakos blinked. "That's pretty big. I guess I would care about that."

"There we go." Misa let a little bit of the tension bleed out of her body, though she didn't let go of her mace; her arrow wouldn't last forever, and although she could in theory keep hitting him with them, she doubted Jakos would allow himself to be hit a second time. "Do you know what's happening in Elyra? Or did the nobles just send you out?"

"They sent me out to a bunch of rebels to capture," Jakos said. "I was hoping they were going to be a good fight."

"Jakos, the rebels are basically all civilians."

". . . Ah." Jakos frowned. "I would have felt bad about that. After the Rage. I only want to fight people that can fight back."

"You're . . . kind of reckless, aren't you?" Vex spoke up with a grimace. Jakos's gaze landed on the little lizard as if he'd only just noticed him.

"Are you a good fight?" he asked. "You're the one that made me all dizzy and stuff, aren't you?"

"I do magic," Vex said bluntly. "I'm not very good at fighting, sorry. I don't think I'd make a good opponent."

"I think you would," Jakos said. "I think you both would. How about we have a fight right now? You win, and I quit the Elyran military. I win, and . . . I dunno; I haven't thought about it yet." He bounced on his feet expectantly, the glimmers of a smile starting to emerge on his face.

It was . . . a little bit creepy.

Misa sighed.

"Arrow's worn off," she said, a little regretfully. At least Jakos wasn't being outright homicidal anymore. "Surprised you're not mad about the arrow."

"We were fighting. Everything's fair in a fight. It was a good skill, too—pretty cool, to be honest." Jakos shrugged, then grinned. "I've got better, though. You gotta do more than that if you want to be my rival. Anyway, do you agree to the deal or not? I don't have all day. I have rebels to capture."

Misa grunted. "It's a deal," she started—and before she could finish, Jakos burst into action.

Because of course he did. She'd been expecting it.

Her mace clashed against his fist with a powerful *boom*. The axe he was using had vanished again—some kind of pocket dimension with different weapons, maybe—and he was once again using his fists, but his fists were hard as steel. He knocked her mace away but didn't follow through with the attack, feinting at the last moment only for his other hand to blur toward her stomach. It took all her focus to bring up a second block in time.

He'd figured her out already.

Vex was working quickly, and surprisingly enough, Jakos was giving him the time—evidently thinking that he needed more of a challenge or something equally ridiculous. The second mana vacuum took the breath of both of them but didn't do much more than disorient Jakos. Had he done something to stabilize himself?

Or . . . no. He just wasn't using any mana. As far as Misa could tell, he was attacking her with raw stats, and she was still barely keeping up.

She couldn't have been *that* far behind him in stats, though. Some sort of passive bonus? If she could figure out what it was and disable *that* . . .

Jakos smirked at her, and Misa suddenly felt the force of gravity triple; she almost stumbled as every piece of equipment she was using suddenly felt three times as heavy. Vex let out a yelp as he collapsed, thrown off-balance by the sudden change.

Misa stayed upright, but it was a near thing. She gritted her teeth.

"I hope you have *some* tricks up your sleeve," Jakos said, his smirk vanishing and his tone gaining a touch of doubt. "Or this is going to be a short fight."

Misa almost scoffed, and called upon [**Me, Myself, and I**].

In an instant, a half-dozen copies of her surrounded Jakos. He raised an eyebrow, impressed. "Well. I wasn't expecting an illusionist. You seemed much more of a physical fighter. But illusions won't do you much good against me, especially when I already know where you are."

He dashed at her. Misa didn't move.

One of her clones stepped in his way; Jakos didn't stop, assuming it was just an illusion, and in that fraction of a second that copy slammed her mace directly into his stomach, pitting his own momentum against him. The metallic *clang* told her it hadn't hit him as hard as she'd hoped, but it still knocked the air out of him—

And Vex, that beautiful lizard—he followed up immediately with a spell of his own. He'd taken advantage of his position on the ground to trace a glyph against the street without being seen, and now three entirely different elemental attacks speared out of the air.

Blistering fire seared the ground beneath Jakos's feet. An arc of lightning tore toward him, cracking the air with a blinding flash and an explosion powerful enough that the shockwave would have thrown Misa back if not for the increased gravity holding her down. A tight sphere of water descended, wrapping itself around Jakos's head and staying there.

Misa could see the logic behind Vex's attacks, but she stayed tense. A Platinum wouldn't be taken down that easily.

Sure enough, the gravitational pull doubled, and Misa gritted her teeth as she had to deal with equipment that was suddenly six times heavier than normal. The water around Jakos's head bubbled violently as he blasted it apart with a *roar*, trembling for a moment and then exploding under the force. Judging by the bubbles, she was almost certain he'd boiled it, which was disturbing enough on its own.

She didn't wait. Three of her clones followed up, two firing arrows of *Restrict* and *Weaken*, and the third one running in with her mace. The arrows missed as Jakos twirled between them, but she'd been prepared—a fourth and fifth copy grabbed the arrows as they shot past, and darted in to stab Jakos directly with them.

The orc's eyes were wild with the pleasure of battle, and Misa couldn't help but grin slightly in response. He kicked one of her out of the way, and spun and ducked beneath the other in a sudden feat of flexibility; the third he took head-on, bashing his own skull against her mace and then tackling her in the stomach.

That clone dissipated almost immediately. Vex was already preparing a new spell, his eyes furrowed in concentration, and Misa considered and discarded her options one by one.

But one thing still bothered her. She was so similar to Jakos. She liked fighting, she liked challenging herself—they weren't all that different, in the end. Something about that thought pulled at her.

She liked fighting, but she was different, because she fought for a cause.

[You have taken another step on the Path of the Endless.]
[New Epic-Grade Skill acquired: [The Flow of the Battle].]

CHAPTER 51

BATTLE FLOW

The skill took effect almost immediately. Misa felt the world slow down around her, like everything was falling into focus; around her were only Vex, Jakos, and herself.

And her remaining clones, of course. There were five of them, spread out in a circle around Jakos, two of them keeping close to Vex in case the lizard needed to be protected—he was still vulnerable compared to her.

Jakos moved, and so did she.

It was a dance. Jakos's eyes lit up with ferocious glee when he realized how much Misa's movements had changed—her style had always been defensive, because she fought largely to steal attention away from others while Vex picked them off with magic. Now she wielded offense and defense in equal measure, and the fight narrowed to just the two of them.

Jakos didn't even glance at Vex. It was through unspoken agreement that they decided that the lizardkin would neither interfere nor be interfered *with;* he would be a spectator in the battle. Misa, Jakos had judged, was a worthy opponent even on her own. Vex's assistance would guarantee her victory, but that wouldn't give Jakos the *fun* that he wanted with the fight.

He leveled a punch at her, and she ducked underneath smoothly; her mace cracked into his stomach once, and she whirled underneath his arm in the same motion so that his follow-up kick hit nothing but air. She twisted, bringing her leg up to kick him in the small of the back.

It was like punching and kicking steel—but she was strong enough to bend steel at this point. Jakos stumbled forward, then ducked into a roll as another copy of Misa tried to swing a punch at his head. That one he caught beneath the chin mid-roll, forcing the clone to stumble back but not quite doing enough damage to dissipate her.

[**The Flow of the Battle**] allowed her to read everything Jakos was doing almost perfectly—it was not unlike what she had been trying to do with her own Endless Echoes, though that method was much more finicky and hard to pull off in the middle of a battle. Changing what she'd done fractions of a second back and acquiring information that way sounded good on paper but was hard to focus on during a fight.

That didn't mean she couldn't still use Endless Echoes. The clones from [**Me, Myself, and I**] helped—they could handle all the extra processing needed to process every alternate reality, every branch of the fight.

And *that* meant she could figure out what skills her opponent had that they were hiding from her.

She stepped a few feet back from Jakos a second before he activated a skill of some sort, blasting the air around him with a buzzing shockwave of electricity; ignoring his expression of surprise, she followed up with an arrow from just outside his range, imbuing it with the concept of a *Lightning Rod.*

A faint smirk touched her lips, but she didn't let it distract her, plunging back into the fight. Jakos was clearly surprised and thrown by the fact that she'd dodged whatever that electrical shockwave was, and so he was a little hesitant to use it again—but the next time she cornered him and he needed to create distance, she saw him reach for the skill.

Just as planned. He expected her to dodge out of the way, just like she had before. Instead, she punched him in the face.

The *Lightning Rod* concept activated, and the electricity he tried to generate bounced back into him, expanding only millimeters from his skin before rebounding and frying him. Jakos let out a cry of shock, and Misa followed it up with another three punches, putting all the force she could muster into each—if she tried anything less, Jakos would recover and punish her for it, no doubt.

She stepped back to duck underneath the next swing, then to the side away from the awkward kick he tried to follow up with. Jakos was flustered now—he was getting less precise with his attacks, relying more and more on instinct. His instinct was still *good*—it was enough to overwhelm any other physical fighter—but with [**The Flow of the Battle**] pushing things in her favor . . .

He didn't have a chance.

He saw it too. Jakos tilted his head slightly, took a step back from her, and then held both of his hands up in a grin. "I yield," he said, suddenly sounding much friendlier. "You're a damn good fighter, you know that? Where'd you learn all those moves?"

"Literally right in the middle of that fight," Misa said dryly.

"The system can be unfair sometimes." Jakos chuckled. "I haven't gotten a cool new move from the stupid thing in *years*. What's the point of it if it isn't giving me new skills?"

"It made you strong enough to do that?" Misa jerked a thumb over to the hole in the wall that Jakos had smashed through. There was, thankfully, no one inside—the move could have caused grievous injury if there had been.

"I mean, I *guess*." Jakos wrinkled his nose, then bounced on his feet. "We should fight more. I bet I can get new skills if we fight more. I haven't been challenged like that for a *while*."

"If you want to fight more, you're going to have to quit the Elyran military like you promised and come join the Adventurers' Guild. Then I'll fight you as much as you want," Misa joked.

She wasn't expecting Jakos to light up. "Deal," he said.

Huh.

Behind her, Vex blinked, then sighed. "I have so many questions," he muttered.

But Jakos didn't seem to hear him. He was already—remarkably enthusiastically—babbling all of Wisfield's plans to them. He didn't actually know much, but he *did* know who he was supposed to capture: it was the blacksmith that had recently been restored, the one that had been lost to rustbite.

Victor. Ingress's father. Vex brightened immediately; they must've figured out a cure using the glyphs.

"When can we fight, by the way?" Jakos asked eagerly.

"Probably sometime after we save the universe?" Misa answered, trying not to laugh. Jakos was almost like an overexcited puppy when he wasn't an enemy.

"Right, right. That does sound important," Jakos said, sounding entirely unconvinced.

Vex sighed. "Let's head back. We're going to give Helix a heart attack from us staying out this long as it is."

I heard that.

"I know."

Derivan knew something was wrong almost the moment they stepped through the portal.

Both Shift and Patch were reporting things that didn't match at all with what he was looking at. Shift often felt like little strings in space that he could push and pull, forcing them to vibrate at different frequencies and opening up paths to different layers of reality—using it to teleport was difficult because he had to path his way to a different layer and then back again.

More crucially, he had what was functionally the ability to sense the different positions of objects with Shift, because every object registered slightly differently to his senses. The mental map of the area it was providing him didn't match what he was looking at at all.

With Patch, he could sense the system itself and how it was attached to people. That, too, looked wrong. Illyr was standing in front of them, but Patch reported no apparent system there; instead, it was a little to the left.

Derivan kept his gaze carefully focused and reached out telepathically to Sev. *We're in an illusion.*

Sev's hand tightened on his staff. *I figured.*

Illyr was a lizardkin—tall and imposing, though Derivan had no idea if that was his true appearance at all. He wreathed himself in a cloak like it was a shield and glowered down at the two of them.

"You want something from me." It was a statement, not a question.

"We'd like for you not to capture the rebels like you were sent out to do, yes," Sev said dryly. "Any chance we can work out a deal?"

"No." The answer was short and immediate. "I have my duties, and I will fulfill them."

"The stakes here are much higher than your duties," Sev said. Derivan paid attention to what the lizardkin was doing outside the illusion—he could sense *someone* moving around, but he didn't seem to be gearing up to attack them or anything.

Yet.

"I would be nothing without my duty," Illyr said. "And so I apologize for what I must do."

"Illyr—" Sev began. Derivan noticed something strange through Patch—the system around the cleric shifting and undulating in some way, centered around his brain. Sev winced and clutched at his head, but it was nothing Illyr was doing, as far as Derivan could tell.

He's familiar, Sev whispered to him through their link. *I don't understand why he's so familiar. I've never seen him before.*

Derivan couldn't spare the attention to think about it. The ground around them was shifting, the buildings picking themselves up and walking forward; for all that this was an illusion—for all that Derivan *knew* that the buildings hadn't moved, that they weren't truly there at all—they felt real. The wall next to him pressed against his armor and physically shifted him, even though nothing was truly pressing against him.

He knew with certainty that he would be crushed if he allowed it.

Derivan grabbed ahold of Sev, who seemed to be half-disabled—he didn't know if Sev was seeing something different from him, but it didn't seem likely—and moved quickly. He kept a fair distance away from Illyr, trying not to make it obvious that he was following the man and could sense where he was. He tried to make it look like he was just dodging the buildings.

At the same time, he prepared a spell.

Grace and Intensity hadn't seen a lot of use after he acquired the stats. He still didn't know which one he'd gotten from whom, but he'd discovered the effects of each stat during his downtime in Vex's bonus room. They were simple but effective. Grace made him more fluid, more physically flexible; it operated together with Slime in a way that gave him almost full control of himself physically. He suspected at a high enough level, he'd be able to outright shapeshift.

Intensity, on the other hand, gave him a force of presence. It made him harder to move, harder to influence, and harder to *change*. It was, thankfully, active rather than passive—a trait he could turn on and off at will. He couldn't imagine what problems he'd have if it were always on.

Now he used them both.

Grace let him flicker between buildings with only a small space between them, even while carrying Sev; he was cautious at first, in case the cleric was experiencing a different illusion—he didn't want to crush his friend against a wall he couldn't see—but it was increasingly clear that Illyr could only maintain a single illusion of this complexity at a time.

Intensity let him increase his presence when he needed to and allowed him to go *through* buildings instead of between them. When it was active, he could ignore the buildings entirely and move through them as if they didn't exist—his presence overwrote that of the illusion and, by extension, Sev's as well, since he was carrying him.

Entire sections of Elyra uprooted themselves and crashed against him. He had to roll through a window, duck beneath a street, and swing around a horizontal lamppost just to keep up—and he had to do all this while holding on to Sev.

Fortunately, Sev dragged himself out of whatever was going on in his mind after a few minutes of this. "Are we still close?" he demanded.

I've been keeping us close, Derivan said. *He is about a street away, to our right.*

"Can you get us there?"

Derivan didn't answer. Instead, he diverted his route, activating Intensity and smashing through what few walls remained between them and Illyr; Illyr stopped in his tracks as Derivan appeared in front of him, staring directly at his invisible presence.

"You can sense me," Illyr said, narrowing his eyes. The invisibility—and the other Illyr, which Derivan had been ignoring—faded.

Sev took a deep breath and ignored the conversation. "I know who you are, *Sylix*."

The illusion cracked and fell apart like it was little more than glass. The real streets of Elyra showed up in front of them, devoid of people.

Illyr stared at Sev, something other than rigidity showing in his eyes for the first time. Derivan saw the sudden flicker of panic that stole his breath, though Illyr tried to hide it.

"How do you know that name?" he asked.

CHAPTER 52

HISTORY

"Because I know you," Sev said. "I met you before. I adventured with you. We were friends."

Derivan shifted, then gently put him down on the ground. Sev took a step forward, not yet completely understanding the memories he'd just unlocked, but working his way through them. There were so many things that were *wrong* with those memories . . .

. . . but there was one thing that was important, and that was the night he had spoken to Illyr in his own tent. They were curled up together, side by side, Illyr's head resting on his shoulder.

"I'm sorry," Illyr said. "I'm too old to be running to people in the middle of the night."

"Bah," Sev said with a laugh and a friendly nudge to Illyr's shoulder. "We all have our own shit to deal with basically all the time. Not your fault yours is worse than most people's. You got a nightmare, I'm here for you. What are friends for, right?"

"Right." Illyr sighed. "I never really understood that until you and the others."

"Not your fault either." Sev was silent for a moment. "But I'm here if you want to talk about it."

"I don't know." Illyr fidgeted, the normally stoic lizard apparently finding it difficult to find the words. It took a full three minutes before he spoke again. "I wasn't always Illyr."

"You've hinted at your mysterious past before," Sev said, with a hint of a smile, and Illyr grimaced.

". . . Illyr is just a name I picked," he said. "My real name is Sylix; Illyr was my brother at the orphanage. He died. I killed him—it was an accident. I didn't know what I was doing, I swear. I was testing my illusions—it just happened—it wasn't

supposed to kill him—you have to understand, I didn't know what I could do, I really didn't—"

The words came out in a rush, like he didn't want to say them and forced them out anyway; the lizardkin pulled away slightly and hugged his knees to his chest, looking for all the world like a child in need of comfort.

Sev hesitated slightly. He reached out, but Illyr—Sylix?—flinched away at the brush of his fingers, and he sighed and sat down in front of the lizardkin.

He was so young. Barely nineteen years old, and still haunted by the past.

"I believe you," Sev said simply.

"What?" Sylix looked up at him, red-rimmed eyes visible even through the scales.

"I believe you," Sev said again. "You wouldn't kill anyone on purpose. You wouldn't even hurt a fly. Is this why you're so afraid to use your illusions?"

"I . . . Yes." Sylix looked down at the ground. "We were just playing. It wasn't supposed to be a dangerous illusion at all. Just, Illyr was so much younger than me, and he hadn't seen snow before, and I wanted him to see the snow . . . He got cold so fast *and it didn't stop when I turned off the illusions . . ."*

Sylix buried his face between his knees. "They can keep the illusions if they want to," he said quietly, half to himself. "Even if I turn it off, if they want to believe it enough . . . it keeps going. And I can't turn it off. And it didn't matter how many coats I put on him or how many illusions of fires I gave him, he just kept getting colder and colder, and I couldn't . . ."

Sev hugged his friend.

He didn't say anything. What could he say? He wouldn't believe "It's not your fault." A dozen platitudes wouldn't save his brother.

Sometimes, the best thing you could do was just be there for a friend.

"I think there's still some soup outside," Sev said. "Do you want to get some? Some warm soup will do you good, and then we can talk about it."

"Yeah . . . yeah, I think that's a good idea." Sylix managed a small smile. "Thanks—"

The memory cut off there. Sev had the strange feeling that there was something *off* with the memory, but the major details were correct; Illyr-or-Sylix had lived a life as an orphan in an orphanage, with only his younger brother as a companion—and then, when trying to show his brother the magic of winter, he'd accidentally killed him.

A skill that could continue even after you turned it off was cruel.

"What are you talking about?" Illyr's voice was ice. He sounded so different from the Illyr in his memories; this version of him was *older* by almost ten years, it looked like. He seemed colder. He seemed like someone who had never made any friends, who had to come to terms with what had happened to his brother by himself.

Sev didn't even know what he was supposed to call him. Sylix? Illyr?

"We were friends," Sev said. He didn't even know if this was the best thing to say—Sylix looked like he was getting increasingly angry, but he'd already started down this path. He could only hope what he had to say would calm him down. "We met when you were trying to find a job in the Elyran Guild, but no one would take you in. I said I'd let you join me. There was a fight that day between an orc and a lizardkin, and you split them up with barely any effort."

"I recall the fight," Sylix said, his voice still cold. "But I did not meet *you*."

He said it as a fact, too. Sev remembered that day so clearly, all of a sudden—everything up to inviting Illyr to join him, and the faces of two other people he no longer recognized but was pretty sure were also his friends . . .

The timeline didn't add up. He couldn't have done this. He remembered where he was on that day—he was halfway hiking through the Outskirts.

Why did he *also* remember this?

Because you've done it all before.

The answer was a startling whisper in his own mind.

"You didn't," Sev agreed, his mouth dry. "But we did meet in another time. Another place."

"I don't believe you."

"You don't have to." Sev didn't fully understand where he was going with this—but something in him resonated. Small memories surfaced, things he'd never actually done, moments that he'd never actually had.

Aneryn, too, the shadow elemental that died in the shade of a tree just across from the Festival. Xothok, the bandit that led the team against him.

Misa. Vex.

He'd met them all before.

"Put me in that illusion." The words escaped him before he understood them. Sylix paused, startled, and then his eyes narrowed in a mixture of anger and confusion and some indiscernible third *thing*; something like fear and panic rolled together into one.

"You don't know what you're asking me to do." Sylix's voice was tight, controlled.

"Elyra wants you to capture me, right?" Sev kept his gaze and his words even. "I won't die. I can heal myself."

"You'll never feel warm again."

"I will. Because I know how that illusion works, Sylix, and I know how to break out of it."

Sev told himself he wasn't nervous.

They'd worked on controlling it. They'd worked on understanding exactly what it was that made Sylix's illusions tick, back when he'd finally told them what happened; he was afraid to use his most powerful illusions because of the way they stuck to their victims. It seemed that even this version of him—the one who had been picked up by Elyra, who used his skills for Elyra's benefit and leveraged his illusions for the sole purpose of carrying out their orders—

He was still *afraid.*

Elyra had never done anything to help him with his skills. [**Winter Fantasy**], the illusion that had killed his brother—they no doubt thought it would be an asset to them. But Sev had seen what Sylix was capable of when he really understood his own illusions, and what they'd seen just now—the warping buildings that threatened to crush them—that was nowhere near his limit.

He hadn't grown. He'd been stuck, and the only thing Elyra offered him was a false acceptance. They were the only people who wanted him; of course he'd gone with them.

Sev felt the air turn cold. He saw the shimmer in the sky as clouds began to form and snowflakes danced across the wind. A thin layer of snow began to build up on the streets, along with the phantom lights of Christmas . . .

An old Earth tradition. Sylix's strongest illusions drew upon their victims to give them what they wanted. For Sev, it was a small piece of home he no longer remembered.

"Are you happy now?" Sylix asked, his voice bitter. "Is this the point you wanted to prove?"

It was cold. Sev drew his robes around himself, shivering, and cast a small divine spell of warmth; it curled down around him and vanished, just as it had done the first time he'd tried that, back when they were friends.

"I wanted to prove that you can be more than a soldier," Sev said quietly. "And that you are not a killer."

That had been Sylix's main contention—that his skills were only good for killing, that his illusions could do no real good. It made sense that he had ended up as a soldier, even if he hated every second of it. He could almost guess what the Elyran nobility had told him. *We'll make sure you use your skills the right way.*

Sev took one last glance at the winter wonderland that surrounded him. It was genuinely beautiful. Butterflies made of snow crystals fluttered around in the sky; shadows stood behind windows, having warm Christmas dinners. He knew those things were true, because the illusion delivered that information to him, giving him a feeling of warmth and comfort that was easy to get lost in even as his real body began to freeze.

He was standing knee-deep in snow.

But he wasn't, really.

The key to [**Winter Fantasy**]—and any one of Sylix's more advanced illusions—was that they weren't really meant as combat illusions at all; they would be rather cruel if that were the case. Sylix had created it because he had wanted to create *art*, to bring a moment of joy to his brother, and poor Illyr had been drawn in so deeply that he had wanted it to last forever.

Most of Sylix's victims did, really. But they weren't *meant* to.

Because when Sylix had made that illusion for the first time, he'd had one image fixed in his mind, and they'd never completed it.

Sev reached down to the ground, packing the snow into a snowball. He threw it toward Illyr without much fanfare at all and watched as the ball of snow hit him in the head.

"Boop," he said simply.

The illusion faded away. He stopped shivering.

Sylix just stared.

CHAPTER 53

ALLIES

Sev had a lot to deal with, concerning whatever he'd just figured out about his memories—but Sylix was sitting on the ground, holding his head, and Sev felt a little responsible for that.

"Are you all right?" he asked. He cared, he really did, but he didn't know how to deal with this. The way his memories were scrambled didn't help. He would have helped past-Sylix in a different way, gathering him into his arms and allowing the lizardkin to cry into his shoulder.

Something told him this Sylix wouldn't appreciate that.

"No!" Sylix snapped, and Sev didn't blame him. "You just told me I could have saved him if I—if we had just—"

He broke off into a sob, burying his face in his arms. Sev sighed. He sat himself down next to the lizardkin, keeping a respectful distance; Sylix wasn't nearly as close to him this time around, and he was pretty sure Sylix was actually *older* than him, too. What that meant, Sev wasn't sure.

But Sylix had been through a lot. That remained the same, across realities, across whatever it was had changed.

"I'm sorry," Sev said. He didn't meet Sylix's eyes. "Maybe the way I did it was a little cruel."

Sylix shook his head. He didn't respond for a long moment, but when he did, it was quiet, his voice strained from the crying. ". . . I wouldn't have believed you if you hadn't done it like that."

"I know."

It had been a long time since they had last spoken. A long, *long* time, if he understood his own memories correctly, and he wasn't sure he did. But there was a part of him that understood who this lizardkin was, and that part of him told him that the Sylix sitting in front of him was no different from the Sylix he'd known, once upon a time.

The only difference was that this version of Sylix had never grown up. Years of service to a military had done nothing for the more-emotional side of him; he'd never really found any friends, never really found any *value* in any aspect of himself other than the part that killed.

But he'd never stopped wanting to.

"You should sign up for a spot with the Adventurers' Guild," Sev said. "They'd be happy to have someone like you."

Sylix laughed, but it was a bitter laugh. "You think Elyra would let me go without consequences?"

"Would they be able to stop you?"

Sylix was silent at that.

The truth was that they couldn't—Sev was certain. As much a master of illusions as he was, Sylix could escape just about any situation if he wanted to. Wisfield wouldn't be able to find him even with their ability to read minds; Sylix had, after all, been working with the nobles for years. He no doubt had ways around their abilities already.

"I need time to think about it," Sylix finally said. Sev inclined his head slightly. He didn't protest when Sylix faded from sight.

It was sudden, but it wasn't unexpected. Sylix retreated from conversations like that frequently, even the better-adjusted version of him that Sev knew. He ran out of energy quickly when talking to others and simply retreated when he was out of it.

In fact, if his memories were right, Sev knew exactly where Sylix had gone. He'd be at the top of the west Elyran clocktower, looking out over the city.

He wouldn't go looking for him, though. If Sylix wanted to find them, he would.

Derivan approached him hesitantly. "You are certain he will not go after the rebels still?" he asked.

"He won't," Sev said. "Where do your senses say he's headed?"

"West." Derivan said. "Wrong direction."

"Then he's not going to capture them. He's a lot of things, but for all that he's an illusionist and tricks people in battle . . . he's really bad at actually lying. Maybe that's why he's an illusionist."

"Hm." Derivan didn't say anything for a moment; he seemed to consider his words carefully, and then he decided to broach the topic. "Sev, your memories . . ."

"They're coming back," Sev confirmed. He sighed. ". . . I don't know if that's a good thing. I'm still not sure what's going on."

"We should inform the others."

"Yeah."

Gathering back within the jewelry store was, thankfully, a simple matter. Helix's reaction was not.

"You *recruited* them?" Helix sounded absolutely scandalized. Jakos was standing in a corner of the shop, picking his nose, and Misa had her arms folded and an eyebrow raised at Helix.

"What would you rather we do?" she asked.

"I mean, don't get me wrong, I'm not *angry*, but . . . do you know how *illegal* it is to recruit a kingdom's Platinum?" Helix asked. "It's basically a war crime! And everyone tries to do it anyway, and no one succeeds!"

Misa gave Helix a flat look, and even Vex looked puzzled. "Helix, you're part of a rebellion intent on overthrowing the Elyran government," Vex said. "I think we've thrown legality out of the window a long time ago."

Helix folded his arms across his chest. "Yeah, well . . ."

He deflated a little. "How did you manage to *recruit* him?"

"She's a good fighter." Jakos jerked a thumb toward Misa. "She promised me a duel."

Helix rubbed his temples. "Of course she did," he muttered. "You know, not too long ago, I would've liked fighting too . . ."

"Do you want to?" Jakos immediately looked eager.

"No," Helix replied flatly. "You'd kick my ass. My combat spells don't match up to a Platinum."

"Bah," Jakos said. "Misa isn't Platinum either, and she did just fine."

"All three of my brother's friends are abnormal for their level," Helix said dryly. He shook his head and tried to move on. "More importantly, we need to figure out what to do next. Whatever Wisfield's done has basically completely halted our attempts to evacuate the city—we're attacked on sight. I don't even know how they're identifying us."

"Same way they're controlling everyone," Sev said. "The Elyran zeitgeist knows, and so does everyone that's a part of it. The only way we're going to stop all this is by getting to the source, and the source is with Wisfield."

"Are we breaking into the Wisfield estate, then?" Jakos asked. He was leaning against the wall of the shop, tossing a dagger around in his hand; where he'd gotten the dagger, no one knew. "That sounds fun! I know all the best routes."

"Are the best routes the ones that keep us hidden, or the ones that have the most fighting?" Misa asked.

"The ones that have the most fighting, obviously."

Misa sighed. "Can you please take us to the *worst* routes."

"You guys aren't any fun." Jakos pouted. "I guess it wouldn't be much of a challenge, anyway. Fine."

"We can't portal in directly?" Misa asked, and Derivan shook his head.

"If we knew where to go within the estate, we could," he said. "But we will need to search. I can get us close, but Jakos's guidance will still be crucial."

"I guess that makes sense," Misa grumbled.

Sev hesitated. Derivan was giving him a *look*, like he was waiting for him to say something—and he knew he *should*. But he didn't understand what was in his own head yet. Small pieces of memories were coming back, but none of it was anything he expected.

He still didn't remember anything of Earth. Instead, he remembered more and more bits and pieces of people that he'd never met—places that he'd never been.

He didn't understand.

"There's something I need to talk about," Sev started, and then sighed. "But . . . maybe not yet. I don't understand it myself just yet. Give me a bit of time to figure it out, and then we'll talk about it."

"Wanna give us a quick overview?" Misa asked. "You know, just so this doesn't come back to bite us in the ass."

Sev snorted. Misa was grinning at him, a small, knowing grin, and he couldn't help but grin back. "I'm remembering," he said. "But none of my memories make any sense. It's all stuff that I'm pretty sure never happened—stuff that *couldn't* have happened. I remember places that I don't think exist. So . . . yeah."

"Huh," Misa said. "Anything important?"

"If there were, I would've said already," Sev said dryly, but he cast his mind through his memories to be sure. "Nothing. Just what I remembered with Sylix, and you already know how that turned out."

"Just checking." Misa grinned. "Don't want you to remember something crucial at the last minute, like you secretly knowing who this half-formed Elyran demigod is or something."

—

"Oh my gods," Sev said. "I know who the Elyran demigod is."

Misa stared at him. ". . . Do you really?"

"No, but I've been waiting to make that joke for the past five hours."

The fact that the Wisfield estate was this large was, in Sev's opinion, disgusting. It took them less time to wander through the streets of Elyra itself, though that was in large part because the streets were *organized*. The Wisfield estate was an absolute maze of rooms and corridors and nonsensical entrances, some of which were located *in the ceiling*.

There was a part of Sev that felt that this was absolutely overboard, and another part of him that wanted to get a castle that was something like this.

The way you were *supposed* to navigate—because Sev had pointed out early on that anyone trying to make their way through this place would be completely lost—was by using the mindstones that Wisfield left scattered all over the place. Approved guests could touch them and receive a set of directions that would take them to their destination.

It seemed far too convoluted for the purposes of having a guest over, but evidently it worked for security, because they didn't encounter a single security guard. Part of that was Jakos leading them along the "worst routes," but the other part of that was just that they didn't employ that many guards.

Whatever the case, they were getting close. Sev knew that because he could feel the strength of control he had over the divine domain decreasing—every so often, he had to pull the radius of his own control in closer around himself. The influence of this god was stronger here, and while that was *dangerous*, it also gave them a direction to go in.

Even if they did have to pack in closer and closer.

It was obvious, though, when they finally found the spot. The familiar doors of the Vault loomed over them, high over their heads, and Misa stared at it, her face pale.

"I thought they couldn't open this," she said.

"I thought they couldn't, either." Vex stared up at the doors. ". . . You should open them. It doesn't make sense. The Vault was just *one* thing, right? There aren't multiple versions of it. It's stable across all Shifts, all realities. It shouldn't even be *here*."

"It is," Derivan confirmed.

"So how did they get it here? How did they get in?"

CHAPTER 54

SEVEN

The doors were silent when Misa pushed them open. They slid open easily, like they had been oiled.

That was the first sign that something was wrong.

Well, not really. The first sign was that the Vault—or something that looked very much like the Vault doors—was here in the first place. But the fact that the doors were this easy to open told them that they *had* been opened; it had been a struggle to open the doors back in the Elyran ruins, where they had been abandoned for centuries.

The room that stood behind the doors was the same. It had the same grandiose marble, the same gold and white, the same pedestal in the center. The primary difference here was that it was that there were people in it. Eight people exactly, standing in a circle around the pedestal; at the top of it was a strangely glowing orb that was not unlike the Grand Anchor Vex had claimed.

And yet . . . different. Incomplete, somehow, like it was only a smaller piece of a whole. It was cracked and fragmented.

"The Wisfield elders," Vex whispered, staring at the men and women circled around the pedestal. His voice echoed in the room, and he grimaced, but not a single one of the elders reacted. They were too engaged in . . . whatever they were doing.

Sev stepped forward, his expression concerned. "The whole room's . . . *vibrating*," he said, his fingers drifting through the air like he could sense something within it. "The divinity in it."

"What does that mean?" Misa asked, casting a glance at their cleric.

"It means this is the birthplace of a god," Sev said. He took a breath, stared up at the orb, and tried not to panic. "We already knew they created an artificial god, but this is worse than that. This is a forced ascension. A forced ascension isn't . . . It isn't safe. It's been tried before."

The last words were almost whispered. Sev winced slightly and clutched at his head, and Misa hurried over to him, supporting him by an elbow before he could fall to his knees. Sev staggered and leaned his weight onto the half-orc, gazing up at the orb like he was desperately trying to *remember*.

"We lost so much when we tried," he said, his voice a half-whisper. "Divinity is one of the few things left keeping this universe together. Reality, Magic, and Divinity—it's a trifecta. We need all three to keep the universe operating. But if you force an ascension, you drain all the divinity out of a place . . . and it collapses."

Sev went pale. "That's what happened to Enkiros," he said.

The word resonated strangely.

"That's why this is our last try," he said, grabbing at Misa's arms desperately. She stared at him, confused and uncertain, not knowing what he was getting at. "Misa, we've—this whole time we've talked about *the three Prime Kingdoms*. Haven't you noticed? We've never said the name of the third. We talk about Elyra and Anderstahl, and the last Kingdom's name is *gone*, because the whole kingdom is gone."

"Anderstahl represents Reality. Elyra represents Magic. As kingdoms, they focus on the development of those aspects, and those three Prime Anchors kept this continent stable. It's the only one we were able to save. But with Enkiros gone—with the Divinity anchor erased—we're running out of time."

"Sev," Misa tried. Vex and Derivan were both staring at Sev; Vex was clutching at Derivan's arm, slightly frightened by the intensity in Sev's tone. Sev's eyes were glazed over and unfocused, and memories seemed to be flooding back into him; there was a resonant echo from him, a feeling in the air that *changed*. That resonance fed back into the false ascension happening in the middle of the room only a few dozen meters away, and a strange feeling began to build in the air.

"This is the last try," Sev said. "That's what my name is. What I represent. Not Sev, but *Seven*. Our last try of seven."

The feeling in the air built up. The flow reversed.

In the middle of the room, above the false anchor, a crack in the air formed.

The Void was here.

CHAPTER 55

OUT OF TIME

Sev reached out and froze time.

Something in his demeanor had changed—no doubt from the memories he'd just clawed back from the Void, something that shouldn't have been possible to begin with. Even the spread of the Void slowed down under the effect of his skill, though it was incomplete. The end of the universe didn't really need to respect a concept as trivial as *time*.

And yet, with divinity here as strong as it was—with the Grand Anchor for Magic present, a half-anchor formed from nothing floating in the middle of the room, and Misa's own reality anchor—reality was too stable. The Void had made its way in, drawn here by something or the other, but cracking through was a process that was incomplete.

All around the room, small distortions began to manifest, wriggling wildly against whatever they were touching. Derivan recognized them instantly.

"Void Wyrms!" he called out. "Don't touch them!"

It was hard to avoid them, though. They were manifesting en masse, spawning from the edges of the crack and quickly crawling all over the pseudo-Vault. The Wisfield elders still had their eyes closed, were still holding hands and channeling whatever skill they were using for this false ascension. It was pretty clear they were locked in a trance.

The question was why no one else was around. This was a crucial operation, surely, and if they couldn't respond to anything that was happening around them—like the situation they were in *right now*—then they should have had other Wisfield members standing by in case there was an emergency. Someone that could wake them up.

Jakos walked up to one of them and poked them in the shoulder. When that didn't elicit a response, he tried slapping them.

"Uh," Misa said.

"I think they're dead," Jakos declared. "We should leave them."

Misa rolled her eyes, stalked forward, and forced two of the hands apart. It took surprising effort, despite her strength; it was almost like something about the ritual was trying to keep itself going.

It didn't stop her, in the end.

The effect was instantaneous the moment the circle was broken. Sev felt the presence of the nascent god fade, still present but no longer strong enough to exert its influence without a focused will to direct it. All eight of the Wisfield elders stumbled apart, several of them gasping for air. Two seemed bewildered, glancing around like they had no idea who they were or what they were doing here. One of them collapsed.

"What are you doing here?" one of the elders asked. He glanced around, finally seeing the crack in the air—the now-visible squirming of dozens and dozens of worms crawling all over the floor and his robes. He flicked them off with disgust, but they clung to his fingers, sticky clumps of nonexistent mass.

Which would have been fine, had small pieces of his fingers not immediately begun to fade.

The elder stared at his own hands with panic, not comprehending. It was hard to tell exactly what was going on unless you knew the nature of the Void—as far as the elders were concerned, he had always been missing one finger. Then two. Then he had never had fingernails—

Sev stepped forward, and in one brutal flash of light, sliced off and regrew the hand. The elder gaped, reeling from both the pain and the sudden *fullness* of his hand; as far as he was concerned, he'd never had the full set of five fingers. Not a single healer had ever been able to restore his hand.

Sev's expression was tight, and his jaw was clenched. "We need to run," he said grimly. "Do *not* touch the worms, whatever you do. They will eat away at everything. Get moving. *Now.*"

Whatever it was Wisfield had done here—for all that they had potentially been the *cause* of this, even—they didn't deserve to die like this, uncomprehending of their own deaths as their own bodies were eaten away.

The elders barely seemed to understand what was happening, anyway. Sev doubted that they were the masterminds who had orchestrated this whole thing—more than likely, that was the Wisfield head. That they'd been left in the pseudo-Vault to keep plugging away at this ritual . . .

Sev didn't know what Wisfield was getting at. Having a god under their control would give them a lot of power, certainly; was that really the full extent of what they wanted? And if that were the case, if this ritual was so important, why didn't they have any guards stationed here?

It didn't make any sense. There was something more going on.

But there was no time for speculation. Now that the ritual had been stopped, the crack in reality had stopped spreading—but that didn't mean that the Void stopped pouring through. The timestop he held was only barely slowing it down.

He needed everyone to *move.*

Thankfully, he didn't need to speak for his team to get the idea. They each gave Sev a concerned look, but there was a mutual understanding in their gaze when they locked eyes: *We'll talk later.*

It was more important now to get everyone out of the Vault, lock the doors, and then evacuate the rest of Elyra. Sev doubted that what had begun here could be stopped, not until the entirety of Elyra was consumed. Wisfield's actions had almost certainly fully destabilized the Elyran Prime Anchor. That would be the reason they hadn't received their rewards properly, and the same reason skills didn't function entirely correctly.

Misa grabbed two of the elders, one under each arm; Javok saw this and immediately grabbed hold of three, as if he needed to outdo her. Derivan grabbed one and threw them over his shoulder.

Vex didn't bother trying to pick any of them up. He cast a spell to lift the remaining two elders, making them float behind him, and all of them made for the exit.

Sev was the only one who stayed behind.

He did it just long enough to mutter an incantation, calling on the divine connection he held; with the ritual stopped and the divinity that was laying claim to Elyra slowly dissipating, the remaining gods could slowly filter back in and lend him their power. The request he made was a simple one.

Seal.

A collection of hexagonal golden barriers formed in the air, sealing themselves around the Void crack. It wouldn't last forever, but it didn't need to.

It just needed to last long enough.

He'd seen all this before, after all. The worms would stop when they reached the edge of Elyra, when the surrounding reality anchors forced them back; that was the whole reason the anchors were set up the way they were, to limit the spread of the Void should there be an incursion.

But now evacuating was a necessity. It was a good thing the rebels had already started the whole process, or Sev wasn't sure that there would have been enough time.

He hurried out of the pseudo-Vault after his friends, glancing behind him to make sure the seal held. It was already filling up with worms; the rest of the room was still covered in them, and a few of them stuck to his clothing. A quick brush of divine magic forced them off, and he kept that barrier active as he ran out.

Misa shut the doors behind him.

"We don't have much time," Sev said without preamble. "I'd say we need to track down the Wisfield head, but I don't think that's actually important right now. He's doomed no matter what we do if he doesn't want to leave. If he does, we'll deal with him once everyone else is safe. I don't want to compromise anyone's safety to go after him."

"I agree," Vex said. The lizardkin waved his tail about anxiously, and Derivan put an arm around his shoulders.

"I could always go kill him, if you want," Javok said cheerfully. "Then you don't have to worry about it."

All four of the adventurers turned to stare at him. He stared back, his gaze innocent, as though he'd just suggested he go and fetch them some water.

"And if I don't kill him, then at least I die in a really fun fight," he added.

"I think you should probably just help us with the evacuation," Misa said dryly.

None of the elders protested as they were summarily dragged out of the Wisfield estate—perhaps because they had observed exactly what effects the worms had on them, or perhaps because the dark crack in the air had been sufficiently frightening.

It might also just have been the very frank discussion of what was happening between Sev and the others.

"How much time do we have to evacuate Elyra?" Misa asked. She was uncharacteristically serious.

"Not that much," Sev said. "Three days at most. The seal is powerful but not that powerful."

"That's not a lot of time." Vex sounded worried. "Not for how many people there are in Elyra."

"With the compulsion gone, it'll be easier to convince people to leave. We just need them to believe there's a problem." Sev frowned.

"It probably won't be that hard." Helix was the one that spoke up there. Sev and the others had gone straight back to the jewelry store to fetch Helix and his team, and the entire group was now headed toward one of the rebel gathering points, ignoring all the stares they were getting. Now wasn't the time for secrecy anymore. "We're all getting notifications about how our skills aren't working properly anymore. It was just letting me break the limits at first, but now a few of them just aren't working properly. Or they do something completely different."

"Some of them are dangerous," Larok said quietly—Helix's clerk teammate, if Sev remembered correctly. The lizardkin fidgeted nervously. "I tested a few because I thought it might let me fight better. It kinda does, but if the skill backfires . . ."

He winced. "It took a chunk out of my tail. Just an entire chunk of flesh. I drank a healing potion, but it wasn't pretty, and it hurt a lot."

Sev grimaced with sympathy. "I don't think we need to worry about that, since we're tied to Misa's anchor and not Elyra's," he said, glancing to Misa for confirmation; she nodded at him.

"I can tie you guys to my anchor, too," she said, "but I'm not sure how much it can support. It's already responsible for a whole village of people."

"J'rokksur might become even more important in the coming days," Sev muttered. Misa glanced at him, and he saw the question in her eyes, but he shook his head slightly.

Not yet. First, they had to make sure Elyra was empty when the Void came to consume it.

"Call everyone you can get ahold of," Sev told Helix. "The nobles, too. We don't have time to fight with one another anymore."

"You say that," Helix said, "but I don't know that they'll listen."

Sev's grip on his staff tightened. "We need to try," he finally said. "If it comes down to it . . ."

He left the sentence unfinished. Vex stared at him, almost frightened. Misa seemed mostly concerned, and Derivan watched him contemplatively.

Then he reached out, placing a hand on Sev's shoulder.

"You are not alone," he told him quietly. "Seven or not, you are Sev to us. And we have always found another way."

Sev stared at Derivan for a moment, and his composure cracked. Something like pain and a heavy, heavy burden suddenly became visible in his shoulders, and he visibly sagged.

"Okay," he said quietly.

CHAPTER 56

CONFRONTATION

The problem with logistics was that they took a lot of time. Getting people to organize, especially any large number of people, was a process that could take hours—and when their time was limited to seventy-two hours, every single one of those hours was inconceivably precious.

All of this was the reason Misa was working overtime in a job she hated. Having a dozen copies of herself was useful for tasks other than combat, it turned out, even if that wasn't anything Misa *preferred*.

That was the case for all of them. They were far outside their comfort zones, working to evacuate the kingdom; for the most part, at least, people took the threat seriously.

And it would have been fine. Their efforts were *working*; the people of Elyra were slowly but surely leaving, convinced by either the rebels or their neighbors that staying was a bad idea. The Guild and the rebels together had coordinated a number of caravans that would carry enough supplies for the citizens to make the trip to Anderstahl. The old and infirm, the ones who had the most trouble moving—they used the Guild's teleporters to move, though the mana supply it ate was, according to the Guildmaster, exorbitant.

Which was about the moment the nobles chose to interfere.

Mostly, it was Wisfield. But Ashion was there too. Vex's eyes darkened when he saw his father standing proudly with the other nobles, his arms folded across his chest like not a single thing was wrong.

"I need to go," Vex said shortly.

Derivan glanced at him, concerned. "Do you need—"

"No," Vex said, and his eyes softened a little as he took in Derivan's worry. He shook his head and gave Derivan a small hug. "No, this is something I need to do alone. We need you to help with the evacuation. You're the one with Shift, remember?"

"I am." Derivan accepted Vex's words, and his next ones were said with affection. "Be careful."

Vex nodded.

Derivan's portals were by far responsible for the most movement; he kept a portal open in the center of each district they were evacuating, and it was the job of the rebels and the other people in the area to slowly corral everyone toward it. He watched as Vex left, keeping his portal open for the civilians to file through, and hoped the lizardkin wouldn't be forced to fight.

Not against his own father.

Not again.

—∞—

Vex took a deep breath.

Karix and the other nobles stood atop the wall on the northern edge of Elyra. They stood *proudly*, too, like they were standing against all that was evil and wrong; the head of the Wisfield house was there, right down to the glorious gray beard that stretched down to his knees, his arms folded across pure-white robes.

"Elyra is stronger than this!" he called out. His words were amplified with Karix's magic, thrown out throughout the kingdom. The northern gate was where they were evacuating everyone; it was closest to Anderstahl, and all their caravans were kept outside, just beyond where the nobles were making their stand. Vex was almost afraid to look, worried that Karix would have destroyed them.

But the Guild had defenders around each caravan. They would be all right, he hoped.

"We can weather any storm!" the Wisfield head continued. He had no name—the head of House Wisfield went by the title of Speaker. As far as he understood it, it was some grandiose attempt to make themselves seem like they spoke for Elyra. "We do not need to run like *cowards*!"

The civilians were muttering among themselves. Not all of them looked convinced; if anything, most of them seemed annoyed. But there were those among them that seemed like they were arguing with their fellows—telling them how they'd been right all along, and how evacuating was unnecessary . . .

Vex sighed. He found that he was *tired*.

He'd been dreading this moment for years. He knew he'd need to confront his parents eventually—his mother was there too, Prissa, a proud yellow-scaled lizardkin that stood tall next to his father. The other nobles who stood alongside them, he didn't care about, except to briefly worry that they would interfere.

At least Riss wasn't here to see this.

The flight spell to bring him up to the wall was simple. The Speaker stopped as he came into view, and Karix faltered, the amplification rune he was using flickering out of existence as Vex stared quietly at them. He wondered briefly why this had taken him so long.

It shouldn't have, he thought. He'd been scared of Karix, and while he didn't blame himself for feeling that way, he no longer understood *why*.

"Dad," he greeted.

"You may have noticed we're in the middle of something," Karix said. His voice was tense, and so was his posture; Vex wondered what he was thinking. Karix knew he'd sided with the rebellion, surely. He couldn't have thought that they would just be ignored.

"What are you trying to do, Dad?" Vex asked. He was almost surprised by how he sounded—not frightened, not angry.

Just tired.

"We're trying to fix your mistakes," Prissa snapped at him. Vex looked at his mother, and something about the look in his eyes made her glare back at him indignantly. "Don't give me that. Look at what your father and I have to do just to—"

"Mom. Dad." Vex's voice was quiet. "Elyra is *dying*. We're losing our home. I wanted to give the kingdom back to the people, but I didn't want this place to die."

"Then you shouldn't have—" Prissa began. Vex waved a hand; [**Silence**] was a useful spell in times like these. It didn't escape his notice that neither of his parents could dispel it, even though his mother tried.

Karix didn't bother trying. He simply watched Vex. Vex didn't know what his father was thinking—his expression was unreadable. His mother looked outraged, but it wasn't like she could say anything.

The Speaker, too, was just watching them. So were the rest of the nobles. Vex didn't know why they were being so polite, but in that moment, he didn't care.

"Elyra isn't dying because of anything the rebels did," Vex said. "What Wisfield did with that god they tried to make . . . that sped things up. But they didn't cause it either. Elyra was already dying. It began dying ever since growth spells stopped working, and now it's going to be erased. There's nothing we can do about it. We haven't figured out how to stop it yet. The best—the *only* thing we can do is to get everyone to safety. Do you understand?"

Prissa didn't, he could see. His mother was still struggling against his spell. The Speaker was still silent, but he saw the stubbornness in the way the man stood. The only person who seemed to pay him any actual attention—the only person who was listening to what he had to say—was Karix.

Which came as a surprise, he had to admit. Vex wasn't sure what he'd expected when he'd come up here, but it wasn't for anyone to listen to him. He was expecting a fight, maybe. He was expecting that he'd have to defend himself, to run away; as powerful as he was now, he wasn't guaranteed victory in a fight against this many combatants. Maybe in his dragon form . . .

But no one was fighting. Many of them looked at him condescendingly, sure. Most of the nobles didn't believe a word he said, save for one or two that seemed uncomfortable.

For now, Vex only had eyes for his father. Karix's expression still seemed unreadable.

"I had a dream the other night," Karix finally said. His voice cut through the silence, mild and strangely subdued all at the same time. "Did you have anything to do with that?"

"Dad, I cannot *possibly* know what you're talking about."

"I was guarding a door," Karix clarified. Vex didn't respond for a moment, but his mind raced. He remembered that moment clear as day, as much as he tried not to think about it. It wasn't even all that long ago.

He remembered the copy of his father Irvis had summoned to protect the Ashion part of the dungeon. He remembered being forced to fight him.

And then, when they'd instead reached an understanding, Irvis had killed that copy. Karix had fought back, had used the last of his strength to freeze Irvis and give Vex the time he needed to work out a solution, but . . .

He still remembered father dying in front of him.

That wasn't him. Not really.

But it might as well have been.

"Irvis is dead now," Vex said. Karix stared at him for a moment and then nodded, as though satisfied.

"Good," he said, and then he turned to the Speaker. "Effective immediately, I resign from my duties as the head of the Ashion House. Our magics are no longer yours to use, and our people are no longer yours to command. Not that we ever were to begin with."

"*Karix,*" Prissa hissed. Vex blinked at her; she'd managed to dispel his magic. Good for her. That was more than she'd have been able to do years ago, so she'd been practicing.

"It's for the best, my love," Karix muttered, his voice low. "It seems we have underestimated our child."

To her credit, Prissa didn't argue with him. She looked angry, but she seemed willing to listen to what Karix had to say. Vex didn't fail to notice that that was more credit than she'd ever given *him*; she didn't consider what he had to say seriously unless someone else vouched for him first.

"He is our child, I suppose," Prissa said, resigned. Vex held back the response he *wanted* to give, that he'd earned all of this on his own, and that the implication that he'd achieved it only because he was their child was . . . insulting.

Fortunately, he was distracted by the Speaker choosing this moment to speak. "You cannot do this," he said. His voice was calm, but the grip he had on his staff was tight; evidently, he hadn't expected Karix to side with his son or to pull back so suddenly.

"I think you'll find that I can," Karix said calmly. "If you stay, I hope you enjoy your time in Elyra. It seems like your remaining time will be quite limited."

The Speaker gritted his teeth. "Fine."

Vex watched the interplay between Karix and the Speaker, then glanced at his mother, whose gaze was focused somewhere in between the two of them. He'd spent a long, long time learning to read her expressions, and something about her expression here was strange. It was almost . . . smug.

Vex sighed.

He was, he decided, really quite tired of all this.

CHAPTER 57

A LONG-NEEDED CONVERSATION

"Come on, son," Karix said. He placed a casual hand on Vex's shoulder, which the lizardkin was tempted to shrug off. Neither of them had really earned his trust, and while he was *cautiously optimistic*, the more realistic part of him thought that this was quite likely just another ploy on his parents' part. Karix seemed genuine enough, but then his father had always been a good actor.

His mother, though? She wasn't quite as good at acting. There was nothing apologetic in her gaze, though she gave him a loving hug and patted his head in the most condescending way he could imagine. He'd enjoyed those, once—seen them as a sign of hard-earned approval—but now they didn't hold a candle to when his friends did it. *They* didn't do it to be manipulative.

Or perhaps he simply wasn't being charitable.

"Where are we going?" Vex asked, not moving.

"We're going to help you with your evacuation efforts, of course," Karix said. He seemed surprised, and Vex wondered how much of that was a front. Then he wondered how much his parents had poisoned him against them, that he was so suspicious of a simple offer of help. "I'm sure you need help. There's quite a lot of people to evacuate."

Vex considered his father's words for a moment. "I think we should collect Riss first," he said eventually. His little brother was undoubtedly still holed up in the Ashion estate. If he wanted to test if his parents were being genuine, then that was where they could start. All his older siblings were undoubtedly there as well, with the exception of Helix; he was still out there, helping with the evacuation efforts.

Part of him was worried, though. They'd interrupted whatever Wisfield was doing in their estate, but that didn't mean that the process was *halted*; it only meant that it had been interrupted. What if that nascent god was still growing, this time without Wisfield control? What if his friends needed help?

Vex checked the system somewhat anxiously. There was no message from Derivan or any of the others, which comforted him somewhat; they'd update him if anything went wrong, or if Sev noticed anything was happening with the divine.

He still couldn't entirely believe that Sev was so *old*.

Lost in his thoughts, Vex barely noticed his father's change of expression—Karix seemed thoughtful for a moment before that expression smoothed over and became something more guarded. "Home it is," he said.

Prissa seemed annoyed, folding her arms across her chest. "I'm sure Riss will be fine at home," she said. "The evacuation should be our priority."

Vex stared at her. "Riss will have to be part of the evacuation," he reminded her.

"But he'll be safe there!" she argued.

"Prissa," Karix said. His voice was surprisingly gentle—Karix always spoke to her that way. For all their flaws, Vex did believe that the love between the two was genuine. "We should get Riss. It's not safe anywhere in Elyra right now."

At least Karix seemed to understand.

Prissa, on the other hand, just sighed. "Fine," she said. "If it's so important, I'll go on ahead and get the rest of our children. Some of them are in their own homes, which you'd know if you'd stayed with us."

The last part was directed at Vex, who flinched; Karix's hand rested on his back almost protectively, and he gave Prissa a *look*. His mother's expression tightened for a moment before she gave her husband a nod, and then she disappeared in a flicker of magic.

Karix sighed. "She does not understand yet," he said. "But she will."

"Are you sure about that?" Vex asked. He glanced at where she'd left, watching the way the mana flowed in her wake; it was erratic and irregular, far from the usual result of a teleport spell. "System skills aren't exactly safe to use right now."

"Do you know why that is?" Karix's tone was curious, edged with a small amount of what Vex thought was genuine worry. He started to walk, leading the way as they chatted along the path back toward the Ashion estate; Vex no longer thought of it as his home, but the road was one he was intimately familiar with, down to the cracks and crevices in the brick.

"Because the system is failing, Dad." Vex sighed. "You've seen the signs. We've all seen the signs. There's no noble that hasn't. We find all these little tricks and loopholes in the system—you can't tell me no one's noticed that the loopholes just keep getting bigger. Things are possible now that weren't possible before. Everything Wisfield is doing, for example. Everything they *did.*"

"Ah, yes, their god plan," Karix said. Vex nearly stopped in his tracks at the disgust in Karix's voice—he glanced up at his father, who saw his expression and snorted. "I did not approve of that plan. It was foolish."

"Tell me about it," Vex muttered. "We stopped their ritual, but I don't know what that means. I don't think their plans are over."

Karix was silent for a moment. "They are not."

Vex glanced up. His father wasn't looking at him—instead, he was staring off into the distance, arms folded behind his back. Vex remembered walking with his father in the noble district just like this years earlier. The only difference now was how quiet everything was.

"The Speaker is contaminated with divinity," Karix said. "A broken form of it, I think, but it already exists within him. He is waiting for the right moment to use it."

"What is he going to use it *for*?" Vex hated that he couldn't help the alarm in his voice, but Karix didn't seem to notice.

"He wouldn't tell me. He was sure it would fix all the problems with Elyra, though." Karix glanced down at his son, and Vex saw a certain intensity swirling in his eyes. "Tell me, son. You don't think this problem is solvable, do you?"

". . . No." Vex said the words quietly, but firmly. "We're not even close to a solution, and *we know the cause*. Does the Speaker?"

"He believes he does," Karix said. "He believes it's a problem with the gods. That they have failed us in some way."

Vex snorted. "They're as much victims of this as the rest of us."

"Is that so." It wasn't quite a question. Vex was glad, if nothing else, that Karix seemed to be taking his words seriously. "That is . . . concerning."

"Dad," Vex said. He searched for the words for a moment, trying to convey how serious all of this was—and then he sighed. "It's not the system that's falling apart, Dad. It's *everything*. We can't afford to fight with one another now. You want to know what we learned in that dungeon?"

"I admit to some degree of curiosity."

"We learned that the world *ended*." It was so strange, saying the words out loud to someone else—it made it all feel so much more *real*. Vex stared at the curbside as he spoke, at the flowers that were planted along the sidewalk; they had all begun to wither and die in the wake of the failure of growth spells, and though a few brave, vibrant flowers continued to thrive, most of them were brown and dry. "Not that it's going to end. It ended, a long time ago, and the system is an attempt to keep the last vestiges of the world together."

". . . That is a bold claim." Karix stared straight ahead, keeping his face perfectly expressionless.

"And now that it's failing, we're running out of options." Vex ignored Karix's doubt—he would see it for himself, one way or another. "We need to evacuate. We need to *run*. We need to keep everyone alive as long as we can until we find some kind of solution, or there isn't going to be a world left for Riss to grow up in."

"Do you have any proof?" Karix asked. He didn't say it unkindly, but he said it with no small amount of reservation. Vex just shrugged.

"Is the system falling apart not proof enough?" he asked. "Growth spells don't work anymore. System skills don't work correctly. The dungeon's begun falling apart; the gods were pushed out of Elyra by a *nascent god* that Wisfield created . . . The signs have been everywhere for a long, long time. Why can't we get enough mana crystals to all the smaller villages? Why don't we have Anderstahl's technology? Why can nothing *spread*, even if we try?"

Vex had never articulated all of this out loud. He curled in on himself slightly as he spoke, realizing the extent of the damage that had been done to their world . . .

. . . and then he straightened again.

He would not let himself be brought down by this. He had Derivan and Misa and Sev, and Sev had—without any of their knowledge—been working to find a solution for this for *centuries*. He trusted them, and they trusted him; if anyone was going to find a way to fix all this, they would.

Karix watched him. Vex was oddly conscious of his gaze—he saw out of the corner of his eye the way Karix's expression flickered in response to his resolve, the way there was the barest hint of regret and something *else* there that he couldn't quite read. The expression was foreign and out of place on his father, and vanished as soon as he noticed it.

And yet, after a moment had passed, Karix spoke.

"Your friends have been good for you." It wasn't a question. There was instead something almost akin to wonder in his voice.

"They have been." Vex's answer was quiet. There were words there that remained unsaid—*They did for me what you could not.* It seemed too harsh for him to say out loud, yet it hung in the air between them, creating an odd tension.

Karix sighed.

"I did not lie about the dream," he said eventually.

Vex cocked his head. "But you did lie," he said. It wasn't exactly a surprise.

"Figured it out from your mother, did you?" Karix seemed resigned. "Yes. But . . . perhaps that plan is foolish. From what you have revealed to me . . ."

"The gods can't help us solve this, Dad." To his own surprise, Vex found he was speaking gently. He saw the tension in Karix's shoulders, saw the listless way his father fidgeted as they walked. The Ashion estate wasn't far now—it could be seen in the distance, tall towers of sapphire and gold built into a veritable mansion. "They're as much a victim of all this as we are."

"If that is true . . ." Karix hesitated. "What makes you so certain we will find a solution? If we need something more powerful than what Wisfield has accomplished, with all their money and resources . . ."

"As powerful as they may be, they're kind of close-minded," Vex said dryly. "We can't solve this with any of the tools we have. We need something new. What do you think my friends and I have been searching for all this time?"

"Hence the glyphs," Karix said.

"And more," Vex said, although he didn't elaborate. Karix glanced at him as if waiting for an explanation, but shook his head when he didn't continue.

"You don't trust me anymore, do you?"

". . . That you have to ask that question at all is telling." Vex glanced up at his father. "You *just* admitted you were planning on betraying me."

"At least I admitted to it."

"Congratulations, you've done the bare minimum." Vex couldn't help the small bite of sarcasm that came out of him; it felt like something Sev would have said, not him. He could picture the cleric grinning at him and giving him a thumbs-up, though.

Karix sighed. "I suppose you're not wrong."

Vex raised an eyebrow. He hadn't been expecting Karix to *admit* to it. He didn't say a word, though, instead slowing to a stop as they came to the gates of the Ashion estate. Vex gazed up at the tall walls, the garish blue-gold towers that he'd once admired—at the place he'd once called home—and wondered how such a majestic building could feel so cold.

He'd spent nights with his friends out in the open, with barely a blanket to share between them, and that had felt far warmer than this.

The good thing was that he now carried that warmth with him.

"Are you on board with evacuating?" Vex asked. "I'd really rather not fight."

Karix eyed him. "Seems I missed my son growing up because of how stubborn I was," he muttered, mostly to himself. ". . . I will help you. We will make sure our family is safe."

Vex glared at him.

"We will make sure *everyone* is safe," Karix amended.

CHAPTER 58

EVACUATION

Derivan's eyes glowed as he focused on keeping the portals open. The effort involved was immense—this was more than he had ever stretched Shift, and he could feel the way it was pulling at *something* fundamental to him, like it was unraveling a piece of his very soul.

Evacuating an entire city was, it turned out, not under the purview of Shift—especially when teleportation gates were more of a workaround than they were the intended purpose of the thing.

Small fights were breaking out all over the city. Evacuating was a serious matter, and not everyone believed it was necessary; the Wisfield Speaker's words hadn't helped the situation.

"You'd think they'd *understand*," Misa muttered. "The system is telling them to evacuate."

And it was.

[Elyran Prime Anchor at critical integrity. Evacuation is highly recommended. Do not delve the Prime Dungeon.]

Far, *far* too many civilians were claiming that this notification was merely a trick. They stayed in their homes, stubborn and angry, and refused to listen when their sons and daughters begged them to leave.

It was . . . tragic. Derivan had seen it personally, more than once; he couldn't help it. Shift made him more connected with space itself on a very fundamental level, and he had to push through two entire layers of reality just to get his portals functioning. He caught whispers from different homes, saw his own friends as they tried to convince different people to come with them, or resolved various crises begun by those who were too afraid to accept what was happening.

He didn't even entirely blame them. They were being asked to uproot their entire lives; it was no surprise that many of them would rail against it, look for any excuse to stay. The fact that some of their leaders were insisting that nothing was wrong no doubt helped them in that process.

And yet to leave them here was to leave them to their deaths.

There would come a time when they would have to force those remaining to leave, he thought. That time wasn't there yet, but it was close. For now, they focused on bringing anyone willing to go with them and getting them loaded into the caravans that were waiting for them outside of Elyra.

It was a long, *long* line of caravans.

"You doing okay?" Misa asked him quietly as she walked past him, slowing down just for a second. She was carrying a large sack of what he knew were the belongings of a poorer family that lived in southern Elyra—nothing too valuable, but precious to the family in question. They were woodcarvers, and the sack was full of small toys they made for their children and distributed among their neighborhood.

"No," Derivan admitted. "It is . . . difficult. There is no battle to be fought here."

"We're used to solving problems with our fists, huh?" Misa said, laughing slightly. The laugh was a tired one, though.

"We try for alternatives when we can," Derivan said. "But there is no alternative here. It feels as though we lose, no matter the outcome; the best we can hope for is to save the lives of the people here."

"I mean." Misa adjusted the sack she was carrying, giving it a significant glance. "Is that so bad?"

"I suppose not." Derivan smiled a little.

"We're doing good out here," Misa said. "Maybe we can do more; I dunno. But if we're doing the best we can do, I think that matters."

"You have a way with words."

"Damn straight I do." Misa grinned. "I gotta get going. You gonna be okay for a bit?"

"Of course." Derivan nodded.

Truth be told, he was straining himself, even now. Shift wasn't *made* for transportation like this, and while he could exploit it to make this happen—especially with the high levels the stat had reached—he couldn't maintain it forever. Derivan felt something inside him struggle to keep every portal open, to maintain his awareness of reality and the way it extended through space.

But he could keep this up for a little longer. He could keep it up for long enough.

He kept telling himself that, even as the weight within him grew and grew.

—∾—

Sev tried not to flinch when a divine connection suddenly sprang into place within him. **We are out of time**, Tempus said. The god sounded worried, and Sev didn't blame him; he could *feel* the divine domain in all of Elyra starting to stretch and crack, like an egg being ruptured from within.

No doubt an effect of what House Wisfield had done. They'd stopped that nascent god from being born, but that apparently didn't stop all of its effects. Whatever they'd set into motion was continuing.

He couldn't blame them entirely, though. There were so many compounding factors—the Elyran Prime Dungeon having to host an entire separate timeline, Irvis's presence taking it over and infusing the entire structure with his flesh . . .

"Derivan," Sev said. The poor armor looked exhausted. It wasn't apparent in any human way, but Sev could see that the lights in his eyes were dimmer than they usually were, and the rock-solid steadiness of his movements had become something a little shakier, a little more uncertain.

Derivan inclined his head slightly to indicate that he had heard him but otherwise stayed focused. Sev took a breath, hating what he had to ask of his friend.

"We don't have time to do this the right way anymore," Sev said quietly. "Elyra's going to collapse. We have to force the issue."

In the center of the city, a gaping hole in the Divine was forming. It was right above where the Prime Anchor was situated, and the hole was only expanding. Sev knew that Derivan would be able to feel it within moments.

Sure enough, Derivan shuddered slightly, glancing in the direction of the hole. "Elyra is falling apart," he said. It wasn't a question.

"Think you can push yourself just a little more?" Sev asked. He placed a hand on Derivan's shoulder. "I'll keep you healed up."

Derivan's voice was grim. "I believe I do not have a choice."

—∾—

Misa was mid-step when she felt the shift in the timelines. She kept a version of her Echoes running almost all the time now, just so she could feel out the different possibilities created by her taking different actions; a good half of her potential selves just *vanished* into a hole in the center of the city.

She stopped, dropped what she was carrying, picked the nearest two people up under her arms—though they screamed in protest—then used [**Me, Myself, and I**] to duplicate herself. A dozen new copies of her flickered into existence, and each one of them sprang into action, grabbing different civilians and hauling them toward the nearest portal.

She didn't care if they argued. There was no more time to wait for them to come to terms with what was happening. Not if the entire city was collapsing. Street after street was starting to vanish in her mind's eye, and although she couldn't necessarily remember that those streets were supposed to be *there*, it was easy to map out the hole by the absence of her alternate selves.

Elyra, she was pretty sure, was not supposed to be a ring.

Misa kept moving. Some portals flickered and failed, and Misa felt Derivan's attention elsewhere, but she couldn't spare him any more attention than that; she had to focus her attentions on the evacuation.

She only hoped things were going better for her friends.

—ɯ—

"There," Vex said. He was calmer than he should have been. His heart was pounding in his chest, but his voice came out steady and strong, and he kept the anger from his voice. "The center of the city. Something's *missing*. You have to be able to tell—there's no *mana* there."

"That's . . . strange," Karix allowed. He sounded confused. "But it's always been like that. Hasn't it?"

"If there was a *mana void* sitting in the center of the city, we would have bent all our efforts towards studying it, and you know it," Vex said dryly. His father couldn't deny the logic there. "It's new, and we need to get everyone out. You promised to support me."

"And I will," Karix said. "But the level of magic we need to evacuate the city . . ."

"We need a spatial anchor to keep the ritual stable," Vex agreed. He was stronger now. Strong enough to teleport an entire kingdom out of its borders? No.

But Derivan's portals could improve their reach, as long as he could open enough of them.

—ɯ—

"Deri," Vex said. Derivan opened exhausted eyes to greet his boyfriend with a faint smile, though that smile dropped slightly when he saw Karix standing next to him. The older lizardkin held his hands up in surrender.

"Peace," Karix said. "I'm here to help."

"He is," Vex confirmed. "We need your help to evacuate the city."

"I am doing everything I can," Derivan said quietly. If the big, central hole in reality was the only one he had to worry about, it would have been easier. As it was, dozens of smaller holes were opening up all over the kingdom, harder to spot but just as dangerous. Keeping up with the portals was straining him deeply now, as difficult as it was for him to admit it—he could no longer open static portals. Instead, he opened portals as needed to capture people who were on the verge of being erased and deposit them outside. It was a task that was taking all his concentration.

"I know," Vex said quietly. The lizardkin's voice—full of confidence and affection—along with the light touch of scales on metal, did a measure of work to restore his failing focus. "Once we do this, you won't have to keep your focus up. Think you can do it?"

"What do you need of me?"

"Six portals, one at six different equidistant points around the borders of the city, and a seventh one right here," Karix said, interrupting. Derivan cast a tired glance at him but acquiesced when Vex nodded to confirm it.

Compared to opening dozens of moving portals around the entire kingdom, a mere seven portals was easy. The only problem was the amount of people that would be lost if he did that. At the rate the holes were expanding . . .

If he wanted to save everyone, he needed to keep all seven of those portals while keeping up his efforts in rescuing everyone.

Derivan had no teeth to grit, but he forced his will into steel and began opening yet more portals.

CHAPTER 59

A FATHER'S POINT OF VIEW

There was no single system spell that could be used here, and nothing the system provided was reliable at the moment, anyway. Karix, for the first time, had to rely entirely on what his son was telling him—had to guide his mana according to Vex's wishes rather than play by his own rules. As much as he'd tried, he had no idea how these glyphs worked and didn't understand how Vex could grasp them so intuitively.

And yet grasp them intuitively he did. His son painted a glyph in a circle around the portal that the armored man made, though the edges of that portal wavered indistinctly in the air. Derivan was clearly struggling to keep it open, and his eyes flickered back and forth within his helmet, like he was splitting his attention with something unseen.

Karix couldn't remember ever feeling this useless. He'd promised his help to his son, and he intended to follow through, but all his accumulated spells and knowledge and skills meant nothing—all Vex needed access to was his vast stores of mana.

It made him wonder what it had all been for. If his methods of seeking out power had truly been so . . . shortsighted.

Karix sat back, waited, and thought about everything he'd done.

He wasn't usually the type of lizardkin to dwell on the past. Whenever he made a mistake, he moved forward and corrected it—he didn't dwell on how things *could have been,* didn't let himself get emotional over things that he'd done wrong. It made him seem cold and aloof, he knew, but dwelling on his mistakes seemed like a waste of time to him.

Now seemed like it was the time for change. There wasn't any "moving forward and correcting this" without understanding what he'd done. He still didn't see eye to eye with his son—he didn't see anything wrong with the Ashion way of mana enhancement—but maybe he needed to *try*.

A long time ago, he'd been the one to undergo those exact same mana treatments. His attitude toward them had been vastly different from any of his children—his mother had drilled into his head for a long time that there was a *duty* that came with being a noble, and though he was young at the time, he took the duty as seriously as anything else. The pain was just something he had to endure.

Not all of his siblings felt the same way, of course. There was a reason he'd ended up as the head of the Ashion House and not one of his brothers or sisters; each of them ended up in their own branch families, and they didn't speak to one another very often. Karix tried to remember a time when he was as close to a sibling as Vex was to Riss or Helix.

And he couldn't.

For the first time, he considered the question of what duty *meant* to him. He'd always considered it important—it had been drilled into him that his duty was important. But he'd never questioned it, not really; he'd never considered the *why* of his duty. For all that he was the head of a House, he might as well have been subservient to Wisfield.

Duty, for him, meant acting in Elyra's interests. Was Elyra that important to him?

Karix couldn't say.

He didn't love his kingdom. Not exactly. It was the kingdom he'd been born in, and he was loyal to it, but that loyalty was rooted in his birth, not in anything Elyra had specifically done for him. Everything his father had given him had been something his father had earned, not a gift from the kingdom, and he didn't spend enough time out among the people of Elyra to really care about them.

Even when it came to his duties, he thought of it as keeping order in Elyra. He didn't *know* the people of Elyra—not the way Vex did, or even the way Helix did, in recent years.

He didn't love his wife, either. The marriage had been an arranged one with a smaller noble house that had dissolved and merged their two houses together under the Ashion name. Prissa was beautiful, and she *did* love their children, but she could also be spoiled and stuck in her ways.

"You look like you're lost in thought, Dad," Helix said. Karix nearly jumped—he hadn't seen Vex's older brother appear at all.

"Aren't you supposed to be helping with the evacuation?" Karix asked.

"Not much I can do at this point." Helix shrugged. "It's all going to be down to your spell. I don't have the best idea of what's happening, but I can tell Elyra's a lot smaller than it *should* be. Wisfield should be panicking right around now."

Curious, Karix checked his system logs—the chat, specifically. There were a half dozen panicked messages from the Wisfield Speaker demanding he return and meet up with them to reevaluate their plans.

"They are," Karix said dryly. He felt glad he wasn't on their side, for once; a small smile curled up along his snout.

"Is that a real smile from you, Dad?" Helix asked in faux surprise. "Damn, I don't think I've seen one from you for years. Halfgold for your thoughts?"

"Just thinking I wouldn't like to be in Wisfield's position," Karix said dryly.

"Can't believe Vex managed to get you to change your mind, honestly," Helix told him. "Considering you helped me get arrested and all."

Karix winced. "I was hoping you'd have forgotten about that. Would you believe me if I said it was mostly your mother's idea?"

"Yes," Helix said. "But you don't get to absolve yourself of blame just because Mom came up with it."

Karix didn't have a reply to that. He glanced toward Derivan and Vex again—his son was nearly done painting the glyph. The paint almost hurt to look at, with how much raw mana was contained in its substance, and Karix could *feel* the magic growing slowly around the symbol. Even without it being active, space was already beginning to warp around the glyph.

"What was on your mind, anyway?" Helix asked. "Never seen you so deep in thought."

"I was just thinking," Karix said. "About my place in this kingdom, and what duty means to me."

Helix raised an eyebrow. "Can't say I was expecting that."

"Neither was I." Karix let out a low chuckle. "Times are changing, I suppose."

"No kidding." Helix was silent for a moment. "You got an answer?"

"No," Karix said. It stung him to admit.

"Then let me ask you something." Helix paused, trying to find the words. "Do you actually know what makes you happy?"

Karix didn't answer.

Happiness had never been something he'd actively pursued. He'd never considered it important. All those hobbies that other people took up, the various forms of entertainment they pursued—whether it was watching a play, reading a book, or finding a tavern to drink and flirt in—he'd always thought about it as beneath him. It struck him as laziness, for someone to have spare time and not to spend all of that spare time in singular pursuit toward a goal.

Now that he actually questioned himself, he realized he had no idea what his goal *meant* to him. He'd considered it important, certainly, and the train of thought made perfect sense; Elyra was a powerful kingdom, and he was proud to be able to contribute to its success.

And yet.

What did his pride mean to him? What did *Elyra* mean to him, besides being the place in which he was born? If it was merely serving a powerful kingdom that brought him satisfaction, then he would have been just as satisfied serving Anderstahl—but that thought rankled at him. He didn't want to serve Anderstahl.

"Dad?" Helix raised an eyebrow at him.

Karix huffed. "I'm thinking."

"Careful you don't overheat," Helix said dryly, and Karix restrained himself from the urge to snap back at his son.

He hated to admit it, but Helix wasn't *wrong*. He hadn't spent much time thinking about his motivations.

"If I say that I didn't think happiness was a particularly important pursuit," Karix said, "what would you tell me?"

"I'd call you an idiot," Helix said promptly. "Vex would too, but he'd be nicer about it than me. I mean, I'm not saying happiness is the end-all-be-all, but you've gotta have *something*. Satisfaction?"

He certainly felt satisfied with his job. But he didn't know if that satisfaction was something that he wanted, exactly.

"Hard to make a choice when you haven't experienced anything different," Karix finally said.

Helix—to his surprise—laughed. "That's the first smart thing you've said."

"I should ground you for that."

"I'm an adult, and grounding me never worked, anyway." Helix mimicked tracing a hole with his finger, letting a flicker of fire-aspect mana rise to the tip of his claws; Karix recognized the ward-destruction embedded in the magic. He smirked at the expression on Karix's face. "You missed a lot, believe me."

"So it seems." Karix wanted to say more, but he didn't know what to say. Instead, his gaze slid over to Vex, who was talking with Derivan in silent murmurs, encouraging him as he finished the final touches on his glyph. "You think Vex will forgive me?"

Helix's face dropped slightly, the casual amusement fading into something more serious. "That's up to him," he said. "If you ask me, I think he was a lot more hurt than the rest of us. I had to learn to care. Vex cared from the beginning, probably a little too much. Riss does too."

"And he knew that," Karix murmured. It wasn't a question.

"Yup." Helix lounged back against the same wall Karix was leaning on, then bounced off of it with a foot. "Better get back to work. And by work, I mean flinging fireballs at the Speaker. See ya!"

"What—" Karix began to protest, but Helix vanished nearly as quickly as he'd appeared. The older lizardkin groaned. The Speaker had defenses, and while he trusted his children . . .

"Dad," Vex said. Karix looked up at him; Vex wasn't quite looking him in the eyes, and he hadn't for a while. "We're ready."

"Okay." Karix didn't argue. He set himself up on the glyph, opposite to Vex. "Just channel mana into the glyph?"

"Yes. You first."

Karix supposed he deserved the lack of trust. He sighed, knelt opposite Vex, and began to channel his mana. He'd have to moderate the amount of mana he put into the glyph—he and Vex had to channel roughly equal amounts, so he'd have to—

The flood of mana from Vex interrupted his thoughts. Karix's eyes went wide, and he slammed his inner gates open, flooding as much mana into the glyph as he could—barely enough to match the sheer flow of his son's power.

When had Vex grown so *strong*? How had he missed it all?

For the first time, Karix thought he felt an inkling of what it was he wanted out of life.

CHAPTER 60

THE END OF ELYRA

It took effort for Vex to hold back his mana as much as he did. A not-insignificant part of him wanted to unleash it all, in no small part driven by the frustration he still felt with his father—but he gritted his teeth and held it back. The dragon transformation had done a lot for his mana channels, and the amount he could now hold exceeded even Derivan, whose Slime stat also let him carry far more mana than the average adventurer.

There were so many other ways to store mana. If his family had just bothered to *look*—

Vex forced himself not to think those thoughts, and he thought he caught Derivan giving him a sympathetic look, though the armor's focus was mostly on maintaining the portals.

Just gotta complete the spell.

It was easier said than done. For all that he understood glyphs better now, the working he was trying for wasn't something he'd done before—it was a combination of several glyphs, including Derivan's personal Sign, a spatial glyph, a transportation glyph, a directional glyph . . .

Derivan's Sign was what held it all together, and if the armor hadn't donated a portion of his mana, the spell likely wouldn't work at all. Even now, it was complicated enough that it was taking an immense amount of mana and no small amount of time. Karix, to his credit, was putting his full effort behind completing this spell; Vex no longer thought his father was trying to trick him.

It was only a small relief.

Trickles of mana spilled out of the glyph they were empowering, flowing out through the kingdom of Elyra. If he focused, Vex could sense the way each trickle split and separated, making a connection with every remaining individual—but that quickly became impossible to track.

"How . . . much longer?" Karix asked, gritting his teeth.

"Two minutes," Vex said.

It was just a guess, but it was an educated one. At the rate mana was flowing out, they needed to maintain the state of the glyph for another two minutes—which was already remarkably fast, considering how much ground the spell had to cover—and then they could activate the spatial-transportation part of it and teleport everyone out.

Vex was aware that with every passing second, more and more of the kingdom was being taken by the Void. Derivan and the others were doing their best to keep everyone away from the telltale cracks in reality, but only those connected to Misa's anchor could really tell that they were there at all.

[**Prime Anchor has reached critical integrity. Please evacuate.**]

"We're trying," Vex muttered. Karix read the same message on his system with an impassive expression, though Vex felt the flow of mana from his father increase slightly as he strained.

If nothing else, he was at least taking the threat seriously now.

—∞—

The Speaker was furious.

He'd be hard-pressed to pinpoint exactly *what* was making him so furious. The defiance of House Ashion was a major factor in it—he'd sensed the exact moment Karix had changed his mind on his allegiances and decided to help his son instead, despite all mental scans not indicating even the slightest chance of that happening.

But that wasn't the only thing going wrong. Of the three Platinums he'd sent out to capture the rebels, only one of them still reported to him, and he had no idea what she was thinking; Liz had somehow found a way to lock him out of her mind entirely. The fact that she was still doing what he told her was a small miracle, considering the other two had stopped responding entirely.

The Ascension Project was very close to failing. The nascent mind and divinity were still stored within the Wisfield estate, and the rebels disrupting the ritual hadn't dispelled it entirely—but without the Wisfield elders maintaining its domain, the other gods flooded back into Elyra, strengthening it with their various divine protections. It made him *weaker*, made his projects that much less effective; no longer could he control the populace.

And yet.

And *yet*.

He wasn't done. Not by a long shot. He had contingency plan upon contingency plan, and although most of them had failed to some degree, he still had enough control to make it all work. If the damn Ashion heir would just stop throwing *fireballs* at him and his team—

"Can you not kill him already?" he snapped to one of his guards. The man flinched back, looking nervous, and shook his head.

"He's very strong," he explained quickly. "Every time we get close, he heats up the air around him so much we can't get any closer. And he's got some kind of flash shield that incinerates any arrow we send towards him."

"What about Liz?" the Speaker growled. "She can kill him just fine."

"She's preoccupied with your other orders, sir," the guard said. He didn't meet the Speaker's eyes, and that was fine; the Speaker preferred it that way. He'd forgotten about his orders. He'd asked Liz to go to the Wisfield estate and retrieve the divine anchor they'd built to store their divinity—what was taking her so long?

"Fine," the Speaker growled.

It didn't matter. They had their own mages who could hold off Helix, even if they had to take turns just so they could counter the lizardkin's massive mana pool, and his personal protections would prevent any type of mana from coming into contact with him even if those mages failed him. The Ashion heir couldn't do a thing to him—the fireballs were an irritation, not a true threat, and once Liz returned . . .

The divinity they were building was based on the combined mental weight of all of Elyra's citizens. Once he had it in his hands, he could force it to awaken, nascent creature or not—and once he had the power of a god in his hands, he could fix *everything*.

He knew he could. The god had been able to do so much. It had been able to direct the attention of the Void, to make it consume something *specific* rather than eat away at everything in sight. Choosing it to eat away at the concept of Growth had been a necessary sacrifice; it would prolong the Void the longest, according to their diviners . . .

The Speaker blinked.

In the span between one moment and the next, everyone around him had vanished. The mental weight around him had similarly disappeared. To all his senses, Elyra seemed devoid of people.

"This isn't funny, Illyr," the Speaker said. He took a step forward, and the sound echoed through the empty streets of Elyra. ". . . Illyr?"

But the city was empty.

"That should be everyone," Vex said. He was panting, strained, and his father was even worse off; the older lizardkin was outright unconscious from mana overuse, forcing Derivan to carry him around. They were, as far as he knew, the only three people left in all of Elyra. Now all they needed to do was evacuate.

"I am unable to check," Derivan cautioned him. "I have exhausted the part of myself that can use Shift. If anyone remains . . ."

"No one *should* be able to stay," Vex said, frowning slightly. "We'll keep an eye out, but that spell should get through most if not all mana defenses. You'd need something divinely ordained to block it, and all the gods in Elyra are on our side."

Derivan nodded at that, though he looked uncertain. "Then we should meet with the others. They will be at the northern side of Elyra."

The streets of Elyra were . . . strange, for lack of a better word. Vex had traveled them often, as a young child and then as a teen; they had never been this *empty*. The silence was unnerving, and the outright missing buildings were even worse. Holes in the street where he knew one of his favorite shops should have been, or alleyways that were entirely missing from the city he was so familiar with.

It felt, in a lot of ways, like a bad dream.

Derivan nudged him gently with a shoulder. "Are you all right?" he asked, concern clear in his voice.

"As much as I can be," Vex said. He tried to put on a brave smile, but even that seemed like too much effort; it lapsed again as his attention wavered. "Just hard to believe we're saying goodbye to my home. If the Elyran Prime Anchor collapses, I might never see any of this again. I spent all my life wanting to get away, but . . . I'm still going to miss this place. I have a lot of memories here."

"At least you will remember them," Derivan said quietly. "To have someone remember the true state of things is perhaps the greatest gift in a world where no one can."

"You would know, I suppose." Vex remembered what Derivan had told him of the Void and what he'd seen in it—all the people that had lost their homes and large swathes of their memory, just waiting to dissolve into nothing. "I wonder if any of us really remember anything at all, compared to Sev."

"Even he does not remember everything. He . . ."

"Doesn't have most of his memories, I know," Vex said with a small sigh. "I just . . . It's sad, how much we've lost, don't you think?"

"It is." Derivan was silent for a moment. "But as long as we are alive, we can always work to get it back."

"Misa did get her family back, after all." Vex managed a small, real smile then. "Come on. Let's go meet with the others."

CHAPTER 61

CONFLICT RESOLUTION

The northern gates of Elyra were absolutely teeming with people. If it weren't for the massive, *massive* barrier that Helix had erected, no small number of them would likely have surged right back into the streets of Elyra—but the barrier created by the Ashion heir was absolute, and none of the higher-level elites seemed willing to help them break it.

Not even Liz, who was sitting, bored, on a small stool right in front of it. "You're not paying me enough to break the barrier," she told the guard that was blustering at her.

"You'll be paid, but our treasuries are *inside*," the guard growled. Liz shrugged at him with a smirk.

"Guess that means you can't pay me." She yawned exaggeratedly. "Come back when you can."

The guard gave a frustrated growl and threw his axe at Helix's barrier; it bounced off, useless, and almost hit him in the shin. Liz laughed at him.

The same thing was happening in all the listless crowds around Elyra. Vex was surprised that a fight hadn't broken out yet—it seemed like it was only a matter of time—but Misa had summoned multiple copies of herself *and* copies of the people from her village, and they were doing a remarkable job at keeping everyone calm, even the angry ones.

And then there was the fact that about half the people who were angry would suddenly stop themselves mid-argument, forgetting what they were angry about as their homes disappeared into the Void and they forgot they had ever had one.

It helped, but it was a little chilling. Vex saw a little bit of the light leave their eyes every time it happened. Losing your memories of your home would do that. His connection with Misa's anchor kept him safe, but that was only the smallest bit of comfort when he could see it happening to everyone else.

Even the rebels.

"Come," Derivan said gently. "Let us get your father situated."

There wasn't anything more they could do.

—❧—

It took some time to get everything in order. The confusion didn't help, as vast swathes of people lost their homes and forgot large sections of their pasts; they connected as many people to Misa's anchor as they could, but it was a tenuous thing, and it didn't have the integrity to host the entire kingdom of Elyra.

In theory, they would regain some of their memories as they traveled and connected to the nearby anchors. For now, they prioritized those individuals who helped the most in keeping things organized and stable. The Platinums were connected, any leading authority among the rebels, and the friends and family they chose. All in all, about a hundred additional people were connected with Misa's anchor.

"This sucks," Misa grumbled.

"Would you rather we all forget?" Helix asked her. He sat in the seat opposite to her in their respective caravan—but they didn't have enough wagons to carry all of them. They were mostly reserved for the elderly, for the pregnant women and children who needed them.

It had taken some effort to convince Misa and the others to take a caravan at all. They had to be told they would take turns before they climbed in, sucking in a breath of relief as they collapsed into their respective seats; four adventurers plus Helix, who had taken it upon himself to follow them in.

And his father, of course. Karix's still-unconscious body lay on the floor between the five of them. Their mother was still out there somewhere, but Vex hadn't cared to look for her, and Prissa seemed wholly on the side of the people who wanted back into Elyra, for all that she had pretended otherwise.

"That's not what sucks," Misa said with a sigh. "What sucks is the fact that we can't *stop* all this. I've been watching people forget their homes all day. It's . . . exhausting, and I'm not even the one doing the forgetting."

"Oh. Right." Helix's voice turned almost meek. "Uh, thanks for letting me connect to your . . . anchor. Thing."

"Don't mention it," Misa said dryly. "I don't think I could let Vex's cool family members forget all their character development."

"You don't have to put it like that," Vex grumbled.

"It's true, though," Misa countered.

Through all this, Sev remained silent, his eyes closed and his hands clasped in silent prayer. For him, of course, that meant he was communicating with the gods; there was no small amount of worry about the collapse of Elyra, and a few unreasonable demands that they find a way to rescue the kingdom.

We don't know how, Sev answered those demands. *We've tried for multiple cycles. The best we can do is hold it back and run. The entirety of the system was built to fight it, and even that's failing us.*

You've had seven cycles by your own account, someone said; Sev didn't recognize the god, and he didn't care to. **Seven cycles, and you couldn't find a solution?**

Seven cycles, and the combined effort of every forgotten god, every genius and lost practitioner of magic, every researcher that studies the Void, Sev answered. *And we still couldn't find a solution. I don't see you helping.*

There was an angry grumble at that but no retort.

The truth was that Sev was just as worried. Tempus was playing defense for him, drawing the ire of some of the angrier gods so he didn't have to deal with them all clamoring for his attention—but a lot of them were worried, and rightfully so. Establishing a religious base within one of the Prime Kingdoms was a massive achievement for a god, and now that base of power was being not only destroyed but erased.

There were devout followers now who could no longer remember their visits to their temples, the small favors that they had done for one another within those grounds. There were faithful who now no longer believed. Some gods were hit harder than others—those gods who still had temples within Anderstahl were fine, for example—but not a single god was escaping the destruction of Elyra unscathed.

And they weren't close to a solution. Not really.

Misa's anchor was helping. The glyphs were knowledge they had never had before, a whole alternative system of magic that could combat the Void in its own way, even if it was imperfect. Derivan had his Remembrances, small tokens carried forward from things that should have been forgotten.

And even with all those tools at their disposal, Sev didn't see a way to bring it all *back.*

The glyphs had been able to reconstruct reality but at a cost; even in that other world, they were slowly losing to the encroaching Void. Give it a few more years, and reality would lose enough cohesion to be a chaotic mess that no life could exist in. Remembrances weren't truly able to bring anything *back,* for all that they could call upon powers that no longer existed. Misa's anchor had a limit, and could be strained and destroyed just like the rest of the anchors.

There *might* be some way to put it all together—to anchor the glyphs to one of the system's reality anchors and stabilize what was left of reality without the anchor slowly degrading.

But for that, they needed time. They needed time, and understanding, and the people and tools to do the research; they'd lost most of the people that could do that a long time ago. He loved his friends, and Vex would surely have stood among the top researchers, but he didn't know if that would be *enough*.

Sev sighed, trying to loosen the knot of tension that had formed in his chest. His friends, of course, noticed.

"You doing okay there, buddy?" Misa asked him. She slung a friendly arm around his shoulders. Sev grumbled slightly but leaned into her; her presence was a comfort he needed.

"Just worried," he admitted. "I don't know how we'll fix all this."

"We'll figure something out," Misa said confidently. Sev didn't know where she got that confidence, but something about it was invigorating. He managed to smile a small smile. At least *someone* was confident.

"How about you tell us some stories?" Vex piped up. The lizardkin was clearly dealing with some emotions of his own—Sev saw the way he kept glancing towards his father's unconscious body—but he put on a brave grin and a cheery voice. "You're really old, right? You have to have *some*."

". . . You don't have to put it like *that*." It was Sev's turn to mirror Vex's earlier words, apparently.

Though Vex wasn't wrong.

The truth was that his memories were still a bit of a jumble. Sev had been trying to sort them out for the past several hours without much success. With the evacuation of Elyra being a priority, he'd had little time to actually focus on it, and even now that he did have time, he found he didn't know where to *start*.

His memories didn't come back in any particular order. Sev had trouble identifying which memory came from which life, or even which ones came first. Having Derivan, Vex, and Misa with him helped. The memories of *this* life, at least, were anchored by their presence. Everything else?

"I don't know where to start," Sev admitted out loud. "It's all a mess."

Derivan hummed, then—to Sev's surprise—reached out to place a hand over his own. "We will help you sort through them."

Sev blinked, surprised by how much that comforted him.

Then he took a deep breath and began with the first memory that came to mind.

CHAPTER 62

AND THE WORLD KEEPS TURNING, EVER SMALLER

While Sev told his story, the evacuation of Elyra began in earnest. Misa helped provide a few extra bodies, but by and large, it was carried out by those more experienced in handling *people*—the job of an adventurer, after all, was not typically that of organization and management. So they left the task up to those that were suited for it.

Still, the process was not without its complications. The Adventurers' Guild, while they had the personnel trained and willing to help, weren't particularly trusted by the people of Elyra. The rebel leaders, on the other hand, were mostly well-respected members of their communities. There just weren't enough of them.

So more than a few arguments erupted surrounding personal belongings and personal property. There were those who tried to take advantage of the chaos, of course, hoping to score something that would give them a better start with their new lives.

And yet . . . there were many who *didn't*. There were many who took it upon themselves to help, to offer up what limited food and resources they had to ease the evacuation process. A few families were on the verge of starving, and most of the food went to them so they would be strong enough for the journey ahead.

It took a long time. During that time, the Void spread, though it was just within the bounds of Elyra—it stopped at the walls, as if bound to the Prime Anchor that had previously kept the kingdom running.

It was a small mercy, but it was a mercy, and at this point, they were willing to take what they could get.

—~~—

Far away from Elyra, in a different branch of the Adventurers' Guild, Xothok paced around listlessly. His men had all retired for the night, their loyalty not quite enough to keep them awake just to stare at their boss's agitation. He was fine with that—no reason they all had to stay awake with him just because he couldn't sleep.

But Elyra was *dying*. Elyra was dying, and he couldn't do anything about it.

Not too long before, he wouldn't have cared. He would have said the kingdom deserved what it got, for what it did to those like him. A part of him still felt that way even now; he had little sympathy for the noble houses, for those who had repeatedly snubbed him when he needed help.

Now, though, he remembered. Small bits and pieces, and he saw those memories through a lens of separation, like they weren't quite his own—but he still remembered.

He remembered a kind old woman who had split the little bread she had left with him. He hadn't even asked her for it. Apparently, he'd just looked hungry, and that had been enough for her.

He remembered the musicians that would always be playing a block from his home, that would always smile at him and toss him a halfgold from their little collection box when he passed.

He remembered a little boy that insisted he would found an organization of guardians that would defend everyone, not just Elyra. What had happened to him? Xothok thought the face looked somewhat familiar, though he couldn't quite place it.

"Having a little trouble there?" Max raised an eyebrow at him.

Xothok scoffed, leaning back against a nearby wall and putting on as nonchalant an expression as he could. "No," he lied.

"We've *talked* about this," Max said, her voice playfully reproachful.

Xothok rolled his eyes and remained quiet for a moment more before speaking. "Worried about what's happening in Elyra," he said shortly. "Didn't think I would be, but I am."

"The Guildmaster did offer to let you help," Max pointed out, and Xothok grunted.

"Bad idea. Too much bad blood between me and a lot of the nobles there. I'd just as soon punch half of them as help them."

"At least you know your limits."

"Wish I didn't," Xothok grumbled, then unfolded his arms and walked over to Max. "What about you? Weird that you're here."

"What, because I'm supposed to be everywhere and everywhen I'm needed?" Max smiled brightly. "Guess I'm here because I need to be here! *Weird*."

The word was pointed. The entire lobby was empty save for the two of them. Xothok knew full well what she was implying. "I didn't *need* you here," he said.

"System doesn't seem to agree," she said with a smile and a shrug. "So, what can I do for ya? Need to talk about your sorrows?"

She was enjoying needling him, he thought. More likely than not, it was just one of the now-common system glitches. She'd keep bugging him until he said *something*, though, so . . .

"I have more of my memories back now," he said. "There's this little boy I used to know that dreamed about creating an organization to defend the world. Kind of like the Guild, I guess. You seem to know about all kinds of things. You happen to know what happened to him?"

"Her," Max said.

"What?"

"What happened to her." Max cocked her head. "You said it yourself, didn't you? It's kind of like the Guild."

Xothok paused. A dozen loose connections formed.

"Oh," he said. "Can . . . can I talk to her?"

"I think she's been waiting for you to remember." Max gave Xothok a soft smile. "Come on. Let's go find her."

Velykos felt more alive than he had for years. From the look of his fellow adventurers—he supposed that was what they were, now, true-and-proper adventurers, a life he wouldn't have imagined for himself not even a year ago—they were feeling the same way.

It was the six of them against a horde. Dungeon breaks were getting more and more common these days, and the Guild could no longer keep up or keep track. Velykos and his team were in the unique position of being able to commune directly with the gods, and with that divine assistance, they were able to head off dungeon breaks before they happened.

Or, in this case, arrive just after it happened and hold off the monsters as long as they could until everyone in the vicinity could evacuate to the nearest Guild branch.

It wasn't that he *wanted* to fight. In fact, Velykos was barely fighting at all—his skills were best suited to defense. He could sculpt barriers made of earth in seconds, blocking off passageways and directing the monsters toward his more-combat-capable friends while defending the Guild branch from direct attack.

But this felt like something Onyx would have wanted him to do. He couldn't stay in a temple forever, hiding from the world.

No. The thought was carved into his very being now, a small, abstract image of his new friends etched into the upper half of his back.

He could make a difference with whatever meager power he held, and so he would.

—∾—

"I'm really sorry it came to this," Novice said. The lizardkin sat in the center of a glyphic circle—an invention of his own that Raltis had helped him with, combining old magic and system magic for something that had some of the benefits of both. Raltis sat next to him, the otter's eyes stone-cold and steady, an unusual expression on the usually nervous archmage.

Helg stood across from them, angry magic sparking ineffectually from her.

Key word: *ineffectually*.

Her words were lost in the buzz of her own spells as they clashed with the antimagic barrier they had set for her. Novice had no idea if she was cursing their names or pleading for mercy, and she wouldn't stop casting for long enough for him to figure it out.

Given the nature of the spells she was casting, though, it was probably the former.

Helg's paranoid control over Teque and Fendal had lasted far longer than it should have. Most people had agreed with her at first—fear drove them, as Raltis had known it would, because that same fear had driven him—but over time . . .

Over time, they'd gone out and seen the effects for themselves. Raltis and Novice were not the only two to trigger the system to offer them a [**Soul Link**], allowing them to build on that essential substance that allowed them both to live as full, complete individuals. There were others. The two Anyatis, the innkeeper in Fendal and the magic-shop owner in Teque, had apparently triggered theirs before the two Norams ever had; they'd simply kept it a secret, and communicated privately while working to try to convince others to give this thing a chance.

They had the influence and charisma to do it, too. While Raltis and Novice worked on the magic, the two Anyatis worked together to charm anyone who came by their shop. The innkeeper left her own inn to its own devices—as long as the system was running things, she didn't really need to be there to manage it. Instead, she moved pretty much fully into Teque.

Slowly but surely, the people of Teque realized things could be different. That fear wasn't necessary. One way or another, the people in Fendal were reflections of themselves. Whether this was a result of the system, pure coincidence, or some strangeness in the way the timelines had split—it didn't matter in the face of overwhelming evidence.

The two Anyatis could accomplish more than a single one of them could. Raltis and Novice could accomplish far more with magic, too, with Raltis's experience supplementing Novice's creativity and eagerness to learn. They were the best of two worlds, grown from the experiences they had gained from two different timelines.

And Helg's influence slowly waned.

Her own counterpart within Elyra had died shortly after the beginning of the separation between Teque and Fendal—no surprise there, and no mystery as to who had done it.

"I'm sorry too, Helg," Raltis said. The otter looked sad. Novice could feel through the [**Soul Link**] how much Helg had meant to him. She'd saved his life a number of times.

Now she was blinded by fear and paranoia. That by itself might have been fine, but she wouldn't stop fighting. Wouldn't stop trying to kill the people of Fendal, and at this point, with the [**Soul Link**]s in place, that would just kill them all.

She was too dangerous to have around.

"I can do it myself," Novice told Raltis. "You can close off your bond with me."

"No, I . . . I have to do this." Raltis clenched his hands.

Together, they surged mana into the glyph beneath them, and the barrier surrounding Helg flashed.

When the light faded, she was gone.

—∞—

"How's Anderstahl's stability looking?"

"Not great. Seventy-five percent across the board. We're not on the verge of collapse, but it's close. Our Prime Anchor is already pulling from every other anchor nearby, and it's destabilizing everything surrounding us. Part of it is the addition to our dungeon, but part of it is just the natural decay of the system."

"We're lucky we remembered when we did. Lucky Seven left us all these manuscripts. Do you think he did something to make us remember?"

"Almost certainly. He's the only loose variable. Everything he touches . . ."

"Every*one* he touches, too."

"Heh. Touches."

"Shut up, Gerald."

"They're headed here next." A small pause. "We should get ready for their arrival. There will be a lot of refugees."

"Any luck finding a solution?"

". . . No. Seven might have left more behind, but we haven't found anything. I don't think we will, either, unless he wants us to."

—෴—

Deep within the Void, there was a silent *click*.

ABOUT THE AUTHOR

Silver Linings has been writing for over two decades and has finally decided to direct that creative energy into authoring complete books, preferably ones about kindness and compassion. He is also attempting to spread across all the clouds in the sky and give them a silver lining. This is not a metaphor. Do not panic, and stay indoors at all times.

www.ingramcontent.com/pod-product-compliance
Lightning Source LLC
Chambersburg PA
CBHW030928120726
47906CB00002B/528

* 9 7 8 1 0 3 9 4 3 6 6 2 6 *